The Hollander

Forbidden Love in Feudal Japan

By *DR. BETH FOGLIN -*
BEST WISHES
Dan WS

Dan Westerlin

The Japans:
A World he could not understand
A Gift he could not refuse
A Promise he could not keep
A Battle he could never win

Facebook: The Hollander

Cover artwork created by Dylan Vermeul: www.dylanvermeul.com

Forward

The Dutch trading post of Dejima is very real. It exists today in Nagasaki Japan on the archipelago's southernmost island of Kyūshū as it has since 1634. The story began when Japanese merchants first excavated a canal to separate a modest peninsula from the mainland creating an islet. Today it is well inland, the harbor being filled in over the years, and the restored grounds and buildings are the destination of tourists, students and those interested in history. The small fan-shaped artificial island was approximately 30 acres (12 hectares) in size, and although the distance between the city of Nagasaki and Dejima across a simple wooden arched bridge known as the "Dutch Gate" could be measured by a stone's throw, in the island's long history this seemingly tiny and inconsequential property has played a unique, isolated and pivotal role. For centuries Japan and the island's inhabitants might as well have existed in different worlds, for in a very real sense, they did.

Soon after taking power in 1603, Japan's first centralized government – the Tokugawa *Shōgunate* - realized that the Catholic Church, mostly represented by the Jesuits, was a threat to their stability and authority and began the long and difficult process to permanently ban all foreigners from visiting Japan - and all Japanese from leaving the island kingdom - under *"Sakoku"* or the "Closed Country" policy. They also forbid the practice of Christianity under penalty of death. Thousands of Japanese converts were subsequently brutally martyred to purge the Catholic influence.

Tokugawa Iyeasu was the first in a line of fifteen Tokugawa rulers that would command Japan from 1603 until 1867, and advising him in consolidating the *Baikufu's* power was Englishman William Adams - the real-life model for John Blackthorne or "Anjin-san" – in James Clavell's epic 1975 masterpiece <u>Shōgun</u>. Not all foreigners were to be excluded.

With the expulsion of the last Portuguese (Catholic) in 1639, Dejima was subsequently leased to the Dutch East India Company (Protestant) in 1641. The Dutch wanted profits, not converts, and only Dutch and Chinese ships would be allowed to trade in Nagasaki. To eliminate further foreign influence, no religious symbols or ceremonies, including marriages, funerals or Christian holidays, could be held on Dejima by the order of the all-powerful *Shōgun.*

The bounty of the world including such diverse products as silk, sugar, coffee, ivory, leather, and perhaps most importantly, scientific books and modern devices which were eagerly studied by Japanese scholars, crossed the wharves of Dejima. These one-way "Dutch studies" which flowed into Japan through Dejima were known as *"rangaku".*

In return Japan traded copper, silver, porcelain and lacquerware. Ship arrivals in the Spring were monumental events bringing trade items, news from home, and an exchange of Dutch personnel. Import goods were closely inspected by Japanese officials, and any forbidden items, such as religious books, would be confiscated and destroyed. Japan allowed no maps, botanical samples, or other information to be sent out. When the trade ships once again departed in the Fall, the outpost returned to its remote solitude. It remained completely isolated for months at a time from both Japan and the western world. For Europeans the Japans remained a consummate and far-away enigma.

The Dutch traders could not venture from their lonely outpost, and access to the island by the Japanese was severely limited. Those locals who worked on the island included clerks, cooks, and interpreters who came and went, including also *"yuujo"* or "pleasure women". The senior Japanese overseer was the *"Otona"*. An assignment to Dejima could be a profitable honor or an ordeal, for both the Dutch and the Japanese.

While Japan largely remained a medieval nation, the world around continued to progress in science, medicine, art and politics with increasing Western attempts to break the island nation's self-imposed barrier erected against outside influence. In 1825 the *Ikokusen Uchiharairei* – "Edict to Repel Foreign Ships" – was enacted, forbidding any intrusions under any circumstances, again with the exception of the Dutch on Dejima.

In 1837 the American merchant vessel MORRISON attempted to land at Uraga with the intention of returning seven Japanese sailors whose vessel had been lost at sea and were subsequently stranded in Macau. The MORRISON and the Japanese castaways were driven off by cannon fire.

1839 became pivotal when *yōgaku* - Western scholars - were purged following their criticism of Japan's isolationist policies with the *Bansho no Goku* – "Indictment of the Society for Western Study" – and the country became ever more divided both economically and politically. The strong nationalist movement to maintain *Sakoku,* and the power of the *Shōgunate,* became ever more intense and often deadly against those demanding reform.

Once again the Americans came to Uraga in 1846 when Commodore James Biddle of the East Indian Fleet arrived with two warships and attempted to initiate trade negotiations, but was refused and left empty-handed. Japan was a nation seething with discord and teetering on revolution, held together only by the power of the Tokugawa *Shōgunate.*

The Hollanders abandoned their trading post in 1853 when Japan's centuries of solitude were finally broken by the European and American "Great Western" powers. For over two hundred years this tiny islet had been Japan's only window looking out across the vast oceans. Suspended over the chasm between the European and Asian worlds, for those who served there, isolated for years at a time with little contact from the outside, Dejima existed as its own reality, alone and separate from all else.

3

The Players

(Family names first for Japanese)

Cas Janssen: A tall and darkly handsome scoundrel with smoldering good looks, he is the Best Man at the de Wolfe/van Courtlandt wedding and Hendrik's good friend. His one passion, and he gives himself diligently to it, is women. He loves them with his dark flashing eyes, and they love him right back.

Hendrik de Wolfe: In his late-twenties with bright blue eyes and blond hair, everything about him is "not quite". He has accepted a two-year assignment with the Dutch East India Company to manage their trading post in the far-off Japans. An only child from a poor single-parent family, he is determined to climb the social ladder through hard work.

Camilla van Courtlandt: Rich, spoiled, manipulative, beautiful and impulsive, she knew she would marry de Wolfe the first time she met him, but could never really understand or explain why. He was a possession that she must have, and less than a year later they were wed in Amsterdam's *De Nieuwe Kerk*.

Joost van Courtlandt: The patriarch of the van Courtlandt family and fortune, the estate has been handed down through the generations from a lucky cultivation of brightly colored "broken" bulbs during the Tulip Mania, and a senior Board member of the Dutch East India Company.

Kamimoto Daikichi: The *Otona* – Japanese overseer – of Dejima. He has spent almost his entire life on the small artificial island, and speaks perfect Dutch.

Abe Akio: An unattractive, dark and malevolent warrior from Fukuoka in his early thirties, responsible for all security on Dejima and the safety of the Dutchmen.

Chief Samurai: The senior officer of the *Obugyō-sama* - Magistrate - of Nagasaki and a Master Swordsman in his youth, but now his skills are dulled by drinking and gluttony.

Sawabe Keishiro – The Challenger: Well-known throughout central and southern Kyūshū, and his nickname *Chosensha* – the Challenger - referrers to the four duels to the death he has already fought to bolster his rapidly growing reputation.

Shindo Taka: The beautiful and innocent oldest daughter in a merchant family, all are arrested and condemned for practicing Christianity during the "Closed Country" period. She may save her family from death, but only if she betrays everything she believes in.

Captain Ostrander: Master of the *VERGULDE DRAECK*. A lifelong seaman with great experience in the Japans, having sailed there for over twenty years. With a stout body and matching white hair and full beard, he is a man to be believed and trusted.

Gerhard Schuck: The accountant on Dejima: Fat, sweaty and continually mopping his brow with a handkerchief that never seems to leave his hand.

The Chakunan: The eldest son and heir of the *Obugyō-sama* of Nagasaki, he serves as a guard on Dejima.

Obugyō-sama of Nagasaki: The local Japanese Magistrate that rules all of the Nagasaki *Bugyōsho* on behalf of the *Shōgun*. His infected leg was saved by medical treatment from Dr. Franz, but he has walked with a limp ever since.

Parcifal Bleeckier: The unofficial Reverend of Dejima. He always seems physically out of control, fluttering and flapping like some giant heavy bird trying to take off. He is impossibly tall and scrawny and his suit is too small, with pallid white skin showing at both pants legs and sleeves.

Dr. Philipp Franz: The jocular rotund physician, always joyful and willing to burst into song and dance at the slightest invitation. He has married a Japanese woman, and intends to spend the remainder of his life in Nagasaki.

Captain Nolan Powell: The newly "elected" English master of the pirate ship PHANTOM with a dangerously mercurial and unpredictable bi-polar personality.

Mr. Barton: The cruel French First Mate of the pirate ship PHANTOM.

Armored Samurai: A mysterious figure that attacks the Nagasaki delegation on their path to Edo and demands the Dutchmen be executed on the spot.

Shōgun Tokugawa Ieyoshi: The second son of the 11th *Shōgun*, he gained power in 1837, but died from congestive heart failure soon after Perry's 1853 arrival in Edo, the modern capital of Japan, today known as Tokyo.

Suzuki: A former *Otona* of Dejima, and now an advisor to the Shōgun, he speaks Dutch with only a slight accent. He was relieved of his duties at the trading post in 1839 for his involvement in the *Bansha no Goku* – the rebellion against foreign involvement in Japan.

Sergeant Major: The senior non-commissioned Marine officer aboard the American Black Ship SUSQUEHANNA, and a favorite of Commodore Perry for his steadiness in combat. His only two great passions are the American flag, and the Marine Corps.

Commodore Matthew Perry: Leads the American expedition to the Japans in 1853 to deliver a letter of introduction from President Millard Fillmore, and to negotiate a Trade Agreement with the *Shōgun*.

Shōgun Tokugawa Iesada: The 13th *Shōgun*. He ascended to power in 1853 immediately upon the death of his father *Shōgun* Tokygawa Ieyoshi.

Timeline

1554: The first tulips are imported to Europe as gifts from the Turkish Ottoman Empire.

1588: The beginning of the Dutch Golden Age, during which Holland's global trading capabilities, science, medicine, military power, and art are among the most acclaimed in the world.

1593: Flemish botanist Carolus Clusius at the University of Leiden plants tulip bulbs and finds they are able to tolerate the harsher conditions of the Low Countries. "Tulip Mania", the world's first speculative financial bubble, is launched.

1602: *The Vereenigde Oost-Indische Compagnie* – The Dutch East India Company or VOC - is established as a Chartered Company when the Dutch Monarchy grants a monopoly for the hugely profitable spice trade.

1609: A concession for the first VOC trading outpost in Japan is granted by Tokugawa Ieyasu, the first *Shōgun*, on the island of Hiradō off the coast of Kyūshū.

1619: The VOC establishes a capital in the port city of Jayakarta – modern day Jakarta - changing the name of the city to Batavia.

1637: Tulip Mania collapses practically overnight at the height of the speculative bubble; vast fortunes – mostly held on paper - are lost. Only a few shrewd investors escape relatively unscathed.

1638: *Sakoku* – the Japanese "Closed Country" policy - is implemented by the *Shōgunate*. All foreigners, except the Dutch, are ordered to leave the island realm.

1641: The VOC transfers all commercial operations in Japan to the small man-made island of Dejima in Nagasaki Harbor. It is the only foreign access point to Japan.

1796: After the Fourth Anglo-Dutch War, the VOC is a financial wreck, and operations are nationalized in the new Batavian Republic, but still largely managed from Holland.

Spring 1851: Hendrik de Wolfe and Camilla van Courtlandt are married in *De Nieuwe Kerk* – the New Church - on Dam Square in Amsterdam.

September 1851: De Wolfe signs a one-year contract as the *Opperhoofd* – literally head man – of Dejima. Including transit to and from, it is a two year assignment, and he sails for Batavia in early December aboard the Dutch trading ship *HALVE MAEN*.

Spring 1852: The *VERGULDE DRAECK* arrives in Japan with de Wolfe aboard.

Fall 1853: The American "Black Ships" of Commodore Matthew Perry arrive in Japan. Tokugawa Ieyoshi, the 12th *Shōgun*, dies of congenital heart failure soon thereafter.

PART I

An Old and Proud Tradition

De Nieuwe Kerk

The *Oost-Indisch Huis* – the East India House - the former world headquarters of the Dutch East India Company in central Amsterdam, was massive and still somewhat impressive, but tired, neglected, and only a ghostly vestige of its former power and glory. Like an old bull mastiff sleeping in the morning sun and secured at the end of a stout chain, its muzzle grey and moving slightly in the heat as it slowly panted in its dreams of chasing rabbits, the brick offices no longer inspired either fear or joy. The building's condition was more akin to narcolepsy than restful slumber.

In 1602 the *Vereenigde Oostindische Compagnie* - the Dutch East India Company - or VOC, had been founded with hope, typical Dutch practicality, diligence and precise organization. With the full and dedicated support of the Monarchy, the Company had built a quasi-military corporation that spanned the globe and established the Netherlands as the world's leading trader. They utilized the most modern technologies in sailing ships and navigation, reinforced by military power, to quickly expand their rapidly growing and highly profitable empire. It was an era that sponsored the finest artists and created untold wealth while building Amsterdam as one of the most prosperous cities ever seen.

Times change, and all great empires must fall, and in 1798 so too did the Dutch East India Company, broken and dissolved into smaller pieces. For decades prior, what was the world's first multinational conglomerate had been in decline, with further hints of decay, deterioration, and even less prosperous times ahead. It was a once proud trading giant that now desperately clutched at the tattered remnants of its previous glory.

Over fifty years later, the records were still here in the old headquarters. In the few remaining offices of the mostly empty monolith were kept the maps, the ledgers, the customs documents, the old sailing logs, and it still retained much of its former political power. Vast fortunes of old-money were still controlled from the *Oost-Indisch Huis,* and the commercial scale of the enterprise may have been smaller but the labor was much more intense, and the schemes ever more devious.

The coming Summer of 1851 would be dry and hot, and this warm Saturday morning in the late Spring was a precursor to those sultry months ahead with the cobblestone streets beginning to shimmer from the bright sunlight. High above, wispy white clouds indicated a coming change in the weather, but today was fine and perfect.

8

An ornate black carriage pulled by two matching *Ostfriesen* mares passed the Tuscan-style pilasters of the *Oost-Indisch Huis*, passed through the small tunnel that led to the inner courtyard with its elegant facades in Amsterdam Renaissance style, and stopped in front of a door capped with the VOC logo – a large central "V" with its arms intersected by the "O" and "C" – and waited. Vaguely, in the distance, church bells could be heard rolling across the city.

The heavy wooden door beneath the sign was flung open and a thin young man bolted into the afternoon's sunlight as if fleeing a house fire. The figure was already loosening his tie and unbuttoning his shirt as he raced from the doorway. He was immediately followed by two clerks, waving documents and crying "Mr. de Wolfe! Mr. de Wolfe!" as he jumped into the dark carriage and it started off. Finally both clerks cried "Hendrik" together in frustrated unison, shaking the papers they held for emphasis, before they turned back to their offices in exasperation.

As the carriage started off, Cas Janssen peered nonchalantly out the window and said "We'll be late," and de Wolfe smiled guiltily back as if they had almost been captured during a burglary. It was not quite an accusation and not quite a rebuke, but merely a statement of fact.

So much about De Wolfe seemed just "not quite". He was taller than the average Dutchman, but not by much. In his late twenties, he seemed younger. Thin, but certainly not skinny, and had blond medium length hair that was neither white nor mouse brown. The only real distinguishing facet of his appearance were the eyes, bright blue that would catch the sunlight and sparkle when he infrequently smiled. Walking the streets of Amsterdam he seemed fairly much like a thousand other pedestrians until he smiled, and in that instant people would turn in his direction as if a light had been shone upon them.

Janssen was wearing a long black frock coat with a wide velvet collar despite the early heat, its somber tone set off by a brightly colored blue silk vest. His long dark hair was tied in back by a matching blue ribbon, and rather than a fashionable full beard he had several days stubble closely manicured along his jaw line. He was strikingly handsome in an eastern European, almost Arabic, manner. He was nearly the same age as de Wolfe, and they had known each other since boyhood. His family was rather well-to-do, although no one seemed to really know where their money came from. And while de Wolfe had concentrated on his studies and then his career, Cas had neither applied himself nor even seemed to care. His life seemed a continuous lark and his success had been apparently assured. The one matter that did greatly interest him, and he gave himself diligently to it, was women. Pretty young women, and lots of them. He loved them with his dark flashing eyes, and they loved him right back.

Next to Janssen on the seat was a full formal suit, and de Wolfe began changing from his business attire, struggling to make room in the tiny carriage as its wheels clattered along the cobblestones.

A small silver cross bounced across de Wolfe's chest as he pulled on a clean white shirt. His torso was full and relatively hairless, and he was clean shaven, even though a man of his age was expected to have begun growing his beard by now. The truth was that his beard was too thin to be impressive, and it was far easier to shave than to maintain facial hair. He was thin, but fit, and it was always the combination of his blond hair and striking blue eyes that most people noticed first anyway, usually set off by the dark somber business clothing of the era.

Janssen spoke up again, "How long this time? How many hours since you've slept?" as de Wolfe was squirming to pull on his long pants.

"I'm not sure," answered de Wolfe, "since yesterday. There is just so much work to do." Outside the carriage the daily life of Amsterdam at the dawn of the industrial age passed by: Canals, shops, pedestrians, farmers selling their wares on a street corner, and beggars.

The beauty of modern Amsterdam was the rival of any European capital, even the fabled London with its vast infrastructure projects and improvements made under their Monarch Victoria. England was the world center for advanced engineering and technology, but Amsterdam was nearby and only a short step behind. The Netherlands were making huge strides in transportation, public health, manufacturing and a dozen sciences, all to the benefit of the rapidly growing population. This "Golden Age" of industrialization was proving to be a truly wonderful time to be alive.

"Well you missed your own bachelor party while you were ensconced at your desk," Janssen scolded him. "Fortunately for you, I drank enough French champagne for the both of us, so you were not missed in the slightest. And, there was a beautiful red sky this morning!! In any case, the van Courtlandts treat you like a slave."

"Be nice," de Wolfe admonished him as the carriage passed several prostitutes that were arguing at an intersection. The women paused their squabble momentarily as they spotted the two young finely-dressed dandies in the carriage, and began to leer and beckon. De Wolfe hurried to do up his trousers and pull on his frock coat as they passed the street-women, and Janssen blew them a kiss through the window. The mares soon carried the carriage past, and the prostitutes immediately returned to their quarrel, which soon threatened to become physical. The church bells became louder and more strident, as if urging the horses onwards.

The driver navigated the coach through the broad and always crowded Dam Square and stopped in front of *De Nieuwe Kerk* – the New Church – so called even though construction had begun in 1408 when the nearby *Oude Kerk* – the Old Church – was deemed too small for a growing Amsterdam.

De Nieuwe Kerk was the home of the Dutch Reformed Church, and its leaders had been greatly influenced by English Puritanism, creating an odd mixture of demonstrable pragmatism supported by glitteringly rich patrons. The church's heavy stone façade dominated Dam Square and the tall spires seemed to leap from the cobblestones and into the bright sky above. While internal squabbles over policy had caused a fracturing among multiple ministers over the past twenty years, the edifice itself remained solid and stoic, dominating and seemingly eternal over the capital of the Netherlands.

De Wolfe and Janssen stepped down from the carriage and had to push through the busy crowd, fighting their way into the church. Inside was an event that no one in Amsterdam wanted to miss out on, and the attendants who were closely inspecting invitations barely gave de Wolfe and Janssen a glimmer of recognition as they made their way through the immense wooden doors.

The two finely dressed swains stopped just inside the massive church, dumb-struck by the spectacle. The cathedral had been opulently decorated the year before for the Investiture of King William III, and the ceremony today was even more grandiose. Hundreds of flower bouquets jammed every available space, including many still hugely expensive tulips, and the pews were over-flowing with the elite of Dutch society. The crowd turned their heads like a herd of cows, all staring in silence directly at de Wolfe as he entered, and he was momentarily caught in their gaze, unable to move.

Standing in a vestibule nearby, although it seemed so very far away across the assembled throng, a bride in a flowing white dress stood, her raiment specifically modeled after what the English Monarch Victoria had worn at the royal wedding to Prince Albert of Saxe-Coburg and Gotha eleven years earlier. Camilla's father – Joost van Courtlandt - stood to her right, and she was attended by six resplendent bridesmaids.

Cas brought his arm up and waved to the bridesmaids grinning at them, and two from the group smiled and returned a shy hand. He nudged de Wolfe, "There! The one on the end! That could be the new Mrs. Janssen!"

"Could you please just stop it! For one day, I beg of you! Stop it!" de Wolfe whispered.

"Oh, but they are soooooo pretty!" Cas whimpered back. "Can't I have just one? Please?" Cas smiled rakishly, winked and waved again.

Following the crowd's attention, slowly the bride's father's head turned to the entrance, staring with rancor directly at de Wolfe, and then looking at the ornate pocket watch in his hand and began tapping its face with irritation.

"Well?" said Janssen as the pastor standing at the alter in the front of the edifice hurriedly motioned them forward, "Let's go!" The two men quickly moved self-consciously up the aisle to join the impatient pastor. Then, booming across the church immediately sounded the deep sonorous organ playing Wagner's Bridal Chorus, also known as "Here Comes the Bride", as the six bridesmaids paced forward and Mr. van Courtlandt escorted his daughter Camilla van Courtlandt down the aisle.

Cas moved to the left side as Camilla's entourage joined de Wolfe at the alter and then the bridesmaids shifted in a line to the right, followed discreetly by Mr. van Courtlandt. The clergyman lifted a large book inscribed with "*DE HEILIGE BIJBEL*" in large gold letters. The pastor opened the Bible and Camilla raised her veil revealing a striking beautiful face framed by long flowing blond hair. De Wolfe and Camilla exchanged vows, their hands touching over the Bible as he stared into her light green eyes.

The formal ceremony raced by, and the rising notes of Mendelssohn's Wedding March soon focused everyone's attention as the newly consecrated groom and bride began their triumphant walk back down the aisle to the bright sunlight flowing in from the exit.

A Great Opportunity

An entire hotel on the edge of Dam Square had been reserved for the luncheon reception, a short walk for the guests as they passed through the multitude filling the open space, and the wedding party ducked quickly into the lobby and hurried to the vast formal dining room. Tables were set with light foods including roast goose, dozens of cheeses, multiple open face sandwiches, and of course herring. There were plates filled with the expensive opulence of chocolate, Dutch cocoa – machine-pressed chocolate – made from beans imported from the Company's colony in the African Congo and produced by the new and revolutionary process of adding back melted cacao butter that had been invented in 1847 by Joseph Fry. The hotel's taproom was double manned so that beer and stout could be dispensed by the keg, and for the ladies *hippocras* - a sweet spiced wine.

De Wolfe and Janssen stood awkwardly alone in the throng of well-wishers as the crowd purled and swirled around them. The ceremony had been the grandest of the season, marking the marriage of one of Amsterdam's wealthiest families, and would be widely reported throughout Europe down to the smallest detail. A newspaper reporter was interviewing Mr. van Courtlandt, and Dylan Vermeul, a popular and well-known local sketch artist, was trying to capture the joy and beauty of Camilla as she chatted merrily with her bridesmaids and many admirers.

"My father always said that he never knew what true happiness was until he got married," Janssen quipped to de Wolfe. "But, by then, of course, it was far too late."

The groom smiled back at him, "Oh, you can prance and dodge all you want, but you will soon follow," de Wolfe countered. "Somewhere there is a woman out there that will catch your heart as Camilla has mine."

"Too true my dear old friend, but not just one, a hundred! How can I break so many hearts by giving mine to only one? I am a generous benefactor of women, but not a provider, and that is truly my problem."

Cas held his hand in front of his face and waved his fingers as if a magician were conjuring a spell, "How could I possible deny them all of this magnificence? And, now you have given your own heart away once and forever. A pity, such a pity."

"It is no such thing!" de Wolfe protested.

"Perhaps not a pity then," Janssen conceded, "But with you everything is work."

"I have great responsibilities, and yes, I do take my work quite seriously. My mother…"

"Please! Enough! Not again! We all know the story: An only child, and your father died before you were born, and your mother fought to raise you as a gentleman. Blah, blah, blah."

"It's better than being out digging canals."

"Is it? The way the van Courtlandts treat you? He sits around all day smoking his pipe while you have to keep the enterprise operating? I wouldn't mind if they at least respected you."

"They do respect me!"

Janssen snorted under his breath. "They treat you like a pet animal, leashed to your work. And, Camilla is no better, to her you are a little rat dog she can carry in her purse and either show off to strangers or use to menace small mammals. Well, you're stuck with it now."

"You are prone to melodrama."

"Am I? Well, your master approaches."

Mr. van Courtlandt stood in front of them in silence for a few moments as if expecting something while the two men waited. "Ahem," he finally announced, clearing his throat.

"Ahem," answered Janssen.

"Ahem," Mr. van Courtlandt repeated with slightly greater emphasis.

"Ahem!" repeated Janssen, shrugging his shoulders.

De Wolfe rolled his eyes, "Cas!", and indicated that he should leave them alone.

Not to be totally outdone, Janssen gave one final loud "AHEM!" and excused himself. "Forgive me your majesties,' he intoned with a flourish and bowed to the two of them. "I myself must get to work." Cas then walked directly over to the bridesmaids and introduced himself, kissing each of their hands in turn, and carefully listening to their names. As he spoke with the last one, a pretty though somewhat plump girl, he held her hand and gazed deeply into her eyes until she looked down and giggled.

Mr. van Courtlandt shook his head in obvious contempt and then stared at de Wolfe for a moment before beginning slowly. "A man is often judged by the company that he keeps," he nodded in Cas' direction.

"Yes, he is a bit of a scoundrel," de Wolfe conceded.

"More than a bit I would reckon, but now, to you. Being a van Courtlandt is both an honor and a great burden,"

Not knowing how to respond de Wolfe simply asked, "Sir?"

"You marry one, and you marry us all. My family came from simple tulip merchants and we made our fortune with two traits that have carried us forward: Intelligence and determination. We are a naturally superior breed that has risen to the top simply because we are the best. We now expect the same from you."

"I have always given you nothing less."

"You are a reliable employee, I will grant you that. But you have applied for an assignment at Dejima and I am not sure that is a good idea. In any case, now you must quickly transform yourself into something greater: A leader of society. I am giving you that opportunity by this marriage, and may God grant you the very best success if you are chosen for the assignment in the Japans."

De Wolfe was unsure where van Courtlandt was going with this, he answered simply, "I am fully prepared and it would be an important promotion."

"In so many ways that you cannot possibly imagine. Less than five months until you would depart, and then gone for at least two years. Time is very short. May I expect a grandson before you go?"

"Sir!" de Wolfe was shocked at van Courtlandt's boldness.

"Don't be childish. I need an heir, male blood to carry on the family. That is now part of your responsibilities as well. The Japans and a grandson. See to it. Better men than you have failed."

14

De Wolfe steadied himself, unsure of the older man's meaning. "Failed?" Was van Courtlandt talking about the Japans or the grandson? He glanced over at Camilla, still completely engaged with her many admirers. He looked back to Mr. van Courtlandt. "We merely seek your blessing for our marriage and if I am chosen for my assignment then I ask that you forego your continuing criticism. When I return…"

"If you return," van Courtlandt spit out.

"Sir, I beg of you! When I return," emphasized de Wolfe, "I hope that you may finally appreciate that even those of us who were not born into wealth can still earn our success. And along with that, I am quite confident that I shall gain your respect."

"A plan is always better than hope," van Courtlandt snapped. "You must plan for success!" They stood staring in silence at each other as the post- wedding festivities swirled around them until finally Mr. van Courtlandt slowly extended his hand to de Wolfe, and he in return grasped it firmly.

The whole event seemed to be running out of steam after another hour, during which Mr. van Courtlandt had returned to a group of older businessmen, and engaged in what occasionally seemed to be a heated discussion. Several times they looked over at de Wolfe, speaking of him just out of hearing as if he were not even present. Otherwise he stood alone and few came over to speak with him. Cas was nowhere to be found as the wedding's groom stood quietly with his hands awkwardly crossed in front of his body, not knowing what else to do with them. Camilla entertained a whole line of well-wishers, the women curtsied and the men kissed her on the cheek, congratulating her and then moving away, replaced by the next set.

Finally it came time to leave, and Mr. van Courtlandt collected Camilla and the three of them prepared to depart. De Wolfe had no idea where his Best Man had gotten off to, so he shrugged and Mr. van Courtlandt signaled his butler. Out of the corner of his eye de Wolfe saw Cas hurriedly pulling up his pants through an open doorway, and the plump bridesmaid behind him smoothing her dress. He waved him off discreetly, and Cas placed his hand to his lips and blew them all a kiss good-bye.

As they emerged from the hotel the late-afternoon sun was glaringly bright and shining off of the buildings and pavement of Dam Square as hundreds of well-wishers and gawkers outside began cheering, but out to sea on the horizon dark clouds were swirling and black heavy rain was falling in the distance. The growing crowd was soon joined by the wedding guests, the entire throng now all clapping and shouting. The bride and groom climbed into the van Courtlandt family carriage, marked by a large "VOC" on the doors and highly polished copper lamps and buckles, and pulled by two matching mares with feather plumes attached to their heads. The carriage had brightly colored ribbons tied to the back, and several children chased them as they started off and away.

A Modern Marvel

The honeymoon trip the newlyweds shared to Paris had both started and ended in a blur, though for very different reasons. De Wolfe had not even needed to pack for the journey; everything had been arranged by the van Courtlandts. The wedding night, under Camilla's parent's roof with the clutter of manservants constantly scuttling throughout the house, had been an unfamiliar and uncomfortable experience for him and he was happy to be on their way. He had always done things for himself, and having a finely dressed butler personally assigned to the "young master" even for one night was odd.

It was an exhausting three-day carriage ride to Brussels, half-way to Paris from Amsterdam, spending the first night in Ultrecht, and the second in an incredibly luxurious hotel that he could never have afforded on his own, directly on the beachfront in Antwerp. Then came the marvel.

The line of iron track running north-south between Brussels and Paris had been completed only five years earlier, the first railway connection in the world linking two international capitals. A group of well-dressed passengers boarded at the station in Brussels early in the morning, the steam engine belched black coal smoke, rumbled, and the train of locomotive carriages arrived in Paris that very evening. A comfortable one day journey from Brussels to Paris rather than three or four grueling days by carriage! It was as simple as that! Incredible!

He had walked the city for hours stretching out from their hotel on the bank of the Seine, not far from the *Arc de Triomphe de l'Etoile*, and it would not have held him back if it were a month's journey down the *Champs-Elysees* to see the *Axe historique* – Paris' incredible line of monuments, buildings and thoroughfares - extending from the center of the city to the west. He spent a full day in the *Musee de Louvre*, opened in 1793 and now containing the world's largest collection of artworks.

He had never traveled outside the Netherlands before, and his curiosity was insatiable. Churches, the archaic forts ringing the city, statues, paintings, he could not take it all in. Amsterdam was his home and a fabulous city, but the freedom of modern travel and the opportunity of so many things to see and do in Paris was intoxicating. It was a living demonstration of modern life.

Camilla was far more interested in the restaurants, and he would usually find himself wandering the river bank or broad thoroughfares alone late at night, long after she had begged off, telling him how tired she was. And, of course, shopping. She seemed to buy something from every store, both large and small, that they entered. She would point, pass the shopkeeper one of her father's business cards, and there was no need of immediate payment or further explanation. They knew the price certainly and now the address to send the goods. The transaction was complete.

In truth, as much as he enjoyed Paris and the wonder of speedy rail travel, he was somewhat relieved to board the steam train once again and to start northward and home. There were so many marvels: He had seen the small office where President Napoleon and Queen Victoria had exchanged greetings by telegraph in an instant between Paris and London. Next Spring he learned, the English would host what they termed a "World's Fair" in Hyde Park, to be held mainly inside of some immense "Crystal Palace" that was now under construction. The French were already saying they should plan their own "Exhibition" as quickly as possible.

It had been almost overwhelming. The world of science and technology was changing faster than anyone might fully understand or even comprehend, and no one could imagine where it might lead. The only certainty was that it was coming and would not be stopped.

By the time they had returned to Amsterdam Mr. van Courtlandt had already negotiated the purchase of a home for the newlyweds, and they immediately moved in, the payments deducted each month from his earnings. They settled into married life, and he returned to his grueling days at work.

The de Wolfe Household

It had been another very long day and well into the late evening, and de Wolfe was walking the semi-deserted streets of Amsterdam back to their house, located in the Jordaan District. As taxes were paid based on the size of the lot, the buildings here were each tall and thin, rising four stories and facing the canal and bundled wall-to-wall tightly together. The building had once been a warehouse, and the cost worried de Wolfe, but he knew it would ultimately be a good investment. Much of the renovation work had already been planned and started, and de Wolfe was still debating the merits of installing a modern water toilet rather than utilizing the cesspit that existed under the house and over-flowed into the canal. Most of the neighbors still simply followed tradition, and just continued to throw their waste and garbage into the nearby water.

There was just so much to do at the Company, and so little time. In addition to the accounting and financial calculations he had done for years, he was also trying to read everything he could about the Japans. Ship's logs went back to the 1600s and spoke of storms and hostile encounters, of both the triumphs and tragedies inherent from trading with peoples around the globe. The Dutch East India Company had in the course of two centuries established dozens of colonies around the world, both large and small. South Africa, and southern India were hugely important, but it was *Oud Batavia* – Old Batavia - that still served as the administrative headquarters for the Company. The Dutch had changed the name from Jayakarta in 1619 and made it their capital for all of Asia until 1800. Since then the Company used Batavia as their business headquarters, even though they had been forced to formally transfer governance of this prized possession to the Monarch of the Netherlands.

But now the glory years of the 1600s and 1700s had long passed, and the Company was fighting to remain relevant in the modern age. South Africa, India and Batavia had broken free from their control, but even so the spice trade could still be hugely profitable if carefully managed.

He expected the house to be dark, but was surprised to see bright lights on the fourth floor living quarters, and wearily climbed the steps. When he opened the door Camilla was admiring a long flowing party dress in the mirror. Spread out across the floor were several more large boxes from famous dress makers, still unopened.

"Oh Hendrik!" she exclaimed happily and rushed to embrace him, kissing him on the cheek. "Look what I have gotten us! And, you will be so happy, they were on sale!"

"Camilla, it's beautiful, but... but when would you wear it?"

"Oh, you don't like it," she pouted and turned away. "And, I wanted so much to please you."

"It does please me, but we must be careful and stick to our budget. Getting this house completed and fit to live in, the workman, the materials, we must be frugal."

"I am being frugal," she countered. "I told you, they were on sale. Besides, I hate this house with all the noise and the dust. We should move to a hotel. A nice hotel until it is finished."

"We cannot possibly afford that! I know, and I understand that it is not yet finished. No one enjoys having people here hammering and sawing all day, but the construction will soon be over, and we will have made this old warehouse our home. Just for you, just for me, and for our family."

"It stinks. That old canal stinks!" she exclaimed and walked away from him. "And, I have only one maid to do all my cleaning and she is an awful cook!"

"Then we will find you another one, someone that you will like and who will prepare the foods you enjoy."

"I do not enjoy being here cooped up all day!" she exploded, and threw a shoe at his head, barely missing him.

De Wolfe sighed. It was happening again. The temper, the demands, the yelling, often with small items hurled or broken. He went to the bed and sat down. "Camilla," he began softly, not daring to look at her directly in case she might fling something or raise her voice again. "Camilla, one day soon this will be a fine house, and you will be proud to live here. It will be filled with laughter, and with joy, and with our children. But, we must devote ourselves to making that happen. It may not come immediately, but we can create it together. Here, come sit with me."

She walked over and sat down next to him on the bed. "Well," she explained, having calmed down slightly. "These didn't cost you anything."

"Did you buy them on credit?"

"I did not, I charged them to Papa's account."

"You cannot continue to do that. You are my wife now, and we will pay for our purchases with the money I earn, not taking it from your father."

"It will all be ours someday anyway after Papa's dead."

"That is not something to wish for!" he scolded. "And, until that time comes we will manage our own affairs. I ask you to please return these to the dress makers tomorrow."

"But I don't want to!"

"I know you do not," he soothed her. "But, promise me that you will, and that you will also refrain from buying more." He kissed her on the forehead. "Will you promise me that?"

"Yes, Hendrik, I will."

"Tomorrow. You promise?"

"Yes," she told him, giving him that little girl pout that had first attracted him to her. "Yes, I will." But, she never did.

The Contract

The long days and grinding cycle of work never seemed to slow. De Wolfe was often out of his home and walking to the VOC offices before dawn each day, and just as often back after midnight. The day of his potential assignment for the Japans, which last Spring had seemed both distant and intangible, was approaching far too quickly.

When Mr. van Courtlandt proudly told him of the Company's decision confirming his selection, the reality of the commitment struck home. He was more pleased than worried, but the magnitude of the assignment was overwhelming. Two years away and half-way round the world. Camilla had known it was what he wanted, but she still had not taken the news well and had not spoken with him for several days.

The Company attorneys had provided him with a lengthy contract, detailing in excruciating detail when and how he was to depart, what his duties were both in transit and at the trading post, even during and upon his return. There was even a clause for him to fill in on how his remains were to be handled in case of his death, and the amount, the truly generous amount, of payment that would be given to his benefactor. He had dutifully filled that section in with his own hand, specifying burial at sea – if necessary; plus the dimensions of his headstone – if possible; and Camilla in that order.

When he returned the signed and witnessed document the attorneys informed him that the contract would not become final nor official until he had personally reviewed everything with the Board and it had been counter-signed by all six active members.

So, that was why he found himself completely bored and sitting on a bench outside the VOC Board Room on a Tuesday evening. At least he thought it was Tuesday. Yes, he confirmed in his mind, the Board meets every other Tuesday. Finally, the wide heavy door swung open and a clerk motioned him inside.

There was a long sturdy table with twelve plush seats, although only six of them were occupied. Two clerk's desks sat on either side of the main table, and the room was dark, minimally lit by two candelabras and small lanterns at each corner. The six older men were in the sumptuous leather chairs, and the combination of light and darkness in the room reminded de Wolfe of Rembrandt's "Night Watch" as those men in the corners seemed to fade into the shadows. One of those shadows was Mr. van Courtlandt.

The clerks were excused, leaving de Wolfe alone with the Board. He had seen each of the members individually, of course. He knew their names, spoken with them, even dined with some of them. But together they created something else, a machine greater than the sum of its parts. A mysterious apparatus that could influence events across the globe on a whim, or after great deliberation.

"Have you fully reviewed and signed your contract?" Mr. van Courtlandt began. It seemed that his father-in-law would do all the talking on behalf of the Board this evening.

"Yes, I have sir, and it is satisfactory."

Several of the heads leaned into the light and nodded their approval. "And," van Courtlandt continued, "do you know why we have asked you here tonight?"

"So that the Board may counter-sign the contract, sir."

"Yes, that is correct. But, there is more, much more that you must understand before we reach the final agreement. Things that must not be made public, and things that cannot be put into a contract. Only after we have explained this all to you, and you have agreed, can we formalize your arrangement."

"I am ready, sir. Here it is." And he handed the document down the table.

20

Van Courtlandt opened the contract to the final page, and noted de Wolfe's signature marked with today's date, 3rd September 1851. "Good, good. What you already know: There was a time, not so long ago, that the VOC was the most powerful non-governmental entity the world had ever seen. The colonies of the Netherlands, and our trading posts, spanned the globe. We were the first formal public company, the first corporation to be listed on a stock exchange, and the first company in the world to issue stocks and bonds. The Company paid a consistent eighteen percent annual dividend to our investors for its first two centuries."

"We had the legal authority, granted through the Crown, to wage war, to imprison and execute criminals, to negotiate treaties, and to mint coins. We were in a very real sense the Dutch government."

"All of that changed after our war with the British and the subsequent French invasion. The Company was nationalized in 1800, stripping us of our authority and, on paper at least, transferring the majority of our assets to the Batavian Republic."

"The life savings of many good people were wiped out, our investors ruined, it was a catastrophe. Batavia remained, of course, but the one jewel that could not be stolen, could not be diminished, was Dejima in the Japans."

Van Courtlandt paused, evaluating. "Do you follow me?"

"Yes sir," de Wolfe confirmed. "I believe that I do." It was old history, he thought, interesting, but he was unsure how it would affect him personally. Batavia was a tropical cesspool filled with unknown and incurable diseases, the graveyard of many Dutchmen. Some had died within days of their arrival, struck down by some gruesome malady that barely affected the natives.

But, the mysterious Japans, that was different. Despite his research there was almost nothing that he could learn. The people it seemed were clean, civilized and virulent diseases seemed hardly known. It was the combination of distance and secrecy that had fascinated him. And, it was a stepping stone, a huge advance to his career with a minimal investment in time. The greater the risk the greater the reward, and the reward would be immense.

"Here is the nub," continued van Courtlandt. "The Japans are no longer that jewel in a bottle, and must be made profitable again. Your assignment could determine the fate of the Company. Dejima is the stopper, and for now only we have access to that cork. The Japans have changed little since the 1600s, and there has been no need or desire by them - or by us - for them to change. The Company has always understood the vital importance of that policy, but not everyone else does."

"In 1844 his Majesty King William II, God rest his soul, wrote to us, recommending that we close Dejima and open the Japans. He argued that it would be best for them without understanding the damage this would do to both the Japanese and to the Company. Fortunately, his heir King William III has far too many other distractions to be interested in a small commercial enterprise clear around the world."

"What would you have me do?" de Wolfe asked.

"Keep the cork in the bottle. Keep the Japans separated from any intrusions or outside trade agreements. Let them continue in their peace and isolation as they have since 1641. The Dutch are their friends, and they can trust no one else."

"I can do that," de Wolfe confirmed.

"Excellent!" van Courtlandt exclaimed, and every head at the table nodded in agreement. "I would entrust no one else with this."

"Sir, with all due respect. I have worked diligently here for the past seven years. You are my father by marriage. Each of you gentlemen knows me. There is no one who could be more committed or would labor more diligently on your behalf to complete the tasks that I am honored to receive here tonight. You have my word."

Van Courtlandt opened the stack of papers, signed his name and passed it down the table. "Your assignment in the Japans is of inestimable importance both for the Netherlands and for the Dutch East India Company. And, when you return, you will be granted full and complete lifetime membership to this Board upon my retirement."

"Could that be an addendum to the contract?" de Wolfe inquired.

"There will be no need," van Courtlandt assured him. "You can trust us. Your contract will be kept here under my personal watch, for safekeeping."

Half Moon

The next three months had raced by far too quickly, each day's work crushing de Wolfe under its gathering burden. There was never enough time to get everything done and prepare for his assignment on the other side of the world. One old man who had served as an accountant in Asia around the turn of the century was brought in to help educate him, but that effort had been useless. The old man could barely hear, and despite de Wolfe's shouted entreaties, all the withered curmudgeon would repeat was "Mighty fine! Mighty fine!"

Mr. van Courtlandt met with him often, emphasizing the need for speedy and conscientious work. The Japans being shaped-up was the desperate shrinking ambition of the Company, and might be the only manner in which they could financially survive. He must be clever, and he must be strict, their aspirations were resting on him, and his success was of paramount importance. Quite frankly, he grew tired of the nearly constant reminders.

For weeks the HALVE MAEN, the ship that would take him to Batavia, squatted at the Company's berth, a daily reminder of what was coming. Each time he saw it he felt a mixture of excitement and dread. It would be the beginning of a long and difficult journey that would eventually lead him to a life of comfortable prestige. It was both an opportunity and an obstacle to be surmounted. He could not envision what lay ahead, and resolved to focus on the result rather than the process. He came to view the dark hull with foreboding.

Camilla had retreated into her own world, and he seldom saw her as he arose early and then returned late in the evening. All of his meals were taken at the Company headquarters. He left her light-hearted notes in the morning, and they were gone in the evening, so he assumed that she had read them. When he did see her she had been quiet and subdued, even distant, but also at times affectionate. Neither one of them knew how they would deal with the coming separation. He wanted to explain to her how important this was to him, to the both of them, and the rewards that would come from this sacrifice. But, he never knew how to start that conversation and he seldom saw her at all except when she was sleeping, or pretending to sleep, when he returned home.

He often thought of when they had first met, the laughing happy strong-headed woman who nearly bankrupted him with her expensive tastes in food and wine. But whatever the expense it had been worth it to see her smile. She had proposed marriage to him, and although he was surprised he had readily accepted. She had laughed and told him she knew they would be married the first time she saw him, but she never explained why. He thought about that from time to time, and once during an argument she had rebuked him with "I don't know why I ever married you!" He had held his tongue and she soon apologized, but the sting remained.

De Wolfe knew why he had married her, it was his chance to build something greater than himself. Of course he loved her, and that should have been enough, but the practical side of him believed they could create more. A family, that is what he wanted. Maybe that was the source of the friction between them: Camilla existed for today, and de Wolfe lived for tomorrow. He needed to constantly remind himself to enjoy what was happening now and not to solely concentrate on what would come next. He needed to learn to embrace the world today, in this moment, rather than to constantly plan for the future.

The house, the Board appointment, the family, his life in Amsterdam, everything he wanted, it was all there right before him. But first came the Japans.

They had made love the night before his departure and then again in the morning. She had not initiated affection for months, but neither did she refuse her husband when he touched her. They had made love often since their marriage, ultimately neither out of passion nor affection, but almost as a sense of urgency and duty to ensure her rapid pregnancy. Unfortunately, nothing had happened and she began to hint of some fundamental fault in either his technique or weakness in his "fluids".

She did seem to enjoy the love-making, really, she just …. Well, she had lost involvement. She was there, of course, but not really with him. He was not complaining, far from it, and he understood that the coming long separation must weigh on Camilla just as heavily as it did upon him. But, any marriage problems they may have certainly would not be settled now, and there was nothing more to be done about it. And, despite Mr. van Courtlandt's frequent and increasingly awkward entreaties, there were still no signs of pregnancy when the contracted departure day arrived.

He helped her into the family carriage when Mr. van Courtlandt collected them that afternoon, and rumbled away to the HALVE MAEN. They would sail on the evening tide. No one spoke much as they traveled through Amsterdam to the Company's berth in the Old City. In so many ways he felt like he was dying. Not physically, certainly, but he had made out a will, finalized so many arrangements, told everyone good-bye. Could planning your own funeral really be that much different?

The HALVE MAEN was loaded and ready, and sailors carried his single trunk aboard and stowed it for him. She was a 1,400 ton "East Indiaman" built more for cargo stowage than for speed or comfort. She had been constructed in India under Dutch supervision more than twenty years ago out of hardy teak, and had made the annual trip to Holland and back to Batavia faithfully every year since. Along with her cargoes she carried a few passengers, mostly on Company business, bound for South Africa, India, Batavia, or a dozen other stops along the way. Her annual sailings were carefully timed to catch the eastern monsoon trade winds from India to Asia in the Winter and then return when the winds shifted back westward in the Summer. Then she would re-trace her route from India back to South Africa, and eventually northward, the entire voyage dependent upon the seasonal weather and taking one complete year.

Timing was crucial to catch the most favorable winds and currents on her journey south along the western coast of Africa, and after a quick stop, on past the Cape of Good Hope. From there to India for replenishment and a quick re-sorting of the cargoes aboard, carefully stowing the heaviest at the bottom of the hold to ensure maximum stability, and then on to Batavia.

At Batavia all of the cargoes, fourteen replacement workers outbound, and de Wolfe, would be trans-loaded to a smaller vessel that specialized in the Japans run. With the Captains' sailing skill and good fortune he would be there in half a year or less.

The carriage stopped at the berth, and the three of them climbed down and walked slowly to the gangway. De Wolfe felt like he was caught-up in the rapids of a river, unable to change the course of his path. What events had led him to this pier? Was it when he joined the Company? When he met Camilla? When he had expressed a desire for travel? Certainly, the last eight months and everything that had transpired since had brought him to this point, and like a leaf in the flood it would carry him on regardless of what he now did.

He noted Cas smiling at him from the corner of a building and waved him over, but his friend shook his head "NO!" and pointed at Mr. van Courtlandt. Cas did a pantomime of the older businessman, mocking his girth, and then of Camilla sashaying down the street with an umbrella. De Wolfe suppressed a grin, nodded his understanding and discreetly waved good-bye. Cas blew him a kiss.

At the gangway he held Camilla tightly as she patted his back, and he kissed her on the cheek. There was nothing left to say. Mr. van Courtlandt shook his hand and reminded him in solemn tones, "You gave your word".

It seemed to de Wolfe that he was being swallowed up by darkness as he looked around at Amsterdam and his family one last time before he went up. It was all up to him now. Whatever happened, whatever he might be required to do, he would ensure that his assignment would be a success. He climbed the gangway and boarded the HALVE MAEN, outbound to Asia.

A Beach in Kyūshū

The sun was setting into the ocean in a fiery red ball as the three samurai waited. Abe Akio was an unattractive, dark and malevolent warrior in his early thirties, and he stood alert in silence. Kamimoto Daikichi was sitting in a fisherman's small boat beached on the sand. In contrast to Abe's disheveled appearance, his own kimono was brightly colored and decorated with embroidery of flying cranes. He was older, but handsome and dignified, but also bored. Next to him sat the Chief Samurai, old, fat and slovenly from years of excessive drinking, staring listlessly out to sea.

Emerging out of the trees and into the brightness of the setting sun three other stern looking samurai approached them: The Challenger, young, athletic and obviously angry, and his two Seconds.

Kamimoto was the first to speak, *"Abe-sama, this is unnecessary."*

"I only accepted his challenge Kamimoto-Otona," replied Abe off-handedly as he quickly and expertly sized up the three opponents.

"He believes that he is the finest swordsmen in Kyūshū," stated Kamimoto.

Abe continued to study the other three with indifference. *"I believe that he is wrong."*

The three samurai stopped directly in front of Abe and several paces away from the rowboat as Kamimoto and the Chief Samurai continued to sit. The Challenger bowed to Abe and began, *"I am Sawabe Keishiro, Master Swordsman. My family has served the Daimyō of Saga for five generations. You shall kneel before me, or you shall die!"* He swiftly drew his long sword and stepping back took a fighting stance in front of Abe.

The name of *Sawabe Keishiro,* was well-known through-out central and southern Kyūshū, and the nickname *Chosensha* – the Challenger - referred to the four duels to the death he had already fought to bolster his rapidly growing reputation. Barely out of his teenage years, he was already considered a deadly master of *kenjutsu* – sword fighting – and instructed men twice his age on the Japanese art at the school he had founded two years earlier. But, there has always been a tremendous and important distinction between knowing how to use a sword, and when. He had yet to learn the difference.

Abe rested his hand on the hilt of his *katana* long sword still shoved deeply into his *obi* – cloth belt - his face expressionless. He pulled a long white headband from the sleeve of his kimono and tied it tightly across his forehead, then slowly withdrew his sword a short length partially out of the scabbard.

Kamimoto shook his head. *"There will be trouble if you kill another one,"* he warned.

Abe considered, and then shoved the blade back into its place. He removed both his short and long swords from his *obi*, and placed them inside the boat next to Kamimoto. *"I will not dull my blade on a child that has yet to learn the honor of bushidō,"* – the Way of the Warrior – he called over his shoulder. He then took one of the oars and tested its balance, swinging it in wide lazy circles, and then turned to face the Challenger.

The Challenger seemed unsure of what to do next, but then quickly became increasingly angry. *"Are you mocking me?"* One of the Seconds cursed and then began to step forward, only to be physically blocked by the bulk of the Chief Samurai as he rose from the rowboat. The Challenger screamed, *"I am Sawabe Keishiro, my family has served the Daimyō of Saga for five generations! Are you mocking me?!"*

Abe lowered the oar from in front of himself and then placed the paddle end on the ground, leaning on the handle. *"If a man seeks offence, it will soon find him."*

The Challenger's face blossomed into a bright red as his fury grew and then snapped. He screamed, raised his long sword above his head and charged Abe with a vicious slash towards his ear which was easily blocked with the oar.

The Challenger continued his attack, alternating between slashes and thrusts, all of which were parried. Soon, his breath was coming in ragged pants and gasps, and Abe easily pushed him to the ground with the blunt end of the oar. Humiliated and unsure the younger man looked to his Seconds, not knowing what to do next. He then rose shakily, took a deep breath and charged again, his sword held high above his head.

Abe knocked the sword away, and with the same motion smashed the young man's head, knocking him unconscious. He then replaced the oar in the rowboat and calmly returned his two swords to his belt.

One of the Challenger's Seconds stepped forward angrily, *"You did not fight fairly!"*

Abe serenely replied, *"Your Master is alive. Carry him home and have him return when he is a* man *who understands what it means to swing your blade for honor rather than for glory."*

"Bastard!" the Second screamed and leaped, drawing his sword in one blazingly fast motion. The Chief Samurai, taken completely by surprise, clumsily tried to draw his own sword, but as he stepped back tumbled instead into the rowboat next to Kamimoto.

The Second paused his step and slowly looked down in great wonder towards his mid-section where the hilt of Abe's sword was protruding from his abdomen. He then went to his knees, and fell forward onto his face, lifeless.

The Challenger was beginning to regain consciousness as his remaining Second assisted him to his feet and began to guide him away.

Kamimoto was still sitting in the rowboat, and sucked his breath in across his teeth in admonishment. *"Another death for you to explain, the Obugyō-sama will be most unhappy."*

"I didn't kill him," Abe responded defensively.

"And yet, somehow, one of them is dead."

"Well, I didn't kill the young one," Abe protested. *"But, you are correct, I probably should have used the oar on this one as well."*

The Chief Samurai had risen to his feet and was staring out to sea. Offshore, sailing slowly with the wind in the gathering gloom was a Western trading ship, a Dutch flag flopping listlessly on her stern. *"The foreign devils are arriving, they will be here tomorrow,"* said the Chief Samurai disparagingly.

Abe rolled the dead Second onto his side and pulled out his sword, shaking the blood off of the blade and then wiping it clean on the man's kimono. He then watched the ship fade into the gathering darkness.

The Shindo Family Household

Shindo Taka laughed and skipped as she carried a small bundle along the streets of Nagasaki, the evening gloom lit only by a few small lanterns. She was greeted warmly by shop keepers and passersby. She was young, beautiful and elegantly dressed, the Shindos being among the most respected and prosperous merchant families in the city.

She swung open the household gate and deeply bowed to the elderly gardener. It was a ritual they had shared for many years as she grew into a fine young woman and he aged into his profession. The family had taken him in from the streets and given him a home and dignity. He loved them all dearly for their generosity, and repaid them daily with dutiful work.

Taka slipped off her wooden *geta* sandals at the entrance and called out "*I have returned!*"

"*Welcome!*" her brother and sisters called back in unison.

Her parents, brother and two younger sisters were waiting anxiously at the dinner table as Taka unwrapped the bundle, and inside were sweet treats to add to the simple meal of fish and rice. She carefully set aside one of the treats to give later to the gardener.

"*Thank you, my child,*" her father smiled.

"*Husband! Your eldest daughter is no longer a child! She has become a beautiful young woman!*" chided her mother.

Taka covered her mouth in embarrassment as her siblings grinned and laughed. Her father smiled lovingly also as they prepared to eat. He carefully looked around to ensure that they were completely alone, and then reached under the table to withdraw a hidden book. On the cover was written "*De Heilige Bijbel*". "*Let us pray,*" he began.

The Foredeck

De Wolfe stood alone on the foredeck of the Dutch trading ship VERGULDE DRAECK anchored in the cool predawn darkness of Nagasaki Bay. She was an old and tired "*spiegelretourschip*", build in 1816 specifically for the route between Holland and Asia, with three masts and weighing 1,100 tons. She also carried forty-two old and largely obsolete smoothbore cannons for self-defense and normally manned a crew of just under 200 sailors. On this voyage there were fewer than 100 crewmen aboard in addition to her few passengers.

The journey from Holland to the Company's East Indian headquarters in Batavia aboard the HALVE MAEN had taken less than the planned four months, incredibly fast, with short stops in Africa, India and Siam. Once on the island of Batavia they loaded the Japan bound cargoes onto the VERGULDE DRAECK with Captain Ostrander, stuffed the holds further with even more trade goods, and prepared for the five-week sprint to the Japans. Now, in the Spring of 1852 they had arrived, and anchored last night off the coast of Nagasaki awaiting the dawn and the tide. Breaking the quiet, eight bells were rung from the ship's mast.

Captain Ostrander, the vessel's long-standing master, could see de Wolfe by the starlight peeking through the rigging and walked forward. He was a wizened heavy-bodied old Dutchman with a full white beard that had been making the run between Batavia and the Japans for over two decades. "A red sky in morning," he began.

"I wanted to see it at first light," de Wolfe responded, ignoring the ominous remainder that would have completed Ostrander's refrain, "sailor take warning". The sounds of the crew, muffled orders, the shuffling of men stirring below deck could be heard. In the distance, framed by the rising sun and brightening red sky was a small artificial island – a large Dutch standard flew from a tall flag pole on the lone wharf, and the city of Nagasaki and surrounding hills emerged from the darkness in the background.

Captain Ostrander's visage darkened as he scowled towards the land. "Dejima. That cursed island is more of a prison than a trading post."

Mid-ship a long boat was lowered and several sailors began to descend the rope Jacob's Ladder to the boat. A ship's officer shouted down at them, "Damn your eyes! Lively now!"

De Wolfe called from the foredeck, "You! Easy there I say! Cursing only reveals weakness in the hearts of men!" He then turned to Ostrander, "Captain! As the Company's representative I must again insist that you exert control!"

Ostrander sighed. Their relationship since Batavia, although short, had become increasingly more strained on the voyage. De Wolfe seemed intent on interjecting himself into every facet of the ship's daily routine, sometimes questioning the officers' orders, and even reprimanding them in front of the crew. He may represent the Company, thought Ostrander, but he does not run my ship! Still, the young popinjay would be ashore soon, and life would quickly return to normal. "What brings a gentleman such as you to this?"

De Wolfe turned, "My assignment is to protect the Company's interests in the Japans, and my success here will serve our family well."

"Family? You are married? And, you chose to come here?" asked Ostrander. Despite the ship's cramped and crowded quarters they had never discussed any personal matters on the northbound voyage.

"Two short years apart, and then she and I will be together forever."

"And, that is your plan? Do you know what happens here?" Ostrander seemed a bit surprised and slightly incredulous.

"Oh, yes, my plan is quite simple," de Wolfe countered with a confident air. "One and a half more years, and then forever together." He was not certain that he felt nearly as self-sure as he sounded. His life in Amsterdam already seemed distant, and he sorely missed Camilla. Right now, hearing himself say it, two years seemed to be a very long time.

The sailors stood cowed and quieted in the long boat, waiting, as de Wolfe walked to the railing and climbed down the Jacob's Ladder. "Indeed?" Ostrander called from the railing. "Nothing in the Japans is ever quite that simple."

De Wolfe sat in the boat and called up to the Captain, "And, nothing is ever quite that difficult either. I have found my way here to Dejima after all, advancing through the sweat of my own brow. I may have entered this life with little, but I can assure you that I will leave it with much."

There was a commotion in the distance on the island, angry shouts and commands in Japanese, muffled pleadings, and smoke began to rise from between the buildings. As de Wolfe looked towards the island with alarm, the ship's officer commanded the sailors and they began to row the long boat quickly towards the wharf.

Ostrander watched with slight amusement and chuckled, calling after de Wolfe, "If they don't burn the damn place down first!" He laughed out loud, and then muttered to himself, "red sky in morning". He then turned back to his duties aboard and thought, "simple"? Oh, to be young again.

The Island of Dejima

The man-made island was flat, fan-shaped and about thirty acres. A brisk walk would take a man from one side to the other in less than ten minutes regardless of which direction he chose. It was separated from the mainland by a short arched wooden bridge known as the "Dutch Gate". Blocks of two-story residences and offices lined the westward side facing the ocean, and warehouses filled the eastern landward side. Between them was an open dirt courtyard running the entire length of the trading post. At the end furthest from the wharf were gardens, pens for chickens, and a single cherry tree.

As the long boat reached the wharf and even before they could tie up, de Wolfe leapt ashore, racing toward the open space of the courtyard and the rising smoke. A score of the Dutch staff were being harangued and bullied by several samurai. Abe, his kimono dark and his hair askew, glowered at the cowering foreigners hatefully. Other samurai were bringing books and drawings and piling them nearby a now blazing stack of firewood.

Among the Dutchmen was Gerhard Schuck, standing fat and sweaty even in the cool morning air. He watched de Wolfe approach, and continued mopping his brow with a handkerchief that never seemed to leave his hand. "Where the Hell is Captain Ostrander?" he called angrily.

"Stop swearing!" demanded de Wolfe as he tried to understand what was happening. "What is going on here?" he yelled to no one in particular.

"The Japaners have gone completely mad!" Schuck shouted back over the threats and commands of the samurai.

The fire, smoke, shouting, the Japanese were now pushing and herding the Dutchmen, it was all too confusing, but de Wolfe knew that it must stop at once. "Here, you!" he shouted, "Stop that! Stop that, I say! Stop what you are doing!"

Abe was still yelling angrily in Japanese at the assembled Hollanders, and de Wolfe began moving towards him. The teenage figure of the Chakunan blocked him along with a larger and more mature man, and de Wolfe attempted to push them aside and move past. In return they easily knocked him to the ground, and he leapt up angrily. The two samurai immediately pushed him down again, and then stepped back ominously drawing their long swords.

De Wolfe lay in the dirt looking around, trying desperately to understand what was happening while everyone in the courtyard stopped still, watched, and awaited his next move.

Abe stepped forward, his face entirely expressionless, his eyes dark and malevolent like a shark's, and his right hand moved to the hilt of his long sword. He then slowly withdrew it slightly, exposing just a bit of the shiny razor sharp blade.

De Wolfe could both feel and hear the blood loudly in his ears while all other outside noises seemed to fade away. He kept staring at the glint of the steel of Abe's sword, mesmerized like a mouse in front of a snake. This was the first Japanese that he had ever seen up close: Long black hair bound together on the top of his head, dark eyes, a loose fitting garment of two parts, the top tied in front by a cloth belt, sandals of some kind made of wood, and two swords held securely in his belt, standing imperiously above him.

The contrast between the two men was striking: The warrior of Japan and the businessman of the Netherlands. One dark, deadly and seemingly ready to kill without hesitation. The other blond, fair colored, and at this moment very confused. For de Wolfe, the world only contained the two of them.

It was Schuck that broke the spell between them. He came bowing and smiling at Abe as he reached down and helped de Wolfe to his feet, taking him up by the arm. "So sorry. So sorry you motherless bastard," he said, knowing that Abe would not understand and feigning deference in the tone of his voice. "Rot in Hell you son-of-a-bitch." He continued to bow and pulled de Wolfe a few steps away.

"They came at first light across the Dutch Gate," he explained. "Pushed aside the night guards."

"Where is *Opperhoofd* Westerveldt?" asked de Wolfe.

"Died two days ago…" began Schuck.

"Murdered?" gasped de Wolfe.

"No, no," responded Schuck. "In his own bed. His heart I think. The Japanese took his body for cremation, and…" Schuck indicated the pile of personal effects next to the pyre burning on the ground. "And now his belongings."

"Isn't this Company property?" asked de Wolfe to no one in particular. He looked at a large sheath of rolled papers sealed with the VOC logo, and in defiance walked over and pulled it from the pile, holding it up before Abe.

"This is Company property!" he affirmed in a loud voice, obstinately shaking the thick roll of paper in the Japanese man's face.

In one blurry swift movement Abe drew his sword and slashed the wrist-thick rolled papers into two pieces, narrowly missing de Wolfe's hand and face. He then returned the sword to its scabbard in one motion before the heavier portion of the papers fell to the ground.

De Wolfe looked down, almost to make sure that all of his fingers were still there, and then regained his equilibrium and without fear threw the remaining roll back on the pile.

Abe began pacing and shouting at the Dutchmen in Japanese, *"Liars and thieves! You have betrayed us! You are animals! Do you hear me you stupid animals?"*

None of the Hollanders understood a word of Abe's tirade, and he stopped directly in front of de Wolfe who stood toe-to-toe with the enraged samurai. "Who are you?" the Hollander demanded.

Abe snorted in disgust, *"You smell and sound like sheep. Speak like a man!"* He was growing noticeably angrier, his face turning a bright red, and he moved as if to strike de Wolfe, raising his fist, and drawing it back.

De Wolfe did not flinch or acknowledge the threat, and continued looking directly into Abe's eyes, still unsure of what was happening, trying desperately to gain control over the situation he had thrust himself into, but completely unwilling to back down.

Unable to physically intimidate the younger man, Abe turned his wrath on the cowering figure of Schuck nearby and stepped towards him. De Wolfe interceded directly between them. "No!" He continued glaring at Abe. "Do you understand me?" I am telling you to leave him alone. NO!"

It was a stalemate. In frustration Abe turned away from the Dutchmen and walked to the fire. He selected a burning brand and took it to the pile of Dutch belongings and gave them one last hateful look. *"I will show you how to fix your lies!"*

A voice came from across the courtyard calling in Japanese, *"Abe-sama, stop! You cannot do this!* Kamimoto came forward and placed himself between the burning brand and the pile of goods, his hand on his belt. *"This is a matter for the Obugyō-sama. This could be evidence."*

"When the fox has a chicken in his mouth I need no further evidence," Abe grunted.

"This is a matter for the Obugyō-sama! I am the Otona here! You are dismissed!

Abe's rage was boiling, but he considered briefly, and then began issuing orders to the samurai. The Hollanders were herded back to their quarters, leaving de Wolfe and Schuck alone with the remaining Japanese warriors. Looking up, for the first time de Wolfe noticed Oriental women in gaudy geisha-style kimono and garish make-up watching, pointing and laughing from the windows of the Dutch workers' rooms.

Captain Ostrander joined them from the wharf, and in the background Abe was still berating and ordering his samurai. De Wolfe had had enough. He wanted answers and moved to Kamimoto. "Do you understand me!?" he demanded.

Kamimoto spoke surprisingly good Dutch, "It seems that you and Mr. Schuck have already angered Abe-*sama*."

"How?" asked de Wolfe, still confused by the morning's events.

"Maps, journals, and botanical samples," Kamimoto answered. "Possibly even religious materials. All illegal of course. And, it appears that someone was intending to take them aboard your ship to Holland."

"I most certainly know nothing of this!" interjected Ostrander.

"Who does know? Who is in charge here?" demanded de Wolfe.

"Well, you are now the *Opperhoofd*," answered Ostrander as Kamimoto nodded in agreement. "You are in charge."

"All foreigners possessing such forbidden items commit a crime against the *Shōgunate* punishable by death," explained Kamimoto.

"Maps? What can you possibly mean?"

"There must be an investigation. The *Obugyō-sama* of Nagasaki must determine who is responsible, and the guilty must be punished," Kamimoto explained. "And, if any others were involved, they must be discovered. It is a very grave matter."

"He cannot think that we were involved?" asked Schuck fearfully.

"We are all Dutch, Mr. Schuck," Ostrander said darkly. "Therefore we are <u>all</u> presumed guilty."

"I will begin the investigation," Kamimoto told them and turned away.

"Maps and journals? Punishable by death?" de Wolfe was astounded.

"Oh, the Japanese take their isolation very seriously," Schuck assured him.

De Heilige Bijbel

The elderly gardener was tending a small plot of just sprouted vegetables at the Shindo household. He carefully carried two wooden buckets to the first row and lovingly spooned out a bit of night soil from the first bucket, followed by a splash of water from the second, then worked the fertilizer into the earth with a stick. He briefly admired his work and then moved to the next plant. The mixture was disgusting, and stunk, but he smiled, content in nurturing the plants his adopted family would soon enjoy.

Outside the gate a heavily armed phalanx of six swordsmen marched in a loose formation led by the Chief Samurai. Each of them wore the official kimono of the *Obugyō* of Nagasaki, and the townspeople adroitly stepped aside and shop keepers hurriedly moved their wares as they were passed to avoid being trampled. These were determined men on official business, and nothing would impede them.

The Chief Samurai called the warriors to a halt in front of the Shindo household and pounded on the gate with his clenched fist. His face was flushed and his breathing heavy after the quick trek, and he was inwardly thankful for a brief respite before he needed to attend to his assignment. He pounded on the gate again.

The elderly gardener slowly swung the heavy gate inward, and was immediately brushed aside by the Chief Samurai as they pushed their way inside the compound. The gardener fell to his knees, pressing his forehead deeply into the dirt and averting his eyes.

"Merchant! You are ordered to come out immediately!" the Chief Samurai gruffly called out. *"Merchant!"*

Slowly and shyly, not sure what was happening, the family came out one-by-one, the last being Taka, shepherding her younger siblings onto the porch.

"Kneel! By the order and authority of the Obugyō-sho of Nagasaki I command you to kneel!" the Chief Samurai blustered.

The Shindo family fell to their knees as the group of armed men moved past them and into the household, and began ransacking their possessions while the Chief Samurai glowered at them with menace. One of the warriors soon found the Dutch Bible and brought it to the Chief Samurai. He looked at it with disgust and then threw it into the dirt of the courtyard, stepping on it and smugly grinding it into the earth.

"Stop!" screamed Taka and jumping up pushed him off of the Bible.

Taken by surprise, the Chief Samurai stumbled backward and tripped over the prostrate elderly gardener, nearly tumbling into the vegetable plot before righting his balance. As two of the samurai jumped to restrain Taka, and her family watched with furtive glances, the Chief Samurai looked down and his foot was stuck in the bucket of night soil, and covered with human feces.

Bellowing like a bull the Chief Samurai kicked the bucket off his foot with disgust and clumsily trampled the vegetable plot in his anger. He then walked slowly over to Taka, restrained by his men, and punched her squarely in the face, knocking her to the ground.

The Opperhoofd's Quarters

De Wolfe was very satisfied with his living arrangements. He had several sleeping rooms for himself and guests, a large dining room and kitchen manned by a personal Indonesian cook, – a seemingly jocular fellow named Acawarman, a billiard

35

room, separate work rooms and the largest space had an ornate roll-top desk. The few items he had brought from Holland had been carried off the ship and quickly unpacked

Most importantly he had a wonderful view of the Nagasaki Harbor and a magnificent spy glass so that he could see far out to sea. He could clearly view the VERGULDE DRAECK in the harbor, and briefly wondered if he could carry the spy glass across to the warehouses and look into the City of Nagasaki. Or, would that be "forbidden" as well? The accommodations were good, he thought, actually better than any he had lived in except for the van Courtlandt's house with all of their fine artwork and numerous servants. This was quite comfortable and would be very satisfactory indeed.

He was sitting at the desk, writing a letter to his wife:

My dearest Camilla,

I have arrived and begun my duties with the greatest anticipation. There is much here to learn, and much I do not yet understand, but I blame that on a lack of diligence and discipline quite possibly tolerated or even encouraged by my predecessor Opperhoofd Westerveldt. I will dedicate my initial efforts to remediating these deficiencies.

While I am loathe to be indelicate, I pray the past months you have grown full with the blessed fruits of our union. If our hopes are not yet fulfilled, please consult your doctors on this matter of great importance to both me and to your family. I will certainly place no blame and will do whatever is necessary. We can only pray for resolution.

I must encourage you again to be frugal with our savings, and accept no monies from your father, for I wish to be indebted to him no more than we already are. I am, of course, in constant agony over your absence.

Your loving husband, Hendrik

De Wolfe signed the letter with a final flourish, sealed it with wax in an envelope and then added it to a stack of correspondence to his wife he had already written on the voyage. It would be another six months before she would receive any of them, but it was important to him that he maintain the link to his home and family.

Trade Goods

De Wolfe and Schuck monitored the movement of trade goods from the VERGULDE DRAECK. Unloaded from the cargo ship and onto the long boats, the merchandise was rowed to the wharf and then lifted ashore by a small crane and next onto a hand-drawn cart. In the courtyard each item was carefully inspected by both Dutch and Japanese bureaucrats and then weighed before moving into one of the several storage warehouses. There were bales of silk and cotton, dark brown cones of raw sugar, boxes of books and various manufactured items, the bounty of a productive world, hundreds of tons of it. It would take weeks to unload. Nearby, the pile of Westerveldt's personal items remained untouched next to the cold ashes from yesterday's fire.

As the day progressed, the long boats ferried more and more goods from the ship's holds, which were then laboriously lifted up to the wharf and subsequently man-handled to the courtyard for inspection. It was hot work, and the sailors and laborers were sweating heavily under the direction of Captain Ostrander.

Abe was standing on the Dejima side of the Dutch Gate with two guards as Kamimoto came across leading a procession of senior Japanese officials, including the *Obugyō* of Nagasaki. He was an older man easily recognizable by the distinctive hat signifying his rank, and using a cane to help with a noticeable limp. The Japanese clerks and laborers were shocked at this rare event, and stopped whatever they were doing to gawk while the Dutch workers simply stood in confused silence.

Abe joined the procession as they entered an empty warehouse and Kamimoto approached de Wolfe telling him simply, "The *Obugyō-sama* awaits".

The Verdict

The first story of the spacious store room had a wooden floor and wide sliding doors to accept or disgorge any items – large or small – held for storage. Up the stairs to the second story however was quite different. Here the floor was covered with tatami mats, woven from rice straw, durable, clean and comfortable. Only high-value items would be taken to the second story.

As de Wolfe and the others entered the room the Japanese had already arranged themselves, the *Obugyō* sitting at the far end facing the door with a scribe at each hand. Lining the walls at each side were elaborately dressed officials and older

37

samurai with their swords laid at their sides, including Abe directly to the right side of the *Obugyō*.

Captain Ostrander was already kneeling uncomfortably on a pillow facing the Japanese as de Wolfe, Schuck and Kamimoto entered.

The *Obugyō's* voice was deep and sonorous, and the foreigners had no idea what he was saying. *"You are Captain Ostrander? You are Accountant Schuck? You are Capitão de Wolfe?"*

The three foreigners looked at each other in confusion, not even understanding the unfamiliar Japanese pronunciations of their own names.

The *Obugyō* continued, *"Crimes against the Tokugawa Shōgunate will not be tolerated. Do you have anything to say?"*

Kamimoto quickly translated this to the Hollanders, and both Ostrander and Schuck shook their heads, looking to de Wolfe to explain and to defend them. He considered briefly, and then also shook his head signifying "no".

The *Obugyō* seemed momentarily surprised by this, and pressed again, *"You have no explanation?"*

Kamimoto whispered urgently to them, "If you have any defense, now is the time to present it to the proper authorities".

De Wolfe studied the assembled Japanese: Abe, whom he did not like; Kamimoto whom he did not trust; and a roomful of others he did not know anything about. This was like no other "investigation" or "trial" he had ever experienced. What could they possibly expect him to say? He had barely just arrived in the Japans. Of course he had done nothing wrong, none of them had. Maps and botanical samples? Penalty of death? It was madness, pure madness.

"No," de Wolfe blurted out.

The *Obugyō* looked the three Hollanders over, obviously displeased. He then announced his verdict: *"Capitão Westerveldt has died of natural causes, and his body has been cremated. No further information is available. This investigation is concluded, and the regrettable and unfortunate death of the Hollander and the complete destruction of his personal belongings will be communicated to the Tokugawa Shōgunate. Captain Ostrander, you will have two weeks to transfer your cargoes. Then, you must depart immediately. This Hearing is now closed."*

The Japanese officials then rose and began to depart as Kamimoto explained the *Obugyō's* decision. "Cremated?" asked de Wolfe surprised. "He is not to be given the benefit of a Christian burial?"

"Burials are not our custom in Japan, and are forbidden on Dejima," Kamimoto explained.

"Two weeks?" Ostrander cut in, not sure that he had understood.

Schuck simply asked, "It is over?"

"Yes, it is over," Kamimoto told them. "His body has been burned, and the ashes scattered. Captain you must depart in two weeks, and the matter is now concluded."

"Impossible!" Ostrander protested.

"But, what was the crime?" demanded de Wolfe.

"The investigation was quite rigorous I can assure you, and the *Obugyō-sama* has determined that there was no crime, Mr. de Wolfe. For, if there had been a crime committed, then the *Obugyō-sama* and I myself would have had to have personally explained this failing to the *Shōgunate*." He paused briefly, "Any such report of criminal activities on Dejima would have benefitted no one. Therefore, there could be no crime." Kamimoto turned and began down the stairs.

Each new development seemed odder than the last, this being the strangest of all, and de Wolfe started after him, "There was no crime?" he shouted.

"Exactly!" Kamimoto called back to him. "You do understand Japan!"

The Reverend

De Wolfe hurried down the stairs to catch Kamimoto before he and the other Japanese crossed the Dutch Gate back into Nagasaki. In the courtyard Westerveld's maps and other items were already being burned by Abe as a few of the Dutch workers quickly sorted through the remaining pile retrieving their own belongings. "Mr. Kamimoto, I must protest! *Opperhoofd* Westerveldt was a Dutch citizen and a Company employee. His remains should have been returned to us so that we could have given him a Christian service and burial!"

"A Christian burial?" Kamimoto inquired, a little surprised.

"Of course!"

"Not possible, as you very well know. Burials are absolutely forbidden here on Dejima. All Dutch bodies must be cremated under the Agreement of 1641. In any case, all religious ceremonies of any kind are forbidden."

"Well, a memorial then. Not religious, but to celebrate his life. It is our custom and certainly you would not deny us that."

"Then, you may have a memorial. Sing songs, jump up and down, or run around in circles if it pleases you. But, there must be no Christian services, by order of the *Shōgun*."

Captain Ostrander was close behind, protesting to Schuck, "I have always had the whole Summer to provision my ship and handle the cargoes. Two weeks simply isn't enough time!"

"My dear friend," Schuck tried to sooth him while mopping his own face, "The bookkeeping may get a bit sloppy, but let us trust in our people to make this work out. If the Jappers have said that you must go, then you must. There is just no way around it!"

"No, something else is brewing," Ostrander told him. "Something is amiss. The shipping lanes are busy, and that always makes the Japanese nervous. It makes me nervous too,"

Ostrander is a good man, thought de Wolfe, and if he is nervous then, … but his attention was suddenly distracted and the thought forgotten as he stared. What in God's name is that?

The Reverend Parcifal Bleeckier came scurrying across the courtyard fluttering and flapping like some giant heavy bird trying to take off and completely out of control. He was impossibly tall and scrawny, his suit too small, with white skin showing at both pants legs and sleeves. He had a long hooked nose, uncombed thin scattered hair, and hadn't shaved in several days. Bleeckier seemed perpetually embarrassed by his appearance and kept tugging at the edges of his clothing.

De Wolfe followed this strange sight as it led him into a building.

The Chapel

Inside the small and simple room Bleeckier was humming to himself and turned around a portrait hanging on the wall to reveal an elaborate painting of a cross on the reverse side. A simple table served as a flimsy altar. He was completely oblivious as de Wolfe entered, quickly followed by a panting and sweating Schuck. Seeing de Wolfe for the first time and not knowing what to do the gangly man stood in confused quiet for a long moment, his humming slowly fading way, and then simply said "Hello?"

He then extended his hand, and his sleeve rose nearly to the elbow and he quickly tried to pull it back down, smiling in consternation. "Pleased to meet you, I am Parcifal Bleeckier, I am the Pastor."

Sternly de Wolfe asked, "The Pastor? But, all religious observations are officially forbidden."

"Right! Quite right," Schuck interjected, "But, like so many things here in the Japans, 'forbidden' seems to have many different meanings."

Bleeckier tried to explain, "Not openly, of course, and therefore I am tolerated. But, I am here mainly for the mens' consultation. And, in a pinch, we have even conducted a quiet service or two. Nothing ostentatious. We had a memorial right here for *Opperhoofd* Westerveldt the evening that he died."

"You see? It is always good to have a man of the cloth available," Schuck added hopefully.

De Wolfe slowly turned to Schuck, "There seems to be much that I have not been told. And, where is my doctor?"

At the question Bleeckier took an uncoordinated step backwards and went head over tea kettle across one of the row of chairs that could have served as a pew, and crashed noisily in a heap on the floor. He leapt up in embarrassment with an ease borne of frequent practice and brushed off his clothes.

Schuck was hesitant to answer the question and de Wolfe stared at him in uncomfortable silence. "At home. At home with his wife in Nagasaki," he said finally quietly.

"Speak up man," de Wolfe pressed him. "With his wife did you say?"

"His Japanese wife, yes."

"In Nagasaki did you say?"

De Wolfe came close to Schuck and repeated the questions as Bleeckier tried to retreat. "With his Japanese wife? In Nagasaki? Not here on Dejima?"

It all came tumbling out of Schuck at once, "Dr. Franz once saved the leg of our *Bugyō-sama* with his potions and ointments. The fellow was so grateful that he built our good doctor a home in the city and allows him free rein to come and go as he pleases."

"Are you saying that our doctor is fornicating with a local woman?"

Schuck was unsure how to answer this as de Wolfe's anger seemed to grow. "Well, the term 'fornicating' does seem to be rather a bit harsh. One of the few pleasures afforded to us woeful souls is the companionship of the local women," he said hopefully.

De Wolfe turned to Bleeckier, "I most certainly did say 'fornicating'. Reverend, do you approve?"

Bleeckier stepped back and almost tumbled down again before righting himself. "It is sometimes easier for God to provide forgiveness than it is to dispense happiness," and he smiled weakly.

De Wolfe turned and strode back into the sunlit courtyard with purpose, followed by Schuck and eventually Bleeckier.

The Local Women

De Wolfe stopped in the middle of the courtyard and slowly turned, observing. Courtesans were crossing the Dutch Gate into Nagasaki as Hollanders bid them good-bye, and that became the focus of his attention and he began moving towards them.

Kamimoto was speaking with Abe and the guards at the Dutch Gate and saw de Wolfe coming, and moved to block his path to the women.

"You! You there!" de Wolfe called out at the women as Schuck also moved to intercept him.

"You do not understand!" Schuck pleaded with him. "Give the men time!" All the Dutch workers had stopped to watch what developed next, suddenly both suspicious and defiant. "Look at them," Schuck urged. "You risk a mutiny!" he whispered with concern.

De Wolfe looked about, suddenly very alone and isolated in the crowded courtyard. Not knowing what precisely to do, he confronted Kamimoto, "What is going on here?" he demanded.

"I like whisky," Kamimoto calmly replied.

"I am sorry, what? What did you say?"

Kamimoto tried to sooth de Wolfe, "You want answers, and answers always take time and usually whisky. Bring whisky tonight. We will talk."

Whisky

Despite the small size of the unfamiliar island, de Wolfe asked twice for directions to Kamimoto's quarters, the second time struggling to understand one of the Japanese guards at the Dutch Gate. He kept repeating "Kamimoto? Kamimoto?" as if

42

by saying the word louder and more slowly it would help the poor man understand him. Finally, the guard pointed and de Wolfe set out once again in the darkness.

Now he stood in front of what must be a door, built with little sections of wood and paper, but he could find no handle or knocker. With two glasses in one hand and the whisky bottle in the other, he was stymied. He thought about kicking the panel with his foot, or even bumping it with his forehead to announce himself, but finally settled on weakly thumping against it with his elbow.

Rather than opening inward the panel slid unexpectedly to the right, revealing Kamimoto in a lightweight evening kimono, and behind him a single simple tatami room with a small writing table on the floor and the beginnings of a seascape oil painting on an easel in the corner.

"I thought we might get better acquainted," said de Wolfe and began stepping inside the room.

Kamimoto subtly moved to block his entrance, and looked down pointedly at de Wolfe's boots, covered with the dust of the courtyard. "Excellent," he replied. "Let us go for a walk."

Carefully stepping out onto the porch, Kamimoto slipped into a pair of sandals, and they began a leisurely stroll through the quiet and darkened courtyard of Dejima. The hustle and bustle of the days sorting and counting was concluded, and the trade goods had been stored in the various warehouses, or covered with large pieces of canvas, stoically awaiting tomorrow's resumption of business.

There was the ring of a woman's laughter, and drunken singing coming from the mens' quarters as they passed the Dutch Gate and the bored disinterested guards there. They continued past more warehouses and towards the tall flagpole until they arrived at the simple rock and wooden wharf that ran parallel to Nagasaki Bay.

De Wolfe plopped down on the wharf, his feet hanging out over the water, set down the two glasses and pulled the cork out of the whisky bottle. Kamimoto looked down at the dirt and dried mud on the wooden planks, and then at his clean light evening kimono. Well, it would just have to be washed after. There was nothing else to be done, he decided, and sat next to de Wolfe.

The moon was just setting over the harbor, and several long boats bobbed quietly against the wooden wharf. The VERGULDE DRAECK floated off shore in slightly deeper water, highlighted in the moonlight and serene in her own world. De Wolfe filled the glasses and handed one to Kamimoto. "To prosperity!" he toasted, and they drank quietly for a moment.

"You are the 'Otona" here at Dejima, is that the correct word?" he began.

43

"Over one hundred Japanese translators, inspectors, cooks, laborers. Yes, I am responsible for them. The inventory and the protection of the trade goods, the buildings. The supply and daily operations of the trading post, that is my duty also. In short, I am responsible for you.

"And, did that include the 'forbidden items'?" de Wolfe asked.

"Oh, I am responsible, but not for every item, and not for every moment. My duty is to ensure that the Hollanders have what they need. The damage they do, to themselves or to others, is their own responsibility."

"Who is that man Abe?"

"Abe-*sama* is from Fukuoka, a city to the north, and he commands all of the samurai that protect you."

"Protect us from what?"

"Most often from yourselves. How may I be truthful without insulting you? The Dutch are a relatively uncivilized people."

De Wolfe was surprised by this and also he <u>was</u> insulted. "Holland is one of the most advanced and prosperous nations in the world. Uncivilized? Hardly!"

"I have hurt your feelings, and therefore I am most sorry. The Dutch are very advanced technically, and there is much we Japanese can learn from you. Medicine, machines, weapons, it is wonderful what you can do. However, we here in Japan have little need of such items. Our lives may seem simple to you, but they are rich with art, poetry, discipline, honor, and most importantly, duty."

"We have all of those! Dutch painters are renowned! Poets, romantic novelists, playwrights, we are among the finest artists of the world!"

"Again, forgive me if I have offended you," Kamimoto said quietly. "I truly wish that I could see the art of Holland, but I will never leave Japan. I wish…. Well, there is a wide world outside of Dejima, isn't there? But, the Hollanders that I have known… I do not blame them, you understand, working here is a lonely and difficult life, we must all seek purpose and comfort wherever they can be found."

They drank quietly for a few moments, then de Wolfe started again. "We were speaking of Abe. Was it he who betrayed us to the, what did you say? The 'bug-a-same'?"

"Betrayed?" Kamimoto considered for a moment, amused by the Dutchman's inept attempt to pronounce the Japanese titles. "That is an odd way to put it. Yes, it

44

was Abe-*sama* who reported the forbidden items to the *Bugyō-sho* in accordance with Japanese law."

"Nagasaki, you see, is governed by a magistrate directly appointed by the *Shōgun* that we call the *O-bu-gyō-sama*," Kamimoto pronounced the syllables slowly for the foreigner's ear, "out of respect for his position. He manages the governmental administration that we call the *Bugyō-sho*. As was his duty, Abe-*sama* informed the *Bugyō-sho,* and thus the *Obugyō-sama* conducted the investigation. But, realistically how can one betray his enemy?"

"Why would we be his enemies?"

"Abe-*sama* dislikes all things foreign. His duty is to protect you, but he does not like you. I would recommend that you stay away from him."

"And, he answers to you?"

"To me?" Kamimoto chuckled. "Oh, no. Abe-*sama* answers only to the *Obugyō-sama* of Nagasaki."

A drunken Hollander kissing and groping a laughing courtesan wandered out of the darkness and nearly stumbled over Kamimoto as the woman giggled, slipped and nearly dropped herself into the water before careening away.

"And the women?" de Wolfe asked, nodding in her direction.

"Their lives are far better here than working on their family farms or in some household as a maid. They have traded a lifetime of labor for a fleeting interlude of pleasure. Is that a bad bargain?"

"Yes, I believe that it is. In any case, I would like to emphasize to you that I am most interested in the courtesans that visit Dejima," de Wolfe said trying to understand his options. The thought of open prostitution at Dejima had not previously occurred to him and certainly could not be tolerated.

"Yes, I believe that I understand your interest in these women completely." Kamimoto smiled, neither understanding the other at all. "I can assist you in that. But, forgive me for asking Mr. de Wolfe, why are you here?"

"I am not sure how to respond to your question, sir. I was assigned to Dejima by the Company. I have a contract."

"But, you had a choice?"

"Of course I had a choice. It is a two year assignment, and then I will return to a comfortable life in Holland."

"Interesting," mused Kamimoto. "Your bargain then is to trade a brief interlude of labor for a lifetime of pleasure."

The Japanese man looked out to sea for a long moment. "I was brought to Dejima myself also, as a small boy, taken from what little family I had. I started helping the Batavian cook, cleaning vegetables with my small hands. I would sit in the shadows each night listening to the Hollanders drink and laugh, straining to understand a word, a phrase. I was like a baby listening to its own mother, and learning."

"When I became too big for the kitchen, I moved to the warehouse where I learned how to lift, count, and eventually inspect the trade goods. I slept in the rooms above, and never left the island. Where would I have gone? But, I still listened, and I studied, and I learned."

"Finally I was noticed by the old *Otona*, a bitter old man, speaking my poor Dutch, teaching the *yuujo* a phrase or a compliment in exchange for a treat or a favor, and he beat me with a stick. But then, he took me to live with him and taught me until the day that he left the island in disgrace. He beat me like an animal, practically every day, at the slightest provocation. But, he taught me patience and discipline, and yet I believe that he hated me in every fiber of his body. I have never understood exactly why."

De Wolfe thought about his own childhood in Amsterdam, how it had seemed so difficult and hard to him. But he had never wanted for anything he really needed, and had never been beaten. How easy in comparison it must seem to what Kamimoto had grown up with.

"I have been here my whole life it seems," the Japanese man continued. "And I am certain that I will die here. Or, perhaps I will be taken away in disgrace, just like my predecessor. It seems that just like you, I too was assigned to Dejima. But you? I do envy you. You had a choice, and you will one day leave."

Kamimoto nodded to himself, lost in thought, finished his drink and stood, soon joined by de Wolfe who spoke sternly, "I find this all very interesting, and I will admit that I do not understand Japan, but I too have responsibilities. It is of the utmost importance that the next year be profitable and proceed smoothly."

Kamimoto sighed, "I will be here long after you have returned to Holland. Japan is a country you may not understand, but there is no need for you to understand it either. This is something I believe that we can both agree on."

"I will not be deceived nor bullied!"

Kamimoto handed him the empty glass, "Thank you for the whisky."

46

Papa! Please!

It was just past noon when the hired carriage stopped in front of the *Oost-Indisch Huis*, and Camilla gracefully stepped down from inside, took a few coins from her purse, paid the driver and moved away as the man tipped his hat, cracked his whip above the horse's head and started off.

It had been just over one year since her elegant wedding in Dam Square, and she was now quite used to being Mrs. Hendrik de Wolfe, at least in name. She was expecting to receive a packet of letters from Batavia when the HALVE MAEN returned in the Fall, but for now she was lonely and bored. The work on the house was still not finished, and her friends were themselves getting married off one-by-one and starting their own lives. One of her own bridesmaids had given birth to a little girl just a few months ago, but no one seemed to know who the father had been. It was really quite a scandal! Unfortunately, her own pregnancy had never seemed to come to fruition.

There were only two ways to fill her days, eating and shopping, and the more she ate the less her clothes fit, so she had to shop for new ones. And for that, she needed Papa.

As always she looked quite regal in a broad dress with flaring hoop skirts and a brand-new plumed hat that was topped with the feather of some African bird. Both men and women nearby stopped to admire her as she hurried through the tunnel and into the main courtyard before heading inside the building. She moved with the easy pace of someone who knows exactly where they are going.

Inside the clerks glanced with disinterest as she passed until she came to a large oak door that was open, allowing a breeze to pass in through the window, across the man working at a large desk, and into the hallway. "Papa," she called and stood at the doorway smiling.

"Daughter!" Mr. van Courtlandt called, looking up from the paperwork piled on his desktop. He was always happy to see her for it gave him an opportunity to get up and stretch for a few moments, and mostly because she was still his little girl, even if she was now a married woman with her own household to maintain. "You are beautiful today! Have you come to join me for dinner?"

"That would be lovely, Papa. Yes, let's. I am so bored at home!" She then gave him a twirl and that little girl pout that she used so effectively to get her way.

"Why are you bored?" he scowled. "There is much there for you to do, how are the renovations coming?"

"I sent them away, Papa. They come every day so early, and I cannot sleep! And, there is dust everywhere from whatever it is they are doing. I just cannot be comfortable there at all!"

"You must put up with it just a little bit longer, and it will soon be a beautiful house."

"Can't I come and live with you again Papa? Please? It smells Papa! And, I have only one maid, and it's noisy and dusty, and the food is awful, and everything is horrible, just horrible!" She put on the pout again.

"Alright," Mr. van Courtlandt said, pushing back his chair and standing up. "Let's get down to it. What do you really want?"

"I need money, Papa. There are so many bills."

"You've already spent all of Hendrik's money for the month?

"Oh, Hendrik has no need for money wherever he is in China! And, I have only spent it on things that I really need."

"It isn't China," he scowled, looking up at the expensive wide-brimmed and plumed hat she was wearing. "Alright," he continued and pulled a coin purse from his breast pocket. "How much this time?"

Camilla withdrew a stack of invoices from her own bag and carefully placed them on his desk. "Will you pay these for me Papa?"

Mr. van Courtlandt began sorting through them, "Dresses, hats, jewelry, restaurants…"

"And, a cook," Camilla added. "Find me someone that really knows how to prepare meals for me properly. The maid is practically useless beyond boiling mutton."

He put his hands sternly on his hips and admonished her. "Fine. I will handle these for you, and yes you may find and hire a cook. Have her come and speak to me here about her wages and employment, and I will handle everything."

"Thank you Papa, thank you!" she exclaimed, jumping slightly up and down in her joy and excitement.

"But," he continued, "you must bring the workman back to finish the house. It must be ready for Hendrik and your family when he returns."

"Oh, I will Papa, I will! Now, let us go out into this beautiful day and have a wonderful dinner!"

"Promise me first," he cautioned her, "that you will arrange for the workmen to complete the renovation."

"Of course, Papa, of course!"

She did allow the construction to continue, but no work was to be done before noon, leaving only half days, and the labor proceeded slowly. The tradesmen complained heavily as they were forced to leave one work site at their mid-day dinner and rush to the de Wolfe house in Jordaan to complete the day. Nobody was really happy about the schedule except for Camilla, who could now sleep in until late morning in peace.

The Doctor

Schuck and de Wolfe began their usual morning walk through Dejima observing the daily routine. Bleeckier was assisting staff with the counting of goods, piles of ivory, leather and buffalo skins being carefully inspected, measured and weighed on a large set of scales. As they moved past the Dutch Gate they paused, and several courtesans went by them, giggling and bowing to Schuck who seemed both flattered and embarrassed by their attention. "Happy men do happy work," he smiled at de Wolfe a little chagrinned.

"And, are you sir, a 'happy' man'?" asked de Wolfe tartly.

"Well, why yes my dear friend," stuttered Schuck, clearly embarrassed. "I am, 'happy', from time to time."

De Wolfe was about to say more when Dr. Philipp Franz came literally dancing across the Dutch Gate and into Dejima. He unabashedly made a great production of his entrance, singing and greeting the guards with a flourish of stage bows and fellowship, then grabbing up a courtesan and waltzing her around for several steps before hugging her and striking a pose with his hands on his hips.

"Good morning ladies and gentlemen!" he announced to everyone. "All of you are looking quite proper this morning I must say! Quite proper indeed!"

Dr. Franz was short and round, middle-aged, slightly overweight with thinning grey hair, and incredibly buoyant. He did a small jig before the guards, trying unsuccessfully, at first, to make them laugh, and ended with another stage bow down on one knee. The guards were doing their best to remain somber, but by now even Abe was smiling. They liked Dr. Franz.

49

From the center of the courtyard Bleeckier was trying desperately, but to no avail, to attract Franz's attention, waving his long thin arms like a scarecrow caught up in a strong breeze.

Dr. Franz saw Schuck standing with de Wolfe and rushed over to greet them as well, closely followed by his Japanese wife. "Mr. Schuck," he shouted joyously, grabbing the accountant's hand and pumping it up and down furiously. He then turned to de Wolfe, "And, you must be our new *Opperhoofd*!"

De Wolfe regarded him coldly. "Your local 'wife' Dr. Franz?"

"Truly the love of my life! I could not live without her!" Bleeckier had come up behind de Wolfe and was slashing his hand across his throat and making horrific painful faces in a vain attempt to warn Franz off.

"And, were you with your local 'wife' when *Opperhoofd* Westerveldt passed away?" de Wolfe asked, unamused by the jocular physician.

"Oh, I was sir, I was," he nodded. "His heart you see, all the symptoms. And nothing more could have been done about that. A great pity, was it not?"

"Yes, I see," de Wolfe continued sternly, "And, did you know... that he had collected certain 'forbidden items' prior to his death?"

"I did sir, I did indeed! All academic materials of course, and I gave them to him myself. Quite sorry to lose them, but his passing was very sudden although not unexpected..."

De Wolfe was quite taken aback by this admission, "<u>You</u> gave them to him?" he asked incredulously.

"Why yes, yes I did."

"You confess that you provided the materials which nearly brought ruin to our entire enterprise?"

"Ruin? Not at all," now it was Franz's turn to be surprised. "Japan is a great mystery sir. We must be prepared to welcome her into the fraternity of nations!"

"That is not our responsibility at all, doctor. In fact, it is quite the opposite. Your personal priority must be to your duties here on Dejima, and may I ask you, sir, to commit yourself fully to your obligations <u>here</u>! And," he added, "to immediately cease collecting any such 'academic materials'!"

Suddenly Franz became very serious. "Are you telling me that I cannot return home with my wife?"

50

"Your home is here, doctor. And, it is not proper to allow whores into the men's quarters."

Franz was stunned, and Schuck attempted to intercede on his behalf, "Not whores, Mr. de Wolfe. Courtesans."

"And, there is a difference?" asked de Wolfe, eyeing them both.

Schuck tried to explain, "It is a respected profession. It would not be either Christian or proper to judge them too harshly."

"It is not my place to judge them at all gentlemen, but they will be judged. There is no place for them here. See to it." De Wolfe turned and strode away to his quarters.

Atonement

The grounds of the Nagasaki *Bugyō-sho* - government building - were defined by a stone wall the height of two men. The wall ran in a square with a large "L" shaped courtyard inside leading from the heavy wooden gate to the main building, and atop that section of the stone wall were the wooden offices of minor officials and guards. The walls featured *ishiotoshi* - small downward facing windows - that were used for shooting arrows or hurling stones against attackers. Every surface above the perfectly inlaid stone, both inside and out, was covered with bright white plaster. Grey tiles covered the roof, and large iron caldrons filled with water were at the corners of the courtyard as fire was always the biggest threat. It had been built in a time of war and could easily function as a fortress, or a prison.

Across the stone courtyard and in the center of the compound visitors would climb five stair steps to enter the large administrative main complex, the building filled and divided by a number of small tatami rooms, and one large meeting room for important formal functions such as the discussion today.

The *Obugyō*, his bad leg bent uncomfortably underneath him, kneeled on a pillow at the front of this room, with senior government officials lining both walls. This is how government business was often conducted in Japan, it was a larger version of the "investigation" into Westerveldt's death.

Directly in front of the *Obugyō* knelt Kamimoto and Taka. He wore his usual style of light and brightly colored kimono, which he had changed to silk as the weather grew warmer. She was disheveled, dirty, and almost unrecognizable from her imprisonment. She was feral looking in a soiled kimono and still suffered a dark black eye from where the Chief Samurai had struck her. But, her composure remained both dignified and defiant in the formal and imposing setting.

The *Obugyō* surveyed her carefully and then spoke, his voice rough and grating, *"Christian materials were found in the merchant's household. Kamimoto-Otona, do you have further evidence to offer?"*

"Not evidence, my liege, but I do wish to speak."

"Proceed."

"There is sufficient proof of guilt, and punishment must be swift," Kamimoto confirmed.

"The Shōgun's law is clear," grunted the *Obugyō*.

"Obugyō-sama the law is clear, but might not the punishment also be used to benefit the Shōgunate? The Hollanders have a new Capitão. He is an unknown and also somewhat strange man. This woman understands some of their language, she could be most useful. I believe that she is also acceptable to their tastes," he looked at Taka disparagingly, *"if she is cleaned up."*

The *Obugyō* considered for a moment. *"You are saying she would become a courtesan and asking to use this woman as a spy?"*

"She may seduce the Hollander," Kamimoto explained. *"She will gain his confidence, and report regularly to me. Through her service we may in this manner permit this woman to demonstrate her loyalty to the Shōgun."*

"Is she a virgin?" the *Obugyō* inquired. *"Have the doctors examined her?"*

"Yes, that has been confirmed."

"Would it not be better to provide a woman who has knowledge in pleasing men? A professional, rather than an inexperienced girl?"

"I had considered that my liege, however, it is almost impossible to employ one that does not find the Dutchmen disgusting. This one will comply, because of her family."

The *Obugyō* nodded his understanding.

A tear rolled silently down Taka's cheek, *"Let me die with honor now,"* she said, her voice barely audible.

The *Obugyō* considered quietly, and then commanded, *"Shindo Taka. Do your duty faithfully to the Shōgunate and your family may live. Seduce the Hollander, and report to Kamimoto-Otona. Fail in your duties and you will all be taken to the execution grounds. Do you understand?"*

Taka showed no emotion, but tears continued to fall silently down her dirty face. She and Kamimoto bowed deeply to the *Obugyō*, stood, and then began backing out of the room. The *Obugyō* called out to the Chief Samurai standing guard just outside, *"And, clean her up!"*

She Is For You

It had been another busy day that had raced past de Wolfe, they were all starting to run together now, and he barely remembered which day of the week it might be. The quiet evenings in his residence were a respite, and he valued them greatly. Tonight he had invited Schuck, Dr. Franz and the Reverend Bleeckier to play the card game whist, and Captain Ostrander joined them, conducting a lone assault against the billiard table in the adjoining room.

The Indonesian cook, Aca…., Aca… Aca something… Oh yes, Acawarman had prepared a splendid Dutch meal with pork, cheese and hot fresh bread, and that caused him to wonder briefly what kinds of foods the Japanese ate. He would ask Kamimoto the next time he saw the man.

De Wolfe had been a very unpopular fellow in Dejima since the day he had forbidden access to the island by the courtesans. None of the men would speak with him, or even acknowledge his presence. When he spoke to them they would usually stare at the ground, pretending they could not hear him. The last few days had been personally very trying for him, but he was convinced that he was doing the right thing, if only they would understand. It was all for their own good.

They had settled down to their cards for several hours, and each had consumed multiple comforting glasses of whisky with Schuck winning the tricks regularly. Now, Bleeckier and Schuck were smoking ornate clay pipes, each engrossed in their own personal game strategies. Franz had dealt, and de Wolfe on his left was considering leading with his strongest suit, or perhaps playing a singleton with the one heart he possessed, when he looked up and saw Schuck make a clumsy move to draw a card from his sleeve and replace one of the cards in his hand. Dr. Franz clearly noticed the cheating as well and smiled, catching Bleeckier's eye and winked at him as the Reverend smiled back, rolled his own eyes in acknowledgment, and nodded.

De Wolfe took a deep breath to voice his objection when the room fell silent as the unexpected click-click of wooden shoes began climbing the stairs outside and up to the residence. There was a soft knock, and Kamimoto opened the door, followed by the most amazing creature.

The woman stepped out of her wooden *geta* sandals and in through the doorway. Her kimono was striking, brightly colored and meticulously embroidered with flying birds and flowers. Her black hair was folded into its own design high above her head and held in place by a bright silver comb. Woven into the coiffeur were live small white flowers, which fell off to one side like a waterfall of color, sharply contrasting with the darkness of her hair. Her face was stark white powder, her lips a bright red, and he could not look away from the eyes, dark orbs highlighted by a reddish blush that faded into her high cheekbones. She was doll-like and barely recognizable as human, rather some sort of dream-creature. He could perceive a similarity between the courtesans he had seen cavorting with the men, but it was like comparing a child's pencil scratching with a Rembrandt. He had never seen anything quite so foreign to him and yet at the same time surreal and enticing.

Kamimoto motioned her forward and presented the woman to de Wolfe saying simply, "She is for you. A gift from the *Obugyō-sama*. You may call her *"yuujo"*.

De Wolfe rose from his seat in shock, and began to choke on his whisky.

Taka kept her hands clenched tightly in front of her and her eyes remained demurely downcast, but she tried to observe as much as possible. She could only understand a few words, but had heard the term "gift" and knew it must mean her. Kamimoto calling her "yuujo" - a semi-polite reference to a whore - would have stung her pride at one point, but for now she only brushed that aside.

She had spent the last days being intently instructed on how to carefully apply the bright make-up and complicated clothing of an entertainer, and although it would take years of diligent study to truly master the necessary skills what she had learned would be enough for these foreigners, they would never be able to discern the difference between an artisan and a prostitute.

The room was brightly lit with multiple glass lanterns fueled by some kind of clear liquid to dispel the darkness, and was filled with blue tobacco smoke. She also smelled the familiar odor of men and she breathed out to push it away. She had never even seen let alone been close to a Dutchman before, but everything she had ever heard was quite obviously true. They were large fat hairy brutes with big noses and long beards. Everyone in Nagasaki knew of Dejima, of course, and when they gossiped of it in hushed tones it was often the insatiable philandering of the barbarian men there.

The one choking on his whisky must be the *Opperhoofd*, the man who would rape her. She had known this night would come, and often thought of what it might bring. She would not give the satisfaction of showing the disgust she would feel, nor the pain. She would give him nothing of her. And, after, she would find her way to the kitchen and a knife. Not for him, but only for herself. The punishment of *the Obugyō-sama* would be complete, and she would wash away the stain with her own blood, both her own and possibly her family's. In the meantime there would be no hate, no pain and certainly she would give no satisfaction. Not to them, and not to him.

"She has never been with a man," continued Kamimoto smiling. "She will serve you quite properly."

"No!" de Wolfe finally croaked out, choking. "No! I cannot!"

Kamimoto was puzzled, "What do you mean you cannot?"

"I cannot accept a strange woman into my household!" stammered de Wolfe.

"I do not understand," Kamimoto responded, becoming slightly perturbed. "You said that you were 'most interested' in the courtesans of Dejima. We are providing you with one."

"Yes! Most interested in resolving the problem of the courtesans, but not in obtaining one myself!"

"You can't refuse a gift from the Obugyō-sama!" called Dr. Franz from across the room.

The guests were quickly becoming quite amused at the irony of the situation, de Wolfe having a courtesan in his household only days after forbidding them from the island. Even Captain Ostrander had stopped his game of billiards and was now leaning on the cue, a broad smile on his face. "Good for the goose, good for the gander!" he offered.

"I am a married man!" protested de Wolfe.

Kamimoto was confused, surprised and now angry. He had thought de Wolfe would be pleased, and now he was refusing to take possession of the woman. "She is here, and she is yours." He motioned, and Taka stepped forward obsequiously. "What you do with her is your own concern." He turned and left the five men alone with the geisha.

De Wolfe spun back to his guests, pleading, "No! I cannot and will not accept her."

"Seems like you have little choice in the matter," Schuck observed.

"Maybe we should call her your 'Second Mate'?" enjoined Ostrander, causing the others to chuckle. He then finished his whisky. "Well, it's late. Back to my ship," and he quickly departed.

He was soon followed by the others, laughing and bowing to Taka on the way out, leaving the Dutchman and the Japanese woman alone in the household.

De Wolfe, frustrated and not knowing what else to do, walked over to his desk, sat down and prepared to do some work. Taka stood motionless waiting by the doorway. Several minutes passed until the Dutchman, unable to concentrate, gave up and confronted her. *"Yuujo!"* he demanded, not knowing what else to say.

Taka fully expected this foul foreigner to rape her. What was he waiting for? For the sake of her family she would endure that much she had promised herself. No matter how horrible, regardless of the ignominy and tortures this monster imposed upon her, she would never give him the satisfaction of seeing her break. If her duty required, she could endure anything. But, after, there would be a reckoning. Embarrassed and humiliated, not knowing what might come next, she stood beside him at the desk and awaited her fate.

"I want you to go!" he told her, loudly and clearly. The woman did not move. "Do you understand me? I am telling you to leave. Leave me alone!"

"Cannot," she said, her eyes downcast.

"Cannot, or will not?" he asked sternly.

She raised her eyes to him in defiance, "Cannot!" she snapped at him.

Frustrated, completely boxed in within his own house and not knowing what else to do, de Wolfe fled to his bedroom, slamming the door behind him. After a moment Taka quietly followed, and calmly kneeled in the hallway outside his door.

Morning

De Wolfe heard chickens and could see the first rays of dawn begin pushing themselves through his shuttered windows. There was no lock on his door, and he was most thankful that he had made it through the night undisturbed. What if that woman had attempted to barge in on him? What could Kamimoto have been thinking? Bringing a whore to him! It was absolutely preposterous. He had not seen the irony of it last night, of course, but from a certain perspective it had been somewhat amusing. Well, he chuckled to himself, it was over now, and he would speak sternly with Kamimoto the first thing this morning.

He arose and opened his bedroom door. The woman was still kneeling in the hallway fighting off sleep and rose up when he appeared, her eyes downcast. She had maintained her vigil throughout the night. A gift from the *Obugyō-sama*? He dared not offend the man, but what was he to do now? The situation was impossible, and would take time to resolve.

"Aca…. Acawarman!" he called, and his Indonesian cook came running. "Give this woman some breakfast. And," he sighed with resignation, "then find her a room to sleep in."

Blood

"The world is an odd place", thought Taka. "I will miss it, I suppose." Her idyllic life in Nagasaki had been ripped apart, her family thrown into prison, and she had been sold into prostitution and it had all happened in the blink of an eye. She had planned to be dead already, and would have been too except for that strange Dutchman. She would kill herself, of course, that was certain. She had found the knives in the kitchen, and smiled at that little cook as he bowed and offered her unfamiliar foods, and even picked out the perfect blade to do the job. When she could get alone she would take a knife, would find a quiet spot and slash it across her wrists and throat and that would be her revenge.

She briefly considered using the knife against the Hollander first, but he had done nothing to hurt her. He wasn't gruff, he wasn't brutal, he wasn't anything at all. In fact, he seemed to be mostly embarrassed to have her in his household and worked to avoid her. Not what she had expected.

Kamimoto had coached her in the rudiments of what happens between a man and a woman and emphasized that it was her duty to please the foreigner. She could do this by thrusting her hips against his and groaning or making noises, and it would all be over very quickly. Of course, she would do nothing of the kind, but rather intended to remain perfectly still and quiet until he was done, and then as soon as possible she would kill herself, her orders from the *Bugyō-sho* completed. But, the Dutchman seemed to have no interest in raping her. Perhaps it was because he did not find her attractive? Or maybe somehow the foreigners stored up their sexual energy for months at a time and came into heat like a dog? It was certainly a mystery.

The pattern quickly became familiar: The Dutchman would arise early, she could hear him moving around the rooms and eating breakfast though he tried to remain quiet. Then he would leave and be gone for most of the day, returning after sunset.

She arose after he departed, and carefully dressed and applied her make-up. This artificial façade seemed to offer her comfort and protection, like a warrior's armor, keeping her safe and anonymous. The cook would show her different foods to choose from, and she settled on rice and eggs, and sometimes there had been fish. It was enough.

The remainder of the day she would sit by the window that looked out to sea, watching the fishing boats come and go and the immense Western ship floating in the harbor. There were books too, big thick ones, all in Dutch of course. They were interesting even if she could not understand them. She would go through the pages looking for words she recognized and admiring the illustrations wondering what it all meant.

There were also windows at the inland side looking over the open courtyard, and if she stood away from the opening a bit no one outside could see her. It was quietly busy on the island, and from time to time she would see the Hollander talking or pointing at something and she took to studying him. More than anything he seemed sad. She expected to be dead by now, but instead she was mostly bored.

In the evenings he would return after dark, eat alone and then retire to his room. She avoided him the first few days, but then came to sitting in the same room with him in the evening. He would eat quickly, nod as he passed her, and disappear. They never really spoke. How could they communicate with her poor Dutch skills? What would she say?

Kamimoto came one afternoon, and began to demand to know the most intimate details of the past few days. There had been no blood on the Dutchman's sheets, was he impotent? Was she using her mouth to comfort him? Did she understand that it was her duty to please him? She refused to give him any information and just shook her head and looked away. He left dissatisfied.

Really there was not much she could tell Kamimoto. She had not been raped, she had not spoken to the Hollander, and she was not dead. The world is an odd place.

Departure

The two weeks until the VERGULDE DRAECK's mandated departure had come far too quickly for everyone, and during this time de Wolfe did his best to avoid the woman who had been imposed upon him. He had spent most days and some evenings aboard the cargo ship, but whenever he returned, day or night, she had been patiently waiting for him. They did not speak.

Under normal circumstances the vessel's unloading would have itself taken a month, and the re-loading of trade goods from Japan, copper, silver, porcelain, exquisitely produced lacquerware and such would have taken the rest of the Summer. She would have sailed leisurely south in the early Fall, stopping by several ports in China on the route back to Batavia.

But, this had not been a normal year, and Captain Ostrander yelled commands at his crew and stomped about for many hours each day until he became hoarse from the exertion. Boxes and bales had been piled up in sloppy heaps in the warehouses as the Dutch and Japanese inspectors could not get to them quickly enough. The outbound cargoes had been loaded haphazardly rather than the careful jig-saw puzzle stowage that would have maximized the efficiency of the cargo holds. But, now it was done. They would depart with the morning tide.

The fourteen replacements that had accompanied de Wolfe on his inbound voyage had settled in and were now an integral part of the workforce. The usual contract for the staff was from three to five years, and they would eventually return to Holland to live out their lives as comfortably rich men. Two had died during the course of the past year, including Westerveldt, and twenty-nine were returning to Batavia in transit to home, and had been boarded and berthed last night. The Dutch community of Dejima was becoming noticeably smaller.

A light early Summer shower was falling, and many citizens of Nagasaki loved the warm rains and considered them romantic. Neither de Wolfe nor Captain Ostrander considered the rain to be idyllic at all as they miserably trudged across the courtyard towards the wharf, followed by a laboring Schuck behind them. Taka watched from the window of de Wolfe's quarters. Dutch staff looked up from their work as they passed with dislike and distrust. A lone sailor waited in a long boat at the wharf.

"May I wish you, sir, the greatest success in the coming year," Ostrander began as Schuck hurried over and presented him two thick bound volumes.

"Mr. Schuck has prepared the year's accounts and the trade orders for next year," de Wolfe replied as the accountant carefully handed over the heavy tomes. He then placed a stack of letters bound with a bright green ribbon on top of the books. "I entrust these to you for my wife."

"Of course," Ostrander reassured him. "They are safe in my care."

The rain softened as if to ease the pain of the departure, and as Captain Ostrander began to board the long boat Schuck moved away politely, just out of social distance so as not to intrude, but close enough to hear.

Ostrander reached up from the long boat and took de Wolfe's hand. "A Captain must sail not only with his charts, but also with his soul. It can be a lonely life at sea, separated from everyone you love and everything you know." He squeezed de Wolfe's hand in emphasis, "Trust in your companions, they are all you will have on this voyage."

"Discipline, first and always, sir." De Wolfe responded. "Discipline. Clear seas to you, your crew, and your vessel, Captain. And, until next Spring then."

As the two men released their grip it seemed that the last link joining Holland and Dejima was severed, taken off like a limb being amputated. De Wolfe looked up at the tall flagpole crowned by the Dutch flag, and then he and Schuck began to walk back across the courtyard.

It Is My Duty

From the second story window over-looking the courtyard Taka could see as Abe watched from the shelter of the Dutch Gate as the two men bid farewell to the white-bearded sea captain, the Japanese man then settled his long swords with a wiggle of his hips, and walked directly towards them in the light rain.

Abe stopped in the middle of the broad courtyard, his feet wide apart and his hands on his hips, clearly displaying his weaponry. *"It is best for you to remember that all of the Hollanders are guests here in Nagasaki,"* Abe growled at the Dutchmen in Japanese, blocking their way and halting their progress.

Schuck stepped back, fearful and intimidated, but de Wolfe stood his ground. Even though he had no idea what Abe had said, he had grown tired of his cocky bluster. "What gives you the right to insult good men?" he snapped back.

"Men? You are not men! Men will fight. I think that you are little rabbits who will run away!" With that Abe took a threatening step towards Schuck who turned and fled. *"Rabbits!"* he called after him.

Scowling and snarling, Abe then moved closer to de Wolfe until their noses were only a hand's breadth apart. As the rain suddenly strengthened, de Wolfe was unflinching as the two men stood toe-to-toe.

The impasse could not be broken, and neither man would turn away as the time began to stretch out into eternity and the rain plastered down their hair and dripped from their faces. De Wolfe had had enough. Enough of Japan, enough of this island, enough of being ignored and now bullied. He was every bit as ready for a show-down as this ragged ruffian seemed to be. Abe's hand moved to his long sword, and he pulled it from the scabbard just enough to show the cutting blade begin to peek through.

Suddenly Taka appeared on de Wolfe's shoulder with an umbrella, sheltering her hair and white make-up, and now de Wolfe as well, from the rain. *"Excuse me Abe-sama, the rain is growing much stronger."*

Abe still refused to break eye-contact with the Hollander; he would not be denied his victory. *"Go away! This is none of your business! Leave now!"* he commanded.

"It is my duty," Taka responded, *"to care for him."*

"You are merely a toy to fill his nights!"

Taka ignored the insult, speaking softly and with respect. *"Even we who are not samurai have duties, and I will honor mine. The Obugyō-sama himself sent me to him, and whether it is day or night, whether we are alone or confronted by a bully, it is my duty to protect him!"*

De Wolfe had no idea what was going on, but he would never back down from this man again even as Taka gently pulled him away and she bowed to Abe. He resisted until she took him by the hand, drawing him with her, and leaving Abe standing alone in the pouring rain.

De Wolfe's anger still filled his gorge and he could almost choke on it. All the frustrations of the past weeks had come to this point, and he tightened his grip on Taka's hand and began dragging her towards the makeshift chapel.

When they burst in, Bleeckier was already there and he looked up expectantly. The room was otherwise empty, and the portrait on the wall had already been reversed to reveal the ornate cross on the back side.

"Reverend!" de Wolfe practically shouted, "talk to this woman!"

"Um, about what?" asked Bleeckier mystified.

"About, about," de Wolfe was immensely exasperated and unsure how to express his frustration. "About, how about staying out of the Company's business and my personal life!" He then stormed out, leaving them alone and Bleeckier entirely unsure of what to do next. The Reverend saw Taka staring at the picture of the cross on the wall.

She was astounded at this open display of Christianity in Japan, a crime that would have earned the perpetrator an immediate and excruciating death sentence. But, there it was, for anyone to see! She walked to the front of the room and slowly kneeled, Japanese style, in front of the religious symbol.

Bleeckier noted her reaction, "You have been in a church before?" he asked.

Taka shook her head "no".

He was hugely surprised, and momentarily shocked, and then moved to kneel beside her. Softly, he shifted her hands to the correct position for supplication and indicated she should rise up onto her knees rather than fold her legs underneath herself. As Bleeckier took this position his pants legs rose up his ankles alarmingly, and he tugged at them with little effect.

He had never seen a Japanese like this, and it was incredibly moving. A *geisha* in her full regalia kneeling in prayer before an altar, even if it was not an official or permanent place of worship. She looked like an Oriental Virgin Mary, pure, serene and beautiful. He took a small Bible from his pocket and handed it to Taka.

"What shall we pray for, my dear?"

"He sex, I die," she struggled to form the difficult words, desperately seeking the vocabulary.

"He sex? Who sex?" Bleeckier was puzzled.

"He sex!" Taka emphasized, pointing to the door de Wolfe had just used.

"What do you mean you will die?"

"He sex, hurt much, I die." Taka slashed her hand across her throat in a cutting motion.

"I have no idea what you are talking about! Mr. de Wolfe is a good man, a kind man. He would not hurt you. Are you speaking of suicide? That you intend to kill yourself?"

How could she begin to explain to this man in Dutch? She just didn't know the words, she gave up, frustrated. Then she began again, "I want God kill me," she said slowly and with difficulty.

"Oh, Heavens dear, no!" How could it be possible that someone so lovely could have done anything to earn such a burden, to endure such pain?

Taka opened the Bible and turned to John 14:15 and Bleeckier peered over her shoulder to read, "If you love me obey my Commandments?"

She nodded her head to indicate "yes", and then turned to the Ten Commandments. Drawing her finger down to number seven.

"And, adultery is a sin. I see, I understand." Bleeckier stood up and walked to the painting, turning it back to the portrait side again. "Our duty to God is eternal," he began. "Our duty to man is temporary. They cannot exist separately, and you cannot see how you may serve both."

Taka could not understand what he was driving at, the Dutch too complex and too rapid for her ear. "Render unto Caesar…." he tried. "Sometimes our duty to man is our duty to God."

"Shame. Much shame," was all she could explain.

"I cannot give you solutions," Bleeckier began, "but I will always offer you solace. God gives us burdens, challenges us every day. But, he will not forsake us, and we must not forsake him. If we always seek out the goodness in our fellow man, then we are both blessed and forgiven."

All of this was lost on Taka, and Bleeckier knew it, so he gently touched her on the elbow, and knelt once again beside her. "Let us pray," he started again.

Taka interrupted him, "You teach I Dutch?"

"Yes, of course my dear I will teach you Dutch. But, for now, let us pray."

A Romantic Rendezvous

I'm drunk, Cas Janssen told himself as he walked down the street of the Rembrandt-Plein in the late evening. He was going to meet a woman, a married woman, and he wanted his head clear when he arrived.

He had spent the evening gambling, and had already had one whole bottle of champagne all to himself. He very much enjoyed the thrill and the risk of the cards, and the sweet bubbles of the champagne, but now it was time to get down to work. He shook his head to clear it and quickened his pace.

The one constant, the one thing that he loved so dearly in life was women. Women of all shapes and sizes, woman of all levels and types, royalty or charwomen, he loved them all. But, the rich ones were the best.

He would have entertained and bedded them for free, of course, but the rich ones were the best challenge and the best reward. For, after he had seduced them, or allowed himself to be "seduced" by them - sometimes for months - eventually the affair withered and died. That's when it became profitable. His absence and his silence were easy to secure, if only for a very small and regular price. There were four women who supported him now to protect their reputations, and to avoid the wrath of their cuckold husbands. The four payments arrived regularly at his lodgings the first of each month. His earnings more secure than a bank loan!

Strange that they all became eventually offended when something that was so easy for them to give, a few small coins per month in exchange for his romantic attention – or his silence - was asked for. But, they had all relented, usually after only a few small tears of humiliation. And, that was good. Most of them needed a little dose of humility anyway.

He did the math quickly in his head, a fifth payment from a new patron, blackmail was such an ugly word and he immensely preferred the term "patron", would be most welcome. It was a process, and it would take time to work its way through to the payment, but the result was practically assured.

They had agreed to meet in a small dark café, one that he had frequently used before when he wanted privacy. The proprietor served champagne and light kippered herring snacks. It was quiet, and two people could meet with discretion. When he arrived the married woman was already waiting in a corner booth wearing a broad-brimmed hat with an exotic feather as a plume.

"Good evening Camilla!" he crooned as he slid into the booth across from her. "You must be so lonely with Hendrik gone already for so many months." He smiled at her with sympathy and understanding, and she smiled back.

Fireworks

The hot days of Summer had been brutal, and even the afternoon rains did not cool the weather down. It was comfortable neither inside nor outside the buildings, and de Wolfe had been miserable, made worse by his social isolation. Everyone ignored him. He wandered the island, but no one sought out nor wanted his advice or companionship.

The sun had set, but there was still a glow in the west that came through his seaward windows, brightening the room. He had eaten his dinner alone, Acawarman having set the food out and then fleeing to the cooler environs downstairs. Taka was politely serving him tepid tea as the late-evening darkness gathered. She often joined him in the evening, and they sat somewhat apart in uncomfortable silence. She had protected him in the courtyard, he understood that now, but he had no idea how to thank her or even acknowledge her assistance.

Her kimono was lighter and her hair less ornately decorated, but she still wore the heavy make-up of a courtesan and he was not sure how that was even possible without melting into a multi-colored puddle on the floor. The heat never seemed to faze her though, and she always had the same expression: Never happy nor sad, just... polite.

She had hated the white and brightly colored pastes on her face at first, but now she came to value the protective mask, shielding her from everything outside. Inside she had her own thoughts and life, but to the outside world she was merely a courtesan, one of many and easily ignored. The façade protected her.

She missed her family terribly. She had never been away from her house before her arrest, then suddenly she had been jerked out of her peaceful and happy life and thrown into a dark room with other women prisoners for days. She had never seen a Dutchman up close, let alone lived in the same household with one. Everyone in Nagasaki knew of them, of course, and constantly gossiped, passing on tidbits of their strange mannerisms gleaned from the townsfolk who worked on the island. This one had been nothing like she imagined. She couldn't really tell if he was handsome or not, he was just different from anyone she had ever seen before. He didn't grow a beard like the others, she liked that, and he didn't smell of sweat. Rather he smelled like, well a man. Not a Japanese man, but not unpleasant. The hardest part of looking at him was his eyes, a light blue. She had difficulty looking directly into those bottomless orbs and avoided his direct gaze.

Everything was so different, the food, the language, the household, nothing to connect with and nothing to make her feel welcome or comfortable. She was alone. Tonight she had the opportunity to do something about that. She took the empty tea cup from the table and carried it into the adjoining serving room and refilled it with hot water. And there was what she had been waiting for, a knife. She had never been able to get into the outside kitchen alone to steal one before, but tonight the cook had carelessly left a medium sized carving knife next to the roast he had prepared for dinner. She checked to see that no one was watching and then slipped it into her sleeve before returning to the dining room and setting the tea cup before de Wolfe. The idea that she now controlled her own fate made her feel very free.

"Thank you *yuujo*," he told her off-handedly.

"No, *yuujo*," she said with sudden and unexpected intensity. "I am Taka."

What? She was speaking to him? No one but Acawarman had spoken directly to him in days, and he was a little unsure of his own voice or that he could trust his ears. "What? What did you say?" Surprising him with the few Dutch words.

"I am Taka," she said clearly again.

"Your name is Taka?"

"Yes."

How was she learning Dutch? Bleeckier! That scoundrel! What else might he be teaching her? "Well, 'Taka', it is a pleasure to meet you. How do you do?" He smiled broadly at her. "Will you please sit with me?"

She hesitated. If she were to use the knife on herself she needed to get back to her room where she could cut deeply into her wrists or throat. She wasn't sure that she really had the courage to cut her own throat, but she knew that would be fastest and most sure. She could not afford to be interrupted, or for him to think anything was unusual, so she quietly sat next to him at the table.

Now that she sat with him de Wolfe had absolutely no idea what to say. "Japan good," he finally offered.

What an idiot she thought, what did he possibly know? Is that all he had to say? "Yes, Japan good," she countered.

"Nagasaki good," he continued.

Were they going to go through a childish list of this is "good", that is "good", something else is "good", she wondered? But, before she could respond he offered, "*Obugyō-sama* good!"

The *Obugyō-sama*? That vile old man responsible for ripping her family from their home and sending them to prison? The man who sentenced her to prostitution at the request of Kamimoto? De Wolfe kept grinning at her like some imbecilic cretin completely unaware of what had transpired. To him she was merely a "gift" hiding behind a mask of white paste and garish red lips.

"NO!" she unleashed at him. "*Obugyō-sama* bad! Nagasaki bad! Japan bad!" and she rose suddenly as the knife fell from her sleeve and clattered loudly to the floor as they both stared, the Dutchman with surprise and the Japanese woman with guilt.

De Wolfe stood and quietly picked up the knife. "Do you intend to kill me?" he asked simply.

Kill him? No, that was absurd! He had done nothing, the knife was for herself. "Knife me," she answered lamely.

"The knife is not yours, it is mine," he answered misunderstanding her intent. Everything in this household is mine, do you understand that? Everything," he emphasized, quickly becoming angry.

"No, no kill. Hollander good. Knife kill Taka."

De Wolfe set the knife down on the table and returned to his chair. "Knife kill Taka?" he asked. "You want to die?

"Yes!" she confirmed. "Shame, much shame."

De Wolfe began to understand that there was so much going on besides his own torment, and he had been blind to it all. "Hollander good?"

"Yes! Hollander good!"

"No Hollander, I am Hendrik."

"Your name is Hen-du-ri-ku," she tried hard to pronounce the difficult foreign name.

"Yes," he laughed. Hendrik de Wolfe."

"Hen-du-ri-ku du Worpu," she repeated. "How do you do?"

"Yes," he affirmed, laughing harder now, "perfect! Hen-du-ri-ku Worpu." It felt good to laugh. Then he became serious. Taka, you feel shame and are lonely here, I understand that. You miss your life in Nagasaki, there is little for you here on Dejima. Neither of us asked for this, but here we are together so let us make the best of it."

She had no idea what he was talking about, the words too fast and unknown. He took a new approach. "Taka, knife bad, very bad," and smiled broadly.

Taka could not help but mirror his smile, and returned to her chair. They sat quietly for a few moments as the evening darkened into night. Loud booms suddenly were heard over the city of Nagasaki and de Wolfe was immediately concerned, but the Japanese woman took little notice, so he walked over to the landward windows and saw brightly colored fireworks exploding, highlighted by the dark hills above the buildings. She walked next to him as they watched the display in silence for a few moments.

"What is the celebration?" he asked.

"*Kunchi Omatsuri.* People happy," she sought the words in her limited vocabulary and finally found them. "Whale hunt."

"A festival to celebrate the whale hunt?" he confirmed, and she nodded. De Wolfe thought briefly, and then smiled mischievously. "Let us go see."

De Wolfe started toward the door, and seeing that Taka was not following he took her by the hand and helped her down the stairs.

He led her across the courtyard in the blackness, sporadically brightly lit by the display, and then instantly crashed into darkness again. The Dutch staff was gathered in small groups to watch the spectacle, staring skyward and emitting appreciative "oohs" and "aahs", a ubiquitous reaction to fireworks the world over. As they approached the Dutch Gate, Taka began to sense his plan and stopped abruptly, pulling her hand away from him and stepping back.

"No! Cannot!" she snapped at him.

"I want to see the fireworks!"

"No! Forbidden!"

He started to command her, to tell her that she was his to order as he pleased, and she had no stature to forbid him from doing anything. Her place was to obey him, but no. That wasn't right at all. That's not what he felt. That's not what he wanted. He walked to her and once again softly took her hand, "We are not prisoners here, come with me."

She raised her eyes to his and forced herself to look directly into them. She felt that she could see right through them, see what he was feeling. She had difficulty looking directly into those eyes, there was too much there. Japanese eyes were dark, and often hid their emotions. But, these light-blue eyes were very different, and she could only see kindness behind them.

The Dutch were not allowed off the island without permission, and it would be a major violation. But what allegiance did she owe either the *Bugyō-sho* or Kamimoto? They had thrust her in with the foreigners, and no matter what else might happen, she suddenly realized that her loyalty was now to only him. She had come into this household contemplating humiliation, disgrace, and death. Instead she had been treated with compassion and kindness, and however strange it seemed or might become, this was her only path forward. She would be with this Hollander, no she corrected herself, she would be with Hen-du-ri-ku.

"Let us go for a walk," he whispered to her.

He held her hand as they leisurely strolled past the shocked guards at the Dutch Gate, over the arched bridge, and into Nagasaki. The samurai watched, too stupefied to move as the couple ambled together into the city, then looked at each other in surprise, and ran off to get help.

Forbidden

Nagasaki was alive with people: Groups of young boys and girls, older couples, families, young lovers, all out enjoying the cool of the evening and the festivities. The streets were brightly decorated with paper lanterns spilling out light from internal candles, and long banners written in the incomprehensible Japanese glyphs spanned across each street. De Wolfe was hugely pleased by everything he saw: The shops, the people, *taiko* drummers and the parade of floats made to look like Japanese whaling ships and the mammals they hunted. There was even one costumed character made to look like a large over-sized rambling Dutchman complete with a tall hat and a huge disgusting nose, which only further amused the Hollander. He was especially taken by the young children playing and chasing each other in their specially made festival kimonos.

The strange sight of a real live Dutchman and a *geisha* in Nagasaki made no less of a stir among the Japanese. Although they were far too polite to point or stare, almost everyone was watching them from the corners of their eyes or from the protection offered by a post or corner. The spectacle soon attracted a discreet crowd that followed them through the streets, watching their every move.

Taka stopped in front of a street side food vendor cooking small treats, and de Wolfe was amazed as his hands slashed and flashed across the pan aided by small sticks, flipping, turning or spearing the food. Taka said something, and the man quickly handed her two, and then offered two more to de Wolfe.

"*Takoyaki*," she shouted over the noise of the crowd.

"Takayaki?" he shouted back.

"No! No!" she laughed. "*Takoyaki*, not Taka! Ta Ko Ya Ki!" she emphasized each syllable separately, then took the round small treat into her mouth and mimed that he should eat one also.

De Wolfe tried the first tentatively, and then ate the whole small bit. "These are good! These are very good!"

The vendor was pleased. A crowd soon began to form around them, and a small boy, no more than five or six years old and wearing a bright green festival kimono stood nearby. De Wolfe tried to entice him forward with the promise of a treat. "Hello! Ta Ko Ya Ki! How are you?!" he shouted, offering the lad the warm ball.

Shyly the child stepped forward, and as de Wolfe bent down to give him the treat the boy tentatively reached up to touch his blond hair, which fascinated him much more than the food.

This made de Wolfe laugh even louder, and he shouted "Hello!"

"Hello!" The surprised boy shouted in return.

De Wolfe picked up the child and they were both laughing and shouting "Hello!" as he turned to Taka. She was looking back behind de Wolfe with concern, perhaps even fear, her emotion barely concealed behind the white make-up. Still holding the boy in his arms de Wolfe slowly turned around.

It was Abe, accompanied by three of his samurai, scowling and standing with his hands on his hips. "Nagasaki forbidden!" he growled with obvious menace. "You go Dejima!"

De Wolfe smiled slightly at the samurai, placed the treat in his own mouth, and gently set the boy down who bowed and then scurried away into the crowd of the festival.

Abe glowering, de Wolfe smiling and slowly chewing, they stood there for a long moment before Abe placed his hand on his sword hilt and withdrew it slightly.

De Wolfe broke the stalemate. "What are you going to do Mr. Abe? You and your terrible sword? What will you do?"

"Nagasaki forbidden!" Abe snarled.

The crowd around them was now packed, jostling both him and Abe. There was almost no room to move, certainly not enough for Abe to draw his sword. It would be almost impossible for them to leave now even if they had wanted to. This was the third time that this bully had accosted him, and it was enough. De Wolfe chuckled to himself and said, "There is no point in having a sword unless you intend to use it".

De Wolfe began bowing, smiling and shouting "HELLO!" to the crowd surrounding them. "How do you do?" he asked making a grand flourish of a stage bow and moving to the next person. "Madam?" he went to a knee in front of an elderly woman and kissed her hand, causing her to jerk it away in surprise and embarrassment, but she was immensely pleased as well.

The crowd continued to swell and jostle until both de Wolfe and Taka were engulfed as he kept shouting "Hello!" and "How do you do?" Several of the townspeople began shouting "Hello!" back to him. Soon even the samurai were smiling at the odd situation while Abe himself silently fumed.

Finally, de Wolfe turned to Taka, "I believe we have had enough of a walk for this evening, why don't we go home now?" He took her by the arm and shouted across the crowd to the samurai, "Mr. Abe! Would you please take us home now?"

Abe had been bested, and not knowing what else to do, he issued brief orders. The samurai began parting the crowd, and the Hollander and the *geisha* began moving back towards Dejima with Abe and his men as an Honor Guard.

They crossed the Dutch Gate as Abe glared at the night guards and they kept their eyes sheepishly downcast, and climbed the stairs to de Wolfe's residence.

Stopping in front of his bedroom de Wolfe was still laughing and mimicked Abe standing with his hand on an imaginary sword hilt and scowling, "Nagasaki forbidden! You go Dejima!" causing Taka to laugh and cover her mouth.

"Well, thank you for a wonderful evening, <u>Taka</u>." he emphasized the pronunciation of her name. "Goodnight."

Taka bowed and began to kneel in front of his bedroom door for her nightly vigil.

"No," de Wolfe told her. "No, not tonight." He took her hand again, very gently, and helped her to rise, watching her eyes intently. After a moment he led her to her bedroom door and stopped. She turned to him, barely apart, almost touching, and he could smell her hair and make-up, feel her soft breath on his face. Unbidden his hand slowly moved up along her sleeve and towards the white doll-like coloring on her cheek.

She still didn't seem real to him in so many ways, so different from anything that he had ever known. He could not bring himself to spoil that perfection.

"Cannot," he whispered, and retreated to his own room.

Advice

Early the next morning de Wolfe made a point to find Bleeckier and confronted him. "You have been teaching the Japanese woman the Dutch language?"

"Your *yuujo*? I could see no harm," he stammered.

"Her name is Taka," de Wolfe corrected him. "And, no it is quite alright. I do not mind. But, what do you know of her?"

"Well," Bleeckier considered for a moment. "I think that she is afraid of you."

"Afraid of me? Why on earth could that be?" de Wolfe protested.

"Because you are a man, and she is a woman. It is really quite obvious is it not?"

"It most certainly is <u>not</u> obvious! I would never...."

"Oh, please. She has been given to you by the *Obugyō-sama,* and as far as the Japanese are concerned she is yours to do with in whatever manner you like. Take her or leave her, they have no concern."

"Well, you must tell her that is not the case."

"I do not think that is possible."

"Why not?" de Wolfe exploded.

"Because my Japanese is non-existent and her Dutch is minimal. If you want things explained, then take her to Kamimoto to translate for the both of you."

"I cannot do that," de Wolfe told him with finality.

"Then, you have only one option, and here is my recommendation: Treat her with kindness. There is never harm in kindness."

"Brilliant!" scoffed de Wolfe.

"You asked for my advice and I am giving it to you. What are you afraid of?"

"Because," de Wolfe hesitated, "Because I am... I am a man, and I have been tempted. I can assure you that I would never act on my desire, that is certain. But, I admit that I am weak and that I have been tempted. I would like to remove the problem. Would you please take her? I will make arrangements for the both of you, but she cannot remain in my household."

"I am afraid that would never do," Bleeckier shook his head. "She was given to you, and you alone must assume responsibility for her. Listen to me. I know that you are a good man, each of us here is a good man," he screwed up his face in thought for a moment. "But, we are here, and everything that we know is impossibly far away. I cannot even begin to suggest what you should do, but be kind, and what happens will work out, I am certain of that. No one can take this responsibility from you as long as you are here."

"That's all? That's it? That's your advice?"

"My dear sir, what did you expect? A magic incantation that washes away problems like soap? You will have months and months of sheer and utter boredom ahead and the opportunity to think long and hard about what you want. You will find your own solution."

"Will you continue your Dutch lessons?"

"I will, and when she has learned enough, you can explain everything to her yourself."

"Thank you Reverend," de Wolfe said and turned to go.

"You see," Bleeckier said beaming. "I _am_ useful! This is what I do!'

"And," de Wolfe laughed, "you are very good at it."

A Ship!

Summer continued its oppression of heat and boredom, and de Wolfe preferred to arise before the dawn and work quietly at his desk until the temperature upstairs drove him to find a cooler location. The evening breeze off of the ocean could be quite pleasant, but the days were becoming mind-numbing and had continued to blend together. On several occasions he had invited Kamimoto over in the evening for whisky, and that had been a bit of company to ease the tedium.

He established a routine: Rise early, work for several hours, have breakfast, seek refuge from the heat, he often skipped his mid-day dinner, and then he and Taka shared a light meal after sunset. She began testing some of the Western foods, and soon took a liking to several, especially the sweets. He wished he could offer her some ice cream, made up with a pot freezer tub filled with ice and salt and cranked with a handle, but where would he get the ice? She also liked pickles and potatoes, but turned her nose up at anything made from ground meats.

He enjoyed their quiet time together, and he augmented Bleeckier's teachings with his own vocabulary terms. It was a child-like parade of nouns such as "ear", "tea cup" and so on that soon graduated to pantomimed verbs like "walk" and "drink". She was a very quick learner, and there was soon a "point and ask" arcade of "How do you say?"

Taka had given up the notion of killing herself, at least for now, and actually began to enjoy her time with de Wolfe. Everything was new and different, not better or worse than the Japanese way, but bringing a whole new perspective. She had never thought of life outside of Nagasaki, but now began to wonder what it might be like to visit Edo, or even Holland. She learned that it took the trade ships over six months to sail to Japan and couldn't begin to imagine how far away that must be.

She met some of the other Dutchmen as well, including the sweaty Schuck and the jovial doctor with the local wife. His Japanese was absolutely atrocious, and the grammar he used was just like a woman, but she was pleased that he had taken the effort to try. As far as she could tell, the doctor was the only foreigner that had even tried to learn the language.

From time-to-time Kamimoto would try to question her about sleeping with de Wolfe, but she avoided giving him any direct answers and that frustrated and angered him. Good.

De Wolfe never mentioned, but he often thought about, the night of the festival. The soft smoothness of the kimono on his fingers as his hand brushed along and rose towards Taka's face, and the bottomless black orbs that stared back into his own eyes. The scent of her skin and hair. It was best to just forget it all.

He had been up early working, and had just extinguished the lone candle at his desk as dawn began to peek up over the hills behind Nagasaki and brighten the sky, when heavy footsteps pounded up the stairs. "A ship! It's a ship!" exclaimed Schuck with excitement as he shoved his girth in through the doorway panting and mopping his brow, and was soon followed by Bleeckier.

Off shore they could see a large two-masted brig-sloop, fortified with eighteen heavy guns, as she dropped anchor in Nagasaki Harbor. De Wolfe moved to the mounted spy-glass at his window and scanned the deck, not a single person could be seen, but on the stern flew the Dutch flag.

"Who are they?" asked Bleeckier.

"They are from Holland, must be a Company ship," speculated de Wolfe. "But, we were expecting no more vessels until next Spring, and she certainly doesn't look like a trader."

"She wouldn't have much stowage," noted Schuck. "And, with that shallow draft she could snuggle right up next to the shore. Not to the wharf though, too shallow there. She'd be fast too."

"But, who <u>are</u> they?" pressed Bleeckier.

"I have absolutely no idea," responded de Wolfe.

He peered through the spy glass again, and now a lone figure stood amidships, tall and thin with a scraggly beard, staring back at de Wolfe through a spy glass of his own. De Wolfe slowly raised his left hand and waved broadly, and the man raised his own hand and waved back. "It's a complete mystery."

Dr. Franz joined them asking, "What's the hubbub?"

"It must be a Dutch trading ship," Schuck answered.

"What do they want," Franz asked taking de Wolfe's place at the spy glass.

"Who knows," Schuck continued.

"Why don't we go out and ask them?" suggested Bleeckier after a moment's confused silence.

"Yes, let's," confirmed Schuck. "Could be news from Holland, valuable additions to our manifest, any of a hundred reasons."

"Then, let's go," ventured Bleeckier.

"Pull myself up that Jacob's Ladder on the ship? Hardly!" laughed Schuck.

"I will go," proposed Dr. Franz.

"Alright," de Wolfe said. "But, be careful. At least until we know more about their intentions."

The Brig-Sloop PHANTOM

Bleeckier, Franz and Schuck man-handled one of the long boats out of a warehouse and carried it to the wharf. The trading post was just beginning to stir, and the only persons watching were the two guards at the Dutch Gate who observed from afar.

They boarded the boat and Bleeckier rowed out while Dr. Franz sat at the stern and Schuck watched from the wharf until they were underway, and then he returned to de Wolfe's residence.

As they approached the ship they could see the name PHANTOM on the stern, but no home port below that. Only the Dutch flag hanging limply in the dead morning air. Leaning over the railing was the tall man seen earlier through the spy glass, and he seemed to be alone. It was all very strange. They tied up on the ladder and climbed aboard.

The tall man greeted them enthusiastically, grinning broadly, laughing and pumping their hands. On deck they could now see crew members who studiously avoided their gaze and kept at their work, but glanced at the Dutchmen from time to time.

"Good morning! Good morning gentlemen!" the tall man introduced himself in English. "I am Captain Nolan Powell!" He wore no special uniform and except for his easy style of command looked little different from the other crewmembers. "Welcome aboard the PHANTOM!"

"You're not Dutch?" asked Bleeckier, switching to English nervously as Powell eyed them for a long unnerving moment.

"No, we have a rather motley crew," Powell answered. "But no Dutchmen. Tight as a gnat's chuff the Dutch, don't you know?"

Dr. Franz stiffened at the insult, and looked about warily, sensing that the crew was beginning to close in around them. "What manner of ship are you?"

At the question Powell dropped any further pretense and motioned to his crew, "We have our hostages. Raise the flag Mr. Barton. Keep all boats away."

"Aye-aye, Captain," Barton replied with a heavy French accent as several members of the crew responded and turned to complete his commands.

The Dutch flag on the stern was quickly lowered and replaced by a pirate's Black Flag, signifying that no mercy was to be asked or given. Hatches on the side of the ship were lifted up to reveal the nine long guns on the landward side, which were rolled out and now faced Dejima.

Through his spy glass de Wolfe was watching it all unfold. He turned to Schuck and said softly, "Please get Mr. Kamimoto".

The Captain's Cabin

Captain Powell had been staring at his prisoners and scratching at his beard for a very long time as the Dutchmen introduced themselves. Bleeckier withdrew a clay pipe from his pocket and stuffed it with tobacco, his hands shaking slightly. "Do you, do you suppose?" he asked pointing at the fire in the lantern sitting in the middle of the table between them. The sole lantern was the only light in the cabin, and curtains blocked any of the outside brightness from gaining entry.

Bleeckier opened the lantern's glass door, inserted the bowl of his pipe, carefully puffed until it was lit, and then leaned back in his chair.

"The Dutch have had a monopoly for far too long here in the Japans, don't you agree?" started Powell.

Neither of the Dutchmen knew what to say until finally Dr. Franz asked, "What are your intentions, Captain?"

"Oh, yes, the newly elected Captain," Powell responded, and then added wryly, "Though by no great margin. Do you two appreciate the responsibilities of a Captain? Many men want the power, with absolutely no idea of the burdens." He looked over meaningfully at Barton.

"I am sure that it is difficult," offered Bleeckier.

"Difficult!" shouted Powell and slammed the table with his hand. "Do you know what happens to a Captain that cannot provide for his crew? What hunger will do to a man? That Captain can swim home for all they care! But, of course, he would never make it that far."

He worked to regain control of himself, "Where is your Captain?" he smiled and asked politely.

"But, we have no Captain here," argued Franz, puzzled by Powell's sudden and mercurial shifts of mood.

"The VERGULDE DRAECK then, where is the GUILDED DRAGON all fat and sassy with Japanese copper and silver?"

"Why, she left weeks ago," offered Bleeckier.

"Please, gentlemen! You are in no position to play coy with me."

"She has already returned to Batavia," confirmed Dr. Franz.

A cabin boy brought a cup of hot tea to Powell, although he offered none to the Dutchmen. "An expensive cup of tea this is," the Englishman told them. "A Chinaman traded it to me for his life. Pity, for he was playing 'coy' with me also."

He took a sip of the tea. "Alright," he continued. "Let us agree for just a moment that the DRAECK is gone. But, you have stores ashore still don't you? Trade goods? Treasures? Foodstuffs?"

"We have sugar! Ivory? Books?" Franz tried to explain. "Goods that may be of great value to the Japanese, but hold nothing for you."

Powell seemed uncertain for a moment, and then decided. "Well, so be it then. Tell that to my hungry crew." He signaled Barton standing behind the Hollanders, and the Frenchman and another burly crewmember grabbed them from behind and stood them up.

"We'll let them stew for a few hours I think. Spread a little terror, see if we can get a reaction. But first, your friends ashore need to be very clear about our intentions," Powell threatened them. "Mr. Barton!"

"Sir!" Barton held onto Franz tightly by the scruff of his neck.

Powell smiled broadly again. "The doctor or this pitiful man of God?"

Mr. Barton looked over at Dr. Franz and then nodded towards Bleeckier.

Corde!

Through the spy glass de Wolfe could easily see the growing commotion on deck, crowded now with more members of the crew. Kamimoto had joined him, and Taka stood off to one side quietly observing.

What is happening?" asked Kamimoto, his voice quickened by concern.

"They've brought Mr. Bleeckier and the doctor back on deck," he replied.

He had never seen a pirate's Black Flag before, but its meaning was evident and evil. What had started out as a mystery only a short while ago had quickly devolved into a crisis. He still had no idea what they wanted, or how this might be resolved.

He offered the spy glass to Kamimoto who peered through it intently, also trying to discern what might be happening.

The Dutchmen were kicked and pushed forward, both of them falling several times and being beaten until they rose and continued on. Now they were surrounded by the crew who were shouting and cursing at them in multiple languages, several of them simply howling like wild beasts. There seemed to be neither rhyme nor reason, just madness and blood lust. Powell stood back and let events develop, his arms folded in front of his chest.

"*Corde!*" screamed Barton, and a length of rope was brought to him. He tied it off to a bitts on the railing, then threw it over the mainmasts spar and quickly tied a loop off at the end.

Barton walked over to both Dutchmen looking them over carefully, then grabbed Franz by the collar, "Doctor might be useful!" he shouted as the crewmembers hooted and hollered. And then he dragged Franz over to Powell.

Barton walked slowly around Bleeckier twice, looking him up and down, and then began kicking him towards the railing. As the Reverend stumbled forward he was lifted up to his feet by crewmembers who shouted, cursed and leered into his face, then shoved him forward. They bounced him back and forth between competing mobs, knocking him one way and then the next, striking his face and back with their open hands, the whole ship taking part and the vessel itself seeming to howl and scream with an animal's rage.

One heavy sailor smashed Bleeckier directly in the face, splitting his lip and sending a front tooth flying across the deck, and the cabin boy scampered after it and held it aloft as if he had plucked up a coveted and valuable prize. At the railing Barton grabbed the Reverend by the neck and, as Bleeckier grimaced in pain, placed the loop over his head, tightening it with a sudden jerk.

"No, please! Have mercy!" begged Franz

"*Merci? Merci beaucoup* to me!" Barton laughed, and then with a sinister snarl, "He must thank me. For I am sending him to Heaven."

"Beg the Lord to forgive my sins!" Bleeckier cried out to Franz.

Barton grabbed the slack end of the rope and began hauling in, lifting Bleeckier to his toes and then off of his feet as the poor man clutched at the noose tightening around his neck. As his victim rose into the air, Barton tied off the end and swung him to the railing while Bleeckier's legs kicked and sought the deck that was far beneath him. "*S'envoler Révérend!*" The First Mate hooted as the crew laughed and cheered. "Fly away little birdie!"

The Frenchman grabbed the flailing legs and pulled down hard, putting his full weight into it until the kicking weakened and then ceased. He then swung the body overboard, and Bleeckier hanged suspended, gently rocking back and forth above the ocean, his white legs protruding from the pants, and the crew cheered.

"We will, Reverend," Franz said quietly. "We will."

De Wolfe stumbled back away from the spyglass, having witnessed the horrible spectacle. Taka was unsure of what had just happened and watched with concern as Kamimoto said, "I must inform the *Obugyō-sama* immediately," and left.

The Decision Is Made

Kamimoto had returned that afternoon, and now as evening approached he and de Wolfe regarded each other tensely while Taka watched. They had been arguing for hours. There had been no signals from the pirates, no demands and no attempts to communicate. Bleeckier's body still swung from the spar, and occasionally Dr. Franz could be seen on the deck, sometimes in passionate argument with his captors, sometimes looking forlornly towards the island.

"The decision has already been made," Kamimoto announced with finality. "Abe-sama will soon have enough samurai here and he will end this attack."

"No!" de Wolfe countered angrily. "They will kill Dr. Franz. We will give them whatever it is they want, and they will be gone!"

"Without wind they cannot sail, and for now they are as much our prisoners as Dr. Franz is theirs. They must pay for their crimes with their lives!"

"Let me negotiate with them!" de Wolfe insisted.

"Negotiations are strictly forbidden!" thundered Kamimoto.

De Wolfe and Kamimoto glared at each other in frustration, neither making any progress in arguing their strategy.

"*You must listen to him Kamimoto-Otona,*" Taka said softly.

"*Perhaps you would do better to keep your mouth shut rather than your legs!*" Kamimoto countered.

"What are you two talking about?" asked de Wolfe, offended to be left out of the conversation they were having in Japanese.

"Make pirates go. No fight. No kill," she said, switching to Dutch.

"*This is a dangerous game you are playing, not a time for women or children,*" Kamimoto warned her.

Taka made a slight bow in deference to Kamimoto as he also switched to Dutch, "The final decision is neither mine nor yours. The *Obugyō-sama* has decided, and Abe-sama is responsible in these matters."

"Then, I will take it up with Mr. Abe," said de Wolfe and strode to the door.

A large group of samurai had already assembled at the wharf when de Wolfe arrived, and several of them moved to block his path. Abe was looking over a map, and glanced up to see who it was, then signaled his men to allow de Wolfe through, "Let me take a boat," he began. "Let me negotiate."

"No," Abe said and turned back to his map.

"You must listen to reason. Dr. Franz's life is at stake."

"You go, you die too. You understand?"

"Then, just give me time. I will think of something. I need time."

Another group of samurai arrived at the wharf, further bolstering the growing numbers. "More samurai come, we fight," Abe said with finality, and in frustration de Wolfe began to retreat to his residence.

Aboard the PHANTOM Captain Powell was livid and growing angrier by the minute, scanning through his spy glass and then screaming into Dr. Franz's face, "More samurai? Do you see that man! They think they can threaten cannon with swords and arrows! Perhaps they do not fully appreciate their situation!"

The crew was restless and also growing more nervous. The cabin boy called out, "Hang the other one!" Barton stepped toward Franz and drew a long knife from his belt, "Skin him alive," he hissed.

Powell grabbed Franz by the throat and lifted him to his toes, "No, something more grandiose I think. Show them our true power. Perhaps that would quiet your friends ashore?" He paused for a moment, and then continued, "Mr. Barton, you know what to do. The carronades, roundshot I think." The heavy smooth bore cannons had been produced by the Caron Company ironworks in Falkirk, Scotland in 1787 and were considered obsolete, but were still devastating at short range.

The cannons were rolled back in from the gun ports and loaded with their thirty-two pound solid shot. Once all nine on the Dejima side were ready Barton dropped his hand and the broadside discharged, hurling heavy iron towards the city.

The solid shot began falling into the structures on Dejima, smashing and skipping across the courtyard or plunging directly into buildings. Several rounds sailed over the island and landed indiscriminately in the City of Nagasaki.

The samurai on the wharf scattered for cover as de Wolfe sprinted towards his residence. There was chaos as tile roofs shattered, walls were knocked out of buildings, and people bowled over.

As the thick smoke shrouded the vessel and Barton cried "Reload!" Powell released Dr. Franz and began dancing and swinging his arms as if he were conducting a monstrous symphony urging on the "booms" of the bombardment, singing "Again! Again!" As soon as the carronade were reloaded they began firing individually like the beat of a huge throbbing drum.

Taka and Kamimoto were watching from the seaward window as a thirty-two pound cannon ball slammed through the wall and destroyed the billiard table scattering shrapnel, both of them disappearing in the dust and debris.

De Wolfe was choking on the dust as he climbed the stairs two at a time and burst into his residence crying "Taka! Mr. Kamimoto! Where are you?" He was nearly blinded by the haze and barely able to breathe, but heard a weak voice croak, "Here!"

He tried to peer through the thick dust and could just make out Kamimoto on the floor and Taka lying next to him unconscious. He rushed to her and cradled her head, feeling something warm and wet. His hand came away red. He picked her up gently and carried her outside.

Powell scanned the carnage through his spyglass, pleased by the obvious destruction his guns had caused. In the distance smoke was beginning to rise from several places in Nagasaki. In the gathering darkness firemen could be seen rushing to help, and climbing ladders to rescue those who were already trapped in burning buildings.

The Englishman laughed loudly and pointed to the fires telling Franz, "Cannon negotiate far more eloquently than diplomats ever can, don't you agree?" Then he turned to Barton, "Stow the guns, let them think that over until morning. Keep a strict watch for boarders."

De Wolfe laid Taka on a bed in the infirmary, and a medical assistant came up and examined her. The bleeding had slowed, but not stopped, and Abe and Kamimoto, still dirty from the attack, stood nearby.

"Her head….. help her," de Wolfe pleaded. Her heavy white make-up was smudged and her carefully arranged hair completely thrashed.

Kamimoto tried to console him, "Tomorrow, at dawn, we must answer."

"We fight, pirates die," Abe assured him.

De Wolfe turned to them, "And, Dr. Franz will die! And samurai will die!"

"We have no more time," Kamimoto consoled him. "We have no more options."

"She really needs Dr. Franz," the medical assistant interjected.

De Wolfe wet a small piece of cloth and began softly wiping the make-up from Taka's face. Seeing her natural beauty for the first time was striking, and he paused, then looked at the white powder on the cloth. He had an idea.

Last Chances

Aboard the PHANTOM the ship's officers were seated for dinner in the captain's cabin, surrounding Dr. Franz. The cook spooned an unappetizing mix of slop onto their plates, shrugged with resignation, spit on the deck, and then left them alone. Powell took one spoonful of the gruel, made a face, and then pushed his plate away. The atmosphere was tense, the stinking smell of the close-packed men and the greasy uneatable stew made Franz queasy.

Powell was staring at Franz, "Still waiting for their samurai are they? Not a signal, not a sign, who makes the first move?"

"Tell them what you want," Franz reassured him. "Give them your demands. I will carry them for you, I will negotiate on your behalf to get you whatever it is you need."

Powell retrieved a long curving knife from his boot and laid it on the table. "I need those samurai on the wharf gone. I need food, whatever you've got. Most importantly, I need information on the DRAECK, not so hard is it? Where did she go? When will she be back. Not so difficult. Why do you deny me this?"

"I have told you," Franz reiterated, "over and over again, she is gone. She will not return until next Spring."

"No, not possible I think," Powell purred. "Not possible. What are you hiding?"

"Nothing," Franz answered. "We are hiding nothing. Tell them what you want, we will give it to you and you may go."

"What do I want?" Powell slammed his knife into the table, "Everything! And, this is how I will get it! Tomorrow morning, if we do not see a flag of surrender high up on the pole at Dejima, why then you will join your friend in his little dance among the masts!"

"You will force them to fight?"

"Fight? Heavens no! I do so abhor a fight, but I always enjoy a good thrashing. We will simply blow your little island to Hell, and then we will take what we want."

Dawn

The mood aboard the PHANTOM was grim as the sun first peeked over the hills behind Nagasaki, highlighting the damaged Dejima in the morning light. An empty noose hung loosely from the spar next to Bleeckier's lifeless and slowly swinging body. A sailor pulled the empty noose inboard with a boat hook and near to Dr. Franz. Upon a hand signal from Powell the cannon were once again rolled out of their ports.

"First, another small demonstration of our intentions, and then our thirty-two pounders. Unfortunately," he turned to Dr. Franz, "you will not be with us to admire our military superiority." Three crewman moved to restrain him.

Dejima was deserted. From the deck of the PHANTOM a far off lone figure could be seen dragging a long boat towards the wharf. He paused at the flag pole, and brought down the Dutch flag that was flying in a stiff off-shore breeze. Slowly the flag came down to be replaced by another: Plague.

Powell watched through the spy glass as the figure pushed the long boat into the water, climbed in and began rowing towards them. "*Peste*," growled Barton, and the word began to spread through the crew, carrying with it fear and dread.

"Plague? How bad?" Powell asked Franz with suspicion.

"In the Orient?" he responded. "Who could know? It could be any of a dozen diseases."

The sickly man rowed within hailing distance of the ship, and the crew on the deck rushed to the railing and then clearly recoiled with fear. It was de Wolfe, his face white and mottled, his eyes dark and sunken. He coughed deeply, and paused to catch his breath, the gasps coming in short shallow groans.

The crewmen holding Dr. Franz looked at him in dread, let him go and then backed away.

"How bad!?" demanded Powell.

"I don't know, I promise you I do not know," said Franz, truly confused.

Captain Powell signaled to a crewman holding a blunderbuss, the shotgun like smoothbore that could clear an entire deck or cut multiple men apart with one shot, took the weapon from him and pointed it at the long boat. "Belay there! Stand off I say! What do you want?"

"It took several tries for de Wolfe to call back loud enough to be heard. He gathered his breath, tried to stand, fell back and shouted, "Give us our doctor, I beg of you. So many sick, so many dead," then collapsed back into the boat. He gathered his strength again, "Please! We will give you anything. Food, water, silver, anything."

It started making sense to Franz, and he began to cough heavily into his hand, then scratched his back as if being bitten.

The crew shifted further away, now giving him a wide berth. They were grumbling and moving closer to panic.

Barton came close and whispered to Powell, "It will all be rotten with plague."

Powell looked at the long boat with suspicion, and then studied his crew, already muttering among themselves and looking at him with distrust. He must do something, and quickly, before the fear spread any further. He decided, "Mr. Barton, cut that boat loose, raise sail, get us out of here!"

"Captain?" asked Barton pointing at Dr. Franz.

"And, throw that man overboard."

There were shouts and rapid fire orders as they prepared the ship to leave. Several crew members were arguing with Powell, and Barton took one last long suspicious look at the doctor before pushing him over the railing, and Franz spun mid-air and then landed in the water with a huge splash. De Wolfe was hunched over, with barely enough strength to lift his head. Franz began swimming towards the long boat, and with effort was able to pull himself aboard as de Wolfe began weakly rowing back towards shore.

"Are you sick man?" Franz asked with genuine concern, but then looked at his hand where Taka's white face powder had come off easily, smearing across his wet fingers. De Wolfe began rowing with increasing strength towards Dejima.

Bleeckier's body was cut loose and hit the ocean with a dull thud, quickly sinking out of sight.

"Let us get out of here," de Wolfe said with urgency, and Dr. Franz smiled with understanding. As the long boat approached the wharf, the PHANTOM could be seen under full sail, rapidly making her way out of Nagasaki Bay.

Is That What You Want?

The Dutch staff were waiting in a nearby storeroom, and they rushed out in celebration as the long boat landed and the two men stumbled out. De Wolfe was the man of the hour, and everyone wanted to shake his hand and congratulate him. Abe stood back, curious.

From the back of the joyous crowd Kamimoto called out, breaking the happy mood, "Your little lie seems to have succeeded. I congratulate you."

"I would never lie!" de Wolfe called back, offended. "It was merely a deception. They themselves chose what to believe."

"Drove them off you did, my friend, single-handed!" Schuck called and slapped him on the back, handing him a towel to remove the now ruined white make-up.

De Wolfe grabbed Dr. Franz by the arm and pointed, "Taka has been injured, Doctor, can you…" but the physician was already gone before the sentence could be finished.

Kamimoto came closer, "She will be fine, and she has already been taken away."

"Taken away? On who's orders?"

"She is obviously strong-headed and quite troublesome to me, and she is no longer of any concern."

"Where has she gone?" de Wolfe demanded suddenly angry.

"She will be sent to a *sake* house or a brothel. There are many men there who will find her pleasing."

De Wolfe was enraged, "She was my gift from the *Obugyō-sama*, and she is neither yours to command nor to take away. You have no authority over her, do you hear me?"

"As she could not 'comfort' you, I assumed that you would not mind."

The blood was pounding in de Wolfe's ears, he had never been this angry in his entire life. He had never struck anyone before, but he was very close to it now. He spoke slowly, "Listen to me very carefully. She is mine. I want her taken to my room. She will be taken care of there. Do you understand me?"

Kamimoto considered the implications of this carefully, and then smiled. "Perfectly. I understand you perfectly. And, if that is what you wish de Wolfe-*sama*, of course that is what you will get."

By that evening Taka was sleeping in de Wolfe's bed. For the first time her hair was down and she was wearing no make-up, entirely natural and beautiful. De Wolfe stroked her hair tenderly out of her face as Dr. Franz entered the room.

"You have finally accepted responsibility for the *Obugyō-sama's* gift?"

85

"Kamimoto would have sent her to a brothel," de Wolfe answered darkly.

Franz considered for a moment, and then offered the best advice he could: "The most dangerous aspect of taking a mistress is that you may grow to love her."

De Wolfe pretended he had not heard and inquired, "How is she?"

"A blow to the head obviously, but not serious." He paused for a moment, "They tell me that several people were killed in Nagasaki. Many feel that the Dutch are to blame."

"Maybe the Dutch are to blame."

Not knowing what else to say Franz turned away, "I need to go."

"Then go," de Wolfe responded, never taking his eyes off of Taka.

The Chapel

De Wolfe was standing in front of the flimsy alter in the make-shift chapel facing the painting of the cross. He could not bring himself to kneel. He spoke clearly and distinctly, as if addressing a large crowd.

"May you protect and keep the Reverend's soul, for I could not save him."

He waited in silence in the quiet gloom, as if expecting some reply. "You simply watched as evil took a kind and gentle man and abused and murdered him. Why would you allow this? Have you sent me here simply to test me? Where are you? Do you have even the slightest care?"

Dejima. He understood now why Captain Ostrander had called it a prison. He had endured months of hardship and travel to come to this? To be isolated with no family or friends, no one he could talk to or confide in? "Do you even have the slightest care!?" he thundered again into the silence.

What had he expected in accepting the assignment here? Two years, and then what? Back to Holland and Camilla and the life of a van Courtlandt? Is that what he had wanted? Lazy self-absorbed elites thinking they were better than everyone around them? "Do you even exist!? If you are all powerful, than breathe life into the Reverend and take me in his place! Will you?" His voice trailed off in despair, "Will you?"

"Better men than you have failed," van Courtlandt had cryptically told him, and perhaps he had been right. But, de Wolfe had never failed in anything he had started.

If he took a challenge he would finish it, even if everyone hated him, even if he was alone, even in this Hellhole in the Japans. With or without his God.

"Do you care? Or, are we all just fodder for your amusement?" He turned away from the cross and the makeshift chapel and returned to his residence.

Taka was awake when he arrived, and he smiled at her. He examined the bandage on her head, and it was dry, the bleeding had fully stopped. He brushed the hair away and began softly, "Your wound, well, Dr. Franz says that you will be fine."

He knew her Dutch was rudimentary, that she could never understand what he wanted to tell her, but he needed to say it anyway. "Perhaps," it was all there, he could feel it in his heart, he just had to put the words together, maybe more for himself than for her. "If I have seemed uncaring. That is not what I have wanted."

Now he was lost again. She stared up at him from the bed and he turned to sit down next to her. "I have much to thank you for, and little that I can do or give you to repay you." No, that was not right, she had given him nothing. She had been by his side though for weeks, and had always turned up exactly when he needed her. And, she had asked for nothing in return for her kindness either. She had been there to soothe him and help him, and he had been polite, of course, but he usually had just tried to ignore her. That had been easier when she had been hidden behind thick cloth and make-up. Now though, seeing her in the bed devoid of any artifice, she was simply a woman.

"I do not understand you," he stammered, and whispered, "And, I will not love you. Cannot." He said with finality.

Taka's hand rose from the bed to stroke his face, and he touched it tenderly. He looked at her in the dim light, it was all so perfect in that moment as he sat next to her in the silence of the night. He took her hand from his cheek, kissed her fingers, and left the room.

PART II

BERTRAYAL

Blackmail

The note from Papa to "Come urgently at once," had been hand-delivered by the family butler, and the carriage driver and butler had both waited outside for over an hour while she arranged her make-up and hair and finished dressing. It was late morning, but as was her custom she had been barely out of bed when the summons came. She wondered what the matter might be as they rumbled across town. Had he gotten the latest set of bills from the dress maker and decided that this time she had abused his generosity? Perhaps the exotic foods the cook had ordered and the amount of entertaining she provided for her circle of friends? But, he wouldn't deny her having a few close friends would he? Maybe that the work on the household was proceeding so slowly? That must be it she convinced herself. It's the renovations.

The carriage arrived at the van Courtlandt estate and she got out demurely, thanked the driver, and put on her best "I'm so sorry" little girl face. The heavy doors were opened without knocking by a man-servant, and she was formally shown into the front room, as if she didn't already know the way.

Papa was there plumped down deep into his favorite chair as he so often was in the late afternoons, and sitting across from him on the sofa drinking coffee was Cas. Her heart jumped, and she pushed it down, kissing her father on the cheek and giving Cas a brief curtsey before sitting. Damn! Why was he here?

"Mr. Janssen is here with a proposition," her father began simply.

"A business proposition?" she asked innocently, and Cas smiled.

"No, but I wish that it were that easy," her father reprimanded her.

"Then, what could he possibly want?" Cas smiled at her, but kept quiet. Her mind was racing and cursing, THAT BASTARD! She screamed inside, but returned his smile. She had freely given herself to him and asked for nothing in return, and now he was betraying her to her father?

"Perhaps I should ask Mr. Janssen to explain," Mr. van Courtlandt said and then turned to Cas.

Cas looked down and a dark shadow crossed his face, although his inky eyes glittered. "It is my mother," he began. "She is most ill and has called for her only son to return to her side before she passes. It is not an inexpensive trip, and I was hoping that a sum of money, a very reasonable and modest sum of money, might be provided so that I may travel to her before, well, before she..."

"And," Mr. van Courtlandt interrupted, "this fellow seems to believe that I will provide him with the money. Though it is not in any way what I would consider to be a 'reasonable and modest sum' at all."

"It is indeed a sad and tragic story," Camilla offered, "but, why is this any concern of ours?"

Cas dipped his head and looked at her sideways, lifting one eyebrow. He had often made the same face while they were lying in bed and she had said something that he believed to be foolish or naive.

"Mr. Janssen has explained to me," distress rose in Mr. van Courtlandt's voice, "what 'close friends' that you and he have become, and that there was little chance that your relationship would receive – shall we say - public attention if he went away. Of course, none of us would want your 'friendship' to be ... what was the word you used Mr. Janssen?"

"Promulgated?" Cas offered.

"Yes, 'promulgated' that was the term you used several times," van Courtlandt echoed, obviously displeased.

So, the cat was out of the bag. Camilla was thinking fast now. If the slightest rumors of her infidelity got out, she would become a social pariah. None of her friends would have anything to do with her. She would be really alone and isolated in that half-built house in stinking Jordaan. She was trapped and caught, but not yet tied up. Cas going away was the perfect solution for her. For everyone, she concluded.

"Well," she began, "he is a dear and close friend of Hendrik's, and the van Courtlandt's have always been most generous to those less fortunate."

"Yes!" Mr. van Courtlandt took a drink of his own coffee. "He <u>was</u> a close friend of Hendrik's," implying that he knew much more of her foolish dalliance. "And, that makes your 'friendship' with Mr. Janssen even more troublesome to us all, and why we must be discreet." He took a deep breath, and looked meaningfully at Cas. "How long do you suppose you would be gone?"

"Oh, at least three and maybe as long as six months," Cas lied easily. He had no intention of leaving at all, of course. This is how the game was played: Get the lump sum up front from the father or the husband, and then lay low for a while. After a short time an innocent note to the wife with a polite request, and then the regular stipends would begin. Much smaller than the initial payment perhaps, but regular. He liked that. This would make five, each arriving promptly on the first of each month, and he could begin working on number six. He could easily live on four, but six would be so much better.

"Yes, I do believe that it would be good for Mr. Janssen to go away for a while, a long while, for the benefit of all of us." Mr. van Courtlandt scowled meaningfully at Cas. "A very long while," he emphasized. "And six months, I believe, would be not nearly enough. I had been concerned that it would be Mr. de Wolfe that might bring dishonor onto the van Courtlandt name, but it turns out that I was unable to foresee it from my own daughter, and we will obviously require more permanent solutions."

"Papa!" Camilla squeaked and gave the both of them the little-girl pout as Mr. van Courtlandt continued. "I will make the arrangements for Mr. Janssen to go away personally." He turned to glare at Camilla, "I think you should both go away."

"What?" both Cas and Camilla asked together.

"If you want something done right, then one should do it himself, and I intend to do this myself. Camilla, you may go for now, I will advise you of what I have concluded. Mr. Janssen and I will continue our discussion, and he will be gone, one way or another, by this evening."

Mr. van Courtlandt looked meaningfully at Cas and repeated, "One way or another". He reached over to the side-table and rang a small bell, and two burly men appeared instantly at the hallway. She had never seen them before, but they reminded her of the scruffy fellows she had seen on the docks, with unkempt hair and heavy calloused hands.

"Off with you!" her father insisted, and Camilla stood up, glanced over at Cas and squinted at him in anger before practically fleeing out to the waiting carriage accompanied by the ever-present butler.

The room slowly became silent and increasingly uncomfortable. "Well, I should be off myself," Cas offered with a brightness he did not feel and stood to go.

"Those are very nice boots," Mr. van Courtlandt noted, his left hand stroking his white beard. "They must have been quite expensive?"

"These old things? Oh, no! Not in the slightest. A combination of both fashion and function really, and well, they were practically second hand, and...."

"You came here looking to finance a trip," the older man interrupted. "And, I am now going to offer you something even better, a job. There is a slave ship heading for loading cargoes in North Africa and then to the Dutch Antilles. Your boots should be aboard that vessel."

"That is most kind, Mr. van Courtlandt, however my mother is quite ill, and I could not consider leaving at this time…."

Van Courtlandt looked frustrated, and then continued. "I'm sorry if you may have misunderstood me, for it was meant to be a bit of a threat you see. But, I suppose I am not very good at threats, and quite a bit out of practice. Let me be clear. A man cannot be a true success in business unless he is able to draw on a broad range of potential assets. One of those is finding employment for persons. Another is completely eliminating problems. I am combining those two talents. Either your boots will be working aboard that slave trader when she sails in the morning, or they will be floating in the canal. Your feet will be in them. There, that's a better threat don't you agree?"

"Sir, I came to you seeking a kindness!"

No, sir, you most certainly did not. You came to blackmail me. You came here today to threaten my family and to extort money. I am not unaware that you have done so to others as well. This is the end of the line for you sir, here and today. As I have repeatedly said, one way or another."

"I see," Cas mumbled, and then appeared resigned. "Well, I have much to do then before we sail. I must, well, I must bid farewell to my friends and family, and I must pack my belongings for the journey to the New World!" He feigned for the first time to be enthused at the prospect, while desperately seeking a way to escape.

"None of that will be necessary," and van Courtlandt nodded to the two men who moved to each side of the playboy. "Everything will be provided to you aboard."

"I cannot just pick up and disappear!"

"On the contrary Mr. Janssen. That is exactly what will happen."

Cas started to make a dash for the heavy front doors and was quickly swept up and then dragged outside.

"*Goede reis* Mr. Janssen!" van Courtlandt called out as the doors were softly closed from the inside by the house man-servant. "Have a good trip!"

A Holiday

De Wolfe had fallen asleep at his writing desk, and was suddenly awoken by an excited knocking at the door. From outside he heard Kamimoto calling, "De Wolfe-*sama*! Good morning! Mr. de Wolfe!"

91

He wiped his eyes and stumbled over to the entrance, but before he could open the door Kamimoto barged in and rushed past him. "Good morning! I have wonderful news!" he started, unable to contain himself. "You are an eidolon!"

"I'm sorry, I am a what?" the Hollander asked, struggling to come fully awake.

"An eidolon. I am certain that it is a Dutch expression. An ideal person, you defeated the pirate's like an apparition. An eidolon. Isn't that the correct word?"

"I really don't know, I can't say. I have never heard that word."

"You do speak Dutch don't you?" Kamimoto teased him. "No matter. You have saved many Japanese lives, and even Abe-*sama* was greatly impressed. He has convinced the *Obugyō-sama* to give you a gift!"

De Wolfe glanced towards his bedroom door which was slightly open, and Kamimoto followed his gaze. Both men could clearly see Taka looking back at them from de Wolfe's bed.

"I, er, I don't think that I can accept another gift," he began, but Kamimoto did not let him finish. "A holiday from Dejima!" he proudly announced.

"I may leave the island?" de Wolfe asked astonished.

"Every Sunday," Kamimoto assured him. "You must be escorted, but only so that you do not get lost, and you must be back before sunset, but yes! You may go anywhere you like!"

"Can Taka take me?"

"A wonderful idea," Kamimoto beamed.

"Today is Sunday."

"You may go today. And, every Sunday if you like."

"Then we will go today."

"Splendid! You should ask Acawarman to pack you both lunches. Now, what about Dr. Franz?"

"Must he go too?"

"Oh, no, of course not! But…. You have restricted him to the island, and what is it that you Hollanders say? Something about a goose?"

"Yes, and a gander."

"What's a gander?"

"A female goose, and if the male goose....., well never mind, it isn't important."

"The doctor does have a wife and a home in Nagasaki," Kamimoto pointed out. "If you are allowed to leave the island....."

De Wolfe considered. He desperately needed to get off of Dejima, if even just for a few hours, and it would not be fair for him to leave the trading post while confining the good doctor. Besides, after what Franz had been through he would need his wife's solace. "You're right, of course. I will let him know that he can return to his home immediately, as long as he first completes his duties here."

"Splendid," smiled Kamimoto. "Simply splendid."

Let Me Taste You

The trail up the hillside left de Wolfe winded and slightly sweaty, but he quickly began to cool as soon as they reached the crest and felt the soft breeze off of the ocean. Taka was wearing a light Summer kimono and carried a Japanese wooden lunch box in a sash. De Wolfe's long woolen pants trapped the heat, but a thin linen shirt and a broad brimmed hat kept the direct sun off of him. He had his own lunch, a picnic blanket and a jacket in his small backpack if he needed it.

They continued across the hill and then slightly down until they found a flat spot near the beginnings of a stream, and there laid out their preparations for the mid-day meal. De Wolfe spread the blanket from his backpack, and Taka opened her lunch box, neatly packed with rice, fish and pickles. The view was spectacular; sweeping broadly across Nagasaki Bay and the ocean, and encompassing the entire city and hillsides, now in the beginnings of their Fall colors.

"This is the perfect location for a house," de Wolfe exclaimed. "Right here, facing the ocean, and already with fresh water. The porch would be here," and he walked over to a spot and pointed, "the dining room here," he stepped two paces to his left, "to admire the view and to catch the afternoon trade winds. The kitchen here, and three bedrooms in the back." He could see it all in his mind, a tile roof, and bright plaster walls, colorfully painted inside. It would be perfect.

"Where do you live?" he asked Taka, and she indicated down the hill to Dejima.

"No, I understand, of course," he laughed. "But where is your family?"

She pointed into Nagasaki at the large *Bugyō-sho* governmental building including its prison where her family was still being held, and the execution grounds. De Wolfe only saw a large well-kept compound, and not knowing better was suitably impressed, thinking it must be a palace of some kind.

"Do you have any brothers?"

"One brother, two sisters."

I never had anyone," de Wolfe told her, opening up his personal life for the first time. "Except my mother. I never knew my father at all, so she had to raise me alone, and it was quite hard on her. She died while I was still in school."

Reflecting on his life in Amsterdam, the many decisions and events that had brought him to this point, de Wolfe became somber and pointed out to sea, "My home is out there, very far away. Everything that I have worked for, everything that I want is there."

"What do you want?" asked Taka.

De Wolfe shrugged, "Money, I suppose. Money brings freedom and the opportunity to do many things. My wife's family is quite wealthy. A home, of course. A family, with children. Everything I suppose that I never had when I was growing up." He hesitated a moment, and thought carefully before proceeding. "I have a beautiful wife," he told Taka.

"I know," she replied.

De Wolfe opened his shirt and took the small silver cross off of his neck and showed it to Taka. She touched it reverently, admiring its simple workmanship. "I have worn this for many years," he said softly. "I want you to have it," he slipped it over her head and onto the nape of her neck.

"Thank you."

She offered him some foods from her lunch box, and he looked carefully, but shook his head, and then took a meat and cheese sandwich from his own. She had a small jar of tea capped by a stopper, and he had a bottle of whisky. He offered her a drink and she smelled it, made a face and shook her head.

"Let me taste you," she offered.

"What?" he said, not understanding.

"Drink."

He took a swallow of the whisky, and Taka leaned forward and kissed him, tasted her own lips, then sat back. "Better," she said.

De Wolfe took another drink, held it in his mouth for a moment, and then leaned forward and kissed her. She held his face softly, looking directly into his eyes as she laid back onto the blanket.

The Slave Ship MEERMIN

Cas Janssen had been dragged by the two ruffians to the slave ship waiting at the harbor, the very same berth where he had waved farewell to Hendrik so long ago, and they immediately hustled the scoundrel aboard, handing a letter to the ship's master before throwing him into the darkness below decks. There was a yelp as he hit the deck at the bottom of the ladder and someone, or something, scurried away in the darkness before the hatch was slammed shut above him.

Cas jerked the handkerchief from his breast pocket and held it tightly to his nose as the stench of unseen fetid unwashed bodies and an unbearable miasma of rot engulfed him, but the stink penetrated everywhere and everything in any case. He leapt back on the ladder and pounded futilely on the hatch for a few moments before he realized that no one was coming to him, no help would be given.

By now his eyes had become more adjusted to the dimness and he could make out other forms scattered into the corners and crannies of the hold, small white orbs all staring back at him with either disinterest or in some cases open hostility or fear. He warily moved to find an unoccupied space he could put his back against, but tripped over a solid metal ring bolted to the deck. He finally found a space in the gloom and settled in to wait.

It was some hours later that the hatch was pulled up, then an immense boom of an angry voice penetrated the blackness, and the First Mate began beating the men in the hold onto the deck with a weighted leather cudgel. A long boat had a line secured to the ship's bow and the smaller boat was pulling the larger ship into the stream. It must have been the middle of the night, but he had no way of knowing the time as he and the other prisoners stumbled up the ladder to meet the emotionless faces of the regular crew and the scowling officers all seeming to be staring at him and his expensive clothing and polished boots.

"Aloft! Aloft! Get your lazy arseholes aloft!" the First Mate screamed and began sheparding the confused and disoriented men toward the rigging. He began pushing and beating Cas with the cudgel he carried, shoving him onto the ropes and then smacking his heels to quicken his climb.

Cas hustled up to the first yardarm where he saw others laying over the spar and holding onto the tied ropes that bound the sail to the wood and quickly found an empty space. A dirty man with a broken tooth tried to push him to the side, to take his place on the spar, but Cas shoved back and the man then continued up the rigging to the higher yardarm above them and took a position over that sail. The First Mate seemed satisfied for the moment and went forward to badger the sailors rowing the long boat, exhorting them to greater efforts to get the vessel moving into the ebb tide that would take them out of the harbor and begin their voyage to Africa.

"God help me," Cas muttered to himself, "God help me," looking down at the clumsy and unfamiliar movements of the men who, like himself, had been forcibly impressed into this terrible journey. Mixed in were the regular sailors, familiar with the ship, but who seemed to be the lowest dregs of the ocean. Above them all were the officers, the Captain standing stoically on the aft deck while the cruel First Mate moved swiftly, shouting and kicking any whom he fancied were moving too slowly, sometimes striking them with his weighted club.

"Well, God better help you," the man hanging over the yardarm next to him sneered. "If He won't, then nobody else will."

Below he could see the First Mate swinging the cudgel, beating other men to their stations. It was nearly as long as from his wrist to his elbow and stitched together with black leather. One end of the weapon was a covered wooden handle with a loop on the end to avoid having it pulled from his hand. He most frequently beat the sailors with that while cursing and kicking them. The other end was a monkey's fist filled with some type of lead that he would use to deliver crushing blows: Huge welts would spring up where the leaden end struck, or a blow to the head would instantly knock a man to his knees.

Cas felt light-headed and dizzy, and suppressed an urge to retch onto the canvas in front of him as he gripped the sail weakly. "Better hold on tighter than that," the sailor cautioned. "We'll be hitting the swell when we pass the breakwater, and this high up you will be like a flea on a dog's ass." The dandy from Amsterdam re-doubled his grip on the rope and canvas and waited grimly in the quiet dark night, the only sounds being the slap of the long boat's oars on the water and the First Mate's cursing.

The Memorial Service

The sun was setting as de Wolfe and Taka strolled across the Dutch Gate. They had held hands as they walked down the hillside, but kept a discreet and respectful distance as they entered Nagasaki. They were both quiet and happy.

Waiting for them was Kamimoto holding a medium sized white box bound with black cord. Seeing the box Taka stopped short, looking shocked and saddened while de Wolfe continued on. Reluctantly, she followed several paces behind him.

"Another gift from the *Obugyō-sama*?" he asked happily.

"Bleeckier-sama?" asked Taka.

His ashes," Kamimoto confirmed. "His body was found by fisherman."

De Wolfe was embarrassed by his stupidity and lack of understanding. "We must have a service."

"A memorial," Kamimoto corrected him as de Wolfe hurried off to find Schuck.

It seemed fitting that Bleeckier's memorial service would be held on a Sunday evening, and the make shift chapel was filled with the entire Dutch staff waiting patiently when de Wolfe entered and walked to the front of the room, placing the white box on the altar/table underneath the portrait on the wall, now turned out and concealing the cross behind. Kamimoto, Abe and Taka waited, standing quietly at the rear of the room.

De Wolfe looked out on the assembly of Dutch and Japanese. This was his world now, and they all looked to him for leadership, order and safety and he had provided them none of that. He had allowed events to drive him, and he would begin changing that here and now, this very evening. "Mr. Bleeckier – the <u>Reverend</u> Bleeckier," he began, "was an innocent victim, gone with no farewells, and only we few souls gathered here today to mourn him. His life was kindness, and his death warned us of approaching peril. When we speak of sacrifice, there can be no greater virtue than giving one's life for another. His life, and his death, were service: To the Company, to us, and to God."

There would be no turning back. He knew that what he was about to do was "forbidden", but the Reverend deserved this moment, as do all Christian men. They were in Japan, but stood on Company ground, in an unofficial Chapel, beside a makeshift altar, none of that mattered. What did matter was honoring a good man. "Let us pray," and de Wolfe held his hands together in front and lowered his gaze.

Even if he could not grasp the words or meaning, discerning the start of a Christian prayer, a forbidden Christian prayer, Abe snorted and left the room. Taka closed her eyes and bowed her head, while Kamimoto watched with great interest as de Wolfe turned the portrait around and revealed the cross.

"Lord, we are all flawed sinners who only seek a seat next to you in Heaven. Our days on Earth are numbered, and we never know when we will be called to Your side to stay with You forever. Some believe that the path to your glory is through a lifetime of noble deeds. Others, that a final act of contrition, a confession and admission of our guilt, will absolve us of our sins and gain entry to Heaven."

Kamimoto carefully noted these last remarks, listening intently as de Wolfe continued the eulogy.

"Whatever the measure, the Reverend has earned his place next to you in Paradise with eternal bliss. He was a good man. May you keep him and guard him forever. Amen."

"Amen," the room echoed.

A Bear on Horseback

Kamimoto was delicately working on the oil painting in his room. It was the scene from the evening that he had first shared whisky on the wharf with de Wolfe. There was a horizon line bisecting the dark sea and sky, the rough shape of a ship, and a luminous orb lighting the water. The pigments were bright and vivid, the Dutch had brought extraordinary colors with them to Japan, and he had been told that they had many fine artists in their own country. He had admired the paintings in the *Opperhoofd*'s residence, especially the realism and the use of shadows. Japanese artists had not yet acquired this skill, and often used charcoal or watercolors in their works. But, he most enjoyed using the oils and techniques of the Dutch. He had once wished that someday he would be able to travel to Holland and see these works, perhaps even speak with the artists themselves.

Westerveldt had been a fairly good artist, and one of the old staff from over a hundred years ago had left various paintings which still hung on the walls. They were unsigned, so he never knew who this unknown Dutch painter might have been, but he learned quite a bit simply by studying the brush strokes, and the manner in which the artist had laid out the subject matter.

He had been sitting on his knees and working on the speckles of light, and it was coming along quite nicely. There was a large full moon setting over the water and illuminating a long boat floating offshore. He especially enjoyed the challenge of the moonlight reflecting off of the ocean's ripples.

A voice from outside called, *"May I interrupt you?"*

He reflexively replied, *"Please come in."*

Taka slid open the paper covered door, slipped off her wooden sandals, and stepped inside. *"Good evening,"* she began politely, and sat on her knees on the floor, bringing their heads to the same level.

"Are you well?" he asked. *"Are you enjoying our fine Fall weather?"* He began the conversation with small talk, as usual, but wondered why she had come to him, what it was that she might want.

They continued in this manner for several moments, and when the unimportant subjects had finally run out, she began with the real reason for her visit. *"I am most worried about my family."*

"Of course," he responded. *"I understand completely your concern. I would like to assure you that they are fine and are being taken good care of."*

"I hope that you will convey to the Obugyō-sama that I am most thankful for the pains that he has taken on their behalf."

"I will speak with him directly myself," Kamimoto offered.

"Do you speak with him often?"

Oh, no, he thought, here it comes. And, I fell directly into her trap. What does she want from the *Obugyō-sama*, and how can I possibly avoid having to ask for it?

"Oh no, not that often at all, really," he added modestly. *Very rarely, in fact."*

"But, from time to time?" and she smiled.

"Yes, yes, but, as I just said, very rarely."

"Could you please mention to him, and I know it is such a small matter for such an important man as yourself, how concerned I am about my family, and how pleased I would be if they were able to return to their own home."

"Well, that is impossible of course. They are being held for their own safety, and under the protection of the Bugyō-sho".

"I understand," she said looking down. *"I have never mentioned this matter to de Wolfe Capitão-sama, of course, knowing how much it would trouble him to share my concern."*

"Do you think that your Dutch is good enough to discuss such a complicated matter with him? I would be happy, at any time, to discuss your family with the Hollander myself, so that you would not be troubled."

"That is true, my Dutch is not perfect. However, since Bleeckier-sama died I have spent every day reading the Dutch books, and de Wolfe-sama has been very generous with his time in the evening. I feel that I am making good progress."

Now the bargain was out in the open, her family for her silence. Certainly he did not want the Dutch involved with any local matters, it would complicate things immensely.

"And, did you know," she continued, "that he has asked me to teach him Japanese?"

"Yes, he made the same request to me, and do you know what I told him? I said that a Dutchman learning Japanese is like a bear on horseback. It might be quite amusing to see, but that it has no practical value at all."

"Well, I am quite confident that I would make an excellent teacher, and that he would learn quickly."

Kamimoto considered his options carefully. He cared little about the Shindo family, but what happened with de Wolfe could have an immediate and direct impact on him. The Dutch Gate had always provided a convenient barrier between foreign concerns and Japanese politics, and it was important to maintain that status quo. De Wolfe was headstrong, and it was important that he remain focused on the daily operations of the Dutch trading post. He decided.

"I share your concerns for both your family and for de Wolfe-sama, and I am certain that small matters such as this should never worry him. I will speak with the Obugyō-sama and implore him to allow your family to return home. I am sure they will be much more comfortable. Would that satisfy you?"

"Thank you Otona," and she bowed to him.

"And, he added, "I am quite sure that we are both pleased that such trivial matters as your family or learning Japanese will not take up any more of the Capitão-sama's valuable time. Isn't that correct?"

"Of course, Otona," she said rising and bowed one last time as she left. "Sleep well."

Otsukimi

The weather over the past several weeks had been unsettled as Fall began to transition into Winter, with frequent storms and occasional heavy rain. Everyone on the island was feeling cooped-up, and arguments had broken out among the Dutch staff and even two fist fights. De Wolfe had been called to intervene and render judgement on which party had been right and which party had been wrong, and he absolutely hated that. He knew that he was the authority figure and had to conduct himself accordingly, but who was he to cast moral aspersions? His standard tactic had been to separate the combatants, let them cool down, lecture them both sternly, and then be done with it. It seemed to work, and he was thankful for that.

Company records showed that Winters were mild in Nagasaki, with only sporadic light snow that soon melted away. It was not the weather, or a lack of food, or disease that concerned him, it was boredom. Dr. Franz could leave the island at will, and was often gone for days at a time, off on some grand sight-seeing adventure probably. He and Taka never missed a Sunday to get away, and he valued those short excursions immensely and with a little guilt. But, for the three dozen other Dutchmen living in Japan there was little respite.

Wednesday October 12th, 1852 was just another in the continuing line of boring days. The warehouses held little activity, the garden had been harvested, the buildings fully repaired and everything tightened up for the coming Winter.

He had spent the day mostly with the men who worked for him, getting to know them just a little. Their contracts ran for years at a time, and many of them he learned never planned to return to Holland at all. They had taken Batavian wives and their families patiently awaited their overseas assignments to expire. Others planned to make a go in India or South Africa using their earnings to set up a shop or business of some kind. They would all leave the Japans as "rich" men, at least from their perspectives he thought, and he was a little conscience stricken thinking of the van Courtlandt's vast inherited wealth.

When he returned home at sunset Taka and Acawarman were waiting for him, standing side-by-side in the dining room with their arms crossed and mischievous smiles on their faces. What had they cooked up he wondered, and in fact they had cooked nothing at all. Rather than his usual hot dinner there was picnic fare on the table, food wrapped up in a brightly colored cloth and two blankets.

"Otsukimi!" Taka announced proudly, as if that explained anything at all.

"Otsukimi!" echoed Acawarman with enthusiasm.

"Otsukimi!" repeated de Wolfe. "Huzzah! Now, what is Otsukimi?"

"Moon see!" Taka explained, again leaving de Wolfe completely uncomprehending. "Alright, picnic."

"A picnic? At this time of night? I fancy not, thank you very much."

"Otsukimi," Taka insisted. "Moon see. Let's go."

She handed him the packet of prepared foods, took the two blankets and marched outside as the Hollander followed and Acawarman beamed at the both of them.

She continued through the quiet and rapidly darkening island until they got to the now barren garden where she spread out the blankets next to each other, and then arranged the picnic food on the cloth. There was hot tea, sandwiches, pickled cucumbers, fried chicken, and even an apple that de Wolfe cut in half with his pocket knife.

They ate mostly in silence as it grew darker, Taka's Dutch was still fairly basic, but it was nice, it seemed, well, natural. What would they have talked about anyway? Business? Politics? Heaven forbid, the weather? With Camilla it would have been shopping, but of course they wouldn't have talked in any case, she just would have listed what she had bought while he listened. So, he ate quietly and contentedly.

Before long the bright full moon began rising over the low hills behind Nagasaki, illuminating the picnic and the garden. *"Otsukimi!"* Taka pointed. "Moon see!"

Spending his entire life in Amsterdam, De Wolfe had never actually taken the time to really look at the face of the moon before. Even on the long voyage he had given the moon and the stars little regard, retiring to his shared cabin early, and he now began to realize what he had missed. It was the biggest and brightest moon that he could imagine, its shining face blemished by dark spots, but they gave it personality. Men have been staring at this since Creation, he thought, but not me. Not until tonight.

He laid back on the blanket, and put his hands behind his head, simply watching the moon rise above them. Taka snuggled underneath his elbow and into his shoulder. *"Otsukimi"* she whispered to him.

"Otsukimi," he repeated softly. What a glorious night. He was happy.

A Winter's Walk

Christmas had been a welcome and restful respite, and he and Taka had spent *Eerste Kerstdag* - First Christmas Day - quietly together. December 26th, *Tweede Kerstdag* - the Second Christmas Day - had been a bright and glorious Sunday and they had walked through Nagasaki and then north along a busy roadway. There could be no religious celebrations of the Savior's birth, of course, but no one worked and the trading post was quiet.

The foreigner and his Japanese guide were now a familiar sight throughout the region, but still often attracted crowds if they stopped anywhere for a rest or tea. De Wolfe was merely pleased to be away from Dejima, if only for the day, and let Taka lead him as they meandered through ever more narrow lanes until she stopped at one house in particular and slid open the gate.

Inside was a smallish older man carrying two buckets on a pole over his shoulder and digging with a stick in the dirt. He jumped in surprise and nearly dropped everything to the ground before placing the buckets down and rushing over to meet them with a huge smile on his face. De Wolfe had no idea how old the man was, but he was quite certain that he had never seen someone so ancient and grizzled before in his

102

entire life. The small wizened man was bowing and talking so quickly that it sounded more like a series of knocks and bumps rather than an actual language. Several of his front teeth were missing also, which caused a whistle to come out on certain syllables. The general impression was of a steam calliope being hammered by a child.

Taka returned the old man's smile, and spoke with him briefly. There was a genuine affection between the two of them, set off by what seemed to de Wolfe, to be an animated yet harsh language. He had only seen her speak with deference to Kamimoto and Abe, and this was so strikingly different.

He bowed to the old man, of course he had not understood a word either of them had said, and unexpectedly the fellow reached out and shook his hand pumping it vigorously up and down. The hand was thickly calloused and hard, and when he let go de Wolfe noticed traces of the earth on his own palm and that it now had a rich organic odor. Taka led him to the porch stairs and called out in Japanese.

"I have returned!" she greeted the occupants from outside.

The paper covered door slid open and a man in his mid-forties stood there, surprised and shocked. *"It has been a long time. You are most welcome, please enter my daughter,"* he told her. Behind the man two girls, no more than fourteen or fifteen years old peeked out, and further back an attractive woman about the same age as the man.

"My father," Taka explained. "My mother," she continued.

"How do you do?" asked de Wolfe.

"I am pleased to meet you," said Taka's father.

De Wolfe suddenly realized with embarrassment that this was the family of the woman that he had been sleeping with for the past months, and wondered if they knew and might be offended by, well, by the illicit nature of their relationship. "Your daughter is a most capable assistant and translator," he began. "She is a great help in ensuring that the Company's business here in Japan goes smoothly."

Taka's father looked to her expectantly, and she translated, *"The Capitão-sama says that my work at Dejima has been satisfactory."*

"Your Dutch is much improved," her father observed.

"He is a very strange looking foreigner," her sister interjected from behind the elder Shindo. *"Do you have sex with him?"* she asked mischievously.

"Hiro!" her mother snapped. *"What does a child know about sex?"*

"I am not a child, I am a 'young woman', just like Elder Sister," Hiro announced smugly. "Besides, I've seen the ducks. One jumps on the other and flaps his wings, and then it is all over. It is really quite funny."

"These are my naughty sisters Chizu and Hiro," Taka introduced them and changed the subject as de Wolfe smiled at them. "Where is Kenichi? You were all to be returned to our household."

"He is training to become a samurai in the Bugyō-sho retinue," her mother answered.

"It is alright," her father said. "He is seventeen years old now, and it is time that he learned to protect himself and to become a man."

"But, that was not the agreement that I had."

"Daughter, please do not worry. You have done so much for your family already. We ask you to remain safe, that is what is important to us all. And, when the Dutch ships come again, to return to our household."

"Yes, father, I will. I will return."

Taka bowed with the sadness of separation, and they departed. De Wolfe had understood none of the conversation, but was glad that they did not seem to condemn nor criticize him. They had been, as far as he could tell, respectful and pleased to meet him.

The Winter days in Nagasaki were short, and they continued their walk through the city streets for a while longer, and then returned to the island, as required, before nightfall.

Happy New Year!

All of the damage inflicted by the PHANTOM's cannon had been repaired, but fresh wood clearly displayed the scars from the pirates' attack. In the *Opperhoofd*'s residence there was a small Christmas tree still tucked into a corner, the Dutch long ago prevaricating solemnly to the Japanese that the holiday was a gift-giving celebration having nothing to do with religion. Although Christmas was a strange and foreign holiday to the Japanese, the New Year's Day celebration was accepted and ubiquitous, if slightly different from the Netherlands.

The dinner table was set with European cold dishes and Japanese New Year's foods which Schuck struggled to eat with chopsticks while Dr. Franz loudly sang "Auld Lang Syne" as his Japanese wife, de Wolfe, Taka and Kamimoto watched. Acawarman was given the holiday off, and joined them, sitting quietly on a chair drinking whisky and getting quite tipsy, despite being a Muslim. It was, after all, New Year's Day!

Ever the showman, Franz was boisterous and demonstrative in his rendition of the tune, hitting both high and low notes and emphasizing the lyrics. Everyone was having a wonderful break from the Winter's drudgery.

Everyone that is except Schuck, who was unable to master the art of the Asian utensils and clumsily dropped a piece of food on the floor. "If you want me to lose weight doctor, this will do it!" he called out to Franz.

Dr. Franz paused his performance to demonstrate, and walking to the dinner table speared a piece of fish, held it aloft in triumph, and shoved it into his mouth. "You may eat all the food you like, Mr. Schuck," he called back to everyone's amusement. "With one chopstick!"

De Wolfe rose from his chair and tapped his glass with a fork, quieting the room and getting everyone's attention. "Well," he began, "I cannot tell you how happy I am that we are all here today to celebrate in such fine style!" He raised his wine glass, and toasted, pointing to the Japanese foods on the table. "Fish and rice, Mr. Schuck!"

"Fish and rice!" Schuck toasted happily in return and they all drank.

"And," he continued, "to Dr. Franz and his lovely wife for binding our wounds, for keeping us healthy, and for being my friend."

"To Dr. Franz!" they all echoed.

"To Mr. Kamimoto," and he raised his glass to the Japanese man. "Our trusted *Otona*, for his service to the Company, and on behalf of all of the fine men that he oversees that keep our little community functioning. He is truly indispensable to all of us, and especially to me personally."

"And Taka?" Franz bellowed out.

"Yes," de Wolfe paused and thought for a moment. How can I publicly thank a Japanese woman who has brought me such joy for these past months? He was ashamed that he had once disparaged Franz for taking a Japanese wife. That he had referred to the courtesans as "whores". How naive and self-righteous he had been, and how easily he had passed judgement on matters he knew so little about. That she had shown the strength to endure and to triumph in the worst imaginable circumstances.

"To the strongest and most fearsome warriors in the world!" he toasted. "To the women of the Japans!"

"Hear! Hear to that!!" interrupted Schuck as they all laughed.

"As I was saying," de Wolfe continued, "Taka has given me more than I can ever return. And today, although some of us are far from home, we all have the true joy of celebrating with our loved ones."

Dr. Franz and his wife hugged each other and de Wolfe looked meaningfully at Taka.

"I would like to thank all of you, … all of us… for your diligent labors and for your friendship. Gentlemen! Ladies! To a most happy and prosperous New Year!"

There were shouts of "Happy New Year!" from the group, as Dr. Franz grabbed de Wolfe and started loudly humming a quick-stepped polka. He began a lively heel and toe step, sweeping him around the room faster and faster. Soon Schuck joined in the rhythm booming "Ba-ba-ba-ba! Boomp-baa-boom-ba-boomp!" While the Japanese laughed and clapped.

Breathless de Wolfe broke away from Franz, and the doctor jumped over and pried Schuck out of his chair while the heavy man protested. As the two Dutchmen continued their dance de Wolfe slowly walked over to face Taka, looked deeply into her eyes, and slightly bowed. She giggled and tried to look away, but Dr. Franz's wife was shouting, "Yes! Yes!"

Not to be denied, he swept Taka up and joyfully began to dance the polka around as she vainly tried to keep up with the strange and unknown steps. She was soon laughing uncontrollably at the absurdity, and hemmed in by the restrictions of her kimono. The rhythm was solitary and clumsy at first, but soon everyone took up the fast pace, humming and clapping ever louder to encourage them as de Wolfe was practically dragging her across the floor.

Dr. Franz stopped his dance with Schuck and paused to notice de Wolfe and Taka spinning boisterously.

"Be careful man, she's pregnant!" he called out.

As Schuck stood panting at the center of the room trying to regain his breath, everyone stopped still, the room slowly going silent.

"Pregnant?" Kamimoto demanded of Taka.

De Wolfe stared in shock also. "Pregnant?" he asked slowly.

She gathered up the hem of her kimono and ran from the room.

De Wolfe looked around, unsure of what to say or do.

"I thought you knew," ventured Dr. Franz.

De Wolfe chased her out the door and down the steps.

The snow in the courtyard was already ankle deep, and it was still falling heavily. He rushed after the footprints and caught up to Taka in the middle of the open space, grabbed her by the shoulder and turned her towards him. "When did you know?" he admonished.

"Dr. Franz, he knows. Baby comes Summer."

"I'm going home this year!"

"The baby is mine."

"No!" he blurted out, and then paused. "Well, yes, the baby is yours, but it's my baby too. It's our baby."

"The baby is mine!" she insisted.

He stopped and looked heavenward letting the drifting snow wash over him. He closed his eyes and felt the soft touch of the flakes on his eyelids and then their transition to water as if the skies were crying. There had been no time to consider this jolt to his system or what it might mean for either of them. A child! His first child! He and Camilla had tried for over six months with no success, and now, this had happened so quickly. How was it possible? Of course, it was possible, he should have foreseen it. Why hadn't he planned for this? Half way around the world, and a baby was coming. He had no idea at all what to say or what to do.

"It's all right," he began, cupped her chin in his palm and gently kissed her. "It's all right. Happy New Year."

That evening he was sitting at his desk preparing to write a letter. The guests had all left, and the room had been cleaned by Acawarman. He dipped a quill into a jar of ink and held it over the blank piece of paper.

Behind him Taka went into the bedroom and began preparing the sheets. He watched as she slipped off her evening kimono, revealing the clear skin of her naked back, and slipped into the bed.

He began to write, "My dearest Camilla," and then sat staring at the otherwise empty sheet of paper before him. He had no idea what to say, and after a few moments pushed the piece of paper aside and rose to go to bed.

There was not a single letter to his wife on the desk.

The Clinic

Every Sunday de Wolfe and Taka continued to explore the countryside, even on cold and sometimes snowy Winter days. If the weather was particularly bad they might simply huddle in a tea house all day, or find a shop that served hot noodles boiled over a charcoal burner. And, every day they practiced Dutch. Taka had a good foundation, but would often use archaic or in appropriate terms like "begat" or "go forth" that made him chuckle. He would gently correct her, and she seldom made the same mistake twice.

He had not seen Dr. Franz on the island for over a week, and although no one seemed to miss him or need his services, it was as good a destination as any, and after Taka confirmed she knew where his house was, the matter was settled.

The morning sun was hidden by the marine layer, although the dim orb was high in the sky when they started out, and it was no more than a thirty minute walk into the low hills when they arrived. The house itself was an odd amalgamation of styles, red brick walls with a light-green tile roof decorated at the peaks and along the ridges with porcelain birds. It was larger than de Wolfe would have imagined for just two people, but a crowd of mothers and children mobbed the front entrance while others patiently waited both inside and out.

De Wolfe eased his way through the sea of miniature heads, none higher than his shoulder, calling, "Dr. Franz! Dr. Franz!"

"Mr. de Wolfe," Franz came out. "So happy to see you! An unexpected guest is always lucky."

"It looks to me as if you have many unexpected guests," de Wolfe responded as he pointed to the crowd.

"Oh? No, no these are patients. All patients. Please come inside."

The entire front room was covered with children sitting on small mats, and with only a narrow path cleared between them. Some had their mothers sitting with them, and others dozed or simply waited alone.

"My clinic, Mr. de Wolfe. May I introduce to you my assistants? Mr. Yamado, or Yamato, I must confess I am never quite sure. Mr. Kurose, all the way from Kuma-moto, and... Oh, I am sorry sir, what was your name again?"

"*Otsuka desu,*" the young man happily replied.

"Yes, yes, Mr. Otsuka, I do remember now. They are here to learn modern medicine, come let me show you."

De Wolfe followed Franz into the next room where a young boy with a scab on his upper arm sat on a stool. "Our small pox vaccination room!" the doctor announced proudly.

A line of children waited patiently as one of the Japanese, de Wolfe thought it was the one called "Otsuka", but he could not be sure, pushed gently on the scab until a bit of white pus emerged, dipped a needle, and then scratched the triceps of the first child in line. He then repeated the action with the next child and the one after that.

"We were fortunate to have a case of cow pox aboard the VERGULDE DRAECK a few years back," Franz announced.

"I don't understand," de Wolfe confessed.

"Oh, yes of course," Franz explained. "Well, years and years ago a fellow named Jenner, an Englishman I believe, noticed that milk maids never contracted small pox. Turns out all that milking work chapped their hands, and that gave an entry to the cow pox bug. Once they had contracted cow pox they never seemed to get small pox. It was quite simple really."

"So, this lad here today is our incubator. We will use the infected cow pox from his arm to vaccinate this group of children, and by next week they will have become our new donors. We always keep a ready supply on hand."

De Wolfe noticed Taka speaking with the children; soothing them and making them smile or laugh. "And, the others?" he asked.

"Oh, any number of things really. Some are simply malnourished, or down with cholera. So we feed them a hearty meat soup with plenty of vegetables, instruct their parents on proper hygiene, good food and clean water, and then send them on their way."

"And, then there is catarrh," Franz continued. "A mucus build up. We check for cysts in the nose, but it's usually just a simple case of hay fever."

"You don't bleed them?"

"Heavens no! My goodness, sir! This is not the 1700s! The days of so-called 'Heroic Medicine' are long past. No bleeding, no leeches, and most certainly no enemas. Good food and clean water would clear up just about anything we see here."

"And, this is where you spend your free time away from Dejima?"

"Why, of course, Mr. de Wolfe. Right here, at my home in Nagasaki."

"I am afraid, doctor, that I may owe you a sincere apology."

"Why? What for Mr. de Wolfe?"

"For thinking, for thinking,….. Well, I was wrong, and I am sorry for it. If there is anything you may require from the Company stores…"

"Oh, thank you Mr. de Wolfe! I would not take anything without your permission, of course, or without paying for it."

A boy, no more than ten with his leg scarred and disfigured, limped into the house. As he turned towards de Wolfe one half of his face had been burned and the eye destroyed. "What was the cause of that?" de Wolfe asked, horrified by the sight.

"Oh, he's an orphan now, lives with us," Franz shook his head. "His parents were killed in the pirate attack. One of the shells made a direct hit on their household."

Sakura

By early Spring Taka had become less talkative, and sometimes moody, but de Wolfe attributed it to the pregnancy. He had no idea what to expect, or what might happen, except that there would be a baby, of course, at the end of it all. She had been sick for a while after New Year's, but that passed quickly. The kimono hid the small but noticeable bulge in her belly during the day, but at night he was surprised at how large it was rapidly becoming.

Franz assured him that it was all "natural" and "progressing well", but that did little to ease his concerns. Finally Franz had been bothered quite enough with his constant annoying questions, and bluntly told de Wolfe, "You are not the first father in the long history of the world you know!" He had tried to keep quiet after that.

She continued to read Dutch books during the day, and they had long conversations in the evening, sometimes studying if she had questions on specific words or phrases. Kamimoto would also stop by for a drink of whisky, or to see what they were up to, and de Wolfe always enjoyed the company. Regularly he would call "Kamimoto!" from the window. "Kamimoto! Whisky!" And, invariably, soon after Kamimoto would appear. Taka never drank with them, of course.

The cherry blossoms were full on the tree behind the warehouses, and the vegetable gardens had been planted when Dr. Franz suggested a picnic and promised to make all the necessary preparations. Blankets were laid out under the cherry tree, and Taka, now visibly pregnant even under her kimono, sat next to Kamimoto.

Dr. Franz was admiring a page of pressed flowers that he had collected, when Schuck joined them. "I trust that you will not be asking me to help you smuggle them home," the heavy accountant asked, pointing at the page.

"No, I plan to remain here for many more years, it is just a hobby," Franz told him. "When you and Mr. de Wolfe abandon us, you may depart in peace."

"I myself cannot wait for some real Dutch beer!" Schuck quipped with a smile.

De Wolfe was staring at Taka. He felt adrift today, torn between two hostile shores and unable to swim towards either one or the other. His life in Holland seemed so long ago and so far away. Is this what Mr. van Courtlandt had meant when he said 'Better men than you have failed". "She will arrive soon," he mused.

"The DRAECK?" Schuck asked. "Yes, and bringing a new accountant and *Opperhoofd*." Then he stopped short, and reflected on de Wolfe's situation. "Have you reckoned what it is that you will do?"

"I planned to leave money and a supply of sugar to sell. They will both be comfortable, and the child will be raised properly."

"Have you thought about how to tell her?" Franz asked.

"She knows," de Wolfe muttered under his breath. "She knows."

Kamimoto smiled at the Hollanders, and spoke to Taka. *"He will return to his wife, and you will be left with his half-breed baby and only me to protect you."*

A gust of wind shook the cherry tree, and thousands of blossoms showered the picnic like a sudden snow storm, covering them with a blanket of white and a soft fragrance.

"Brevity is the nature of the *sakura* cherry blossom," Kamimoto observed.

De Wolfe looked up and smiled at Taka, trying to catch her eye, but she turned away.

Today Home

The weather continued to improve day-by-day, although an unexpectedly fierce shower could blow in from the sea at any moment, and then would be gone just as quickly. Each day continued pretty much like the one before. De Wolfe arose, and after breakfast walked the island, sometimes alone and sometimes with Schuck. He checked the men, spoke with them briefly, talked with the cooks, generally just making his

111

presence known. There was little else to do. He would return to his quarters by early afternoon for the mid-day dinner.

He climbed the stairs slowly, and opened the door. Inside Taka was waiting, but today dressed in her full kimono rather than the light household kimono she often wore during the day. He glanced down, and her packed bag was on the floor next to her. They looked at each other in silence.

"Where are you going?" he finally asked, his heart dropping into his stomach.

"I need to be with my family," she answered him in Japanese. *"I must go now."*

He could not understand the words, but her intent was all too clear. "Just like that? It is over?" He had no idea what else to say. "Do you believe that I will beg you to stay? For I will not!"

"No." she responded, knowing this was hurting him, but she had made her decision. "Today, home."

"Should I say that I love you? Is that what you want to hear?" he demanded.

She shook her head. "Today home," she repeated, and picked up her bag.

He would not allow her to carry the bag as it was large and heavy, and he followed her morosely as she led him down the stairs and out into the courtyard. One of the guards at the Dutch Gate rushed over and took her belongings from the Hollander. She stopped at the short bridge and turned back to de Wolfe, smiled slightly, and bowed deeply to him. She turned away and walked across the Dutch Gate and into Nagasaki.

A Spring storm was blowing in, and it began to rain as she entered the city, opened an umbrella and continued on. De Wolfe watched for several moments as she walked away until no more of her could be seen. He would have rather chopped off his own arm and thrown it into a river to be swept away.

Kamimoto was speaking with Abe from the shelter of a warehouse and nodded a greeting to de Wolfe. "It is for the best," he told him.

De Wolfe completely ignored him and began walking dejectedly through Dejima as the rain increased. It was falling hard now, but he barely took notice. There were courtesans peering at him from the second story residence windows or seeking shelter in the buildings. He stepped into a warehouse to get out of the rain and noticed that it seemed half-empty. Puzzled, he proceeded to the next store room and it also was similarly bare.

He saw Schuck speaking with one of the Japanese customs men holding a tally sheet in his hand, and he walked over to them. "The storerooms," he asked, "are they empty?"

"Quite normal," Schuck responded, barely looking up. "We need to make space."

"The sugar? The cotton? The wool, ivory, all gone?"

"We never know what is coming exactly," he explained. "Why, years ago they even brought an elephant for goodness sake, my dear friend, it is quite alright and proper. We must be ready."

In the distance Abe had begun shouting in Japanese and gesturing at Kamimoto. De Wolfe had no idea what the problem might be as he surveyed the empty warehouse. "Trouble?" he inquired.

Schuck seemed only concerned with the tally board and signed it with a flourish before handing it back to the Japanese bureaucrat who immediately walked away.

"Trouble?" he repeated.

"Oh that," Schuck looked, but seemed unbothered. "Just shouting and strutting about. Always sounds like they are fighting though, doesn't it? Never comes to anything."

VERGULDE DRAECK

The weeks continued their achingly slow transition from the short and cold days of Winter to the rains of Spring. There was nothing to do on the island, and every single book had been read and re-read a dozen times. Some of the men took to craft work, carving their wooden travel chests with intricate and fantastic decorations. Others drank or slept far more than was good for them. Bleeckier had been a moderating force, keeping the lid on the boiling tea kettle of cooped-up men on a small and finite amount of ground. Now that he was gone there was no governor of the pressure.

Twice full-blown brawls had broken out, and Abe and the guards at the Dutch Gate had sprinted to separate the combatants before any real damage had been done. When de Wolfe questioned the adversaries, after they had sobered up and Dr. Franz had sewn a nasty gash or two, no one could remember what exactly they had been fighting about. De Wolfe had never known that boredom could be such a destructive force. But, at least no one had died under his watch, he thought, and then guiltily remembered that that one man had, hanged by the pirates.

He had learned to live alone again in his residence, and several weeks had already passed since Taka had left. There had been no word on her or the baby, and he had prevailed on Dr. Franz to tell him the moment that anything happened, either good or bad. He had spent those weeks on the island, although he could have asked another of the Japanese to go with him on a Sunday walk, but it would have felt wrong. He didn't try to communicate with Taka. She had taken it upon herself to leave, and if that is what she wanted, then he must respect her wishes. But, he missed her terribly, and there was nothing to take his mind off of his loneliness.

He had discreetly tried to engage Kamimoto in conversation, perhaps he might know something of how she was, but the *Otona* had been absent for much of the past month as well.

De Wolfe had been in bed just thinking for some time in the pre-dawn darkness when shouting from outside roused him. He rushed to the balcony, and there she was, appearing silently from the mists and firmly anchored in Nagasaki Bay, the VERGULDE DRAECK.

As he raced out the door in his nightgown, hurrying to slip on his boots at the doorway, Schuck came jiggling up the stairs shouting, "They are here! They have come!"

"Send a boat!" de Wolfe grabbed him. "Get the mail! Get the newspapers!" And, with that, Schuck was already gone. In the courtyard the residences were rapidly emptying with the spreading word as the Dutch men began streaming out and jumping up and down in excitement. Courtesans watched mystified at the spectacle, not really understanding what was transpiring. The arrival of the ship meant home, a link to that far off and sorely missed connection to family, loved ones, a real civilization, their culture, familiar foods, everything that was important. Even for those whose contracts would keep them in Japan, it made them feel as if there was hope, that they were not alone and abandoned.

No one wanted to wait an instant longer, and they had immediately sent a long boat out to the ship. Every single man jack was standing on the wharf of Dejima under the looming flagpole when the boat arrived at the VERGULDE DRAECK and began receiving packages. Aboard in the distance they could see small figures moving about the deck as the morning mists swirled in tiny white eddies around the hull, and the long boat disappeared and then just as suddenly reappeared in the growing light. Every second was filled with both joyful expectation and the agony of waiting. The next few minutes seemed to take much longer, but finally the boat was cast off and began rowing back to shore.

Aboard were items of great or urgent importance, the manifest, including a complete listing of the trade goods, bundles of newspapers, over half a year old, but each would be read and passed along until only the tatters remained, and two passengers: Captain Ostrander, and next to him sitting straight upright in the middle of the stern seat under a brightly colored parasol, Camilla van Courtlandt.

My Dearest Husband

Camilla was holding the ornate umbrella that perfectly matched her dress over her head as the long boat tied up at the wharf, not for any rain or to block the sun, but rather for the show. She sat unmoving for long moments before several men rushed forward to help her ashore. De Wolfe himself was dumb-struck, trying to understand how it was possible, how she had gotten here. She looked more mature than when he had left her in Amsterdam, and a little heavier, but still beautiful and absolutely regal. She was in complete command of herself, and those about her rushed to do her bidding, unknowingly compelled by her presence.

The long boat was stuffed to the gunwales with her trunks and bags, and she carefully stepped over them and was helped up to the wharf where she walked directly to de Wolfe and kissed him on the cheek.

"My darling husband!" she announced grandly to all. "You have been gone so long that I have decided to come fetch you home myself!"

Captain Ostrander said nothing, but looked pained as he climbed out of the small watercraft and moved past the crowd.

She stood there for some time looking at her trunks and bags in the long boat and finally said, "Well?" Several Dutch men jumped forward and began hauling her baggage up. There was one very large trunk that took two men to lift, and at least four heavy expensive decorated fabric bags. "The rest will come later," she announced, and began leading the procession in the general direction of the buildings.

De Wolfe skipped ahead to guide the baggage train up the stairs of the *Opperhoofd*'s residence, and the luggage was dropped just inside the doorway before everyone fled, leaving the couple alone.

"Well, it may seem rather small and primative," de Wolfe began awkwardly, still startled by the sudden developments. "But, we do dine here together often. This is the dining room," he pointed, "the billiard room, but the table has been, well the billiard table is being repaired...." As he walked on alone, he turned to see Camilla kneeling and praying in front of the bedroom. Without opening her eyes she held her right arm out, waiting for him to join her. He walked over, grasped her hand and knelt beside her.

"Give us a fruitful marriage, and a happy and prosperous life," she said quietly, "Your will be done. Amen."

Finishing her prayer she stood up and, still holding his hand, playfully led him into the bedroom. She pushed him onto the bed and climbed on top of him, holding him down with her weight.

115

She leaned forward and whispered, "Together! Finally and forever!" And then began rapidly removing the multiple layers of her clothes.

After, as they lay together in the cool of the late morning covered by the sweaty sheets, she chattered on about home and her voyage as de Wolfe stared off into the distance, barely hearing her, but holding her tightly and occasionally nodding.

Gabriel Muis

The dining table was richly furnished with their finest sets of dishware, and there was great anticipation of the sumptuous evening supper in celebration of the ship's arrival. It was always surprising how grandly Acawarman could recreate the style of Dutch foods using locally sourced meats and vegetables. Kamimoto had politely declined his invitation, but, Schuck and Dr. Franz joined him in welcoming Camilla, Captain Ostrander, and the new accountant, Gabriel Muis.

Those who came from the ship were happy to finally be eating fresh dishes again after weeks or months in transit aboard the HALVE MAEN and then the VERGULDE DRAECK. Still, everyone looked slightly uncomfortable in the presence of Camilla as she instructed Acawarman in the importance of the proper serving of the food. De Wolfe watched, but said nothing, as she began to exert influence over his staff and his dining room.

The final newcomer arrived late, and he was small and mouseish, constantly squinting through his thick glasses above his crinkled nose. He was the type of accountant one would picture sitting on a high chair, his legs dangling off of the edge, hunched over a slanted table consulting multiple books of facts and figures, all illuminated by a single candle. A man who knew his job and was incredibly good at it, but was totally unable to connect with those around him.

As the small slouched man shuffled in and stood next to his chair, Captain Ostrander introduced him to the group. "May I acquaint you all with Mr. Gabriel Muis, Chief Accountant, and Mr. Schuck's replacement here."

Muis sat down in his chair, joining the others who had already been seated, and blinked at everyone around the table. "Pleasure, of course, gentlemen, and…. Mrs. de Wolfe."

Acawarman was just starting in from the kitchen with the *amuse bouche* – the small single-bite appetizers - carefully set on a large platter as Camilla began to speak, halting him at the doorway. She bowed her head and held her hands out to each side until everyone had joined hands in a circle around the table. "We thank You for a swift and safe journey to the Japans, and for Your protection from all the dangers of the deep on our travels. We thank You for our companions and our servants, and for Your wisdom in creating the world as it is now, and how it has always been, and will forever

116

be. We thank You for our health and for this sustenance, and for the strength to care for those beneath us. Amen."

"Amen," they all echoed.

As Acawarman served the first course Captain Ostrander proposed a toast. "To your lovely wife, who has been our talisman and good luck charm on the voyage. It was excellent time we made here, and clear seas and fair winds all the way from Batavia."

"And," Muis said barely looking up as he gulped his appetizer, "we have brought the gifts for the Japanese king as well."

"Gifts?" Camilla asked, puzzled.

"Yes, Yes," Muis continued. "I was told the *Opperhoofd* would be visiting Edo this year and required gifts for the king.

"The *Shōgun*, Mr. Muis," Captain Ostrander corrected him. "Not the king, although in many ways they may seem the same."

"Well, the Americans may beat us there anyway," said Muis off-handedly.

"Why would the Americans be going to Edo?" asked Schuck surprised.

"Yes, why?" inquired de Wolfe. The *Shōgun*'s Trade Agreement is explicitly with the Dutch only, and all other trade is forbidden and has been for over two hundred years. The Americans would be violating that Treaty, a serious provocation to the Japanese and the Dutch Monarchy."

"Can't really say myself," Muis told them. Some new urgency. The Americans were meeting with our government to explain things when we sailed from Holland."

"But, how does this concern us? We will be returning home, and wouldn't this be a matter for the new *Opperhoofd*?" asked Camilla.

"Yes," agreed de Wolfe suddenly concerned. "An excellent question. Why isn't..."

"Gentlemen!" interrupted Captain Ostrander. "Please! Let's not talk business at supper and in front of your lovely wife so that we do not bore Mrs. de Wolfe."

The group nodded in assent, and the table went quiet as Acawarman brought in the six second course bowls of soup, and they ate in silence. Finally, Camilla coughed and began tentatively, "If I may?"

Happy for the change in conversation, Schuck brightened and said, "Yes, how may we be of service to you my good lady," and spooned more of his soup into his mouth.

"I have noticed," she said and looked up slyly, "oh, how to be delicate? Women. Local women entering the compound?"

Schuck choked on his food, barely able to keep from spitting out the soup before getting it down the wrong pipe and beginning a loud coughing fit. The other diners all stopped eating and sat in silence with the exception of Muis who kept spooning, oblivious to all else but his soup.

Schuck finally regained his breath and was able to cough out, "Local women you say?"

"Perhaps," she asked tartly, "it has escaped your notice these past years?"

Schuck had no idea how to respond, and looked to de Wolfe for help.

"They are here for the mens' comfort and companionship, dear," he explained.

"Here on Dejima," she feigned surprise and offence. "Well, I do suppose some of the lower classes cannot be stopped from their debauchery."

Acawarman appeared at the door with the pasta entrée that would precede the main course as Camilla set down her silverware and laid aside her napkin. She pushed her soup bowl towards the center of the table, indicating that she was done, and thus the supper was finished. All of the conversation halted, and soon everyone at the table stopped eating as well.

"Sinful and disgusting!" she exclaimed, and stood up.

Acawarman stood holding the next course, unsure what to do, and de Wolfe waved him off. Only Muis was unaware of what had transpired, and finished his soup before adjusting his glasses and looking around quizzically. Slightly puzzled, he laid his spoon down next to his soup bowl, gulped his wine, and set his napkin on the table.

Supper was over.

Camilla excused herself and moved to the bedroom while Acawarman returned all of the unserved food to the kitchen. The men shifted to the empty billiards room, and de Wolfe immediately opened a fresh bottle of whisky and began pouring a glass for each of the guests. He walked to the window to call for Kamimoto, but the only sign of life in the courtyard was a shadowy figure moving towards the Dutch Gate and then quickly escaping into Nagasaki.

"Mr. Kamimoto! Will you join us for whisky?" he shouted. Strangely, no one was visible. No guards, no courtesans, no Dutch staff, nothing was moving.

"Hello? Mr. Kamimoto? Are you there?"

"A word in private?" Captain Ostrander interrupted.

"Of course, Captain," de Wolfe stepped away from the window.

"Straight into the breakers is always best," he began, looking serious. "The Company is asking you to stay on until next Spring."

"Another year? That is neither my understanding nor my contract. I am to return with you this Fall, I have many obligations in Holland."

"I was instructed to advise you that the contract has been amended."

"I would need to sign any such 'amendments' in order for them to be legally binding."

"Nothing is to be in writing. I am also to advise you that all of the remaining provisions of your agreement would remain in effect."

"Mr. van Courtlandt...." De Wolfe began.

"Mr. van Courtlandt himself requested it."

De Wolfe considered, "Is that why they have sent my wife?"

"No," Ostrander assured him. "That was her own doing. We have not told her, of course. But, she will stay here to be with you. And, think of how this will enhance your career. Building on your plan."

"My plan?"

"Of course! One more year, and your wife is already here. 'Together forever' you told me, and you have already accomplished that."

"Yes, I suppose that I did, I mean that I have," de Wolfe mumbled, remembering their conversation aboard ship that tumultuous morning so long ago when he had arrived in the Japans. Had it been only one year? But in his mind he was picturing Camilla in the bedroom, already preparing for sleep, and Taka, away somewhere and the child growing within her.

Ostrander was working hard to keep a positive tone in his voice, "Plus the trip to Edo! Your chance to see the Japans as few of us ever will! Travel the country, meet the *Shōgun* face-to-face! The *Opperhoofd* of Dejima, that's what you are, and with all the pomp and glory that goes with the title!"

De Wolfe stared out at the empty courtyard and took a deep draught of his whisky, "One more year...." he mused.

Do You See?

They had slept in late as was Camilla's custom, and Acawarman had prepared them a breakfast of sausage, eggs, bread and coffee before they met Mr. Muis and began touring the trading post.

They started out by the vegetable garden, meticulously planted and with the first sprouts showing, and the large cherry tree where they had picnicked what seemed so long ago. He took them through the warehouses awaiting the new shipment of imported products, and through the communal kitchens and make-shift chapel. He did not turn the portrait to reveal the cross on the reverse side, nor mention the table that also served as an altar.

They had reentered the bright sunshine and he was pointing out the last few buildings as he glanced towards the Dutch Gate in time to see a very determined and, as usual, enraged Abe strutting onto the island and past the guards, followed by four dour faced samurai surrounding a very pregnant Taka.

His heart stopped as the guards at the bridge snapped to attention at Abe's passing, and the angry samurai began barking commands as those following him ran off in various directions. Taka looked very subdued, and stood quietly with her hands in front of her swollen belly. She glanced up and saw de Wolfe, and standing next to him Camilla who opened her umbrella slowly above her head in a show of dominance.

"Oh, goodness! Do you see?" she cooed.

De Wolfe was caught between the two women as Muis myopically took off his glasses, wiped them, and then returned them to his nose, squinting through the thick lenses.

"Call her over dear, I do so want to take a look! Call her over!"

"I am sure that this affair is no concern of ours, it would be a very rude intrusion."

"Oh, Hendrik, please!" She pouted in annoyance, but also enjoying her mischief, knowing that he would have difficulty refusing her. "I insist, I must see! Call her over."

De Wolfe felt as if he was walking to the gallows as he reluctantly moved to Taka and waited, looking at her, unable to speak.

Taka bowed slightly, *"Abe-sama, may I speak to the Capitão's wife?"*

"Why would you want to?" Abe countered. *"She is disgusting. Her feet belong on a duck, she is as fat as a pig, and she smells like rotten flowers."*

"Please mind your manners and your language, she is de Wolfe-sama's wife. We must show her respect."

"A dutiful wife does not boss her husband around and peck at him like a chicken! Look at her, she carries her umbrella like a beggar's sack at the end of a stick. She has no manners and no delicacy, are you sure that is a woman? How can it be his wife?"

"Abe-sama, please. May I go?"

Abe nodded his consent, and Taka then followed the silent de Wolfe back to join Camilla.

"Delightful!" Camilla preened. "Simply marvelous! See how she walks, and in her condition! Oh, isn't she a pretty one!'

Taka stopped in front of Camilla and stood stock still, each taking the measure of the other. Camilla circled her, looking her up and down, noting every detail.

"See how she glows! Her skin is clear and radiant. I will be radiant too when I am with child, don't you agree?" She asked, turning to de Wolfe.

De Wolfe was in sheer agony, trapped with no escape, and no idea what to say or do next. "Of course," was all he could muster.

"Is she one of the whores?" Camilla asked smiling. "Can they speak? They carry disease you know, the French Pox and worse. Still, a pretty wrapping for such a damaged package! Do ask her dear, what is her name?"

"I do not speak Japanese," was all he could stutter.

"Oh, such a shame. There is so much I would want to know! And, who do you think is responsible for her condition? Could it have been one of the Dutch men?"

De Wolfe did not answer.

"Well, delightful," Camilla concluded. "Simply delicious. Now, send her away."

De Wolfe looked at Taka, he was humiliated and aching, and bowed. Taka maintained her dignity, bowed slightly in the direction of Camilla, and spoke directly to de Wolfe, "You have a beautiful wife."

Camilla stepped back with a start and gasped, "Well! I never..."

Taka turned and with great dignity walked back to wait beside Abe.

Two of the samurai returned empty-handed, and the two others were dragging Schuck, who still held a clipboard in his hands and was protesting vehemently. "What is this all about? Unhand me, I say! You have no right!"

De Wolfe tried to come to his aid, and was roughly pushed aside. "Let go of him," he demanded.

Abe swaggered over to de Wolfe, reached inside his kimono, and withdrew a paper written in Japanese, handing it over for inspection. The Dutchman was desperately trying to make any sense out of what was happening, but the only thing that de Wolfe could read was **"GERHARD SCHUCK"** written at the top, the remainder was all in the incomprehensible glyphs.

"Schuck arrest!" shouted Abe. "Shindo arrest! All arrest!" He jabbed his finger into de Wolfe's chest and growled, "Tomorrow! You come!" The Japanese warrior then strode across the Dutch Gate with the four samurai dragging a heavy and resisting Schuck, meekly followed by Taka, and into Nagasaki.

A crowd of both Dutch and Japanese had gathered, but it was Camilla who spoke first, "What in God's name could they have done?"

De Wolfe watched them go, and then turned to his new accountant, "Mr. Muis, would you do a complete inventory, please? All of the books and all of the inventory in the warehouses? Today, please?"

"Of course," Muis answered, and hurried off to begin.

Schuck's Quarters

All that afternoon Muis had set up camp in de Wolfe's dining room and kept ordering fresh pots of coffee, sending Acawarman scurrying to heat water and prepare the brew, as he continued going over the books they had retrieved from Schuck's room earlier.

From time to time he would click or cluck, and there even was an occasional "Oh, my!" but otherwise he kept his council to himself, raised his glasses from his nose to the top of his head, wiped his face with his sleeve, and persisted on.

It was near nightfall before he suggested that they send for Captain Ostrander as "an unassailable witness" he declared, and they returned to Schuck's room to await. Now, Ostrander stood in the doorway, and they began their search.

A heavy winter coat hung beside the unmade bed and across the room from the fireplace, and there was a stack of clean handkerchiefs folded and waiting on the dresser. Nothing seemed abnormal nor out of place.

"I have seen this type of scheme before, and it was all very cleverly done. It might have taken months to find out, or perhaps not at all," Muis told them as they looked around the seemingly plain quarters.

"What scheme is that?" Ostrander asked.

"Why the theft by Mr. Schuck, of course. He's been stealing for years it seems, and must have been hiding the loot away somewhere. All very cleverly done, as I just said."

"How much is gone?" asked de Wolfe.

"Oh, very difficult to say you see, and that's the beauty of it. There were goods missing from the Company's inventory and the Japanese as well. And, since they were both evenly balanced it would always look like it was equal."

"But, the Japanese don't commonly use any real money, they usually trade in rice to settle a debt or barter." Ostrander objected. "What would be the point? How could Schuck, or anyone else, keep enough rice to be of any use?"

"That is not really quite true Captain," Muis explained. For example, they trade with us don't they, and that's not in rice. The *Shōgun* mints both gold and silver coinage, and also prints notes for large debts. It is not common, but it is not unheard of. We keep a supply of Japanese coins right here on Dejima. But, that is not the case in this scheme, coins and notes are too easily identified. So, our thieves must have something that would be easily stored and transported. It most certainly must be something of high value though, something besides rice."

"What do you mean by thieves?" de Wolfe asked.

"There is no way that Schuck could have managed this alone. He had help. You might say that it was a conspiracy. And, the first suspicion obviously must fall upon you."

"Me!" de Wolfe exclaimed.

"Don't be simple, of course you are the prime suspect. Therefore, unless you want to be charged with the crime then we need to find out what he stole, and that information may tell us who his accomplices are. Captain Ostrander is here to be our witness."

De Wolfe began searching around the room, looking underneath the mattress, which was silly of course, and through the drawers. But, it made no sense. It must be another ruse by Abe to punish the Hollanders, or a huge mistake of some kind. He checked the pockets of the heavy coat, looked down, and then he stopped. "Here. Help me," he said to Ostrander.

Ostrander pulled a short knife from his pocket and they began to explore the brickwork of the fireplace until they found a bit of it loose. They worked the corner off and de Wolfe reached his hand inside to feel something cold and hard. He pulled a long slim rough bar of silver out, and then reached in for another. Soon there were more than a dozen of the ingots on the floor.

"You see, as I told you, he must have had help," Muis confirmed. "He would need help."

The Summons

It had been a difficult night for de Wolfe, and the dawn could not come soon enough. Camilla had not spoken to him at supper and had gone to bed early while he paced and brooded through the long dark hours. Did she think that he had something to do with this? He was drinking coffee at his desk when she arose, and they ate a light breakfast separately. Schuck had been taken, Franz was with his wife, Ostrander had retreated to his ship, and Kamimoto was nowhere to be found. It had been a solitary vigil in an empty room on a lonely island half-way around the world.

It was in the mid-morning that Abe returned with his four samurai and passed over the Dutch Gate into Dejima and waited. De Wolfe walked down the stairs to him, and Abe handed him a single sheet of paper that looked exactly like the one he had seen yesterday. There was one difference: On the top of this one was written **"HENDRIK DE WOLFE"** in large black letters.

De Wolfe looked back at Camilla peering at him through the landside window, and Captain Ostrander came hurrying from the wharf as Muis joined him.

"Mr. Muis, you are in charge of the trading post until I return."

"When will that be?"

"Soon, I hope," and de Wolfe shook his hand and nodded to Ostrander before being surrounded by Abe's men and grimly escorted into Nagasaki.

Before, he had always enjoyed walking in the city at this time of the morning, invariably with Taka, of course, and watching the residents conduct their daily routine. The smells of small charcoal fires, rice or a stew cooking, in comparison to the cacophony of early morning Amsterdam, it was quiet and sedate. There were no large animals, of course, but even the dogs were politely quiet throughout the day. He recognized some of the street corners and shops as they led him to a new part of the city.

The group stopped in front of a large white governmental building complex, and de Wolfe recognized it as the one that Taka had pointed out from the hill top last Fall. A large stone wall the height of two men surrounded the compound, and ringing that was a dry moat that could be flooded when a stronger defense was warranted. Through small downward facing windows he could see the heads of waiting samurai watching him, and four more men guarded the large heavy wooden gates of the open front entrance.

The central building was huge and covered with grey tiles sloping down from a high peak. The doors were covered in paper, but wooden shutters could be closed over them to protect the building from the weather or an attack.

Behind was the kitchen, keeping the cooking fires separate from the main building, and smaller structures were scattered among the carefully tended paths and ornamental gardens.

They arrived at the steps leading up to the main building, and Abe gruffly indicated towards de Wolfe's feet, "Shoes!" he commanded.

The Hollander stood unmoving, not sure what to do, as Abe slipped off his own sandals, put on a pair of slippers from a neatly laid out set of shelves, and continued to point and mime. Finally his demeanor shifted and for the first time he became softer and kinder, perhaps even sympathetic, "Shoes," he said. "Shoes off. You understand?"

De Wolfe pulled off his boots and set them down on the steps, and put on a pair of the many slippers that were there. He then followed Abe through the sliding paper doors and into the building.

Abe led him down long hallways with unvarnished wooden floors, all of it spotlessly clean, and some of them creaked as they walked. He could not believe that it was poor construction technique, and wondered if it might be specifically designed as a warning to the residents that someone was coming? He soon became disoriented, all the halls and rooms looked exactly the same to him, and Abe stopped in front of a plain paper panel.

"May we disturb you?" Abe called out.

"Welcome!" answered a voice from inside, and Kamimoto slid open the door.

125

"Welcome to you de Wolfe-*sama*, slippers off, if you please," and the Hollander stepped through the doorway.

Including the Girl

It was a plain tatami room, barely big enough for a man to lay flat across. Bedding and clothing had been stored in a small closet on the side, and on the floor was a tea service, a small writing desk, and the now almost finished oil painting of the VERGULDE DRAECK in Nagasaki Harbor with the moon setting behind. Kamimoto was very somber, and returned to his painting while indicating that de Wolfe should sit. But, there were no chairs, nowhere to sit. Finally de Wolfe folded himself up and sat on the floor.

De Wolfe was anxious, and getting a little angry, but at the same time completely out of his element. He had been summoned from Dejima to who knows where by who knows who for who knows what purpose. Was he being accused of the theft? He would prove his innocence! He wanted answers!

Kamimoto, on the other hand, seemed at peace, and finally de Wolfe could stand it no longer. "What is this all about?" he demanded.

"You should have brought whisky," Kamimoto responded. "Sometimes I will miss whisky." He continued to paint in silence as if that should have clarified anything at all. Then, after a moment he started again. "Still, it is almost impossible to find the right shade of blue."

"The color blue? What are you saying?" de Wolfe asked, his exasperation growing.

"Blue mixes with yellow to make green. I have the proper yellow, but without the proper blue I cannot make the correct green for the ocean. See?" He indicated on the painting.

"Blue? Yellow? You are making no sense!"

"Have you learned so little about Japan in all the time that you have been here?"

Kamimoto sighed and turned away from the painting to face de Wolfe. "You Hollanders. Westerveldt was bad and you are even worse. You come here feeling so superior and rushing around demanding this and commanding that, it just never seems to stop. 'What is this all about!' you want to know, but you never take even just a moment to inquire how I am or to admire my painting. What do you know of me? When have you ever taken the time to ask about me?"

126

He was right, of course. De Wolfe had always treated Kamimoto with respect as the *Otona* of Dejima, but he knew practically nothing about him. He had never taken the time to ask him about, well about anything other than his duties at the trading post. Despite their time together, he had never treated him as a friend. He had not meant to be cold, he had just never thought of anything else. He now realized with a shock that he had been unintentionally cruel, and that a different approach would be necessary. Kamimoto would not be rushed.

"That scene is quite beautiful, and very well constructed. I especially like the manner in which you have captured the ship's rigging, and how it directs the viewer's gaze to the clouds."

They spoke for some time about the painting, about the weather, about anything but the island of Dejima. De Wolfe soon also began to wish that he had brought whisky. Finally, Kamimoto grew somber again. He was ready to talk, set down his brush, and looked upward. "Do you ever think of death?"

"We all wonder how we will die, and what is beyond," de Wolfe pondered. "There can be no escape, and neither is there any proof of what is beyond except for our faith. But, I do truly believe that there is value in virtue during our time here on earth."

Kamimoto turned back to his painting and made a few strokes, "And, what of your faith, de Wolfe-*sama*?"

"I believe in Heaven, although we cannot see Paradise until we are judged for our deeds in this life."

"What is your Heaven like?"

De Wolfe briefly laughed, not because the question was humorous, but because he realized that he had not really ever thought about it. "Well, it is glorious, and there will be no more pain or misery, and I am not sure that I really know or that I can tell you what it looks like. But, you will be with God."

"If there is a Heaven," Kamimoto asked, "should not all Christians try to get there as quickly as possible to be one with their God? Why would you wait to endure a long and perhaps painful life when you could join him today?"

"Hamlet?"

"Who?" Kamimoto asked, confused.

"Forgive me," de Wolfe started again, "it is the story of a Danish prince. Suicide is a mortal sin. We may not know or understand God's purpose for us, but it is there with us always. 'They also serve who only stand and wait'."

"More Hamlet?" the *Otona* asked.

"Milton, another English poet, but never mind. The point is that suicide is wrong on every level."

"Not here, not in Japan," Kamimoto countered. "Here an honorable suicide can be an act of kindness, or of protest, or of repentance."

The Japanese man continued to paint in silence for a few moments until de Wolfe asked, "Why am I under arrest?"

This caused Kamimoto to laugh, "<u>You</u> are not under arrest, I am!"

"But, why!?"

"Because of my choices, I suppose. You had a choice to come to Japan, and I had a choice also. And, because of that choice I have been arrested for the theft of the trade good. Half belonged to the *Shōgun*, and the other half belonged to the Dutch. By taking them I have stolen from the both of you. The *Shōgun*'s laws are quite clear, and you were summoned here so that the Dutch would be given justice."

"Why would you steal?" Once again it just all made no sense to de Wolfe. "Why would you steal from me?"

Kamimoto sighed, and thought for a long moment before answering. "Can you even begin to imagine my life on Dejima? What it was like for me, day after day, to awaken being choked with the stench and the noise of the Dutch? Being away from any real home, not being able to build a family or a future. Knowing that every day forward would be just like the one past, season after season, year after year until I drop down like a pitiful insect with a broken leg, unable to go any longer."

"I am six months journey away from my home, and the only effort you had to make to leave Dejima would be to walk across the Dutch Gate."

"Do you believe that? That it could be so simple? Do you really?"

"It would have been that simple."

Kamimoto took a deep breath, and slowly exhaled. "No. We Japanese have our duty, and that can never be forgotten or abandoned. From the time I was a small boy out of the kitchens I was told that I must learn *rangaku*, what you would call Dutch Studies, and beaten if I did poorly. How you dressed, what you ate, and most importantly, your language. I was never really a Japanese, you know, but I certainly would never be Dutch either. I was raised to live on Dejima from the day I was chosen by the *Shōgun*'s representative until the day I would die."

"Could you really believe," he continued, "that I would want to spend the rest of my life among the Hollanders on that stinking little island? It was my duty, it was my life but it was never my choice, and I hated every minute of it."

"The silver would not have changed any of that," de Wolfe countered.

"In Japan, no. But it would have given me a life, a new life. Here my duty would follow me like a ghost. But, somewhere else I could be free. Free of my past, free of my duty, free of the Dutch. Possibly in Chosun or China, only a few days sail on a good ship. For a thief, violating the Shōgun's Sakoku Edicts are only a comparatively small matter."

Kamimoto made a few last small strokes on the easel, and then leaned back to admire his work. "A small gift for you." He turned to face de Wolfe once again, "And tomorrow I will pay for my crimes. But, I will not be disgraced."

"And, what of Mr. Schuck?" de Wolfe asked in trepidation.

"That decision will be yours. You may take him away with you, if that is your choice."

"My choice? It cannot be as easy as that."

"Yes, just inform the Obugyō-sama of your decision, and you may take him away with you today. You will be required to board the ship with the criminal, and every other Hollander on Dejima, and immediately sail away, leaving everything behind. The trading post will be closed and burned to the ground."

"Dejima closed?"

"Or, he may share my fate and accept the guilt of his crimes. For," Kamimoto wanted to be very sure that de Wolfe understood him clearly, "if Dejima is to be kept open, then equal crimes demand equal justice."

"Japanese justice?"

Kamimoto sighed, "Why, it must be death, of course."

"Who else was involved?" de Wolfe demanded.

"Only myself, Schuck," and he paused slightly, looking sideways at the Dutchman, "And, Shindo Taka."

"What was her part in this?"

"I placed her in your household as a spy and to occupy your attention. Whether or not she knew anything else I have no idea, but I do not think so. However, the Obugyō-sama believes she did, and is conducting a full investigation."

"Is that why she has been arrested?"

"The entire Shindo family is already under a sentence of death for being Christians. Certainly any involvement in further crimes would seal their fate." He paused before continuing. "It might be possible that my testimony could assist the Obugyō-sama in understanding that she shares no further guilt in this matter. I could help her immensely, if you like. But there is something I would ask of you in return."

De Wolfe waited, having no idea whatsoever the price that would be demanded.

"I am not afraid to die," Kamimoto continued, But, I want the chance to gain entrance to your Heaven. I want to be given Last Rites."

"You are not a Catholic!" de Wolfe protested.

"Today I have no more secrets, so let me tell you one more, my last one: My ancestor was a Portuguese Jesuit. He had come to Japan to convert us, starting with the peasants and farmers. He was tall and handsome and spoke perfect Japanese they say, and many chose to follow his preaching. He offered them a better life than the hardship they knew, if only they would follow the teaching of Christ. Then the Shōgun ordered the country closed under the Sakoku Edict. Christianity forbidden. So many wanted to believe, and so many were tortured and crucified. But, not my ancestor."

"You do not look to be of mixed-blood."

"It was so many generations ago, one drop in a vast ocean. Can you imagine, he worked on Dejima, it's true! He renounced his faith to save his own life, and for many years he inspected trade goods to ensure there were no Christian books or symbols. He had a Japanese wife and many children. Hundreds had died as martyrs to preserve their faith, while he lived. But, my family has been cursed by his betrayal of his God, and it has never been forgotten nor forgiven. Even that one small drop of Portuguese blood makes us forever foreigners in our own country. "

Kamimoto became very intent. "I have always thought that there could be nothing after death. But, when you spoke of Bleeckier-san you said that a confession of one's sins might please God. I began thinking that, if there is a Heaven, why not take a chance on spending eternity in Paradise? Tomorrow I am going to die, and you can give me that chance. You can give me eternal life through your Christian God. You can give me Last Rites. Perhaps I will join my ancestor, or if there is no Heaven, what would I have lost?"

"It is simply impossible. There are no priests in Japan. Even the Reverend Bleeckier could not have done it, would not have done it."

"I understand that it cannot be done properly, but it can be done. That is my price for Taka's life. You now have many decisions that must be made. The investigation will be concluded today, and the verdicts will be decided. If Schuck stays, then you will be summoned back tomorrow so that justice may be given to all. If he goes with you, then you must all be gone. You alone must decide who will live and who will die."

"If you wish to save Dejima, you must sacrifice Schuck. If you save Schuck, then you must go, and the Shindo girl will no longer matter. But, if you believe in equal justice, then give me your oath that you will come early tomorrow to administer Last Rites. Tomorrow there will be justice."

"It would be sacrilege," de Wolfe pleaded.

"No, it is simply your choice, and your decision. If you cannot, I understand completely. I would, of course, be forced to amend my testimony to include all the guilty parties so that justice may be complete. All of them. Including the girl."

"Abe-sama! Would you please take him to the Criminal Schuck?" Kamimoto called out. The door slid open and Abe led de Wolfe outside, the Hollander stopping on the stairs to put on his boots.

Rice and Fish

Schuck was sitting quietly in the darkness of an old storage shed at the edge of the compound, and had used several of the Dutch trade goods boxes to create a table and chair for himself. On the box was a half-eaten container of white rice, a few bits of pickled radish and scraps of some fish that had been heated over charcoal.

Abe had guided de Wolfe past the two bored looking guards, and opened the door of the shed, indicating he should proceed in. Schuck had turned away from the bright mid-day sun and shielded his eyes, squinting to see who his visitor was.

"Oh! Mr. de Wolfe! I am so glad to see you! It has been quite lonely here, quite. And," he indicated the food on the wooden box, "nothing to eat but rice and fish for the past day. It is so good to see you my friend." He turned another box upright and indicated that de Wolfe should sit.

"How are you?" asked de Wolfe with genuine concern.

"I'm so frightened. I am so very frightened, and I have absolutely no idea what..."

131

"We found the silver in your room," de Wolfe cut him off.

"Oh. Oh, yes I see," conceded Schuck with defeat and embarrassment in his voice. "I suppose, well, I knew that you would."

He looked down and took a deep breath. "I am not a strong man, you know that Hendrik. I am not much of a Christian and apparently not much of a thief either." He smiled weakly, "But, with the VERGULDE DRAECK leaving early, everything was all so jumbled, it was the chance of a lifetime, and who would be hurt really? A Japanese despot and an obsolete business that is rapidly going extinct. All I wanted was the chance to live like some people do. It would take so little."

"I would have been hurt Mr. Schuck. Me, personally. I would have been responsible. And, what would you really have gained? You have been in the Japans for three years, certainly you have saved a nice sum during that time?"

"A tidy amount, but I suppose that I became greedy, and wanted more. Enough for a big house, enough for fine wines and stylish clothes, enough for, oh I don't even know, but I wanted more, and this seemed a way to get it."

"These are all only material things Mr. Schuck. I myself came from a poor family, and I do understand your desires, but money cannot buy you respect. It cannot get you health nor a family."

"Of course it can! The only people who think otherwise are those without money. I believe that it can buy you happiness, or at least a very believable façade. It can buy you love certainly, if only for a few hours. Isn't that enough? And, as for a family, you yourself married into the van Courtlandt's for money," Schuck scoffed.

"That is not the case," de Wolfe countered, his feelings hurt. "And, it is truly beneath you. Camilla and I married for love, and with her father's approval I can assure you."

"Perhaps, and if so, I apologize. It was not my intention to insult you. But look what awaits you when you return to Amsterdam. It is everything that I wanted, and it was given to you so easily. I envied that, I suppose."

"But," de Wolfe said after a moment, "you stole from the Company."

"Yes, I confess, that is true. But I would propose an agreement. I will surrender all of my savings, everything that I have earned over the past three years, and relinquish it to the Company in atonement. And, then I will sail away in the Fall aboard the VERGULDE DRAECK, and will never bother you or anyone else again. I will go on my way and build a new life for myself elsewhere."

De Wolfe could not look at him. "I am afraid that is not possible."

"My dear friend, you are a businessman, and I am offering you a just and fair bargain. Of what value to anyone is this tired and fat wreck that sits before you? Only to myself. I am of no use at all to the Japanese, and I have nothing else that I may offer you, except my labor, and that you may have willingly."

"Mr. Schuck..."

"I understand, Hendrik. You are driving a hard bargain, I admire that, and you need a better offer," Schuck countered. "Then, let me propose that I will work here in the Japans without pay for three more years. Everything I have saved and three years added to my contract free of charge and at no cost. Certainly that is an arrangement that the Company would leap at. I so dearly want to go home, you know that! But I will offer whatever is necessary to pay the debt that I have created."

De Wolfe shook his head, and Schuck whined, "I am to be going home soon!" standing up and knocking the box he was sitting on to its side. Hearing the outburst one of the guards peeked in briefly before Schuck continued meekly, "Am I not?" A slow realization began to spread through his bowels and he felt weak and nauseous. "I would be of no use to anyone dead," he offered with finality.

"You have been my good friend, Gerhard Schuck," de Wolfe said with great sadness. "Let us sit together for a while."

Schuck reached down, righted the box and sat in the darkness. "I would like that Hendrik. I would like that very much." The Dutchmen sat in silence together until mid-afternoon when Abe opened the door and indicated they should both come with him.

The Verdict

Inside the large tatami hall of the main building multiple governmental officials were waiting as de Wolfe and Schuck were ushered in. The formal scene was similar to last year's investigation in the warehouse on Dejima, but much larger and infinitely more imposing. Kamimoto was already kneeling on a pillow in the middle of the room facing the *Obugyō-sama*, and there were two empty pillows beside him. A score of senior officials were kneeling along each side of the room, and as soon as the Dutchmen entered a legion of armed samurai formed ranks kneeling behind them. With difficulty the two foreigners folded their legs underneath themselves and waited for the proceedings to begin.

The *Obugyō* looked directly at Kamimoto and growled with a low sonorous voice, *"Criminal Kamimoto. You were given a position of honor and trust, and betrayed both the Shōgun and the Hollanders. You are a thief and have freely admitted your guilt. Do you have anything to say in your defense?"*

"I have brought shame and disgrace to myself and my ancestors, and for this I am truly sorry." Kamimoto bowed low, placing his forehead against the tatami.

The *Obugyō* looked him up and down and then read from a piece of paper that was handed to him by a scribe, *"Criminal Kamimoto, we sentence you to death."* He paused and looked directly at Schuck, stumbling over the difficult foreign name.

"Criminal Gerhard Schuck!"

Recognizing his name Schuck tried to speak, but only stuttered in his fear. He wiped his brow with his handkerchief and then began again. "I am most sorry, and I apologize for what I have done in a moment of weakness. I will give it all back, you can rely on that, and I am to go home soon, so I will cause you no more troubles. I only ask you, I beg you, to have mercy on an old fat man."

The *Obugyō* listened carefully to Kamimoto as he translated for Schuck, and then read from a separate piece of paper, *"Criminal Schuck. You are a confessed thief, and you must be subject to the laws of Japan and the rule of the Shōgun. We sentence you, Criminal Schuck, to death."*

Kamimoto turned his head slightly and said simply, "You are to be executed tomorrow." The sweaty fat man slumped forward in fear and defeat, and peered around the room packed with Japanese nobility and warriors who watched him without emotion. He turned to look at de Wolfe, his only friend in this madhouse.

"De Wolfe-Capitão, do you confirm the sentences?"

"Did he call me *Capitão?*"

"Yes, you are the *Capitão* of Dejima," Kamimoto explained. "It is a position with great honor and authority. That would include the ultimate responsibility for all of the Hollanders on the island."

"And, I may take Schuck away with me. Right now, today?"

"As I told you, *the Obugyō-sama* has been quite clear on this. Take Schuck and close Dejima, or confirm the sentence. The choice and the responsibility must be yours and yours alone."

The *Obugyō* was impatient with their discussion and loudly repeated, *"De Wolfe-Capitão! Do you confirm the sentences?"*

Schuck looked on in horror as de Wolfe answered clearly and loudly, "Yes. I confirm the sentences."

The *Obugyō* announced, *"Take the criminals away,"* and several samurai rose and stepped forward to manhandle Kamimoto and Schuck out as the *Obugyō* continued. *"The Shindo girl remains under investigation."*

Schuck called to de Wolfe, "You would allow me to die?" as they began to drag him from the room.

"My sworn duty is to protect the Company," he replied, trying to stiffen the resolve and conviction that he was not truly feeling.

Kamimoto whispered to him, "I will arrange for you to come early. Remember the bargain that we discussed," and then he was escorted away.

De Wolfe desperately looked for Abe in the hallway and found him standing with a group of his men. "I want to see Taka," he began.

"Today," Abe responded.

"Yes! Shindo Taka today!"

"No, today," Abe said, this time confused.

De Wolfe tried to mime with his hands, "Yesterday. Today. Tomorrow. I want to see Taka today."

"No today," Abe told him, finally understanding. "Shindo Taka tomorrow. Today we go Dejima."

Responsibilities

It was sunset before they moved across the Dutch Gate, and an expectant crowd soon gathered around him shouting questions.

"Safe! You are safe!" Dr. Franz exclaimed vigorously pumping de Wolfe's hand. "Wonderful!"

"It was Schuck and Kamimoto," he shouted so that every Dutchman could hear. "They stole from the trade goods, and they are to be executed tomorrow!"

Franz suddenly stopped moving and dropped his hand as if it had become unpleasant to hold onto, "Dear Schuck? To be killed?"

"Doctor, they have both freely admitted their guilt."

"Then they have earned their punishments," said Camilla as she approached and stood next to him and the crowd grew silent.

After a long pause Dr. Franz implored him, "But he is a fine man! He may have erred, but that does not negate your obligation to protect him, to protect all of us. There was nothing that you could do?"

"Obligations?" Camilla confronted the physician. "We have no responsibilities to an admitted thief, nor to anyone who commits such an immoral breach of trust. We have no obligations to him, nor to anyone else here in the Japans."

De Wolfe spoke loudly and clearly so that every man could hear him. "Listen to me! I have fulfilled my responsibilities," and looking directly at his wife continued, "further, I can assure you that I fully appreciate all of my duties." He turned and walked quickly to his quarters.

The Lion of Flanders

De Wolfe was waiting expectantly the darkness the next morning in his formal clothes when Abe and two samurai arrived at the Dutch Gate. He had packed the outfit in Amsterdam not thinking it would ever be needed, but just in case he would ever have to preside over a funeral, or to be buried in. He carried a thick book under his arm. Dr. Franz and Muis bid him good-bye, but Camilla was nowhere to be seen.

They walked through Nagasaki to the northern residential area, even this early there were already small shops selling foodstuffs on practically every corner, interspersed with restaurants serving grilled fish or noodles. De Wolfe soon began to recognize the streets, and they arrived at the Shindo house. Abe pushed the gate open and called out, *"May we disturb you?"*

The door of the house slipped open, and Taka stepped out to the porch. Abe and his men bowed, and turned away, leaving the two of them alone. She was wearing a light kimono, and moved with difficulty bearing the weight of the child, their child in her belly, and she looked beautiful to him. He thought of the first time he had seen her, painted like a toy, ornate and covered with decorations and heavy embroidered clothing. So much had changed over the past year. Everything had changed.

"I brought you a book, so that you could continue to study," he began, and handed it to her. "It is a famous Dutch novel by Henri Conscience, The Lion of Flanders. It is historical fiction."

"What is that?"

"It's a story, completely made-up of course, but based on what had really happened in the past."

"But, why write such a thing? You should tell the true story."

"Well, just because it is a story does not mean that it isn't true. That is, it could have happened. But, well, it didn't. Telling it in that manner makes it more interesting, I guess."

"Is it a good book?"

"Yes, I think so. It can teach us many things. It is full of action and adventure, and romance, and makes us feel as if we know the people in the book, and as if we might have actually been there. And, if you enjoy the story and maybe learn something, then it is a good book."

"Then, I will read it. Only to improve my Dutch, of course." She smiled at him, "Will you read some of it with me?"

"I would like that."

They sat on the porch and de Wolfe would read a paragraph, endeavoring to breathe life and emotions into the plot and characters, and then Taka would read a paragraph, occasionally stopping to ask the pronunciation or meaning of a word. Her Dutch had rapidly improved this year, and he was both impressed and proud of her. She was still shy, and often made simple mistakes in speaking, but she understood nearly everything he said and avidly listened to any of the conversations among the Hollanders.

They read together for over an hour until Abe returned, signaling that it was time to go. She stood, "I like 'historical fiction'," she told him.

"Please, keep reading the book. When you finish it I will bring you another," he promised, and she bowed to him.

He reached out and took her hand, "Kamimoto told me," he said, "why he brought you to my house. As a spy," he told her with difficulty.

"That is true," she began. "But, Kamimoto had his reasons, and I had mine."

"You betrayed me."

"I betrayed everyone, including God! My family was held in prison. It was the only way to save them. My body was a small price for them to be safe."

"I was a 'price'?" de Wolfe snapped. "I understand perfectly," he said coldly.

"You understand nothing!" she flared back. "I was a gift to you and little more. I knew nothing of the Dutch. I expected to be beaten and raped. I believed that I would be a slave. Can you begin to imagine how I felt? It was my duty to please you. And, I would have done whatever was necessary for my family. I hope that I have pleased you, and if you are finished with me please go."

"That is not what I said! I would never do anything to hurt you or your family," he told her.

"Neither would I," she snapped. "Thank you for the book."

He released her hand and walked back to Abe.

Last Rites

Kamimoto had completed the oil painting, and carefully wrapped and stored it against the wall of his small tatami room when de Wolfe entered and kneeled beside him. The *Otona* seemed distant and dreamlike, and wore a clean pure white kimono, barely noticing his visitor.

"Is there no way to save you?" de Wolfe finally interrupted after a moment.

"Save me?" the condemned prisoner asked surprised. "Why would you want to do that? We all die, and it is a rare man who can create his own death with both honor and beauty."

"There is no beauty in death," de Wolfe scoffed. "There is no honor. There is only death. And, even if you may find it beautiful, I can assure you that Mr. Schuck and I will not."

"Have you come to do what I requested?"

"I do not think that it is right. It is a mockery, and I do not like it. May God have mercy on the both of us."

"But, you will do it?"

"Yes, I will do it."

"Then, what must I do?" asked the Japanese man.

Kamimoto knelt in front of de Wolfe who took two pieces of paper from his pocket and handed him one. "Read this," he began uncertainly. "You, ah, you start with a Confession."

138

"In the name of the Father, and of the Son, and of the Holy Spirit. My last Confession was…" Kamimoto read and then stopped, unsure how to proceed. "What do I say here?"

"Just continue."

"Forgive me for I have sinned. I have lied to those who trusted me and I have stolen. And, I have hidden my thefts."

They continued the Sacred Ritual of Confession, de Wolfe reading and prompting and Kamimoto responding from the page that he had been given. Finally, the Dutchman took a small piece of bread from his coat pocket and placed it in the Japanese man's mouth.

"This is the Lamb of God who takes away all the sins of the world. Happy are those who are called to His supper."

"Lord," Kamimoto read, "I am not worthy to receive you, but only say the word and I shall be healed."

"The body of Christ," they said in unison.

"Amen," Kamimoto intoned.

"May the Lord Jesus protect you and lead you to eternal life," de Wolfe read, finishing.

"Thank you, this was important," Kamimoto said, seemingly content, and then called out, *"We are ready!"*

Abe slid open the door and they departed.

The Execution Grounds

At the rear of the *Bugyō-sho* main governmental complex a tatami stage had been constructed to the height of a man's knee, with two white flat pillows, the kind used as home furnishings or during a meeting to kneel upon. At the center and between the pillows was a small table bearing a short sword. Surrounding the stage completely was white bunting, except for three small steps placed at the rear and leading up. At the back of the stage were four more white pillows in a line.

A crowd of stern looking men filled the space in front of the stage, and Schuck was standing off to one side with two samurai, one of whom de Wolfe recognized from the day of his arrival in Japan, the boy Abe called the *Chakunan*.

De Wolfe, Abe and Kamimoto stopped near the stage and waited briefly until a formal procession came out from the governmental building consisting of Shinto priests in their odd looking hats, two senior officials, and lastly leaning on his cane for support the *Obugyō-sama*.

The *Obugyō-sama* walked directly to Kamimoto, flanked by the officials and Shinto priests and read a paper from his kimono.

"Kamimoto Daikichi! You are hereby ordered by the Tokugawa Shōgunate, the Bugyō of Nagasaki, and the Capitão of Dejima to commit seppuku."

He displayed the paper to Kamimoto and then to those gathered in around the stage, and he and Kamimoto bowed deeply to each other.

Abe guided de Wolfe to the stage and one of the pillows at the rear. The *Obugyō* and two governmental officials joined him in kneeling, and the Shinto priests stood formally on each side of the platform. Kamimoto knelt on the pillow to the crowd's left next to the small table, and Abe knelt on the other side.

The condemned man looked for a moment at the short sword, and then spoke in a low guttural voice. *"I am sorry for the great troubles that I have caused and that you have encountered. I sincerely thank you for your kindness and friendship, and the Obugyō-sama of Nagasaki and the Capitão of Dejima for their fairness and wisdom."* He turned and bowed to de Wolfe and the *Obugyō*, touching his forehead to the tatami stage. They both returned his bow.

The prisoner then reached into his kimono and withdrew a piece of paper. *"Spring came late this year,"* he read. *"But the leaves fall early: Heaven's beauty waits."*

Kamimoto shifted his head and looked directly at de Wolfe, "I have kept my bargain. Taka was never a very good spy anyway. Women fall in love too easily, and always at the wrong time and with the wrong man." He smiled.

Kamimoto turned back to the front and straightened himself, took a deep breath, and looked dreamily off into the distance. He carefully opened his kimono, exposing his hairless chest, and bared himself to the waist. Without looking down he raised his left arm and reached to pick-up the short sword in its scabbard off of the table, and grasped the handle in his right hand. In one motion he unsheathed the sword and set down the scabbard, and then moved the small table behind him with his left hand. He looked happy and angelic.

How could de Wolfe have prepared himself for the events of the next few moments? He had never read of, nor heard of, anything that could be quite so barbaric. He could not have conceived that anyone would allow such things to happen, let alone approve of them.

The concept of death had always been somewhat distant and largely academic. He had watched his mother die. He understood a noble death in battle, of course. From far away he had watched Bleeckier be horribly murdered. He knew these things happened. The concept of capital punishment had been a distant one for him, the stuff of history books, but to witness the reality of it first-hand was beyond anything he could have imagined.

Kamimoto plunged the short sword into the left side of his belly, but there was no change in his beatific expression. The razor sharp blade barely drew blood as he slowly began to draw the steel across his stomach and slightly upward.

Now, with a slight grimace, the pain finally beginning to penetrate, the head leaned forward, and in that instant Abe leapt up, drawing his long sword and striking the rear of Kamimoto's neck from behind with one swift and smooth motion, expertly leaving a small flap of skin at the throat so that the nearly severed visage fell onto the lifeless body's chest and then pitched forward onto the mat. Bright red blood began spreading across the stage and soaking the tatami.

Abe cleaned his sword with a piece of rice paper, and returned it to the scabbard. He then took the bloody short sword from Kamimoto's dead hands, and presented it to de Wolfe for inspection until the Hollander turned his head away in disgust.

Abe then presented the short sword to the *Obugyō* and governmental officials for examination. They nodded their approval, and several men rushed forward to remove the lifeless body.

"Gerhard Schuck!" the *Obugyō* growled in a low sing-song voice. "You have been sentenced to death as a common criminal".

Two samurai dragged and prodded the quivering Schuck up the stairs and to the center of the stage where they tore off his shirt revealing the rolls of fat across his belly while he tried to hunch over and cover his naked chest. He was moaning quietly in fear as the two samurai stepped back and everything went completely silent.

In that single endless moment the sun was bright above and the barest hint of an afternoon breeze brushed de Wolfe's face. The platform he was kneeling upon was dazzlingly white, corrupted by the slowly darkening pool of Kamimoto's blood. On the horizon, high above the white plaster walls and grey tile roofs of the governmental building two birds flew off towards the ocean. His vision pulsed and his heart thumped in his ears as de Wolfe called out, "I will see you in Heaven, Mr. Schuck!" trying to comfort him.

Schuck turned, panting and tears streaming down his face. "Oh, I doubt that very much my 'dear friend'. For you have sent me to Hell. May God damn you!"

141

Fast, very fast, the samurai on the left drew his sword and with a loud and startling shout struck Schuck a deep and penetrating downward blow on the right shoulder, cutting through him past the nipple and nearly to the navel. At almost the same instant, the *Chakunan* on the right swung horizontally and severed the body completely in two at the waist, and the two parts dropped separately onto the tatami mat, the intestines and organs clearly showing through the gore.

The two samurai wiped their swords clean with rice paper, and then brought their weapons to the governmental officials and the *Obugyō* to admire the quality of the blades. De Wolfe would not look at the slaughterhouse the stage had become or the blades that had created this carnage. He simply stared without emotion or thought at the face of the *Chakunan*.

"This matter is now concluded!" the *Obugyō* announced.

Everything had been a blur to de Wolfe since the moment that Kamimoto had reached for the short sword. Schuck's body was taken away for cremation, Abe shoved the oil painting into his hands, and someone, he could not remember who, had escorted him back to Dejima.

It's All Wrong

It had been over a week since the executions, and de Wolfe had done practically nothing and spoken to no one during that time. He had asked Dr. Franz to conduct a memorial for Schuck, which he could not bring himself to attend.

Wracked with sorrow and guilt he spent the days on the wharf under the flagpole staring at the VERGULDE DRAECK, and idly watching the long boats shuttle trade goods from the vessel onto the wharf beside him, then they were man-handled with difficulty into the warehouses. He said nothing, didn't seem to invite any company, nor did he seek any.

Dr. Franz was hesitant, therefore, to approach him, and stopped some distance away for several minutes before he braced himself and walked to the wharf.

"It's all wrong, isn't it?" he began.

"What's all wrong?" de Wolfe asked absently. "In what way?"

"First of all Bleeckier. Then Kamimoto and now Schuck. All gone so quickly, and barely even a chance to say good-bye. We all feel it. We all share in the loss."

De Wolfe did not respond, and looked back out to sea.

"I miss them, each and every one of them, and I wish they were still here," Franz continued. "But, most of all, I miss you. Always alone, walking the grounds at night like some apparition from the ether. They are gone, but you should still be here with us, among the living."

De Wolfe remained distant and unresponsive until finally saying just under his breath as if talking to himself, "Who bears the guilt doctor? The patient or the physician who let him die?"

"I do not get your meaning."

"By not knowing that they were stealing, by not preventing the crime, am I not also responsible? There were so many times that I could have - that I should have - noticed what was happening and stopped it. But, in my own hubris and stupidity, I allowed it to happen. I therefore encouraged it to happen."

"If they had succeeded," Franz pointed out, "it would have been you that was culpable when the crime was discovered. Not them, they would have been long gone, but you. Your life and everything that you worked to achieve would have been washed away. How can you be held responsible for their crimes? They made those choices, not you."

"Then, who shall rot in Hell doctor? The criminal, or the witness that sends him to the gallows?"

Franz paused, understanding the unimaginable pain that de Wolfe bore, and the guilt associated with it. But life is for the living until there is no more of it. This poor man must be brought back from the abyss he had fallen into.

"We men are not perfect," Franz began, "certainly not in this world and probably not in the next. We make our plans, we do our best. Sometimes we succeed, and often we fail as circumstances arise to knock our little tea kettles over."

"I have done what I was sent to the Japans to do. I have protected the Company whatever the cost."

"We make mistakes," Franz continued. "They are not forgotten nor forgiven. Each one has its cost and we carry them burning in our guts like bitter little sacks of bile that we cannot vomit out. Instead, we must learn to live with them."

He leaned directly into de Wolfe's face, "We need you. You have a wife that needs you. And, you have a newborn son."

Slowly the realization began to spread through de Wolfe like a healing balm. Men had died because of him, and he could never forget that. But, despite the pain, he had never really been ready to give up. Now the news that he had brought new life into the world energized him, forcing him to turn his attention away from the execution grounds and back towards the living.

"I must see them!" he told Franz urgently. "I must see Taka and my son. Can you bring them to me?"

"Yes," said Franz beaming. "I will try. Tonight, after supper in my quarters. A son! It's a new beginning!"

Franz was nodding happily as de Wolfe turned back towards the sailors rowing the long boats from the VERGULDE DRAECK to the shore. "I have a son!" he bellowed across Nagasaki Bay, startling both the men and the birds on the water.

Supper

Acawarman had served the five courses in perfect order. The main course had been chicken, followed by cheese and finally coffee. Attending were de Wolfe, Camilla, Dr. Franz, Muis and Captain Ostrander.

"Thank you again for another fine meal," Ostrander commented. "As we have completed the unloading, and there is very little in the way of return cargoes this year, we are making plans to depart very soon. We will sail for the Busan, then the British settlements in Shanghai and Hong Kong and see if there is anything of interest to trade. Possibly some sandalwood in Siam. In any case, I wanted to deliver the gifts for the *Shōgun* into your care."

He walked over to a mid-sized trunk and opened it, taking out each item and placing it on the dinner table. "Candies, of course, quite popular. Here, books on astronomy and medicine in both Dutch and English. A superbly crafted Swiss telescope, and these very unusual items from the United States, a box of 'safety pins'."

"What can those possibly be?" asked Camilla as she opened the box and took one out to examine it.

Ostrander picked one up also and passed it around the table. "Yankees, quite clever don't you know. It folds in upon itself," and he demonstrated by opening a pin and then closing it up again.

"But these, these are my favorites." He turned back to the trunk and took out a smallish box, little more than two hand spans wide and engraved with a stars and stripes flag behind an ornate eagle, all in bright colors. He opened the box to reveal two percussion cap pistols and their accessories.

"Matching Colt 1851 Navy revolvers in .36 caliber, the most modern pistols in the world. Look here," he continued, "each revolver carries six shots!" Six shots, can you believe it? Why, a single man could practically hold off a whole army!"

He passed the box around for the others to see, and the men eagerly examined the revolvers.

"Easy to use?" asked de Wolfe.

"Very!" Ostrander assured him. "Look here. Each cylinder has its own cap, so once it is loaded all you do is pull the trigger six times."

"Is this what the Company thinks the *Shōgun* needs?" asked de Wolfe.

"Certainly not!" answered Ostrander. "But it most assuredly is what the Japanese do want to study as it will change their world. Of course they all love their swords, the boys carry them from the time they are babies. Shooting an opponent though is considered cowardly, not a manly manner to kill a fellow at all. Especially since any farmer can point and pull a trigger, where is the honor in that? The samurai may not like guns, and they may not use them, but they do love to look."

"No," he continued, "without their swords there are no samurai, and without samurai there are no *Daimyō*s, and without *Daimyō*s there is no *Shōgun*."

"And," Muis finished it for him, "without the *Shōgun* there is no Japan."

"Precisely! They live in a bottle, and the *Shōgun* is the cork," Ostrander completed the thought.

"What did you just say? 'The *Shōgun* is the cork'?" The words rang familiar in de Wolfe's ear.

"Rather obvious, isn't it?" Ostrander observed. "The Japanese have lived in their own little world, separate from everyone else since the 1600s, cut off from every social and technological advance. Why, they practically live in the dark ages."

"It works for them," Franz argued.

"I think not," Ostrander shook his head. "Here you are born into a caste. If you are a nobleman or a samurai, well then life can be fairly good. Much better than if you were born a farmer, or Heaven forbid the lowest of all, a merchant."

"Aren't we merchants?" Muis screwed up his squint and wrinkled his nose.

"True, I reckon you can appreciate then where we stand in the Japanese pecking order. They may need us, but they certainly don't have to respect us. Ah, but the merchants can control the money, and that's their little secret. The nobles have the land, the samurai have the swords, but the merchants have the money. The whole system is out of balance, teetering towards collapse and there are only two questions: Will it come from inside or out, and how bloody will it be."

"I believe that a society where everyone knows their place under a king is most practical, and the rest is all nonsense," Camilla voiced her opinion.

Ostrander looked at her from the corner of his eye and started to say something, then thought better of it. "You are most probably right, madam," he offered. "I stand corrected."

There was an awkward silence until Muis asked, "How long will the trip to Edo take?"

"On horseback and by foot? I would say eight to twelve weeks there and back," Ostrander considered, happy to change the subject. "You will want to hurry so that you don't get caught up in the colder weather, especially in the mountains near Fuji volcano. Still, if the Japanese would allow it I could take you there on my ship in just a few days."

The conversation grew quiet until Franz turned to de Wolfe, "I have some items in my room as well for the journey. Will you join me?"

"Certainly doctor, certainly." De Wolfe turned to the others at the table. "If you will all please excuse us for just a few moments?"

Camilla was so engrossed in the box of safety pins she barely noticed them leave, and Muis unexpectedly popped a pin open, pricking his finger and drawing blood. He looked around the table in embarrassment, and seeing that no one noticed, he shoved the finger into his mouth.

Every Day

Taka. Inside Dr. Franz's quarters was the physician's wife, holding a small bundle, but every sense de Wolfe possessed screamed as he saw her standing quietly, looking tired but happy, and everything else faded away. She looked up as he and Dr. Franz entered. She began to bow to him, but he would have none of it. He stepped to the mother of his child, put his arms around her, held her gently to him, and felt life refilling his soul.

Dr. Franz's wife held the infant out to him, and he accepted the baby gingerly as if it was the most fragile and precious object he had ever touched, and looked down into the small face. The eyelashes were long, and the mouth moved as if kissing the air, and then the child crinkled his nose and yawned.

146

"He is beautiful!" he turned to Taka. "Have you given him a name?"

"No, no name."

"His name, his name will be so important! But, I don't know...."

"A name can come later," Dr. Franz chided him. "But for now he is happy and healthy, as is his mother."

"Of course, I am sorry, I meant," the words came tumbling out of de Wolfe. "What I mean is," he turned back to Taka, "How are you?"

"I am fine," she laughed. "Look at what we have done!" She smiled at the baby as de Wolfe cradled it in his arms.

"I will arrange a residence for you here at Dejima," de Wolfe exclaimed. "For both you and the child. I will provide everything that you may need."

"Do not be silly," she scolded him. "Now that Kamimoto-*Otona* is dead, the *Obugyō-sama* has commanded that I live in his household, The child, as he is half-Dutch, is of special importance to him. The women of the royal family are most pleased to have a new baby with them, and are very helpful. I am comfortable there. And, your wife....It would not be right."

"Yes, my wife....."

The baby began to cry softly, and Taka took him from de Wolfe and comforted him. "You have a wife, and I have a child. I came to you as a gift, and you have given me a much better one. I betrayed you, and you have given me back my life."

"How could you believe that you betrayed me? You have brought me joy and kindness. In return, I took advantage, and for that I am sorry," de Wolfe told her. "But, I cannot apologize, for it was what I wanted."

"I was forced to be with you," she touched his face and kissed him gently. "I did not know then that you would become my man, my lover. Being with you was what I wanted also."

"May I come visit you on Sunday?" de Wolfe asked hopefully.

"The *Bugyō-sho* government building the baby and I. We will be there."

"I will find you. Then, I must go to Edo. Wait for me, and when I return I will come for you. After I return from Edo."

The Silver Cross

The Chief Samurai was napping on the porch of the main governmental building, in front of the rooms that served as the *Obugyō-sama's* residence. The late Summer was warm, and he had been drinking heavily until late last night and again first thing this morning. His back was against a post, and his head kept falling towards his chest even though he was nominally on guard duty. There were two small *sake* bottles empty and knocked over next to him.

Quietly at first, and then growing ever more incessant a baby could be heard crying from the inside, and the Chief Samurai began to twitch and squirm as if a small animal was biting at him. He came fully awake with a start, belched, and then looked around to see what it was that had bothered him.

It was that damn merchant girl and her howling half-breed brat. He had no idea why his lord had invited them to live here, but she had caused nothing but trouble for him from the first time he saw her. He thought he had gotten rid of her once already when they found the Bible, but here she had popped up again to torment him. Well, she may live here for now, but he had no reason to be polite to her, and there must be a way to finally get rid of her once and for all. Until then, it made him feel good to bring a little bit of torment into her life. After all, what would she do? Complain to the *Obugyō-sama*?

Focusing on the baby's crying he rose, pulled open the paper covered door and shouted, *"Shut that little bastard up!"*

Inside the small tatami room Taka was startled when the door flew open as she had just begun to suckle the child. Her kimono was undone and her breasts were bare as the Chief Samurai leered at her. De Wolfe's small silver cross was hanging down from her neck and clearly visible above the back of the baby's head. She tried to cover it with her hand.

Wearing a Christian cross! First the Bible, and now this! Oh, this was just too perfect! The Chief Samurai smiled grimly as he anticipated gaining his revenge on this woman for her previous humiliation of him, and once more enjoying a quiet household. He reached into the room as Taka tried to shield the baby, and ripped the pendant from her neck, breaking the chain.

Christians! How he despised them! And, even if the *Obugyō-sama* might be inclined to discreetly ignore the *Shōgun's* Edict, he was still only the local magistrate of the national government. The Chief Samurai knew how to get such important information to the right people. He would pass this evidence directly to the *Shogun's* samurai, and his problem would immediately disappear. His reward for these merchants breaking the *Sakoku* Edict? Peace and serenity for his morning naps.

148

De Wolfe and Captain Ostrander were supervising the loading of the last few trade goods the VERGULDE DRAECK would take to Batavia. There was not much to carry on the southbound voyage, and she had loaded numerous rocks for ballast. Two small but heavy chests were among the last of the items on the manifest.

"The Company will be most pleased," Ostrander noted, checking them off on his tally sheet, "with the silver. I will store them in my cabin for safe-keeping."

"But, so little else, you are leaving half-empty," de Wolfe mused.

"Profit is profit. Besides, since we sail weeks early and have extra time, we'll swing west to Chosun and China and see what we can barter. All in all, you have done quite well."

Dr. Franz and Abe came hurrying to the wharf, and de Wolfe noted that for the first time the Japanese warrior did not walk in a manner that he had so often described as "strutting". In fact, Abe seemed subdued and Franz worried.

"When you go?" Abe demanded.

"We are almost finished loading in all of the cargo and provisions. We will leave in a few days," Ostrander explained.

Abe turned to de Wolfe pointing. "We go Edo! You, me, samurai."

"You? You are taking us to Edo? You and your samurai?" de Wolfe was astonished. He had not thought it through. Of course, someone had to take them to Edo, but he had never imagined it would be the hateful and murderous Abe.

"We go Edo!" Abe pointed at his own nose and then to de Wolfe's chest. He then turned to Ostrander. "You go Holland!"

"Yes," Ostrander was growing exasperated and rolling his eyes. Why bother to explain world geography? "When I finish loading my ship." He counted on his fingers to be sure that Abe understood. "I go Holland, two or three days."

"Your wife," Abe continued, turning back to de Wolfe. "She go Holland too."

"No. My wife is staying here. With me, she will wait here until we return from Edo." He tried to speak loudly and slowly so that Abe would understand.

"No! Cannot! Your wife, she go Holland."

"What on earth are you talking about?" Ostrander asked.

149

"Forbidden!" Abe was also growing frustrated at the language barrier.

As Franz fretted, Abe pulled a scroll out of his kimono and presented it to de Wolfe. It was written in Dutch and officially stamped under the authority of *Shōgun* Tokugawa Ieyoshi.

THE AGREEMENT OF 1641 FORBIDS THE PERMANENT RESIDENCE OF ANY WOMEN ON DEJIMA.

MRS. HENDRIK DE WOLFE IS HEREBY ORDERED TO DEPART JAPAN ABOARD THE VESSEL VERGULDE DRAECK AS QUICKLY AS POSSIBLE.

AUGUST 1853.

Abe continued, "*Shōgun* write, your wife, she go Holland. You, me, we go Edo."

"That agreement was signed over two hundred years ago!" de Wolfe protested. You cannot possibly hold me to that."

"Well, unfortunately," Ostrander sighed, examining the paper. "He is right, and a contract is a contract. And, to the Japanese, it does not matter whether it was signed yesterday or in the Court of King David, it still binds you, and this order is personally authorized by the current *Shōgun*."

"And, it is even worse I am afraid," Franz offered. "They have taken Taka."

"Taken her where?" de Wolfe demanded.

"*Shōgun* samurai," Abe answered.

"The *Obugyō-sama* has pardoned her," de Wolfe protested.

"No, this is the *Shōgun*, and our local fellow no longer has any authority," Franz explained. "Taka was found to be wearing a Christian cross. It will mean certain death of course, for the entire family. Including the boy. She has already been taken to Edo by ship for an investigation while the child and her family are being held here for the verdict."

"My cross!" de Wolfe exploded. "My cross has condemned her? A woman and a child! A whole family? For wearing a small piece of jewelry? Is killing all that the Japanese understand!"

"It will be the *Shōgun*'s decision now, and only he can save her."

150

De Wolfe was shaken. "It is my fault doctor, we must get to Edo. I must explain everything to the *Shōgun*, I must make him understand. Mr. Abe, we must get to Edo quickly! We have to save them."

"Yes!" Abe barked, and Dr. Franz nodded his head grimly.

A Bargain Offered

Camilla was in the chapel, kneeling before the painted cross hanging on the wall. "God is punishing me for my transgressions," she announced angrily as de Wolfe came in, but did not turn to acknowledge him.

"Camilla, please," de Wolfe tried to sooth her. "Do not be melodramatic. The Japanese have their ways."

"Separating a man and his wife! Is that the Japanese way? It is intolerable!"

"It cannot be helped. When I, rather when we accepted this assignment we also accepted the burden as well as the rewards. We both understood that it would be most difficult and involve many sacrifices."

She rose and rushed to him, throwing her arms around his shoulders. "Let Dejima rot for all I care! You have done your agreed one-year term and fulfilled your contract."

"A man cannot run away from his responsibilities!"

"I will explain everything to Papa. He will understand."

"My assignment is to ensure that Dejima endures as it has for the past two centuries. You heard Captain Ostrander, the Japans may very well be on the verge of collapse or invasion. If I abandon the post now, I cannot promise that it will endure! In fact, quite the opposite. By leaving, it may very well ensure to the Company, and to your father, that I have broken my oath and allowed it to fail."

She released him and stepped away. "Perhaps you just want to stay in the Japans," she pouted.

"That is not true."

"Come with me then. Stay with me. I will make you so happy."

He thought back to the first time he had seen that pout, and how much it had pleased him. He had always known that she used her beauty to manipulate men, her father first, and certainly him, but ultimately anyone from whom she wanted something.

151

Taka had given him joy and never asked for anything in return. Pleasing him had pleased her, and even though her arrival had been cloaked in betrayal, she had never said or done anything to hurt him or to actually use him for her advantage.

But, the reality was that he had married this one, not Taka. It was a bond under God that he had broken to his shame, and now was the time for honesty.

"The woman in the courtyard," he began. "The child is mine."

Camilla regarded him for a long moment, thinking back. What was he saying? The realization and understanding came with the memory, and her face darkened. She walked to de Wolfe and slapped him hard across the face.

"Damn you!" she cried out. "Damn you and your whore!"

Camilla broke down and retreated to a chair where she collapsed sobbing. De Wolfe wiped a trickle of blood from his lip.

"They are to be killed," he tried to explain.

He let that settle for a moment before he walked over to the window and stared out. He waited until his heartbeat had calmed before he made his offer.

"He is a boy, healthy and strong. He is here in Nagasaki. I have seen him Camilla, and he is the most beautiful child. You will love him, and together we can save his life. I want you to take the baby home to Holland, and we will raise him as our own."

"As a van Courtlandt?" she asked astonished.

"Yes," he continued, and walked over to her. "I want him to be a better man than I could ever be. Take him with you, and I will follow in one short year. I will have fulfilled everything the Company asked, and we will be reunited forever. But, I cannot leave now with so much yet undone. Imagine him growing as a boy and then into a man, there is so much we can give him, so many advantages. He is the grandson your father so desired."

She stood and turned away from him. "You have been foolish, I understand, men are like that. But," her voice became cold and bitter, "you are asking me to take a child, a Japanese child, and to keep it next to me every day to remind me of your infidelity? This is madness."

"He is neither Dutch nor Japanese, he is my son. He can be our son. That is all that I can see. A family. I am asking you to make us a family."

"I am not barren!" Camilla suddenly raged. "I... we... are already a family! I will give you sons!"

"No, Camilla no. I do not blame you, but you cannot have children. We have tried. It is a medical condition, of that I am certain. It will not work, and I know you want them so desperately, but it ... it is just not possible."

"It is you that is impotent, and not enough of a man to admit it or to give me children!"

De Wolfe tried to catch himself before the words leaped out, but he could not, and he immediately regretted his angry retort. "It would seem quite obvious that I am quite capable of fathering children. The fault can only be yours!"

"Liar!" she screamed and pulled her arm back to swing at him again. He caught her wrist. She became desperate and began to plead with him. "Everything awaits you in Holland. Love, family, wealth, happiness, your entire life. The Japans hold nothing for you now. Come home with me."

They had many times fought over money, her endless shopping purchases, and a dozen reasons, but all that seemed trivial now. Taka and his son's lives were in jeopardy, and he could not allow his pride nor his anger to sweep away any chance they might have, whatever he must do. "Take the child," he implored, "and when I return to Holland in one year I will be whatever it is that you want me to be. I will do what you say, I will become what you want. I will give you everything that you desire. Take the child home with you. I will give you my life for his."

"Is that your bargain? Well, it is impossible. If you have made mistakes, leave those mistakes here. Abandon and forget them forever."

"Camilla," he implored her, "I am begging you for a Christian act of charity."

She shook her wrist loose. "I have heard your ultimatum, and you know mine."

"Circumstances have changed," he shook his head. "I cannot go, and you cannot stay."

"This is a calamity of your own making, and you alone must suffer its consequences." she huffed, and walked out.

The Winds Do Change

Everything had been stowed, and the VERGULDE DRAECK was ready to sail with the morning tide. It was an unaccustomed early rising for Camilla, and she watched unspeaking as the sailors lifted and carried her trunks and bags down to the wharf in the pre-dawn darkness. Dr. Franz, Muis, and Captain Ostrander stood with her and de Wolfe as the last of her baggage was transported out to the vessel.

Much of the talk during the past two days were the threat of the Americans to the Dutch trading monopoly, and whatever political developments may have occurred over the past months since the DRAECK had sailed from Batavia. Regardless of what might have happened, none of them believed that it would be good for the Dutch.

Ostrander spoke first, extending his hand to each of them in turn, de Wolfe last. "You must get to Edo before the Americans. You must not allow them to gain a concession from the *Shōgun*. I will report your mission to the Company, but everything relies on you now. You must not fail."

"You yourself said that Japan is poised for revolution from inside or out. How can I possibly stop it?" de Wolfe asked.

"You most certainly will not be able to stop it," Ostrander cautioned him. "But it can be delayed, perhaps even guided to our advantage. Just don't be the one that's left holding the bag."

De Wolfe let go of the old sailor's hand, "I can assure you that I will travel to Edo with all possible speed."

Camilla ignored the men, and faced towards the waiting long boat and Nagasaki Bay. She then turned to de Wolfe, disregarding the others.

"Everything you have, everything you will ever have, is in Holland." She then turned to the other Dutchmen on the wharf. "For the sake of my family, I trust that the embarrassment of the events here in the Japans will never be spoken of again."

She walked away to the edge of the wharf, and now again looking remote and regal she waited to be helped aboard the long boat as the sailors jumped up from their seats to assist her.

Once she was seated aboard, Ostrander spoke privately to the Hollander. "The winds do change, do they not Mr. de Wolfe?" Then, quite pointedly, "Do not let your passion for this Japanese girl cloud your mission. We are all relying upon you."

He boarded the long boat, lines were cast off, and they began rowing to the VERGULDE DRAECK. The last link between Holland and Dejima was once again broken.

PART III

Changes

Slave Trade

Curacuo is a tiny Caribbean speck located north of Venezuela and scattered in among other islands including the better known Aruba, St. Croix and Tobago. The Spanish had first settled there in 1499 and used it mainly to raise livestock until 1634 when the Dutch West India Company forcibly moved in, fortified Curacuo and four other islands in the Lesser Antilles Chain, and hereafter claimed them for the Kingdom of the Netherlands.

Although Curacuo was small, only 444 square kilometers, its strategic position enabled the Dutch to use it to launch other forays into neighboring islands and even Brazil itself, although none of these adventures were ever quite successful for military, political and economic reasons. Piracy was hugely profitable, and in 1628 Piet Pieterszoon Hein had captured the Spanish Silver Fleet and over 11,000,000 guilders in gold, silver, and trade goods, giving the Company's shareholders an unbelievable 50% dividend that year.

But, neither piracy nor trade were reliable revenue streams, and the enterprise went bankrupt in 1674, was resurrected in 1675, and ultimately collapsed again on January 1, 1792 when all territories held by the Dutch West India Company reverted to the States General of the Dutch Republic. During the following years the Dutch traders on Curacuo may not have prospered, but they had found a consistent profit in enslaved Africans imported into the North and South Americas and the Caribbean.

The United States had prohibited the importation of slaves in 1808 and the British had outlawed the hideous practice altogether in 1834, leading the Dutch to determine in 1848 that the sale and exploitation of humans should be eliminated, but they had not yet taken the steps to end the slave trade. It would continue for another fifteen years.

Cas Janssen had arrived fourteen months earlier aboard the MEERMIN after an interminable two months voyage. He was sunburned, much thinner and fitter now and sported a long jagged scar on his left cheek that ran from just beneath his eye to his lower jaw. It was still reddish and the crooked lines clearly indicated where it had been crudely sewn shut by the ship's surgeon with heavy canvas thread, a "gift" from the First Mate and the dreaded leather cudgel. He had woken from the blow to the sensation of someone grabbing his face and pulling it away, and when he had opened his eyes he could see the large curved needle rising and falling, pulling his lashed flesh back together as the First Mate stood nearby, his arms defiantly crossed in front of his chest.

They had sailed the MEERMIN, a so-called "Guineamen" specifically designed and outfitted to carry human cargoes, from Amsterdam due south past Portugal and

155

Morocco before arriving at the Dutch Slave Coast. The first weeks under sail had been horrific with all Cas' non-watch hours spent imprisoned in the stinking hold below deck, and all watch hours being cursed and beaten by the sadistic First Mate. The former dandy's previously fine clothes had quickly become tatters, although it seemed to matter less and less as they approached the equator, but eventually he was forced to draw from the ship's provisions and carefully sign a chit that the costs would be deducted from his meager wages. He had no idea how much the clothes cost him or how much his wages would be, and it really didn't matter. He had left everything behind, been thrown aboard the slave ship with nothing, and disappeared into the ether just as completely as if he had never existed at all.

They had loaded 409 enslaved blacks aboard at the Slave Coast, carefully guarded by ferocious looking African warriors, the defeated hostages both exhausted and resigned. The prisoners seemed to have no life left in them at all, either staring blankly down at the dirt in front of them, or far off into the distance, seeing nothing. The captors were laughing and singing as they drove them onto the ship. They had defeated their traditional enemies and were now earning a handsome profit and clearing land at the very same time. The Dutch had become their instrument of war, taking the spoils away and gladly paying for them. As each prisoner came aboard they were taken down into the fetid hold where the impressed sailors had previously slept, and then chained to the floor. Cas had been ordered to lodge in the forward chain locker in preparation of their arrival. There was no separation of men, women or children, all went down and were bound together. As soon as the last slave was loaded the Captain paid the slave-traders and they began a sprint towards the Caribbean.

It was a race against time in the heat and equatorial humidity with limited supplies of food, and most importantly fresh water, and raging diseases. There were casualties everyday both among the sailors and slaves. The bodies were quickly thrown overboard without ceremony, and by the time they arrived in Curacuo five weeks later nine crewmembers and nearly one hundred of the slaves had perished. Cas was immensely gratified to see that the First Mate was one who did not survive the voyage. From time to time he would still rub the long scar on his cheek and remember heaving that vile carcass over the rail for the sharks and crabs to feast upon.

This evening he was sitting on a crude bunk in the jail of Willemstad, the largest city on Curacuo, although "capital city" were certainly two words he would never consider to describe the small trading settlement now run by the Dutch government under an *Opperkommies* – a head merchant. There was a soft knock on the cell door, and *Opperkommies* Van de Berg was holding a single candle to break the gloom. He was an older man, rotund and bald, wearing a light cotton shirt and trousers to fight off the daytime heat that still radiated throughout the brick building. He took a key from his pocket and unlocked the cell door, stepping inside and then leaving it open so that a slight draft freshened the hot air inside.

"Well," he began simply, "my overseer will live."

Cas nodded grimly, and then replied "I am glad to hear that."

Van de Berg sat the candle on the floor and sat next to Cas on the hard bunk. "You are a mystery to me," he said, shaking his head. "When you arrived, I was given a letter, written by a very respected gentleman in Amsterdam, saying that I was to punish you as necessary at my discretion, and that there would be no questions asked. I was told that I could break you, imprison you, hang you if I chose. And yet in all this time you have been a perfect employee. You work hard, you have no vices that I am aware of, and there has been no trouble. And yet today you beat my man nearly to death. Why?"

"There was an African," Cas began slowly, "your man was striking him with a horse whip. At first the poor fellow took the blows grimly, but in silence, three, four, five. And, I think that must have been what enraged your overseer, that he was being bested by a black. He continued until the man could stand no more, and then steadily whipped him while he lay in the dirt. I had to do something, and I did."

"Did you know this slave?"

"I did not."

"Then, why did you feel this was any of your affair?"

Cas smiled and shook his head, thinking back. "I had always lived my life as a lark. I wanted for little, and I am a bit ashamed now to admit to you that I loved it. I had fun. But, I came to do things that hurt people. It didn't start that way, but that is what it became. I was selfish, and I did things that I am not proud of. I betrayed someone that was very close to me, my lifelong friend, and I can never forget that."

"But," Cas continued, "I had never known cruelty or suffering until I was thrown onto that slave ship. I had never imagined that such barbarity even existed. I promised myself that I would never stand by again and watch another human suffer. What your man was doing was wrong, and well, I had to stop it."

"He wasn't beating a human, he was beating a slave."

"I see no difference between the two."

"You cannot believe that, of course there is a difference," Van de Berg pointed out. "The Africans are a lesser and uncivilized people. Besides, you own slaves yourself."

"I do not!"

"You have purchased three slaves in the last year alone."

"And, I have set each of them free."

"Then you have wasted your money," the *Opperkommies* scoffed.

Cas rose and stood staring out the door of the cell, "If so, then it is my money to waste."

"They are like children," Van de Berg pointed out. "They cannot read, they cannot speak Dutch, they have no way of living in a modern world. It is our obligation to take care of them."

"You have forbidden them schools, work them all day and into the night, beat them whenever you are dissatisfied, and then place the blame on the slave? You call them uncivilized, but never give them the dignity to find their own ways in the world."

"I have three hundred and nineteen slaves, ranging from those who have yet to walk to nearly seventy years old. Do you believe that they also should fend for themselves as well. It would be a huge mistake to free them. Besides, their value is well over ten thousand guilders."

"Ah, now we have determined the price of your soul," Cas turned towards the older man.

Van de Berg rose to stand facing the younger man. "I agree with you, slavery is abominable, and it must be abolished. It takes time. The Americans have been trying to do so for many years, but slave labor in the rice and cotton fields cannot be replaced."

"Do you know the life span of a slave in the cane fields? A mere six weeks. That is why fresh slaves must be constantly brought in, to replace those who have been worked to death."

"You would free them all?" the *Opperkommies* asked.

"They have been defeated in battle, ripped from their homelands by their enemies, and then sold to the Dutch. Many have grown up knowing nothing but slavery. We have an obligation to help them."

"In Africa they had little and invented nothing. They lived in the Stone Age, how will they ever adapt to a world of machines, technology and culture?"

"We must teach them," Cas insisted.

"And you believe that this debt is eternal?"

"Of course not! There will be a day when none of their children will have known slavery and none of ours will know what it is like to own another human. Some will rise and some will fall, each must take responsibility for their own fortunes. But, we must give them that chance to succeed or to fail. We must help them prepare."

Van de Berg thought for a long moment, stepped through the open cell door and then paused. "Well, you must be punished, and I now need a new overseer."

"I understand," and Cas sat down on the cell bunk.

"Why are you waiting? Come along!" Van de Berg picked up the candle and motioned to Cas. "You are being released to my parole and will live in my house. As overseer, I expect you to manage the slaves."

"Overseer? Never! I will never own another human being!"

"Come along! Come along!" Van de Berg insisted. "As my overseer I expect you to treat the slaves with kindness, and also with discipline when you must. Quietly, and I emphasize that, quietly you may begin to teach them how to speak Dutch and school them in basic reading, writing and mathematics. Begin to prepare them for what must come one day soon. Their freedom. I want you to be a slave-teacher, not a slave-owner."

"Then set them free. Set all of them free now."

"That I cannot do, and neither can you. Not today. But, someday. And, until that day comes they will be enslaved. Slavery will not last forever, although it will seem like it does." They stopped at the end of the hall before Van de Berg continued. "I believe that I have found the right person for the job. You are a good man Cas Janssen."

Three years later when Mr. Van de Berg died, Cas Janssen was made the *Opperkommies* of Curacuo. In 1863 the slaves in all Dutch overseas territories were freed, and their former owners were paid thirty guilders by the States General of the Dutch Republic for each of the formerly enslaved Africans.

The Procession

Muis had prepared two money belts for the sojourn, and stuffed each with gold and silver Tokugawa coins to pay for food and lodging on the way to Edo and back. He entrusted one to de Wolfe and the other to Abe, although the Japanese man seemingly disparaged having to handle actual money. There were more than a dozen horses waiting patiently in the island's courtyard as the procession gathered. Some were for riders, some were being loaded with baggage for the journey, and others were being brought along as spares.

They would be traveling from the deep edge of *Kyūshū*, the southernmost island of the Japanese archipelago, all the way to Edo, and few cities were farther from the capital. The Dutch had no maps of Japan, forbidden items of course, but they all knew that it would be a long and arduous trip.

They would travel north to the bustling city of Fukuoka and the adjacent merchant town of Hakata, and then on to Chikuzen for a short transfer by ferry to Shimonoseki, placing them back on firm ground on the main island of Honshu. They would continue near the eastern coast through Hiroshima, Hyogo and Osaka before arriving in the ancient capital of Kyoto.

From there they would join the heavily traveled *Tokaidō*, the "Eastern Sea Road" linking Kyoto and Edo that would make their travels both faster and easier, and lead them directly to their appointment with the *Shōgun*. Two to three months there and back Ostrander had estimated, and they would want to hurry both coming and going to be home before the first days of Winter.

They would spend each night at inns or villages along the way, some of them barely more than farmhouses while others were quite accommodating, until they reached Kyoto and the thoroughfare between the old and new capitals. After Kyoto there were government sponsored rest-stations on the *Tokaidō* with provisions for travelers and horses. The immensely popular artist *Hiroshige* had himself completed the journey from Kyoto to Edo during the Spring and Summer of 1845, and had depicted each of the fifty-three inns in what had already become a series of best-selling woodblock prints.

The *Shōgun* mandated that each of his over three hundred *Daimyō* or *Hatamoto* visit Edo at least once every year to personally report on the activities in their regions. It was both good government and good politics, but it was also a hardship the further from Edo they had to travel. Nagasaki was *tenryō* – a district under the direct administration of the *Shōgunate* – managed by a *Bugyō* clan that also maintained a permanent residence near Edo Castle that was constantly occupied by close family members and courtiers. The residence in Edo by children, brothers and sometimes wives of the administrators ensured the loyalty of the far-flung provinces. For the Dutch the requirement was once every four years, and since *Capitão* de Wolfe was, at least technically, a *Daimyō*, it was a journey that he was obligated to fulfill.

Along with Dr. Franz and de Wolfe there were numerous Japanese accompanying the group. Six armed samurai for security led by Abe, a flag bearer, and a score of porters carrying baggage in addition to the horses were gathered in Dejima's open courtyard. Only Abe, the *Chakunan*, de Wolfe and Franz would travel by horseback.

All of the samurai, including Abe, were wearing new kimono with a fan shape embroidered into the back to represent the island of Dejima, and the flag bearer carried a standard with the same design. Two Shinto priests were blessing the procession before its departure, waving bright red tassels on long sticks back and forth as they chanted in low sonorous monotones.

The Dutch staff had also turned out to see their countrymen off, and Dr. Franz was shaking the hand of each one of them personally after he had said good-bye to his wife. He continued moving down the line until he came to the Japanese porters, and kept right on pumping hands and saying "Thank you! Thank you!" before he realized they were going with him to Edo, and then laughed in slight embarrassment. "New sights and new specimens," he enthused. "How exciting!"

"We must get to Edo as quickly as possible," de Wolfe said grimly.

"It is going to take weeks," Franz soothed him. "I understand your urgency, but the *Shōgun* is never quick nor arbitrary in his actions. Taka has some kind of value to him, and he will not be hasty. He would not have taken her all the way to Edo without some purpose in mind. It is a very long way for us to travel, he knows that, and it will take time."

As soon as the priests completed their ceremony Abe began issuing commands and checking the preparations of both the samurai and the porters, inspecting gear and pulling straps on the baggage. He looked around and shouted, "We go now!" as he mounted a fine-looking all black steed.

Horses were brought to the Hollanders, and de Wolfe was hesitant, he had never had much experience before on horseback, added to that was his relative unfamiliarity with the Japanese bridle and saddle. He carefully lifted his left leg into the stirrup and pulled himself up. He turned to see Franz slowly chasing his mount in a circle as it stepped away from him, and the pair made at least three complete revolutions until one of the porters put down his bag and rushed over to hold the animal still until Franz could climb up. Then Franz sat on the saddle absolutely beaming with pride over his accomplishment.

De Wolfe was not so ebullient. "Every time I have seen that man," he said to Franz and nodding in the direction of Abe, "something bad has happened."

With Abe leading the procession, preceded only by the flag bearer, they moved across the Dutch Gate, and the Shinto priests once again began their chant and waved their tasseled sticks up and down as the group passed in single file: The flag bearer, the three riders, three armed samurai, the porters, baggage and spare horses, and lastly the final three samurai and the *Chakunan* on horseback.

After they had passed only a short way through Nagasaki Abe suddenly signaled a halt, and dismounted before a large and well-kept house. He swaggered to the gate and shouted, *"It is me!"* while the procession waited.

From inside the house a young boy rushed out, a huge smile on his face and his arms stretched out in front. He seemed barely able to walk, but stumbled and bumbled towards Abe who watched sternly with his hands on his hips.

"Kenichi!" A woman called out, and rushed to catch the child before he crashed into Abe. She halted the boy by the shoulders, and they stood a pace apart from the fearsome samurai as he scowled at them. Then, the mother and child both slowly bowed in unison.

Abe returned the bow with great deference as a smile grew on his face. De Wolfe had never seen the stoic and somber warrior happy or smile on any occasion, and watched with astonishment. Abe reached down and picked the boy up, kissing his cheek and whispering in his ear as the child laughed and giggled. He then reached out his free arm and brought the woman close to him, the three of them standing quietly holding each other for a long moment. He glanced over to de Wolfe, and there seemed to be a small bit of moisture at the corner of Abe's eyes as he let the boy down and once again bowed to the woman.

After that brief moment of tranquility Abe issued a brusque command and mounted his horse as the flag bearer lifted his banner high once again, and they proceeded through the city, a crowd gathering at every street corner, and shop keepers coming out to watch as the grandiose procession passed.

As they neared the northern edge of Nagasaki the houses and shops thinned out, and without any noticeable order being given, the flag bearer began to jog down the road at a moderate pace, followed by the horses at a trot and the others behind them moving just as quickly.

They did not stop for the next five hours.

Sento

De Wolfe had to be helped down from his mount when they briefly paused for the mid-day meal and break. His bottom ached, and his knees were screaming in agony over the unaccustomed outward angle of sitting on horseback.

The column, despite its size and amount of baggage, moved as quickly as light cavalry, and they had already gone a great distance. He had no idea how the small and thin Japanese had accomplished what seemed to be a minor miracle to him. As he had bounced along, each jolt bringing fresh shooting pains, they just continued on and on as if it were no bother to them at all. How could he complain or ask for a stop?

They had kept to the shoreline for most of the morning before turning inland. The path was well traveled, and light bridges had been constructed over streams or gullies as the trail wound around mountains or across meadows. There was a tall peak on their right as they ate a light meal of rice balls and pickled vegetables, but they soon put it behind them as they concluded their brief noon time respite and de Wolfe had planted his sore bottom on the saddle for the afternoon's travel. If they could do it, he could do it, and he had gritted his teeth and kept quiet as they set off again at a jog.

The sun was beginning to disappear before they arrived at a small country inn and Abe called for the column to halt. De Wolfe's agony had increased throughout the afternoon, but this time he was able to painfully drag himself off of the saddle and towards the inn as Abe slid open the paper door and called inside.

Dr. Franz had already circled around and peeked behind the building while the porters began to attend to the horses and settle the baggage for the night. "Hot springs!" Franz called out excitedly, pointing and with his head bobbing up and down with enthusiasm. "It's a *sento!* Hot springs!" he repeated several times and rushed to a wooden building behind the inn.

De Wolfe followed Franz, taking off his boots before stepping inside. An elderly woman was there and the doctor was already stripping off his clothes as she indicated and pantomimed undressing. A bath? A public bath? He had heard of Roman baths, but immersing oneself in hot water could easily allow unhealthful *miasma* – bad air – into the pores. It was simply dangerous to wash any part of the body that could not be seen in public.

But, the doctor seemed not in the least concerned, and if he considered it healthful then de Wolfe would try it also. In any case, it was only Franz and himself. The physician was already buck-naked, holding a towel in front to hide his genitals, as de Wolfe began removing his own clothes with great trepidation and embarrassment. Amused, the old woman roughly helped him undress, directed him towards a small wooden stool, and then took away their clothing.

The doctor was already happily lathering and scrubbing himself clean, rinsed off with hot water from a wooden bucket, and then wincing from the temperature of the water, climbed into a large communal bath carved into the stone and fed to over-flowing by a natural hot spring.

De Wolfe watched to make sure he knew precisely what to do, mimicked Franz's actions complete with the hot water rinse, and then climbed into the tub.

"Hot!" he exclaimed. "Hot! Hot!"

"Do not fight it!" Franz exalted. "Winter is coming soon, and a hot bath is one of the great joys of Japan!" He then began humming a happy tune and sat back to relax in the soothing hot water.

It did feel wonderful, and de Wolfe felt the aches and pains of the long day's road being burned out of his knees and butt.

163

They were suddenly joined by Abe and several others from the procession, who quickly stripped down, washed off, and moved to join them in the tub while one solitary guard stood at the doorway, his hand on his sword hilt. De Wolfe had no idea that others would join them, so he immediately became increasingly more self-conscious of his nakedness as he slid over to make room, but no one else seemed to mind in the slightest.

Scrubbing down next to Abe was the *Chakunan*, but de Wolfe had no idea who the third man was. A samurai? A porter? A complete stranger? The *Chakunan* climbed into the tub and then placed a small white washcloth on top of his head like some silly cock-eyed hat. His action was soon followed by Abe, who put a small towel on his pate, then the other fellow, and then even Franz, all wearing the same ridiculous headdress. De Wolfe, watching the Japanese warily and endeavoring to ensure he would offend no one, placed his own washcloth on top of his head.

For the first time, none of the Japanese looked like a warrior to de Wolfe, especially the *Chakunan*, who seemed simply a harmless grinning teenager. Among the most fearsome swordsmen in the world, they sat in the tub together like happy children. "I have not taken a bath in this manner, especially with someone else, since I was a child," de Wolfe said to Franz.

Franz closed his eyes, sank deeper into the tub, and began to speak mainly to himself, and only partially to de Wolfe. "The Japanese may be different, but not really all that different from us Hollanders are they?"

"I do not see that at all!" countered de Wolfe, just before Franz sank completely below the water, playfully blowing out bubbles.

A Toast

The strange night continued to unfold for de Wolfe. He had been given a light *"yukata"* - an evening kimono - to wear after the bath, then was escorted into a small tatami dining room with multiple low tables. He and Dr. Franz took a table a short space away from the others and, seeing that there were no chairs, took a seat on the soft floor. Within seconds the old woman arrived with hot soup, bottles of *sake*, and various Japanese foodstuffs on a tray.

De Wolfe surveyed the unfamiliar meal, not sure where to begin. He tried the soup, and it was salty and thick. The *sake* was cloudy and unfiltered, but also good. There was some kind of meat on rice in bite-sized portions, so he popped a whole one into his mouth, and then stammered, "This is raw fish!"

"Sushi! Watch out for the green paste," Franz cautioned him. "It will make your eyes water!"

164

He stared at the sushi for a long moment, and then decided that since it was going to be a very long trip, he might as well begin accustoming himself to all things Japanese. Taka had instructed him on how to use the *ohashi*, two thin sticks made of wood in lieu of a fork, to eat his food, so he tucked in and began hungrily eating everything the hostess brought and placed before him.

"Two months or more in the company of that foul man," he said, indicating Abe as he continued eating.

"Abe-*sama*?" Franz asked, barely looking up from his food.

"Yes, Mr. Abe! He is a braggart and a bully. Always strutting and swaggering about as if he were the only one who mattered."

"A braggart? How would you know this? You do not speak his language. Would you insult a man for the manner in which he walks?" Franz countered.

"Well, alright, I admit that is petty," de Wolfe offered defensively. "But, I have seen him to be a bully, and frankly a murderer. I myself witnessed him kill Mr. Kamimoto."

"My dear sir," Franz sighed, setting down his soup bowl. "You may have seen much, but you understand nothing. What you witnessed was an ancient and solemn ceremony of repentance and even forgiveness. The Japanese word is *kaishakunin*, not a murderer, not an executioner, but a trusted second who will faithfully complete the ritual. Abe-*sama* was Mr. Kamimoto's best friend."

"Impossible!" De Wolfe objected.

"Kamimoto specifically selected Abe-*sama* because of their friendship and his skill with a sword. He wanted to ensure that the ceremony was conducted with dignity, skill and compassion."

"Compassion? He nearly chopped his head off."

"Exactly, that is precisely how the ceremony is properly conducted. A less skilled swordsmen might have lopped his head clean off and sent it rolling across the ground staring at all the witnesses. The perfect blow of the sword ended Mr. Kamimoto's suffering and preserved his honor. It was both skillful and compassionate."

"Abe-*sama* was selected by Mr. Kamimoto who implored him to complete the ceremony,' Franz continued. "Do you honestly believe that our warrior friend wanted to be involved in any of that? Kamimoto specifically chose Abe because he was his friend and he trusted him."

Dr. Franz filled his *sake* cup, caught Abe's eye, and toasted him from across the room. Abe smiled, and returned the salute. "And," Franz said with finality, "I trust him too."

The Challenger

From the dining area the sound of the inn's main door sliding open barely registered to the Dutchmen as they sat eating and drinking, but Abe paused in mid-bite, and his hand reached under the low table for his short sword. Words were exchanged in the entrance, and several of the Nagasaki samurai began to notice that something was amiss, but Abe motioned with his hand that they should remain seated.

A figure stepped from the shadows of the hallway and into the dim light, a thin teenager, barely a man, his hair disheveled and his kimono dirty, he surveyed the room until his eyes stopped on Abe.

"Abe Akio! I am Sawabe Keishiro. You cheated me of a fair duel on a beach in Nagasaki. Do you remember?"

"I remember you, the one called Chosensha, the Challenger. Are you here to fight me again?"

"My family has served the Daimyō of Saga for five generations. I defeated four great swordsmen in battle, and established my own fighting school. I was the greatest swordsman in all of Kyūshū. And, you vanquished me with an oar. Because of you I am disgraced, a laughing-stock," he continued. *"My school has closed, My father has commanded me to leave his household, and I am now ronin, a warrior without a master. I have nothing, and it is all because of you!"*

Abe's eyes darkened, *"You were defeated not because of your lack of skill,"* and he poured himself another cup of *sake*. *"But rather your lack of honor. It was not me who defeated you, it was yourself. I bear no responsibility for that."*

"I am not here to fight." The Challenger stepped forward towards the low table.

Abe did not look directly at the wretch standing over him. *"Then, what do you want?"*

"I beg you to take me as your student. Teach me, so that I may learn."

"Learn what?"

"Teach me to fight! Teach me your Way of the Sword."

"Bah!" hissed Abe.

166

"*Then,*" The Challenger went to his knee, "*teach me to be a man.*"

"*I am a swordsman, not a teacher,*" Abe scoffed.

"*Ani,*" the Chakunan interjected, using the term for an older brother. "*if he has come to this result, a homeless vagabond and ronin, perhaps it is also your responsibility. If he wishes to travel until we reach the Tokaidō, let him join us. Perhaps you will both learn something.*"

"*How am I responsible?*" Abe protested.

"*It was your own pride that caused you to accept the challenge.*"

Abe took a deep breath, looked over the thin pitiful figure, and considered for a moment. "*Have you eaten?*"

The young man shook his head to indicate "no".

Abe signaled the innkeeper's wife, and she immediately brought out a bowl of steaming hot noodles and a small cup. Abe slid to the side and beckoned to the Challenger. "*Sit beside me,*" he said, filling the cup with *sake*. "*Let us talk.*"

De Wolfe turned to Franz, "What is that all about?"

"I think that we have just added a new member to our company," Franz speculated, and then resumed his meal.

Fukuoka

Their clothes had been returned to them cleaned and with all the wrinkles carefully smoothed out in the morning. The innkeepers stood on their porch and bowed continuously as the column sorted itself out and the four horsemen mounted up. The Challenger fell in with the other samurai, he had bathed and been given a clean kimono at the inn and his old clothing had been burned. At a shout from Abe the flag bearer once again began jogging, and the procession hustled off as the old man and his elderly wife bowed one last time in farewell.

The column continued with its amazing speed northward, but despite the long days Abe, the *Chakunan* and the Challenger spent several hours together each evening, talking or doing a strange imaginary fighting dance to practice the movements of combat. If they could borrow bamboo practice swords they would fight with those in the gathering gloom, or sometimes even with branches from trees.

In less than four days the procession arrived at the merchant harbor city of Hakata, and the imposing stone barricades of the neighboring Fukuoka Castle. Because of its proximity to Korea the city had been burned multiple times during ancient attacks and the boundaries were still defined by defensive obstacles along the Naka River.

Both of the Dutchmen had been hard-pressed to remain in the saddle during these long days, and desperately looked forward to the hot baths and several bottles of *sake* each evening to replenish their energy. Inside the fortifications of Fukuoka Castle their horses were quickly handled and they were shown to their simple tatami rooms, the bathhouse, and finally a large hall filled with multiple low tables.

Like so many chambers in a Japanese building, this space could be a meeting room, a sleeping room, or a dozen other uses, and tonight it was a celebratory dining room. Abe and a large group sat together chatting and laughing as if they were old friends. De Wolfe and Franz were seated nearby and almost immediately small charcoal burners were brought out and placed on each table along with the ubiquitous hot green tea and several bottles of *sake*, followed by plates of raw and thinly sliced red meat.

"Beef!" de Wolfe exclaimed. "Mr. Abe! Beef?"

"Yes, beef!" Abe shouted back across the room. Chosun way! Beef!"

"Chosun?" Franz pondered. "Why, that's Korea, very near here actually."

De Wolfe began following Abe's example, placing the strips of meat on a metal grill over the coals for a brief time, swirling the hot meat in a salty sauce, and then eating them hungrily. Bowls of steaming rice, dried seaweed, raw cabbage and other dishes kept arriving almost continuously.

"Kamimoto told me that Abe was from Fukuoka, so this is his home?" de Wolfe asked.

"Abe-*sama*!" Franz called across the hall. "Fukuoka home?"

"Yes!" Abe shouted above the noise and began pointing. "Brother, brother, father! Fukuoka family! Fukuoka huzzah!" and he raised his hands high above his head in celebration.

"Fukuoka huzzah!" Franz echoed and then toasted the group.

As the meal progressed two courtesans came into the room, bowed to the guests and one began playing a three stringed instrument, plucking and creating a rhythm while the other played mysterious notes on a flute. The effect was soothing and also fascinating.

It reminded de Wolfe, of course, of the courtesans at Dejima and the manner in which his "gift" had been brought to him so long ago, but even the beauty of Taka paled in comparison to the perfection of these women. Every touch of make-up, every stitch of clothing, every movement seemed sure, confident and practiced. They were a joy to both listen to and to watch.

"And, at one time I believed that they were prostitutes," de Wolfe mused.

"You must be joking, of course," Franz replied. "These are Kyoto-level *Geiko*, Mr. de Wolfe, supreme high-class and not some tea house courtesans! Look at them! They are artisans who have studied and practiced for their entire lives. Would you ask a *prima donna* to sleep with you after the opera merely because she is an entertainer? These *Geiko* are like pieces of fine art!"

"It does remind me of Taka…" de Wolfe began.

"Oh please, stop it! Do not go all melancholy on me. We are hurrying to Edo as quickly as possible, and it will be a long journey, so let us enjoy what we can along the way. Why, look at Abe, he is having a fine time!"

The music had stopped briefly, and one of the *Geiko* was playing a drinking game with the guests as they all gulped small cups of the rice wine.

"They are an odd sort," de Wolfe mused.

"Different yes," Franz chastised him. "I grant you that. But think of them like the knights of old, a strict code of honor and all that."

Again de Wolfe was skeptical.

"Here in Japan, everyone has their own social class," Franz explained. "Have you wondered why some of the samurai walk while Abe, the *Chakunan* and we both have horses? Abe and the other are 'high samurai', and they are entitled to ride and to wear full armor in battle. The ones that walk, well they are 'low samurai' still warriors though, and much higher than farmers or peasants."

"What of that new fellow?" de Wolfe indicated the Challenger.

"Yes, bit of a mystery that one, isn't he? Something to do between him and Abe. But he does carry two swords."

"What do you mean by 'two swords'?" de Wolfe inquired.

"One sword can be carried by a merchant, not that they are really fighters or samurai at all. But, they have begun buying titles for themselves and then having one

169

shorter sword to show off their rank. No good at all in a scuffle. The ones with two swords, those are the ones that you must watch out for."

"The one thing that all true samurai share," Franz continued, "they are warriors. That is, from boyhood they must constantly be preparing for death, to meet death face-to-face in accordance with *Bushidō* - their code of honor - in an instant without fear of success or failure. To strike! To strike in accordance with the principals of *Bushidō*. That is what is most important. But, as you say Mr. de Wolfe," he concluded, "a very odd sort."

The Road North

In the morning they were loaded onto three separate ferries that carried the procession the short distance separating the islands of *Kyūshū* and *Honshū*, soon arriving at the seaside town of Shimonoseki. They spent the next week working their way northward, sometimes along the shore and sometimes through hills, but they always kept the mountains on their left and the ocean on their right. The path was easy to follow, and they stayed the night in several larger towns and cities; including Hiroshima,

The routine of each day was the same: Up before dawn with clean washed clothing, tea and a light meal. Hours of quick travel, then an all too brief stop for what was called a *bentō* – a lunch box - filled with rice and a variety of other foods packed by the previous night's innkeepers, then back on the path until the sun was near setting. The inns were established at regular intervals to allow for a day's journey, but the column was traveling so quickly that they would frequently by-pass several each day.

While the group bathed and rested in the evening, Abe, the *Chakunan* and the Challenger continued to conduct sword practice, sometimes one against another, and sometimes two-on-one. Then, in the evenings the three of them would share their own table and talk in low tones until well after everyone else had gone to sleep.

It was after the group had passed through the city of Okayama one early morning, when they came upon a small village and, in a nearby field, a crying woman. She was in her mid-thirties, and obviously a farmer's wife wearing a broad hat to shield her from the sun, but still with a very dark complexion and heavily calloused hands. The prostrate figure that she stood weeping over was almost certainly her husband. The simple houses and gardens behind them were tidy, but unremarkable. Like tens of thousands of other farmers working in fields and villages across the globe, they were simple people earning a hard living from the earth with their labor.

Dr. Franz unbundled his stiff and sore limbs from the saddle, quickly searched through his baggage for the medical kit, and examined the unconscious figure as everyone waited.

"They didn't want him dead," Franz called back, and soon had the man sitting up. "Abe-*sama!*" he shouted, and waved to him with his palm facing downwards to come over. "*Abe-sama, nan desu ka?*"

"*What has happened here?*" Abe asked the woman brusquely.

"*Bandits!*" the fear still ringing in her voice. "*Bastard bandits! They came this morning and most of the farmers were able to run away into the fields, but they caught the two of us.*"

The husband shook his head to clear it, his voice still weak. "*They demanded everything. Food enough for five days and any money or other valuables we have. We are to tell the entire village. They will return tomorrow, and if we trick them or hide anything they will burn our houses and murder everyone.*"

"*We can ask your Daimyō to send samurai,*" Abe suggested.

"*From where? We are too far from the Daimyō of Hirama or the tenryō of Osaka. There is no one near enough. Won't you help us? Won't you drive them off, or kill them? Please, can you stay until tomorrow?*" the woman begged.

"*We are on an important journey to Edo for the Capitão-sama of Dejima,*" Abe shook his head. "*We cannot be delayed.*"

Franz helped the man to his feet, "*Will you ask the Capitão-sama? We beg you to help us,*" the farmer implored Abe.

Abe pointed to de Wolfe waiting. "*There is the Capitão-sama of Dejima, the Hollander.*"

"*Yes, please ask the Hollander, ask him to help us. Please! We beg of you. Stay with us until tomorrow.*"

Abe walked to de Wolfe, followed by Franz. "Tomorrow bandit farmer kill," Abe struggled to find the words. He drew a circle in the air with his hand. "Tomorrow, you no go Edo." De Wolfe had no idea what he was talking about and shook his head.

"I believe that they are asking us to protect them from bandits," Franz explained. "They want us to stay here."

"But, we don't have a moment to lose," de Wolfe protested. "No, we cannot. We must continue."

"Mr. de Wolfe," Franz pointed out, "I ask you to re-consider. Yes, we must hurry, but think about these poor people. Can't we sacrifice one day? We must help them!"

171

"One day?" De Wolfe got down from his horse, looking slightly ashamed. "You are correct doctor, and I am sorry for my hesitation. Yes, of course we must help them. Mr. Abe! Please tell them 'tomorrow we no go Edo'. We stay, we help."

"Good!" Abe grunted. "The Hollander says that we may stay and help you. How many bandits are there?" he asked the farmer.

"At least four, and possibly more. They are ronin, they have swords."

"Only four? Bah! Take everyone to the next inn and wait for us there," Abe instructed the Chakunan. Chosensha! Challenger! Stay here with me." He turned to the Dutchmen, "You go. You wait. We fight."

As the column moved away, Abe and the Challenger followed the farmers into the village.

Bandits

The next morning the villagers tried to go about their normal routine, but there was a stiffness of anticipation and fear in their actions. The men were working in the nearby fields, and kept looking up in anticipation. The women were cooking on low fires, but no one wanted to get too far from the shelter of the houses and small gardens.

It was mid-morning when the first bandit was sighted, slinking among the trees of the forest like a dog returning to lap vomit. He moved with practiced stealth, and soon it was possible to see three others moving in the woods behind. When there was no more cover they formed into a group and cautiously advanced into the village.

"Farmers!" the bandit cried out. "Farmers, come in from the fields and out of your houses." He may have once been a large and proud warrior, someone who had enjoyed regular meals and hot sake, but that was years ago. Now he was a hungry man with little to lose, and there was a wretched desperation in his voice borne of want rather than greed. The village was poor, but these men were desperate and impoverished.

Slowly the villagers gathered, and soon the group of four armed men were facing the entire population of thirty or so. They were ragged from the ground up, starting with worn sandals and filthy threadbare kimono. Their faces and even their hair were squalid, while leaves, twigs and dirt from the forest still clung to them here and there. They were obviously starving and had slept in the woods with no shelter. The first bandit called out, "Where is our food? Where is our payment?"

Abe appeared out of a house on the left, calmly slid into his sandals and joined the villagers. On the right side, the Challenger came out and stood in front, shielding the farmers, as the bandits moved to form their own line and pulled their swords from the scabbards.

There was no challenge, no warning, and the first bandit lifted his sword and charged forward, only to be instantly knocked down by the Challenger's flashing blade. The three remaining marauders stepped back, unsure of what to do next. They had not anticipated any resistance, and had no real plan.

"Kneel!" Abe commanded, and the three remaining bandits instantly dropped down.

"I am Sawabe Keishiro!" the Challenger shouted. "And, the only fit outcome for bandits is death!"

"We know who you are," one of the threadbare vagabonds spit out, "we are not afraid of you or of death. I am Watanabe from Kumamoto and your family is from Saga. Look at your clean clothes and your full belly. We are dirty and we are hungry, and if we are bandits it is because of you!"

"Because of me? Impossible!"

"Two years ago you killed our master in a duel for sport. Since then no other lord would hire us, and we have become ronin. What were we to do? Do you believe that we want to threaten and rob farmers? This is the only way we can survive."

"You could have become monks!" Abe observed.

"Monks? Begging from village to village for our rice? No, I would rather be a thief or dead. I was born better than that! We are swordsmen, and we will live by the blade or we will die by it. I will not spend my life as a monk, or as a farmer or as a merchant, I am samurai and I will die like one. We have nothing else to live for."

"The penalty for your crimes is death," the Challenger growled.

"I told you that we are beyond fear now. Death can be no worse than what we have become."

Abe pulled his long sword from his belt and walked behind the kneeling man. "You will die as a samurai?"

"Yes!" Watanabe spat out, bowing his head in resignation.

"Or, will you live like one?"

"What are you saying?" the bandit asked desperately.

173

"It is really a very simple question. If you have the courage to die as a samurai, do you have the strength to live as one? You are ronin, samurai without a leader, without honor and without purpose." Abe turned to the Challenger. "And Chosensha, you also have lost everything and are ronin. Are you now ready to become a man?"

Abe walked to the three bandits, and one by one helped them to their feet. "This village is far from the Daimyō's protection, and there are many others like it. They need men who will protect them from the real bandits of the world. Respectable men who will fight. Honorable samurai."

"You would spare bandits?" one of the farmers asked, still unsure.

"I see no bandits here, I only see samurai who live without purpose. They are only ronin because they have no purpose, and they have no leader. Give them a purpose." He directed them to the Challenger, "this man is the finest swordsman in all of Kyūshū, will you follow him?"

"How would we live?" the Challenger objected, surprised at the idea but already considering the outcome.

"I will not beg!" Watanabe told Abe.

"Earning rice is far different from begging for it, but you will need some things that rice alone cannot provide." Abe opened his kimono and lifted out the money belt, counting dozens of the gold and silver Tokugawa coinage. "This is your start, and I would suggest a bath and some new clothing! You may ask the villagers for food, but never demand it. Help them, protect them, and they will provide for you."

Several of the villagers nodded their agreement. "We need protection, and you would be most welcome to visit us often," the farmer confirmed.

Abe looked around at the two groups and grunted "good!" in satisfaction. It was time to go. He bowed to the three armed men, the villagers, then to Chosensha.

"The 'greatest swordsman in all of Kyūshū'?" the Challenger smiled.

"I have always believed so," Abe smiled back. "For the man who knows why he swings his sword is always greater than the man who only knows how to."

"Thank you teacher," and the Challenger bowed deeply to Abe. "I believe that we have found a worthy purpose."

"I will speak to the Daimyō of Hirama and tell him of the service you are providing. Perhaps one day he will choose to take you all into his household."

The samurai again bowed to Abe as he turned to go north, and the farmer's wife went back to her cooking and soon brought back three bowls of rice and vegetables for the famished men.

It was after dark when Abe arrived at the evening's inn, and the Dutchmen had already bathed and were eating dinner. "Do you suppose they killed the bandits?" de Wolfe asked.

"Oh, I suppose so," Franz noted. "Now where's the thin one gotten off to?"

"I don't have the slightest idea," and de Wolfe turned back to his food.

Kyoto

De Wolfe was beginning to feel that he knew Japan, at least until they arrived at the ancient capital of Kyoto and he then realized how sophomoric and superficial his knowledge really was. He had thought the governmental compound in Nagasaki had been grand, Kyoto's dwarfed it. He had thought that Fukuoka Castle had been impressive, but Ni-Jo Castle was infinitely grander. He had thought that the small shrines he had seen along the way were quaint, but Kyoto contained well over one thousand shrines and temples both large and small.

Ni-Jo Castle had been built as the Winter residence of the original *Shōgun* Tokugawa Ieyasu, both for his comfort and as a clear demonstration of his power and authority. Its pure white walls were capped with black tiles, and rose above massive stone walls that were protected by a moat. Several bridges crossed the moat into the castle, and could be blocked by huge yet elaborate wooden gates which were muscled closed each night by a crew of soldiers, and opened the next morning. The grounds inside the compound were spacious and contained well-tended ornamental gardens as well as groves of plum and cherry trees.

My God, de Wolfe contemplated, if this is just the old palace, what must Edo look like? Amsterdam's palace and Paris' broad boulevards were magnificent, but he had never seen such an impressive, and yet heavily fortified building in his life, and had no idea they even still existed.

Abe spent that first night in meetings somewhere deep in the bowels of Ni-jo Castle, and de Wolfe and Franz ate alone in their room. The Nagasaki delegation would spend two nights at the castle resting and preparing for the trip to Edo via the *Tokaidō*, and no one seemed to mind if they stayed within the compound or went, so the Dutchmen took the opportunity to view the splendors of this Japanese wonderland rather than to rest.

Not far away was *Kinkaku-Ji*, the Golden Pavilion – completely covered in gold leaf, and elegantly set off in a reflecting pond at the temple's base. In the garden was a single white pine in the shape of a sailing ship that was over four hundred years old, and was tended like the most precious of jewels.

Built into the mountainside on the eastern edge of the city was the *Kiyomizu-dera* Temple. From the building's veranda, built high up on thick wooden columns, they could see the entire city laid out before them, sparkling in the early twilight as lanterns were lit in front of restaurants.

They walked back in the darkness towards Ni-Jo Castle from the west and crossed the *Kamo* River and passed into the entertainment district of *Gion*. Ahead there was a crowd moving slowly down the road, and as they caught up they could see the elegant outline of a senior *Geisha*, even more impressive than the two entertainers they had seen in Fukuoka. She was walking delicately with two armed samurai as escorts, and everyone was staring, Japanese and Dutchmen alike. She moved with both regal grace and bearing. This was her district in her town, and none could ignore her. She smiled politely and slightly dipped her head to those following her as she discreetly slipped into a restaurant and her two attendants waited outside.

De Wolfe stood quietly for several moments reflecting on the depth and beauty of Japanese culture that he had never imagined. And, he knew so little of it. "We should go," he finally said. "Tomorrow is the *Tokaidō*."

A Conversation in Dutch

The coastal ship from Kyushu that had brought Taka to Edo had been small but fast. It was used to carry important documents and small items between the farthest reaches of the island kingdom, and adding one passenger was unusual, but not difficult, and had taken only days. She had never been on the ocean before and the sweet smell of the land as they hugged the coast northbound and the beautiful vistas were captivating. It had been an incredible vantage point to really appreciate how large and alluring her country really is. The seamen were rough and it was difficult to maintain either your privacy or your decency in such cramped quarters, but they had given her as much courtesy as possible. Especially considering that she was a prisoner.

It had been difficult to leave the boy in Nagasaki, but there was no choice and the *Obugyō-sama's* wife and daughters had assured her that he would be safe in their care and had helped her pack a small bag for the long journey. No one knew when, or even if, she might return.

She had been welcomed at Edo Castle and even treated kindly. There had been glimpses of the *Shōgun* as he moved about the castle, but no one of authority had questioned or even spoken to her. She was largely ignored.

Taka spent her days with the ladies of the court and was invited to attend events in the evening including the most spectacular Nōh presentations, and at other times delicate concerts. She was also provided with beautiful clothing and delicious food, and she often had to remind herself that she was a prisoner rather than a guest. No, not a prisoner, a hostage.

The ladies of the court were kind, but she found them to be quite tedious after a few days. They wore the most expensive kimono, they ate the most fabulous foods, they were invited to the most refined theatre, and yet all they seemed to know was political gossip and they excelled at it. If the men of Japan were the world's finest swordsmen through constant practice and dedication, then the women must be the world's best busy-bodies. Their weapons were a word or a phrase, sometimes the mention of a simple proverb or a glance.

Fall weather was wonderful, and she would often sit in the shade in the garden. The other women avoided the sun, careful not to darken their skin in the slightest, but she adored the warmth and the quiet.

The old man had been watching her from a distance for several minutes before he walked over and bowed slightly then kneeled with her before introducing himself with a simple, *"I am Suzuki"*.

"Should I call you Lord or teacher?"

"I am Suzuki-Otona."

That was an unexpected puzzle, and Taka considered carefully before going any further. Otona could have many interpretations, but the most obvious to her was an overseer at Dejima. But he did not have a Kyushu accent. It was not an Edo accent either, and she could not quite place it. Suddenly it seemed to her quite important to be cautious.

"It is a pleasure to meet you, Suzuki-Otona. You must be from Dejima in Nagasaki."

"Yes, I was, long ago. Perhaps you knew Kamimoto-Otona? I brought him onto Dejima as a youth, a dirty small boy from a disgraced family running the streets and begging for food. I raised him as my own son, and when I departed he was my replacement."

"You showed him great kindness."

"I showed him discipline, and discipline grows to duty and duty becomes love. Although I now understand that he has met with a rather tragic ending. Too bad, but as it is said 'The child of a frog is a frog".

"You knew his parents?

177

"Let us say that I knew his mother quite well," the old man looked at her for a long moment. *"Were you there when he died?"*

"No, I was not," Taka answered truthfully. *"But, I believe he greeted death with dignity and honor."*

"Well, as I said, it was a very long time ago and very far away." They sat in silence for a moment before Suzuki began again. *"And you have a son with the Hollander?"*

"In Nagasaki, yes."

"The Dutchmen are on the Tokaidō now, and you will be with him soon."

"In Edo?"

"In death," Suzuki answered grimly. *"The foreigners will be dead within the day and you will soon follow him. You were brought here as a token in a game, and if there is no game then there is no further need of tokens."*

Taka refused to be intimidated, but now her suspicion had been confirmed, this conversation could have lethal consequences. *"Have you come here to threaten me?"*

"Of course not. I came here to give you the truth. I understand that you are a Christian, and I believed that you might desire some time for preparations as the result may come far swifter than you can possibly imagine."

"The Capitão-sama has done nothing wrong, why would he be killed?"

"He is a foreigner, and that is enough. A Japanese patriot must hate all outsiders, and sometimes you must use poison to overcome poison."

"But, is not it also true that if you hate a man you should let him live?"

"You are truly a clever girl. However, the issue is not a man, but rather the fate of Japan. A few men dying to save a country, is that not a sacrifice worth making? He will die, and then you will die as you will no longer have any value to the Shōgun or to anyone else."

Suzuki rose slowly and with slight difficulty before continuing in Dutch. "And, your bastard son will die also," he said with a smile.

The words stung Taka deeply but she refused to let any recognition betray her understanding or feelings and she smiled back at him blankly. *"I don't understand,"* she replied in Japanese, working hard to look confused.

"Of course you don't," Suzuki continued. "You really are only an empty-headed little creature, are you not? And such a pity. I was so looking forward to having a conversation in Dutch." Still seeing no recognition on her face he bowed and reverted back to Japanese, *"I am not sure that I will meet you again,"* finally turning to go.

"Suzuki-Otona," Taka called after him.

"Yes?" the old man turned and hesitated.

"One who has lived so many years should have far more wisdom than to make empty threats to a woman. You may soon learn that the Hollander is far more clever and difficult to kill than you can possibly imagine. I will soon be with him. You will be long dead, water will be placed to your lips and I will be happy myself to pay the six coins for your passage across the Sanzu River before any harm will come to the Dutchmen."

Suzuki scowled, grunted, and turned away walking quickly.

De Wolfe was in danger Taka now knew, and she had no way to warn him or to protect him. Well, she had no way to protect herself either.

Duty

The long path to Kyoto had been grueling, it had taken several days for de Wolfe to become accustomed to the rapid pace, and he now felt that he was ready for the Tokaidō. He was wrong. The roadway was broader and better maintained, so from before dawn until after dusk they rushed, stopping for the mid-day meal only briefly, the porters and samurai panting from hours of jogging, and then hurried on again. Throughout the day they would pass slower-moving groups who would step aside to clear the way, and then resume marching behind them in the column's dust. Some days they would skip past two or even three roadway inns before settling in, using every available bit of light to continue moving north. Franz would look sideways at each inn with longing, and then turn forward again in the saddle as it rapidly receded behind them.

The journey north had taken them for nearly a week along the familiar ocean side, with ever larger mountains to their left through Nagoya and into Izu, and the procession was moving briskly but wearily after a long day, pushing on to the next inn. The flag bearer jogged ahead, and following him was the implacable Abe who never seemed to change his expression or position throughout the interminable days. They had entered an area of hills and thickets, and the sun was just beginning to set behind the mountains on the west.

Abe abruptly pulled up his mount, creating a cloud of dust as it whinnied and kicked from the sudden pull on the reins. On a hill, silhouetted against the setting sun and perfectly outlined in the bright glow was an astonishing figure. It seemed larger than life and was completely covered in armor constructed of bamboo staves woven together with silk ribbons, leather scales bound together by stout macramé cords, and carefully molded lacquer plates each brightly colored in red.

The headgear was the most astonishing. There was a metal helmet with two highly polished horns reaching skyward, and fully covering the neck both front and back were more fitted lengths of bamboo. The face was completely hidden by a dark red lacquerware mask with glaring eyes, an impossibly large nose, and a scowling mouth. From under the helmet long white tufts of hair protruded along the cheeks, and a matching mane flowed out the back. The effect was supernatural and imposing. The entire procession stopped to stare.

A single samurai wearing a light blue kimono with symmetrical embroidery of a white blossom on the left breast stepped from the brush and bamboo in front of the flag bearer, blocking the path ahead.

"You are ordered to immediately surrender the foreigners!" he snarled.

There was temporary confusion along the procession as the *Chakunan* jumped off of his horse and raced to the front, his hand on his sword hilt. *"Clear the roadway!* he commanded.

The single samurai placed his hand on his own sword. *"Get down! Know your place! Kneel before my lord!"*

"This is the Capitão-sama of Dejima!" the *Chakunan* countered. *"We have the Shōgun's permission and authority to freely travel the Tokaidō!"*

The single samurai stepped forward, placing the *Chakunan* well within the reach of a swipe from his long sword. *"We know who you are,"* his voice a low and threatening growl. He pointed at de Wolfe and Franz, *"And, we know who they are. You cannot protect them!"*

The *Chakunan* flashed his long sword from the scabbard, and stopped it a hand's width from the single samurai's face. They stood frozen like that for a long moment, and then with a single shout a dozen samurai, all wearing the same style of light-blue kimono leapt from their hiding places by the roadside.

Screaming his own war cry back, the *Chakunan* slashed at the sword arm of the man in front of him, and then rushed single-handedly into the opposing group of warriors slashing and thrusting, driving them apart.

It immediately became a confused, disorienting and deadly melee. From behind de Wolfe the remaining six samurai on foot rushed forward, and the battle immediately devolved into a strange mixture of aggression and caution. A single blow from the razor sharp *katana* could be fatal, and it was an intense brawl of glinting steel, strained grunts and calls, and rising dust from sandaled feet. One of Abe's men was struck down, and the *Chakunan* was hit with a glancing blow that cut deeply into his leg. The ebb and flow of the struggle brought the fight towards the procession, and the flag bearer and porters retreated out of the way, the baggage dropped and quickly forgotten along the side of the path.

There was now an ever smaller Nagasaki group defending, and despite the number of blue-clad bodies littering the ground or limping away, they were unable to hold the pathway from the numerical superiority of the attackers. Abe entered the fray, his horse spinning and kicking, well trained in combat, until he was pulled down, and continued to fight viciously on the ground. The Nagasaki men were losing the skirmish.

De Wolfe leapt down from his horse and rushed to the discarded baggage, frantically sorting through until he pulled out the gifts for the *Shōgun* and extracted the ornate box with the eagle on the front and quickly began loading the pistols. The sword-play raged on just steps away as he finished loading and stood up, one in each hand.

The Hollander stepped forward and discharged a round directly into the face of one attacker who dropped, clutching his eye in a cloud of blue smoke and the roar of the discharge. Pointing with both hands he set off two shots simultaneously, knocking two more down and shrouding the battlefield with the haze from the black powder. Stunned by the noise and smoke, the battle paused for a moment and everything went quiet as both sides stepped back breathing hard.

"Kill him!" screamed an attacker and charged towards de Wolfe as Abe's men fought to protect the Dutchman and he leveled the pistols, firing again and again. He knocked down two more, and then killed another only an instant before he would have delivered a fatal blow to Abe's unprotected back. He then kept methodically firing into the attackers with the pistol in his left hand and then the one in his right, wounding several more as the fray waned before him. The tide of battle had now shifted back to the defenders.

"Stop!" The apparition they had seen silhouetted on the hill appeared on horseback above the melee. *"Stop!"* he commanded.

The remaining swordsmen on both sides drew back a few paces, sweating and gasping for breath while the dead lay in the dust and the dying groaned in agony. Through the lingering smoke the armored warrior dismounted and stepped in front of Abe, face-to-face.

"Only these foreign devils must die today," he began. *"Give them to me and justice will be done."*

"They are under the protection of the Shōgun, and you are a bastard bandit!" Abe snapped back.

"A bandit?" the unworldly apparition laughed, *"Don't you know your better when you see him? I am here to protect Japan. I am here to preserve Bushidō! You are here herding sheep."*

De Wolfe had retreated to the baggage, and was quickly re-loading the pistols. "What are they saying doctor?"

"I have absolutely no idea," Franz stammered. "But, I am certain that it is not good."

"We will cut you all down like dogs!" The armored warrior announced to the group, and a dozen more fresh samurai wearing the blue kimono stepped from the brush.

"Fate will determine who lives and who dies here, not your boasts!" Abe sneered back. *"I am happy to die in battle! Bring more of your men! Bring them all!"*

De Wolfe finished reloading the pistols and stepped forward to stand shoulder-to-shoulder with Abe.

The armored man noted the loaded guns, but ignored the implied threat. *"Foreigners are infecting our country, and bring nothing we need, only death and destruction. Do you honor the emperor? Do you obey the Shōgun? I am here to end the infection."*

"We travel under the protection of the Shōgun." Abe reiterated.

De Wolfe slowly raised his right arm, pointing the weapon directly into the red mask before them. Abe stepped in front of de Wolfe, blocking his target and his shot.

"No gun!" Abe commanded.

De Wolfe waved the gun, indicating that Abe should step aside.

"No gun!" Abe insisted.

De Wolfe lowered the pistol, and Abe turned back to his attacker. *"Will you fight me for them?"* he demanded.

"I will kill you for them," came the response, a slight lilt in the voice, muffled by the mask.

"Sunrise?"

"Agreed. Prepare your last letter to your family, or perhaps a death poem you will read?" the voice from the mask sneered. Commands were given, and the attackers vanished back into the brush, dragging their dead and wounded away.

Dr. Franz rushed to the *Chakunan* to staunch the gash in his leg. He quickly checked the others, and one was plainly dead, two more wounded. They were down to just four uninjured men to protect the column. The sun completed setting, and there were only a few moments of dusk left before full darkness.

We Can Escape

The moon had not yet risen, and the procession was huddled in the black night against the gathering mountain chill, sharing what little food had been left over from the mid-day meal. One of the porters was soon able to light a small fire, and they all gathered around seeking its warmth, but also some reassurance of normality and that they might all survive. It was the first uncomfortable night they would have to spend on the roadway without the cherished benefits of a hot bath, fresh food and clean clothes.

De Wolfe was desperately trying to communicate to Abe despite the crippling language barrier between them. "We can escape in the darkness," he insisted. "Why would we wait here to fight and be killed?"

"No," Abe countered, pulling his kimono tightly across his chest. "We go, they follow. We stay, I fight."

"That makes no sense at all! We are under the *Shōgun*'s protection, if we can find a city or an outpost, we will be safe."

"Samurai come from city."

"Rebels, yes, I understand. But there must be others that will obey the *Shōgun*."

"Many samurai hate Hollanders. Hate all foreigners. All foreigners bring trouble."

"But, not the Hollanders. We bring only trade. We bring only medicine. We bring good."

"Hollanders bring guns. Samurai no need guns. You understand?"

"Guns can be used to defend what is right. To protect yourself. Doctor," de Wolfe was growing exasperated, "will you please help him to understand?"

"Let's just hope that red faced fellow doesn't come back," Franz offered.

"Hope? Hope is not a plan! We must have a plan!"

"Alright then, here is the plan. Let Abe-*sama* do what he was born to do Mr. de Wolfe," Franz bowed his head in resignation. "Let him fight."

"Fight? And, if he loses? What then?"

"Use gun," Abe replied. "You understand?"

De Wolfe looked around, and everyone was settling in for the long dark night. In the morning their fates would be determined. Win or lose. "Oh, I will use the gun," de Wolfe assured the Japanese warrior. "I will."

Sunrise

They had used the little fire to heat tea, and sometime during the night a light rain fell, preventing de Wolfe from getting much sleep at all. He had propped his head up on a saddle, bundled himself as best he could, and endured until the first faint glow began to appear off over the ocean.

As the sun rose everyone could clearly see the armored figure in a clearing on the hill above, fully illuminated and standing menacingly in silence in the growing light. The sight was both magnificent and terrifying, and the Dutchmen could not help but stare.

Off to the side of the road was Abe, his head on his own saddle, and he appeared to still be sleeping. Franz looked at him, his eyes shut and his face serene and muttered, "You better have your pistols ready."

Finally, Abe opened one eye and called out, *"Oh, it is a beautiful morning!"* and yawned. He began to move slowly as the minutes passed, and finally rose, *"Is there any hot tea?"*

The morning progressed, each moment passing with an almost painful intensity while Abe sat drinking his tea and eating a cold meager breakfast, and the figure on the hill became more and more impatient. The red masked man began to pace back and forth angrily, like a caged tiger, and then started to shout taunts down the hill.

"Coward! Where are you? Have you forgotten our appointment? Are you afraid to die? Will you come and fight me?"

Abe listened to the taunts and smiled, *"Beautiful morning!"* he repeated.

The sun continued to rise, and the air was warming rapidly as the mists burned off, and the armored samurai continued to pace as his fury increased. Soon he was slashing at phantom enemies, taking a fighting stance and slaying invisible opponents by the dozen as Abe continued to slowly chew and drink tea and everyone else watched with growing alarm.

Abe finished his breakfast, wiped his mouth on his sleeve and walked over to piss in the bushes as the armored samurai continued to shout and rant from a distance. Finally Abe came over to de Wolfe. "I die, you kill many samurai. Then you die good." He then pulled a long white headband from the sleeve of his kimono, tied it tightly across his forehead, and began walking up the hill.

The armored man on the hill was furious, *"We agreed on dawn, and the sun is long risen! Coward! I might have given you mercy, but no longer. Prepare yourself for death!"*

Abe removed his *katana* from his waist, threw the scabbard aside, and smiled. *"Even monkeys fall from trees."*

They were evenly matched master swordsmen, moving carefully and maintaining their distance. The slightest miscalculation in timing or space would be met with a slash or parry and possible death. Like dancers linked by an invisible string they circled and shifted, neither striking, each waiting for an opening that would not expose a counter-strike.

The heavy armor protected the red masked fighter, and his first feints and blows were swift and strong but also constricted. Abe moved lightly and easily, darting here and there around his opponent flicking in lightly, probing the openings between the lacquered plates and bamboo staves, hitting often but never finding flesh. Momentum shifted from one warrior to the other, each gaining and then losing advantage.

Soon however the man behind the dark red mask began to pant, his breath more and more labored and the heat under the armor building in the morning sun. He had used so much energy in his anger and carrying the burden of his artificial carapace that now he was quickly weakening.

Abe saw his opening and leapt forward, closing the gap, the tip of his flashing sword point skittering off the helmet, and briefly locking on one of the ornamental protruding horns. The armored man swung upward and off balance, but Abe had already freed his sword and skipped backward and away.

The mask dipped down, the eyeholes dark slits, seemingly occupied by nothing, but sweat dripped off of the lower edge and into the dry dirt, deep ragged breathing coming from behind the grotesque artificial visage.

Abe attacked again, now raining multiple swift blows from various angles, and each was skillfully blocked or deflected until several crashed through the protection of the sword and against the hard armor, scratching its surface, but unable to penetrate beyond. Stumbling back the armored samurai lost his balance, his sword moved outside its protective vector, and he fought to remain upright.

Abe's right foot lashed out, striking directly in the center of the chest armor and knocking his opponent onto his back on the ground. The Nagasaki samurai pinned the heavy armor down with his foot, shifting his weight and pushing hard as he probed his sword point around the bamboo staves protecting the neck until it penetrated, and then he used both hands to push it through and into the earth behind. Blood welled up from the mouth of the mask as the body thrashed and tremored, held in place by Abe's foot and the sword. Then, it became quiet.

Abe lifted the dark red visor, and the man behind it was handsome and in his early twenties. He spoke with his dying breath, his whisper hoarse and labored, *"Why do you protect these animals?*

"It is my duty."

Abe pulled his sword from his opponent's throat and wiped it on the dead man's pants leg. He picked up the sword the armored samurai had dropped on the ground and inspected it for damage. He plucked the scabbard and *wakizashi* short sword from the body, admired them briefly, and then shoved them into his own belt.

He stripped the headgear off of the corpse, pulled the head upward by the hair, and decapitated the lifeless body. He held the head at arm's length above his shoulder and shouted, *"I am Abe Akio, the eldest son of Abe Tadamichi of Fukuoka!"*

He glared at the hillside, although no one else could be seen, and tossed the head beside the body. He picked up his own scabbard, returned to the waiting procession, and walked directly to de Wolfe.

"His duty, my duty, same. You understand?"

"Was it his duty to murder innocent men?" de Wolfe asked.

"No! His duty, protect Japan. You blame he die."

"You hold me responsible for his death? What did I do?"

"You Hollander, understand? Good samurai fight, die here today because of you."

"No! I do not understand," de Wolfe protested.

Abe walked to the *Chakunan*, and inspected with satisfaction the bandages that Franz had tightly tied around the wounded leg, and patted his arm approvingly. He turned to Franz, "Thank you. He big man. Son of *Obugyō-sama* of Nagasaki"

"The eldest son of the *Obugyō-sama*?" Franz asked to confirm.

"Yes. One day he *Obugyō-sama*." Abe eyed de Wolfe, and then handed the Hollander his two swords, the shorter *wakizashi* and the long *katana,* the very weapon he had used to kill Kamimoto. "Yesterday, you fight good. My sword you keep. You remember. I remember."

De Wolfe had never heard Abe speak so much Dutch, had believed that the Japanese man could barely understand or even speak their language. He pushed the swords through his own belt, swung up on his horse, and the column once again prepared to continue their journey to Edo.

Monstrosity

The wounded men and the one dead body were loaded onto the spare horses, and they continued their rapid pace northward. To the west they began to see a tall cone like mountain that had snow on the top, even this late in the season and despite the hot weather. As they approached it seemed ever taller and perfectly symmetrically shaped with thick forests along its flanks. It was truly spectacular.

They had stopped at the first inn, and left the three casualties to rest and the corpse for cremation. They collected some cold rice balls and paused briefly at mid-day to gulp them down, but everyone was anxious to get to the city of Hakone and out of Izu and its samurai with the light-blue kimono. De Wolfe had kept the ornate box with the pistols inside nearby, in case any of the dead man's friends or relatives might accost them seeking revenge. But, the road had been quiet.

In the late afternoon they climbed a hillside that offered a view of the inactive volcano, and both de Wolfe and Franz were breathing heavily as they crested the top on foot, leading their horses. De Wolfe was the first up and shouted over his shoulder, "Dr. Franz! An ancient volcano! It's Fuji volcano! We are almost to Edo! Hurry up! Dr. Franz!"

Below him Franz was standing stock still, staring out to sea. In the distance was a black-hulled side-wheeled steamship cruising leisurely offshore. Although it had three masts, no sails were raised, and dark oily coal soot belched from a single smokestack.

"What can that monstrosity possibly be?" Franz asked in both wonder and disgust.

"They are burning coal to drive the ship."

"How is such a thing possible? Where could such an abomination have come from?"

The wind shifted, and on the stern of the vessel was a standard with alternating red and white stripes and, barely discernable so far away, in the upper corner a smudge of dark.

"It's the Americans," de Wolfe responded grimly.

Edo

They had spent the night at an inn on a sedate lake in Hakone, surrounded by lush forests and the looming volcano at their backs in the distance. Franz had no idea how many species of trees there were, but counted red pines, cypress, cedars and beech. The countryside was mountainous and beautiful, and under other circumstances would have been greatly admired, but Edo was ahead and they pushed on before dawn.

The pace had been quick for the past two weeks, but now became brutal with both Abe and de Wolfe urging each other and everyone else to go faster. They spent less than six hours resting at Yokohama, before beginning the final push into Edo.

By mid-afternoon they entered farmlands surrounding the city, and Abe paused the procession for an inspection as the flag bearer and porters caught their breath and the straps on the baggage were readjusted. Everyone washed their faces and hands, and as much as possible dust was brushed off their clothing. Abe tightened the column, and they began to march into the city.

They were soon joined by other groups entering Edo, each distinguished by the color and embroidery on their kimonos. Some of them were resplendent in bright greens and purples with huge retinues, and others looked small and drab. Abe remained straight upright on his horse as they moved forward, neither looking to his left or right, his three remaining samurai marching behind him.

The *Bugyo-shō* of Nagasaki permanently maintained a large house in Edo as did many of the three hundred regional *Daimyō* located throughout Japan. It was important to clearly demonstrate their allegiance and to have a comfortable place for close relatives to stay as "guests", although some might consider them hostages, of the *Shōgunate*.

Although the Nagasaki House had its own kitchens and multiple sleeping rooms, they used a nearby public bath that evening, and Abe had ordered it cleared of all other patrons. After washing the road grime away Abe, de Wolfe and Franz settled into the hot tub to soak. They had completed the long and arduous journey from Kyūshū to Edo in less than half the time normally required.

"Mr. Abe," de Wolfe began, "our meeting with the *Shōgun* is most serious and important, and everything must go exactly as I say, do you understand?"

"Uumph," Abe grunted.

"First, we will present him with the gifts from the Company, and express our appreciation and our fidelity. It is most important we remain humble, but dignified and at the same time insistent in what we require."

"And, the Americans?" Franz inquired.

"Yes, next the Americans. We need to emphasize the long and profitable history of our Trade Agreement in the Japans, and the importance of maintaining our monopoly here. The *Shōguns'* long relationship with the Dutch has helped bring peace, security and strength to the Tokugawa reign. The Jesuits were driven out in the 1600s for very good reasons, and nothing has changed in the past two centuries. There is no benefit to having more foreigners in Japan."

Abe shook his head, "*Shōgun* boss, not Hollander. You understand?"

"Yes, yes of course," de Wolfe insisted. "And, our time will be very limited, so it is important that we stick to our plan."

"Shindo Taka?" Abe asked.

"That will be the last point on our agenda. She is meaningless to him, and I will vouch for her and ask that she be returned to Nagasaki as a personal favor to me, a trivial boon and nothing more. That is our plan and our agenda, alright. One: gifts. Two: Affirm our Trade Monopoly. Three: Return the girl and out."

"*Shōgun* boss," Franz said skeptically, "not Hollander."

"Yes, yes, of course! I am just saying that it is important that we stick to the plan. Agreed?"

Song and Dance Man

Abe, de Wolfe and Dr. Franz had walked the short distance to Edo Castle – also known as Chiyoda Castle after the district's title - in the morning, and the citadel was every bit as grand and impressive as de Wolfe had imagined. It was surrounded by broad and busy boulevards and a moat that would take an hour's walk to circumnavigate. Formidable stone walls rose easily twice the height of those he had seen in Nagasaki and Fukuoka. Dozens of pure white buildings topped with grey tile crowded the grounds, and a multi-storied pagoda stood over one corner of a spacious courtyard.

The Dutchmen wore their formal clothes, including top hats that had been carefully sheparded along their path to Edo. They had crossed the moat over a broad bridge, entered the courtyard through huge heavily guarded gates, then waited for hours by a complex of large buildings in the shade of a pagoda as the day progressed. Group after group of ornately dressed officials were shown in and then back out while the foreigners grew ever more anxious. Finally, they were led down a long hallway to a large tatami room with the familiar arrangement of officials and bureaucrats.

At the front of the room sitting on his knees higher than everyone else and elevated by a dais in solitary magnificence was *Shōgun* Tokugawa Ieyoshi, the twelfth direct descendent of the first military monarch Tokugawa Ieyasu. Behind the dais were colorfully painted wooden panels, and advisors came and whispered to him as the Nagasaki delegation entered the room. He appeared sickly with dark circles under his eyes, but the eyes themselves sparkled with an interest in the Western guests.

Both sides of the room were lined with dozens of kneeling samurai, each wearing a distinctive and colorful kimono denoting where they had come from. De Wolfe halted briefly when he noticed two older officials kneeling on the right side of the room wearing the same light-blue colored kimono and symmetrical white blossom pattern embroidered on the left breast as the attackers on the Tokaidō had worn. Neither looked directly at him as the Nagasaki delegation passed, and simply remained passively staring ahead.

Abe led the Dutchmen to the front of the room and then went to one knee as de Wolfe and Franz struggled to imitate him. *"May I present,"* Abe growled in a low formal voice, *"Capitāo-sama de Wolfe of Nagasaki, Kyūshū!"*

The wooden panel behind the *Shōgun* opened and a scholarly looking old man stepped out wearing a high headdress and a spectacularly decorated kimono. He bowed to the *Shōgun*, descended the dais, and bowed to de Wolfe. "I am Suzuki," he said in perfect and nearly unaccented Dutch.

"Please tell the *Shōgun*," de Wolfe began, "that we are here to demonstrate the friendship and the loyalty of the Dutch." The gift box was brought forward and set down beside de Wolfe who opened it and withdrew the items one at a time, giving the gifts to aides who then carried them to the dais and presented them to the *Shōgun*.

"We have brought his Majesty," de Wolfe announced grandly, "the latest books on science and medicine. A telescope, so that he may study the moon and stars. Candies for his enjoyment. And, to amuse him, pins that fold in upon themselves!"

He paused for dramatic effect and then withdrew the ornate wooden box containing the pistols. "And, these American revolvers, each of which holds six shots."

"Americans?" asked Suzuki suspiciously, and he and the *Shōgun* exchanged a glance.

"The most modern of American weapons, for the pleasure and for the defense of the *Shōgun*. And, we now must speak of the Americans....." he began, but the *Shōgun* silenced him with a wave.

The *Shōgun*'s voice was high and quavering, and Suzuki translated for the Dutchmen. *"Thank them for the gifts. Now, tell them to sing."*

Suzuki smiled at de Wolfe. "The *Shōgun* says that he is most pleased with your gifts. He now asks that you sing."

"Sing?" asked de Wolfe totally confused. "Sing what?"

"A song," explained Suzuki. "He would like to hear a Dutch song. Please sing and dance. A Dutch song."

De Wolfe was at a complete loss of what to do. This was serious business, and it was time to negotiate. A song? What was that supposed to mean? He had no idea what to do next. He looked at Abe and Franz in bewilderment.

Next to him Dr. Franz, ever the showman, spontaneously began to hum a tune, and then burst into a bawdy and slightly vulgar old drinking song, his voice rising and solitary in the large room as de Wolfe stared in shock and surprise. As he hit the refrain he stood up and began the steps of a jig in front of the dais, his feet moving quickly and lightly with great enthusiasm. Franz began the second and last stanza as his arms joined his feet in the rhythm and he scowled and smiled to match the lyrics, finishing with a huge flourish on one knee facing away from the packed and kneeling officials.

The room was completely silent as each man stared straight at Franz stoically. The *Shōgun* indicated that Suzuki should come near, and then whispered something in his ear.

"The *Shōgun*," Suzuki announced grandly, "requests that you sing it again!"

"Again?' asked Franz, still breathing heavily.

"Yes, again," confirmed Suzuki.

"Enough!" objected de Wolfe. "Your Majesty, we are here on urgent business!"

The *Shōgun* appeared displeased, and became very serious, whispering to Suzuki. "My lord directs me to ask you what you may know of the Black Ships."

"Ships that burn coal?" confirmed de Wolfe.

"Yes. The Americans have come to Uraga Harbor."

"Please remind the *Shōgun* that your Trade Agreement is with us, with the Dutch alone. The Americans are intruders."

"Well, as you have so easily disposed of the foreign pirates at Nagasaki, the *Shōgun* now directs you to immediately go to the Americans, and advise them to depart." Suzuki watched the Nagasaki delegation for a long moment, and then emphasized, "You may go."

Abe and Franz stood, but de Wolfe did not move.

"You have received your instructions, you may go!" Suzuki reiterated, and turned to speak with the *Shōgun*.

"I have a request," de Wolfe said slowly and loudly, still on one knee. Suzuki and the *Shōgun* stopped their conversation at his rudeness, and several of the officials raised themselves to one knee and placed their hands on the hilts of their swords.

"There is a woman, Shindo Taka, she is under your arrest, and her family is being held and sentenced to death. It is only a small matter, but they are good and honorable people, and I would kindly ask that she be released to me as a token of our two nations' great friendship."

Suzuki stared in anger, and then clapped his hands. The two wooden panels behind him opened and two samurai guards stepped out and onto the dais, the one on the right holding Taka by the arm. The three stopped directly behind the *Shōgun*.

"What is this woman to you?" Suzuki inquired.

Seeing her, de Wolfe's heart leapt into his throat, and he worked hard to keep his voice strong. "She has borne my son."

De Wolfe rose and stepped toward the dais as Abe moved quickly to block his path. Both guards behind the *Shōgun* half-drew their swords and moved to shield him as well.

"Let me speak to her!" he demanded in frustration.

The *Shōgun* stood, and everyone in the room immediately jumped to attention. He stepped in front of the guards close to the Nagasaki delegation. *"Go to Uraga!"* he commanded brusquely.

De Wolfe was staring at Taka, she was the only person in the room as far as he cared, and she kept her gaze demurely on the floor in front of her. Abe pulled on his arm urgently, "We must go. Go now. I have plan."

De Wolfe could barely contain himself, and with difficulty was finally able to tear his gaze away from the dais. There were no other options. The three men bowed deeply and backed slowly out of the room.

Once they had exited, put on their shoes and started walking away from Edo Castle, Dr. Franz turned to de Wolfe. "Excuse me if I am just a little confused, but which part of all that was 'sticking to the plan'?"

"The part where you started singing and dancing," de Wolfe snapped back. "It is absolute madness! Sing us a song? Go to Uraga? What am I supposed to do with the Americans?"

"Well," Franz suggested, "we can always talk to them, find out what they want, why they are here. They have sent ships-of-war, so it is almost certainly not a commercial venture."

"Americans go, Hollanders stay. Simple, you understand?" Abe suggested.

"Alright," de Wolfe relented. "Let us go to Uraga and speak with the Americans, there must be a diplomatic manner for the Dutch government to enforce and maintain its treaties."

Uraga

The three had left Edo the next morning before dawn on horseback, traveling back along their previous path taken only two days ago, and now moving even more quickly unencumbered by porters or baggage. They exchanged their horses at Yokohama and arrived on the low hills overlooking the city at the mouth of Edo Bay by mid-afternoon. Off the coast they could see two black hulled side-paddle ships, individual stacks smoking slightly as they lay at anchor in the calm waters. Their gun ports were open and facing towards the city, and behind them two additional three-masted warships also rested.

"Talk to American," Abe pointed at the four ships. "Make them go."

The ships were formidable, each bearing dozens of heavy guns and manned by well-armed Marines trained in both land and sea warfare. If the Americans wanted to come ashore they would, and nothing he could do would stop them. At this moment in time the small fishing village of Uraga Japan had become the intersection of modern brute force and international political will.

"The world is changing Mr. Abe. But yes, let us speak with them."

"Make them go!" Abe insisted.

They rode down the hillside, and along the main dirt road lined by houses, restaurants and shops that led to a small wooden pier jutting out into the ocean. Uraga seemed not much more than a village, and practically deserted, all the local folk taking shelter inside. There was a sense that they were awaiting someone, or something to happen. The three men dismounted, tied their horses to the posts along the wharf, and de Wolfe walked to the end and began waving his hat back and forth, high above his head.

Soon, a long boat was lowered from the American ship and began rowing towards the shore.

SUSQUEHANNA

The two sailors manning the long boat each wore the exact same style blue trousers and red undershirts in the warm afternoon sun. Neither one spoke in the few moments it took to row from the wharf to the side of the ship, where they indicated their passengers should climb up a Jacob's Ladder and aboard.

Standing at the railing was, what appeared to de Wolfe, the strongest man he had ever seen. The American was wearing the uniform of a Marine Sergeant Major, a dark blue blouse with light blue trousers held up by a pure white belt, the chest crossed by matching white shoulder belts. His sword hilt carried gold tassels that matched the metal tip of the leather scabbard he held in his right hand, offset by the dyed black length of the sheath. He wore a blue peaked hat with a broad short brim, and brusquely waved them aboard.

As the three men scrambled over the railing the Sergeant Major inspected them, backed up my three more Marines. "Armed Jappers on my ship?" he sneered, eyeing the two swords ensconced in Abe's belt. He started to move towards Abe when an older heavy set man hailed them in English.

"Gentlemen! Welcome aboard my flagship the SUSQUEHANNA, I am Commodore Matthew Perry of the United States Navy."

The most striking aspects of the Commodore, besides his girth, were the brightly colored gold and black epaulets on his shoulders and the three gold stripes at the wrist of each sleeve. His collar was white and high up on his neck. Two rows of gleaming gold buttons ran down the dark blue blouse from the collar to the black belt, and his trousers matched the blouse. He seemed genuinely pleased to meet them.

"I am Hendrik de Wolfe, of the Dutch East India Company, and this is Dr. Franz and Mr. Abe."

"Have you ever been aboard a steamship before?"

"No," stammered de Wolfe slightly thrown off stride using the unfamiliar English. "But, I have been aboard a steam train."

"Same principal, only bigger," and Perry started aft. "Come along with me and I will show you."

The Marine stepped in front of Abe, "I'll take the swords, if you please."

"Not necessary Sergeant Major, thank you very much," Perry called over his shoulder. "Please have your men stand easy." The Marine scowled, but the Commodore took de Wolfe by the arm like an old friend and began to show him around, obviously proud of his vessel and its technology. "I despise these monstrosities myself," he confided. "Grew up on great ships of sail, go wherever you please without the constant thump-thump-thump and stink of the engine. Free as a bird, mind you."

"And yet, we left Virginia under steam just seven and a half months ago, and every day made certain and regular progress regardless of the wind or weather. Steam is truly a modern miracle, gentlemen, and you are both seeing and standing upon the future!"

Perry pointed up at the single stack. "Coal goes in, smoke comes out, the paddles turn, and we move along no longer prisoners of the vagrancies of the gods of weather. What could be more straightforward? But, enough of the tour, I recognize of course that you came on business. Now, shall we go to my cabin?"

Old Acquaintances

The Commodore's cabin was mid-ships in front of the stack and just aft of the bridge rather than on the stern as had been the custom of ship builders for thousands of years. After the bright sunshine outside, it took de Wolf's eyes a moment to adjust to the darkness of the interior, and there sitting at a large square table, was the pirate Captain Powell and next to him a leering Barton.

At first Abe did not understand as Dr. Franz involuntarily stepped back towards the door, and then the slow realization settled in on de Wolfe and the Japanese warrior. They had never seen Powell up close, only through the spyglass and from the wharf, but there could be no mistake.

Perry watched the interaction between the two groups carefully as Abe's visage hardened, and his right hand hovered over his sword hilt seemingly unbidden. The Dutchmen's faces both shone with anger and distress at the unwelcome reunion, Franz's glowing a bright red.

"Well," said Powell jovially, smiling and looking at the Hollanders, "you both seem to have made a rather remarkable recovery."

"May I ask, Commodore," de Wolfe bristled, "why these men are here?"

Perry looked at the two groups with equal interest and suspicion. "For now they are here as my guests, as are you," he emphasized.

"They are pirates!" Franz snapped.

"Pirates? Nonsense! We are but peaceful traders, like yourselves," Powell protested. "Competitors most certainly, but merely businessmen."

"These 'businessmen'," de Wolfe scoffed with disdain, "hanged a virtuous man and bombarded a peaceful city with their cannon, killing innocent women and children."

"Commodore!" Powell smirked for effect as if his feelings had been deeply wounded. "I freely offer you my help, and ask for so little in return, and now I am insulted and falsely accused by an unscrupulous adversary."

"Liar!" Franz screamed, and Barton half-rose from his chair.

"Gentlemen!" Perry shouted to regain control, his hand slapping down on the table. He eyed both groups cautiously, and then regarded de Wolfe, indicating they should all sit together at the large table. Reluctantly, the Nagasaki group sat down across from the pirates. Everyone waited in awkward silence as a steward brought mugs of hot coffee and distributed them.

"I know why Captain Powell is here," Perry began again, "and he has made me his offer. The question is, sir, why are you here?"

De Wolfe settled, it was time to get down to business, but he kept a close watch on Powell directly across from him. "We have come to you, as the rightful Dutch representatives in Japan, to protest your unwarranted intrusion on our legitimate trade."

"The 'rightful Dutch representative'?" Perry asked. "Was that the term you just used?"

"Yes," de Wolfe confirmed.

Perry sipped his coffee, "Your 'legitimate trade'?"

"That is correct. We have a long-standing treaty with the Japanese *Shōgunate*, and I am authorized today to speak on his behalf."

"The Dutch now speak on behalf of the *Shōgun*? Interesting. Are you aware that our Secretary of War has fully advised your government of our intentions," Perry countered.

"And, did they offer you their approval?"

"No," Perry conceded. "No, they did not."

"And," de Wolfe added, "neither have the Japanese."

Perry sighed, and began speaking in low tones as if a school master were instructing a small gathering of students. "Gentlemen, we are engaged in a great worldwide industrial revolution. This extraordinary vessel is only one manifestation of the wonders we are seeing. Railroads, steam shovels, the telegraph, did you know that just eight years ago a man named Samuel Morse sent a message from Washington DC all the way to Baltimore Maryland as quickly and as easily as I am speaking to you."

"The advances ahead in transportation, communications, medicine, a thousand different fields, are unforeseeable and will be incomprehensible to those of us alive today. Every country, every soul on earth, will benefit, and no nation – including Japan – can continue to stand alone."

"The Japans are not alone," de Wolfe protested. "They trade with us."

"Sir, Japan still lives in the Middle Ages, not the 19th century." Perry stood, picked up a globe from his desk, and placed it squarely in the middle of the table. "The route from California to Asia comes across here," he indicated, "past Japan to China and beyond. The United States requires coaling stations along the way. My mission is to present the Shōgun with our requirements, and to negotiate a treaty for coaling stations and, if possible, a Trade Agreement."

"At what cost?" Franz pointed out. "Japan is perfectly content in her isolation. She neither desires nor needs your interference or your modern machines."

"Japan is like a canary that has been inside a cage for too long. Even when the door is opened the bird is too frightened to venture outside. This will be to the benefit of Japan and to the Japanese people. We came to negotiate...."

"It is certainly not to the benefit of the Shōgun," de Wolfe interrupted.

"If negotiations don't work, there are always other methods of persuasion," Powell chimed in.

Perry shook his head. "I must emphasize that we have come in peace."

"The Shōgun has directed us to ask you to leave immediately," de Wolfe insisted. "He does not want a 'coaling station', he does not want an 'industrial revolution', and he certainly does not want a Trade Agreement with the United States!"

197

"My mission is political," Perry sighed. "But, this is a ship of war and we will not be ordered about by foreign governments." He paused for a long moment before he continued, wanting to make sure that his meaning was very clear.

"The *Shōgun* cannot have what he wants, so he must learn to want what he has. And, he <u>will</u> have a Trade Agreement with the United States of America. May I suggest that you return to him with this information? Sergeant Major!"

The Marine non-commissioned officer entered the Captain's cabin and saluted briskly. "Sir, yes sir!"

"Would you please show our three guests to the long boat?"

"My pleasure, sir, but if I may?"

"Yes?" Perry asked. "What is it?"

"Bit of a crowd of the Jappers gathering in the city, sir. Looks like it could be getting a trifle rough out there."

"I see your point," the Commodore considered. "Take a detachment, fully armed, and see that these Dutchmen get safely back to the wharf and their horses. After that I will bear no more responsibility for them."

"I can assure you Commodore that nothing untoward will happen to us," Franz countered.

"Probably right, of course," Perry nodded. "But, you came aboard my flagship in one piece and I will see to it that you are returned to the land safely as well. After that, you are on your own."

While Powell and Barton stayed aboard talking with the Americans, the three men were shown out of the cabin by a waiting Marine. They climbed across the railing and down the Jacob's Ladder to the long boat joined by the Sergeant Major, and waited while a second boat was lowered and filled with eight Marines along with two sailors.

As the American Marine suspiciously eyed the Japanese warrior, Abe continued desperately trying to understand the body language of the earlier conversation in what was the completely foreign English language, endeavoring to comprehend what was happening. Finally, he turned to de Wolfe and spoke to him in Dutch, "Black Ships, they go?"

"No, I am sorry Mr. Abe," de Wolfe answered him resigned. "Black Ships they stay. You understand?"

Abe merely grunted in reply and looked grimly determined.

The Sergeant Major saluted up to the Commodore on deck and the sailors began rowing for the Uraga wharf. At the railing of the SUSQUEHANNA Captain Powell waved and blew kisses towards the longboats as they departed, placing his hands on his hips and sticking out his thin chest. Somehow it vaguely reminded de Wolfe of the farewell that Cas Janssen had given him so long ago.

The Wharf

In the few moments it took to row ashore a growing unruly crowd had gathered along the main street of Uraga and pushed itself onto the wharf. De Wolfe could see the mob was composed solely of men, young fit men. There were no spectators, no women, no children, and more than the total possible population of this small fishing town. The clothes they wore appeared dirty and tattered, but it seemed more stagecraft than an occupation, as if they were dressed for a theatre production. Many of them had headbands or cloth over their heads to hide their identities, or perhaps the long styled hair of a samurai. They did not appear to be armed, but who knew what kinds of clubs or dirks could have been carried or concealed among them?

The other craft landed first, and several Marines scrambled out of the long boat and onto the wharf, pushing back the leading edge of the crowd. They were soon followed by the others, and they formed a perimeter and cleared a space for the second boat to pull up allowing the Sergeant Major and Abe, De Wolfe and Franz to disembark. The two long boats then backed away.

The mob began pushing forward, and were repelled back again by the Marines who were physically larger and better organized. It immediately became a shoving match with the Americans on one side and the Japanese on the other, the Marines using their strength and gun butts to clear the pier.

As they reached the dirt street the mob parted to reveal a dozen fully armed samurai wearing the familiar light-blue kimono with the embroidery on the left breast and holding their hands on their swords, fully demonstrating their intentions. The three horses the Nagasaki men had left tied to the pier were nowhere to be seen.

By now the mob was shouting and screaming, and out of the corner of his eye de Wolfe saw Abe deliberately signal to one of the blue clad samurai who nodded back at him grimly. He was sure it was one of the men he had seen yesterday during his audience with the *Shōgun*.

The Sergeant Major touched de Wolfe on the shoulder and shouted into his ear, "Off you go now!" Abe grabbed the Dutchmen and pulled them through the crowd and away from the wharf while the horde's focus remained on the Marines.

The samurai moved forward as a group until they stood only a few paces in front of the Americans as the mass of Japanese shoved forward hooting and hollering incoherently. Abe kept urging de Wolfe and Franz away, but they were making slow progress careening through the tightly packed throng.

The eight Marines stood silently shoulder-to-shoulder at the intersection of the wharf and the street, their rifles held horizontally in front and sealing off the pier. The blue-clad samurai formed a similar line opposing them, and the roar of the throng increased with shouting, insults and shaking fists as the Sergeant Major calmly assessed the situation from behind his line of armed men.

"Ranks of four, gentlemen, if you please. Bayonets!" he commanded. Four Marines slid smoothly behind the four in front as blades were pulled out of scabbards on their waists and mounted on the single-shot carbines, effectively converting them into spears as well as firearms.

The samurai opposing the Marines were infuriated by this action, and began stamping their feet and fingering their swords as the tension grew and the rabble continued to shout and press forward.

"Front rank, prepare to volley fire! On my command!"

The first four Marines lowered their rifles to point at the men in front of them and the crowd, a sharp steel barrier commanding the wharf. At this provocation one of the older samurai in a blue kimono screamed and charged forward towards the Americans.

"Fire!" the Sergeant Major calmly called, and four rifles discharged in unison filling the air with thunder and blue smoke, and knocking down the charging samurai and several others standing beside him. The front four Marines then smoothly stepped two paces backward through the four behind them and began to reload. As a group the remaining samurai charged the wharf.

"Rear rank! Volley fire!"

The four rounds hit several of the samurai, but more broke through and the Marines held them away with their bayonets as the Americans stepped two paces backward.

"Volley fire!" and thunder and blue smoke followed the command.

Aboard the SUSQUEHANNA Commodore Perry watched through a small pair of Galilean binoculars as the distant heavy dark smoke continued to build in the calm early evening air, followed several seconds later by the deep boom of the carbines. He sighed and with obvious regret softly ordered "General Quarters."

200

"Powell stood next to Perry and sneered, "I told you that it is impossible to bargain with these heathens."

Perry lowered his binoculars from his eyes, and regarded Powell and Barton. "Nor, will I bargain with pirates," he replied. "With all due respect, 'Captain'," he said with obviously no respect at all, "I ask that you stay below until the PHANTOM returns at sunset and then get the Hell off of my ship."

"Commodore!" Powell protested.

And," Perry continued, raising his binoculars once again and dismissing them, "may I further suggest that you use all speed to depart these waters."

"You will regret this Commodore," Powell announced to no one in particular. "You may have the constraints of diplomacy, but I can assure you that I do not. Besides, the hunting here is too damn fine."

The Japan You Knew

Abe continued to drag de Wolfe and Franz through the mob as gunfire and screams went off behind them. From where they were no one could see what was happening on the wharf, but the blood-lust and madness was growing in the Japanese as the Dutchmen shouldered and bullied their way through. They had no idea where their horses had gone, where they were going, or how to get to safety. But, they needed to get away from the wharf while the rabble ebbed and flowed like waves against a rocky shoreline and men began to point and grab at them.

Ahead a horse whinnied and rose up on its back legs, and Abe drove them towards it. At the edge of the crowd a man was leading their three horses away as Abe knocked him down and de Wolfe grabbed the reins while Franz desperately tried to keep up. The throng was pulling at de Wolfe as he mounted and spurred the horse in circles, clearing a small space for Franz to climb on his horse, and they rode hard for the hills.

On the wharf the Marines continued to fire into the mob and leapfrog back along the wooden pier two paces at a time. The strategic retreat was very efficient, and the attackers tripped over or were forced to drag away the dead and wounded on the narrow pier before pursuing the Americans, unable to get close and held back by the deadly bayonets.

A Japanese *ite* - archer - ducked in and out of the swirling battle looking for his opening, trying to get a clear shot at the Sergeant Major. He drew back his bow and let fly, hitting a Marine in the shoulder while he was re-loading his rifle and knocking him to his knees.

"Fire at will!" The Sergeant Major ordered as the bowman moved forward in the melee for another shot, and was then targeted and himself knocked down by a bullet as the Marines continued their step-by-step retreat to the waiting boats.

With loud booms the cannon from the Black Ships began to toll like distant bells, and heavy solid shot screamed over the wharf and struck buildings in the village, sending splinters flying. The Marines reached the end of the wharf and began jumping down to the waiting boats and loaded the wounded man aboard. The Sergeant Major stood alone and holding his unsheathed sword on the pier until the last of his men was safe, then he stepped down into the long boat as the frightened sailors began rowing vigorously for the flagship.

Abe, de Wolfe and Franz paused on the hillside overlooking Uraga, both the horses and the men breathing hard. The Dutchmen had deep scratches on their arms and hands where the mob had grabbed at them, but there was little blood and no serious injuries.

They watched in horror and dismay as cannon shot bowled through the attackers like ten pins, scattering body parts and smashing houses and shops, clearing the last of the riot from the wharf and the city. One shell lay smoking in the middle of the dirt street and several men came to stare at it curiously until it exploded in a tremendous flash and obliterated them.

De Wolfe watched in distress, thinking back to the damage and death suffered by Nagasaki from a far less efficient bombardment. Down below he knew that dozens, perhaps hundreds had been killed and the town was devastated after only a brief shelling.

"I must go back, I can help," Franz began and turned his horse towards the devastation.

"Do not be daft, doctor, de Wolfe cautioned. "They would tear you limb from limb. "And you, Mr. Abe," he continued. "I saw you! You are part of this. Did you help organize this attack? Was this your plan all along?" he demanded.

Abe thumped his chest. "My duty, number one," he said holding up one finger, "protect you. My duty number two," he emphasized holding up two fingers, "Protect *Shōgun*. My duty number three," he screamed, holding up the third finger, "Protect Japan! Perry," he had difficulty pronouncing the heavy double-r sound, "Perry friend pirates!"

"What?" de Wolfe was surprised. "The Americans are no friends of the pirates."

"Pirates Perry ship," Abe insisted. "American kill samurai. Perry friend pirates!"

Of course that is what he must believe de Wolfe understood. Powell had seemed quite at ease aboard the flagship, and the battle with the Marines and subsequent cannon fire only confirmed in the samurai's mind that the Americans and pirates were cooperating. But, how could he explain that to Abe, how could he prevent a full-scale war between the Americans and the Japanese? The American's use of the weapons of war provided by the technology of the Western world were devastating, and such a war would only bring destruction to the Japanese.

"You may have just destroyed the Japan you know," De Wolfe told him, and spurred his horse towards Edo as the afternoon sun began to set behind the hills in front of them.

Peering through the gun port aboard the American ship Powell turned to Barton, "Leave it to the Americans," he smirked. "Compared to them we knock nice and easy and ask politely, while they just kick the bloody door wide open!"

The Frenchmen spit on the deck and muttered "*merde*".

"*Merde* indeed Mr. Barton. However, I believe that it will be quite possible for us to scupper the Yanks tidy plans, and at the very same time turn a profit for ourselves. *Merde* indeed!" and he rubbed his scraggly beard in glee.

Go Back to Nagasaki!

The three riders traveled as quickly as possible through the gathering dusk and then into darkness, but it was still well after midnight before they arrived back at Edo Castle. Abe pounded on the large wooden gate until a small portal opened and they entered the courtyard, leaving their horses outside. They were led to an unremarkable side building, told to wait, and spent the next hour in the gloom and silence. Finally, they were escorted back to the main building once again, and entered the large audience room.

The *Shōgun* was sitting on the dais, with Suzuki to his right and Taka, her eyes downcast, on his left. De Wolfe could barely restrain himself from going to her side. The room was barely lit by four small lanterns, one at each corner of the dais, and despite the hour the two men wore full formal kimono, and their eyes glittered in the reflected light.

Suzuki ordered all of the guards from the room, leaving them alone, and began, "You were ordered to advise the Americans they must immediately depart Japan".

"We met with the Americans," de Wolfe answered.

"But, they have not departed?"

"No."

"And, now the Americans have attacked our people with cannon," Suzuki snapped angrily.

"The Americans have…." de Wolfe began.

"Silence!" Suzuki demanded. *"Abe-dono. What did you see?"*

"The American's have great warships with many cannons and guns. They are also capable of fighting on land with great courage. They would be formidable enemies."

Suzuki whispered in the *Shōgun*'s ear, and they conferred for a moment. "De Wolfe!" Suzuki had dropped all pretenses of courtesy and honorific titles. "What do the Americans want?"

"The Americans are a young country, but they have learned quickly. Twice they have defeated the British, the most powerful empire on earth. You have seen the marvels that they can build, and now they have brought a powerful war fleet to your shores."

"You have not told the *Shōgun* what they want."

"The Black Ships burn coal. They want ports to store the coal and power their vessels. They want to expand their reach from California to Asia, and Japan stands before them. They want to travel the oceans and trade with the world."

"For rocks that burn? They have murdered innocent townspeople for rocks!"

"The Americans were attacked by armed Samurai!"

Suzuki turned abruptly, seething, *"Abe-dono, what is the truth?"*

"There were pirates aboard the American ship. The same pirates that fired cannon into Nagasaki. And now, the Americans have fired cannon into Uraga. Perhaps next it will be Edo itself."

This took a long moment to sink in. The *Shōgun* remained seemingly unemotional, then called Suzuki close and spoke to him. "Pirates?" Suzuki questioned de Wolfe. "The Americans have formed an agreement with pirates? The very pirates that are raiding our ships and cities? The pirates that are raping and murdering our people?"

"No, I do not believe that is so. The Americans are traders. The pirates are animals. If you command, the Americans will go away, but then how will you protect your people from the pirates? And, if it is not the Americans, there are others, the English, the French, the Spanish. Some nations will seek only trade, but others will seek conquest."

"The world is moving quickly forward," de Wolfe reflected, seeing the developing situation in a new light. "And the Japanese are not. You were a powerful nation, united and strong. But now, even the smallest modern enemy can attack you and you will have no way to defend yourselves."

"The Hollanders have not protected us."

"The Hollanders are a peaceful people."

"The Japanese are a peaceful people!" Suzuki barked.

"The Black Ships bring change," de Wolfe said low.

"Japan has no need to change!" thundered Suzuki in return.

"How do you fight an enemy, an invader that sails off of your coast and fires cannon into your cities?" the Dutchman asked in resignation.

Hearing the translation, the *Shōgun*'s face grew red with anger, and Suzuki snapped back to de Wolfe, "Do not question or instruct the *Shōgun*!"

"Japan will join the modern world. You may fight against it, delay it, but even the *Shōgun* cannot prevent it."

Suzuki translated this to the *Shōgun* and then the old man measured de Wolfe carefully. "You know that this will mean the end of the Hollanders? The end of Dejima?"

"Yes, I know."

"You also know," Suzuki continued grimly, "that the samurai will rise up again against all foreigners and will spare no one. Especially the Dutchmen?"

"The Dutch have been your friends and allies for over two hundred years."

"The Dutch have allowed war to come to us. You are no longer our friends or our allies."

Suzuki conferred quietly with the *Shōgun*, who clapped his hands twice and two guards emerged from behind the wooden panels and stood, one on each side of Taka. *"Abe-dono, you may return to Nagasaki and await the Shōgun's wishes,"* Suzuki commanded.

205

De Wolfe stood, and stepped towards Taka. The guards bristled, and quickly blocked him at the front of the dais.

"If I stop the attacks, will you spare the girl?" he pleaded.

"Do you truly love this woman?" Suzuki cocked his eye and questioned.

"Yes, yes I do," de Wolfe answered loudly.

The *Shōgun* and Suzuki spoke briefly, and the anger slowly left the *Shōgun*'s visage, replaced by mild amusement. He turned his head to Taka and asked, *"Do you love this man?"*

She lifted her eyes briefly, *"Yes, your Majesty. I do."*

The *Shōgun* nodded, curling his lip, and then spoke in his high singsong voice at de Wolfe standing next to the kneeling Abe and Franz. *"Tell him that if he stops the attacks she will be spared."*

Suzuki translated, and de Wolfe was both over-joyed and terrified. How could he possibly stop the attacks? He had just given a promise that he had no inkling of how it might be fulfilled. Abe and Franz rose and they all began backing out of the audience room.

"Wait!" called the *Shōgun*, looking directly at Franz. The doctor halted dead still, not sure what might happen next and looking quite worried. *"I liked your Dutch song,"* the *Shōgun* smiled, then watched as the Nagasaki men turned and walked out of the room.

As soon as they departed Franz stopped de Wolfe, "Did you see the *Shōgun*?"

"Of course I saw the *Shōgun*."

"No, I mean did you really look at him? The blue tinge to his lips? The swollen ankles? The wheeze of his breathing?"

"What are you driving at doctor?"

"It was the same as with Westervelt, his heart that is. That man does not have many days to live."

"Then what happens to Taka?"

"Whatever debt there may be is between you and this *Shōgun*, not the next one. If you have a plan on how to proceed, act quickly, as there may be very little time."

Nagasaki House

They returned to the Nagasaki House in Edo for a few hours of sleep, but it was still well before dawn when Abe was quietly awakened and told that he had a visitor. He ensured that his two swords were nearby, within easy reach standing ready in the corner of the room, and then it was just another moment before Suzuki entered.

"My apologies for disturbing you," the old man began. He looked smaller than before, and infinitely more tired as if exhausted from carrying a great weight. Outside of the governmental palace, without all the trappings of State, he seemed frail.

"I have been told that you fought an exceptional duel on the Tokaidō, that it was the equal to myths and legends, two great giants in battle."

"I fought in the hills beside the roadway, as for the rest, I cannot say."

"Tell me about him, your opponent."

"He was a great warrior," Abe considered. *""A better swordsman than I am, certainly. His kenjutsu was flawless."*

"How is it then that you were able to defeat him?"

"That is for others to determine. He was a powerful warrior, but perhaps he fought with too much passion rather than skill. In a duel we make choices, and ultimately it is the mind that must defeat the opponent, not the blade."

"I see that you have taken his swords, Suzuki glanced at the two weapons propped up in the corner. *"He was my nephew,"* the old man whispered with great weariness, *"and he was an exceptional young man,"* Suzuki sighed.

"I understand, my sincere apologies," Abe replied with sadness, bowing deeply. *"Please accept them, and return them to their rightful owners."*

" No. You have won my family's swords fairly and in battle. They are yours. The old man slouched forward, near exhaustion. *"Let me tell you of my nephew; he was not only a master swordsman, he was a scholar, and a poet."* Suzuki paused, sighed again deeply, and then continued. *"From the time he could toddle, I knew that he would be special, that there was something about him. His father is the Obugyō-sama of Izu, and he surely would have followed. He was a living example of the kind of great men that Japan can produce. Do you think that he was correct?"*

"Regarding what?"

"The foreigners, of course. I know the Dutch well from my own time serving the Shōgun as the Otona on Dejima, even though I have been gone from there for many

years after my involvement in the Bansha no Goku Rebellion. Those of the Society for Western Study argued that Japan must be opened to all countries. I had observed the Dutch closely and knew the idea of opening Japan must be suppressed. Some wanted all of the foreigners banished or put to death, but it was finally decided that the deaths of the rangaku scholars were sufficient. It seemed the only way to protect the Emperor and the Shōgunate, don't you agree? I chose the side of patriotism, and that became the end of my time at Dejima."

"This is not for me to decide," Abe protested.

"But you must agree," Suzuki insisted. "You too have lived among them, you truly have seen and understand the corruption they bring that will poison our country, and that will destroy everything we know and believe. And yet, you still protect them?"

"The Dutch have always brought change, even if you could not see it. Now the Americans may join them, and others, but it will be the Japanese alone that decide whether that change will be deadly poison or healing medicine. Yes, I defend them, and I will safeguard them from anyone who means harm. That is my duty. And, I will always do my utmost to protect both the Capitão-sama and Japan as well."

"You are a fool. You killed a great man, and you owe me a life!" Suzuki spit out, venom in his voice. "The Hollanders must be stopped, and if you are too cowardly to do this thing yourself, then I will go to them and finish it now while they are asleep. I am an old man, but I am samurai, and my arms are still strong enough for one last act of rebellion."

"I owe you nothing. And, as for rebellion, against what? Against the Dutchmen? Against all foreigners? Or, is your uprising against the Shōgun himself? I have told you, it is only the Japanese that can decide our future. Not the foreigners and certainly not one bitter old man."

"Then fight me! I challenge you to a duel! Give me the honor of a quick and glorious death in battle!"

Abe shook his head. "Ridiculous! Even drawing one's sword against a Shōgunate official is punishable by death. If you want to die, do it yourself, do not ask me to be your executioner."

"I would happily give my life to protect Japan from this foreign scourge. You may live to see the end of the Shōgunate, but I can assure you that I will not," Suzuki said with finality, and rose to depart.

The warrior from Fukuoka remained impassive. "If you can no longer serve the Shōgun then may you find your peace in seppuku. One man's death will neither speed nor hinder what is to come. May I humbly offer to serve as your kaishakunin, and complete the ceremony? I have made my choices, and I know where my duty lies. I carry no guilt nor fear."

"No," Suzuki answered. "My duty remains to translate the lies and filth of the Dutch, and I will do so faithfully. However, you will see that I will not be silenced, nor will I allow the mind of the Shōgun to be poisoned without protest."

"You speak of the mind of the Shōgun as if it were known to you," Abe scowled. "I am a servant of Japan, and will do as my lord commands, and not attempt to control him. That is your duty as well."

Abe closely watched Suzuki leave the Nagasaki House to ensure that he was gone.

Sergeant Major

The city of Uraga was deserted, and the damage caused by the cannon fire was the only testament to the battle two days earlier. Buildings were half torn apart, and one had caught fire and burned to the ground, but its neighbors were unscathed. Several deep furrows had been scoured by cannon shot along the dirt road through the village and into the woods and hills behind. The fishing boats had all been pulled ashore and squatted in unattended solitude on the beach, the nets hung over their sides.

In déjà vu, once again the three men tied their horses to the wharf and de Wolfe stood at the end of the pier, waving his hat at the American ships at anchor in the harbor. The gun ports on the SUSQUEHANNAH were still pulled up and cannon were already rolled out, their barrels protruding like the quills of a porcupine. A boat crewed by a single sailor soon began rowing to shore.

As the Nagasaki delegation once again boarded the flagship and stood on the deck the Marine Sergeant Major blocked their path. "I'll take those swords," he ordered sternly, looking Abe up and down with distrust.

Abe had no idea what was happening, until the Sergeant Major pointed at his waist and a Marine stepped to either side of him to ensure his compliance. Understanding now that they meant to disarm him, the samurai stepped backward, clearing room for himself, and pulled his long sword from its sheath, holding it with both hands above his head, prepared to strike in an instant.

There was absolute quiet on the mid-deck as sailors hurriedly scrambled away and several other nearby Marines readied themselves to rush forward. "Hasn't there been enough killing already?" de Wolfe called out, breaking the silence.

"It wasn't us who started it," said the Sergeant Major watching Abe carefully.

"Perhaps not, but you also killed civilians and destroyed a village. You do not trust the Japanese, I understand that. But, they do not trust you either. In any case, we are here to see the Commodore," he insisted, starting to move past.

"Of course," the Sergeant Major refused to budge, "but, I'll have those swords first."

De Wolfe moved to stand in front of the samurai. "Mr. Abe, may I have your short sword please?"

Abe shifted the position of the *katana* from above himself to the front to protect him from a sudden charge, and with his left hand gave de Wolfe the smaller *wakizashi*. The Hollander pulled it from its sheath, twirled the blade in his hand feeling its weight and balance, and then threw the empty scabbard to Franz. "And," he menacingly lowered the sword point and asked the Marines facing them, "who will start it this time?"

The Sergeant Major pulled his pistol from the holster on his hip, cocked the gun and pointed it directly at Abe's head.

Commodore Perry opened the door of his cabin and strode onto the mid-deck, everyone frozen in front of him, no one wanting to make the first move, until the Sergeant Major broke the spell, "Attention! Commodore on deck!" and all of the Marines snapped to attention. Perry waved his hand and the Marines melted away, leaving Abe and de Wolfe standing alone. Abe replaced his long sword, and de Wolfe retrieved the scabbard from Franz and returned the short sword to the samurai.

"We are here," he began, "to negotiate on behalf of the *Shōgun*."

Silver

The morning was bright and fine as a light wind moved the PHANTOM slowly off the eastern coast of central Japan. There was a heavy fog lingering offshore, but that would burn off well before the forenoon watch finished, and there was much to do before then.

Expectancy gripped the crew as they waited for the action to begin. The past weeks had been hungry ones, and even though Powell had managed to beg some foodstuffs from the American Commodore a few days ago, there was still never enough to eat, and depression and lethargy prevailed. The best pickings were fishing boats returning from a day's haul, but you could never count on what they might be bringing back to market. Sometimes edible species, and sometimes the oddest beasties and muck from the ocean bottom: Sea urchins, large worms and the like. Disgusting filth they had pitched overboard along with the boats' frightened crews. After all, they could not allow word of their hunting to be reported.

210

Twice there had been minor gossip of mutiny and the election of a new Captain, and Barton remained a crew favorite to replace the Englishman Powell. Each time the ringleaders had been flogged and tied up in the stinking bilge until they begged forgiveness. Powell had promised to keel-haul the next traitor and then leave him to rot with the crabs.

There were also signs of scurvy appearing among the famished crew, and everyone knew that they had to get fresh food before it became rampant. So, today promised to be both a profitable and healthful day, and it was time to get started.

Powell surveyed the coastline and town through his spyglass from between the two masts on the mid-deck, noting the tall brick smokestacks on the edge of town. He called from the aft quarterdeck near the ship's wheel. "Mr. Barton, this is where they refine the silver! Raise the flag!"

"Aye, Captain!" and Barton attached an American flag to the pole protruding from the stern and lifted it fluttering behind the ship.

"So much for the diplomatic efforts of those Yankees," laughed Powell. "A pox upon them all! Now, let us begin our own negotiations!"

The thirty-two pound cannon on the shore side were rolled out of their gun ports, and with a nod from Barton the PHANTOM fired a broadside into the helpless city, the Stars and Stripes clearly visible on her stern.

The pirate ship made multiple passes back and forth, firing port and then starboard broadsides as she went, seeking out targets of tall buildings or groups of people cowering among the carnage. Powell had joined Barton on the quarter deck and carefully monitored the bombardment. "One more pass I think, Mr. Barton, and then dispatch the landing party. I want no man left alive on that shore."

"Understood, Captain!"

"But the women, at least the pretty ones, keep them together for later. First thing first! Food, silver and then women, in that order! Do I make myself clear?"

"Perfectly, Captain. Perfectly!" Barton was smiling broadly in anticipation.

From The Fog

The Sergeant Major was watching the PHANTOM with a deck-mounted targeting telescope on the flying bridge as the SUSQUEHANNAH cleared the marine layer and into the open sun. "They're firing into the city, Commodore," he reported.

Perry was watching the developing scene through his own binoculars from inside the bridge, and then spoke with a ship's officer and the Marine, "General Quarters. A single warning shot across her bow. Sergeant Major, prepare your boarding party."

He then turned to de Wolfe and Franz standing next to him. "Our apologies gentlemen, and especially to you Mr. de Wolfe, for my earlier doubts. That is an act of piracy, and under false colors no less."

The Nagasaki men had retrieved their weapons from the horses in Uraga, but de Wolfe sorely wished he still had the American pistols he had given as gifts to the *Shōgun*. He unsheathed the long sword that Abe had given to him on the roadway and set the scabbard on the chart table, leaving the *wakizashi* short sword in his belt, and they started to follow the Sergeant Major off of the bridge. They could see the Marine boarding party began gathering on the bow, and Perry reached out and held him by the shoulder.

"This is their job, not yours," he told de Wolfe.

The Hollander stood close to the Japanese warrior. "This is our fight, Commodore," he responded with finality. "We will see it finished."

"Well then," Perry opened a drawer and withdrew a heavy single-shot pistol finely decorated and showing signs of wear and tear.

De Wolfe was skeptical. "Why, the *Shōgun* has better guns than this!" he exclaimed.

"It was my father's," Perry smiled.

"Then Commodore," de Wolfe accepted the weapon, and tucked it into his midriff. "I will take it proudly."

He withdrew the scabbard containing the wakizashi from his belt, handed it to Perry, and they shook hands. The Commodore nodded, accepting the exchange, and with great deference bowed to Abe.

"Oh, and," he smiled again, "don't get yourselves killed."

Turn Us Mr. Barton!

Everyone aboard the PHANTOM was watching the spectacle of the final broadside devastating the city when the warning shot from the rapidly moving Black Ship splashed directly in front of the brig-sloop. Barton rushed to the seaside port railing on the quarterdeck, and pointed, "Captain!" There was no need for further explanations.

The two steam-driven side-paddle wheels of the SUSQUEHANNAH were churning white froth, and the ship's speed generated bright sea-foam at the bow, what sailors called "a bone in her teeth". Dark smoke billowed from the warship's stack as her black gang furiously shoveled coal into the single boiler. The American vessel was charging directly towards the vulnerable bow of the pirate ship as it continued to cruise leisurely parallel to the shoreline and had no warning, the crew's attention focused entirely on the landside, when the Americans had come upon them.

"Turn us Mr. Barton! Turn us into her! Bring our guns to bear!" Powell screamed, and looked around at his sickly scurvy-ridden crew. They had not eaten well in weeks, many of them with pale thin skin and dark deeply-sunken eyes. "Tell them to fight! Fight for their lives, or we will all be food for the fishies!" Barton shoved the seaman on the wheel aside, spinning it rapidly while shouting orders to the crew.

The bow of the Black Ship made a narrow target, even if the PHANTOM's port side cannons had been re-loaded. The pirate ship's gun crews scrambled to get her heavy cannons with the thirty-two pound shot ready, their very survival in jeopardy.

From this angle the SUSQUEHANNAH could only fire her smaller twelve-pound rifled bow gun, but was only minutes away from "crossing the T", sailing directly before the path of her target and utilizing the full power of her broadside. On each beam she carried six Dahlgran smoothbore guns and one Parrot rifled cannon for long-range attacks. She would not need more than one or two volleys to destroy the smaller pirate ship.

But, if the PHANTOM could turn inside her attacker she would bring her own broadside to bear, and with luck could disable the side-paddle, leaving the American flagship turning in helpless circles while she escaped. It would be a very close thing.

On the bridge of the SUSQUEHANNAH Commodore Perry immediately understood the tactic and ordered, "Ten degrees starboard, prepare for ramming." And a bugler immediately signaled the maneuver as the helmsman swung the wheel.

Naval maneuvering is such an odd thing, and often seems to take place with an unescapable inevitability, everyone seeing and knowing the outcome sometimes minutes before the result. The courses of the two vessels were now set, and their fates determined. Each crewman made his own separate preparations for the anticipated inexorable and violent encounter of the hulls.

The American ship smashed into the bowsprit of the brig-sloop, toppling the bowsprit sails and sprit topmast, tumbling gear and fouling the foredeck with rope and canvas as the crew of both ships held on tightly from the impact.

The collision drove the bow of the smaller ship sideways and down, and except for the distant thumping steam engine and screaming tortured wood of the scraping hulls there was almost silence as everyone watched to see what would happen next.

As the PHANTOM righted herself, the paddle-wheels of the SUSQUEHANNAH stopped their momentum and began to spin backwards. The pirate vessel was now blocked and the American ship was safely angled across the bow so that it could not be fired upon. The wind powered sloop had been easily out-maneuvered by the steam-driven frigate.

The SUSQUEHANNA fired a broadside along the length of the PHANTOM, tearing huge holes in the cannon deck, and then her port paddle started forward again, turning the two slowly separating combatants bow-to-bow and then bringing them back steadily closer.

"*Merde*! We are helpless!" Barton screamed.

"Prepare to be boarded you fool!" commanded Powell as he kicked his First Mate in the trousers. "Keep them off of us Mr. Barton!"

High in the foremast of the American ship Marine snipers began firing down into any groups of pirates that showed themselves above deck, while grappling hooks and lines were thrown over and teams of sailors pulled hard, bringing the ships closer and closer. The Marine boarding party gathered on the bow, their weapons ready to protect the sailors and to push over the gap as de Wolfe and Abe shoved their way to the front.

"Stand down!" commanded the Sergeant Major. "We will handle this. The United States Marines have a long history with pirates, to the blackguards regret. This ain't no tea party or formal dance, it's gonna be rough over there."

"Not on your life, Sergeant Major," de Wolfe retorted. "We owe these pirates something as well."

"Well then civilian," the American snorted and indicated towards Abe. "Tell him not to get in our way."

The Marines waited expectantly as the gap between the two ships closed, unable to see through the tangle of ships gear and with the still swirling smoke from the cannon fire. "Gentlemen, prepare to board!" ordered the Sergeant Major.

Before anyone else could move, Abe athletically leapt across the gap and onto the deck of the PHANTOM, alone as several pirates suddenly moved to surround him. Barton led the attack, and swung a cutlass in circles in front of himself while indicating that Abe should come closer. "*Allez*, monkey," he taunted.

214

Barton charged Abe, swinging his cutlass viciously, wielding it expertly with strength and speed while Abe skillfully deflected his charge and then began to toy with the Frenchman. Other pirates would appear out of the mist, be struck down with a single blow from the Japanese swordsman, and then disappear.

But, despite these sporadic attacks, Abe's singular attention never seemed to waiver from Barton, and he methodically kept driving him back until the pirate was pinned against the railing on the bow. Then, with two incredibly fast strokes Abe took off the First Mate's sword arm at the wrist and then at the elbow, the glistening meat falling to the deck.

Barton held up the stump and stared at it just in time for the final slash to decapitate him. The headless body staggered for a moment in apparent confusion, and then fell.

Several other pirates half-heartedly continued their attacks on Abe, and then retreated, leaving the bow deserted except for the lone samurai. The Marines had been watching this display of expert Japanese swordsmanship from the bow of their own vessel in silence, and then a single man let out a joyous hoot and was immediately silenced by a stern look from the Sergeant Major. The boarding party hesitated, there was no more immediate fighting, it had all been done by one lone man.

Abe waved them aboard the PHANTOM, and one-by-one they began climbing across the railing. "You might want to tell your men," de Wolfe suggested to the Sergeant Major, "not to get in his way."

Pirate!

De Wolfe and the Marines easily climbed unopposed across the railings between the ships as another broadside thundered below them, blasting into the guts of the pirate vessel and shrouding them again with thick blue smoke. "Bayonets! Form a line!" The Sergeant Major ordered, and the Marines spread out across the bow just past Abe in a skirmish line, a mobile razor-sharp steel barricade. Out of the artificial gloom glimpses of pirates could be seen, barely visible for an instant and then lost again.

As the threatening wisps of the danger coalesced in front of them, edging forward in the smoke, bodies and debris littering the deck, the Sergeant Major stood firm. "Gentlemen!" his loud authoritative voice rang out. "Prepare to defend yourselves!" Then came the attack.

It was chaos and every man for himself, stabbing and hacking, and de Wolfe felt his blade hit something solid that screamed and then pulled away. The pirates tried to overwhelm the Marines again and again, each side jabbing with sharp steel, the Americans refusing to yield, relentlessly moving forward.

215

The Sergeant Major withdrew his pistol and discharged it directly into the smoke in front of him, and there was a yelp of agonized pain. "Prepare for volley fire!" he commanded, and then after a moment to check his men, "Fire!"

The rumble of the volley echoed across the ocean and a cheer went up from the SUSQUEHANNA as the smoke further obscured the battle for the main deck. "Forward!" he ordered, and the Marines once again began moving ahead, their bayonets ready, an irresistible force as they stepped over the bodies of dead pirates.

Unseen, pirates began rising from the hatches behind the Americans like avenging apparitions. The marauders gathered, and then began moving silently towards the Sergeant Major and the unprotected backs of the boarding party, completely engaged still fighting the enemy at their front. It had been a trap.

From the smoke emerged Abe, standing defiant between the skulking pirates and the Marines. He charged at them alone, swirling in and out of the dense smoke relentlessly, fighting against impossible numbers until only two opponents were left, circling him warily.

De Wolfe stood next to the Sergeant Major pointing with the pistol that Perry had given him, barely able to make out who was who only a few paces away. "I cannot get a shot!' he screamed in frustration.

"Wait for it!" the Sergeant Major spoke calmly.

A sudden light gust cleared the smoke, and Abe was backed against the railing as one pirate pulled him forward and off balance with a sharpened boat hook, while another cut at him with a broadsword.

A single shot rang out from de Wolfe's hand and the man with the boat hook fell away, freeing Abe to cut down the other before he could escape. Abe had been slightly wounded, checked his left arm, and nodded his appreciation to de Wolfe.

"Forward boys! Forward you magnificent iron-gutted leathernecks! Forward!" the Sergeant Major rallied the boarding party.

The line of Marines moved across the mid-deck fighting, brief individual battles ebbing and flowing as the cornered pirates struggled for their lives. Powell stood on the aft quarter deck above them, trying to rally his men, and De Wolfe fought madly while Abe's tactics were controlled and deadly even though he could only use one arm.

The pirates began to weaken, and then surrender in wholesale numbers while de Wolfe fought his way up the starboard ladder towards Powell. The sailor at the wheel held up his arms in surrender, and the Englishman kicked him away and then back-handed the man next to him that was holding a blunderbuss in one hand and the other high in the air.

Powell grabbed the blunderbuss, smiled in victory, and leveled it at de Wolfe as he crested the ladder. The Hollander stopped cold, looking down the dark gaping maw of the hand-cannon pointed directly at his chest. "Good-bye Mr. de Wolfe!" Powell called out.

"Pirate!" Abe screamed from the port ladder and charged Powell, his long *katana* beginning to swing in a wide horizontal circle, and the buccaneer fired blindly in that general direction. Abe staggered several more steps towards Powell and then collapsed, the multiple lead projectiles from the blunderbuss peppering his body.

De Wolfe's vision went red, blind to everything other than the smirking vile evil man standing in front of him holding the smoking weapon as Abe collapsed to the deck. There was no plan, no tactics, only the raw senseless need for vengeance. Revenge for Abe, for Taka, for all the innocent victims of Nagasaki, of Uraga, and of the smoking ruins ashore. He leapt.

Powell tried to kick, to bite, to gouge, anything to keep the mad dog that was attacking him off, and de Wolfe smashed his fists into him time and again, unmindful of anything except his boiling rage.

De Wolfe knocked Powell down and jumped upon him, smashing his face again and again as the pirate struggled to pull the knife from his boot, barely getting it into his hand before de Wolfe knocked it away.

The Hollander drew Perry's depleted pistol from his waist and smashed it into Powell's face, knocking out a tooth and jarring his head sideways. "Goddamn you! he screamed. "Goddamn you!"

As Powell weakened and then went quiet de Wolfe continued to batter the bloody mash that had been his face, screaming and smashing. He had lost all control. "Goddamn you to Hell!" he half-screamed, half-sobbed.

"Mr. de Wolfe," the Sergeant Major said almost quietly as the Hollander kept smashing the corpse.

Louder now and more insistent, "Mr. de Wolfe! He finally physically pulled him off of the pirate's body. "It's over."

De Wolfe settled, panting and spent. Covering the deck were the bodies of pirates and several injured Marines. There were wounded everywhere, and the PHANTOM's motley crew were being herded together with their hands raised. He looked up and the smoke and fog were completely gone. It was a bright clear morning, with a sweet cool wind blowing across the blood-stained deck. He wanted to vomit from the adrenalin pounding in his veins and from what the lust of battle had done to him. He had succumbed to the lowest instincts of a barbarian; shed the veneer of civilization, and become a rampaging murderer. Every bit of his soul had been given over to just one purpose: To kill.

The sky was the same, the earth was the same, but he could never be the same man again.

He rose and went to Abe, kneeling next to him. Blood trickled from the mortally wounded man's mouth, a sure sign that he had been shot through the lungs and belly. The samurai was weakly trying to reach his *katana*, his hands slowly moving as he dragged himself across the deck.

"You are dying Abe-*sama*," de Wolfe cried as tears filled his eyes.

"Help me die." Abe begged him.

It took a moment, and then de Wolfe understood. "Like Kamimoto?"

"You understand?" Abe whispered, his strength almost gone. "With honor."

De Wolfe helped him into a kneeling position, and then gently withdrew and handed him his *wakizashi*. Abe could not hold the short sword, and de Wolfe placed it into his open palm and then closed the fingers around the hilt.

As Abe waited on his knees, the breath wheezing in and out from his tortured lungs, de Wolfe lifted up his *katana*, stared out across the sun-dappled waves and took a deep breath of the salt sea air. The Hollander stepped back, paused momentarily, and then swung the blade deeply into the back of the samurai's neck. The body pitched forward.

The Sergeant Major stepped up and gently took the sword from de Wolfe's numb hands. "That man," he began, "I have never seen anything like it, and I've been at war my entire life. Who was he?"

"He died doing his duty," de Wolfe began slowly. "He is Abe Akio, the eldest son of Abe Tadamichi of Fukuoka." De Wolfe stood tall in the bright sunshine among the gore of hand-to-hand combat. "He died protecting his country." He looked up at the sea birds that had returned to wheeling and turning above the ships. "He was my friend."

The Sergeant Major signaled two Marines to wrap Abe's body in canvas and carry it away as he cautioned them, "Easy men. Gently now."

Perry was with Dr. Franz on the foredeck of his flagship when the boarding party returned. "Sergeant Major," he commanded pointing to the Stars and Stripes on the stern of the PHANTOM. "Have your men salvage that flag, you may scuttle the rest."

The bodies of the two Marines and Abe were handed up, and immediately covered with blankets, and those of the pirates, including Powell's, were simply weighted and thrown overboard while the prisoners were escorted below.

"What will you do with them?" Franz inquired.

"They have done little to harm the U.S. Navy, so I have no interest in them. Their crimes have been against the Japanese, so let the locals decide how justice may be found."

De Wolfe stood in a daze; he had no strength, nor any interest in moving. He wanted to sleep, to forget the events of the day. He wanted to be home, but could not recall where that might be or how he might get there. He handed Perry the pistol he had been loaned, and the Commodore took it gingerly by the barrel, avoiding the muck of hair and blood that covered the grip, before handing it to a crewman.

"Let's go to my cabin," Perry suggested, and they climbed the stairs from the main deck and into the cool darkness.

A steward brought strong hot coffee and then retreated, leaving the three of them alone. "I am very sorry about your friend," Perry began.

De Wolfe was staring into space, reliving the battle on the PHANTOM over and over again in his mind. How Abe had boarded the pirate ship alone and single-handedly cleared the path. The screams and grunts of the deck struggle, the wood slippery with blood and cluttered with bodies and wreckage. And finally, how he had, my God, how he had ended the poor samurai's agony.

"Mr. de Wolfe," Perry spoke through the mists. "Mr. de Wolfe, drink your coffee, it will help clear your mind."

"Yes, of course," and he took a deep swallow. "I promised to help you. What do you require?"

"The United States has, for many years, unsuccessfully endeavored to establish commercial relations here in Japan. In 1837 we tried to return Japanese sailors who had been ship wrecked from Canton, and when they arrived at Uraga aboard the merchant ship MORRISON she was immediately attacked and driven off."

"In 1846 Commander James Biddle came to Edo with the seventy-two gun COLUMBUS. He was told that Japan was closed and that he must negotiate with the Dutch in Nagasaki."

"All together since 1790 twenty-seven American ships have attempted to call Japan, and all with the same result. Each time we have been turned away."

"I said that I would help," de Wolfe confirmed. "We had a bargain, and I will fulfill my promise."

"Excellent, there are three requests," Perry continued. "One: I want to meet with the Shōgun himself. No diplomats, no lower level underlings, no Dukes or other bureaucrats, the Shōgun and only the Shōgun. Is that possible?"

"Yes," the Dutchman considered for a moment. "But you cannot enter Edo Castle as an invader or a war party. You must come as a friend. That means no weapons, nothing that could be perceived as a threat."

"Agreed. Myself, the Sergeant Major and a few Marines, all unarmed. Two: I have a Letter of Introduction from President Millard Fillmore. In it he promises that our venture has no religious purposes, and that we come only for friendship and commerce. Our only desires are trade and coal. I would ask you to convert the document from English into Dutch on our behalf so that I may present it to the Shōgun."

"I can do that for you," de Wolfe assured him.

"Three: Come as my official translator to the meeting."

"That is certainly not feasible," de Wolfe shook his head, "I am an employee of the Dutch East India Company and a citizen of the Netherlands. In no way is it possible for me to assist your venture to that degree."

"Sir, our mission is doomed without your involvement. I ask only that you arrange a meeting, translate a letter, and then provide a simple facilitation between the Shōgun and myself. I do not ask you to take sides, nor do I desire you to do anything that would damage your own enterprise in any way."

"And, if the Japanese ask for my recommendation?" de Wolfe countered.

"Then you are absolutely free to give it. I could ask nothing else. I do not ask you to betray your enterprise. Agreed?"

"Agreed," confirmed the Hollander.

The SUSQUEHANNA had caused quite a stir when she anchored in Edo Bay, not far from Chiyoda. Wild rumors had spread detailing the tragedy at Uraga, and none of the citizens of the capital were quite sure if the Americans were now preparing to do the same to their own city.

The Dutchmen were rowed to shore, and they immediately departed for the Nagasaki House, and did their best to explain to the *Chakunan*, through gestures and pantomime, what had happened and what they planned next. It was the following morning before they returned to the Black Ship, this time with horses, and accompanied Commodore Perry, the Sergeant Major and a small contingent of Marines to the grounds of Edo Castle.

Perry was in his full formal uniform with gold epaulettes and plumed black two-pronged bicorne hat. The Sergeant Major and his men were cleaned and polished as well, and the Americans made an impressive sight moving through the streets of Edo as the Commodore and the Nagasaki delegation rode on horseback followed by the non-commissioned officer and a single Marine pounding on a bass drum while six other leathernecks marched behind them.

When they arrived at Edo Castle the *Chakunan* indicated that the Marines should stay outside, and Perry held the Sergeant Major's arm tightly indicating that he must come also. The *Chakunan* quickly understood, and motioned that the four foreigners should follow him inside. De Wolfe and Franz slipped off their boots, and Perry soon did also, but the Sergeant Major was reluctant.

"I would rather not Commodore," was all he repeated until Perry finally lost all patience and ordered him to remove his boots. When he did, the big toe on his right foot protruded through the sock and into the morning air, causing Franz to laugh and Perry to roll his eyes. Then they all went inside.

The large tatami meeting room was especially crowded, packed by dignitaries and visiting *Daimyō*, but an unfamiliar figure kneeled in the middle of the dais. Suzuki kneeled on his right, his face pale, and from time to time pain flashed across his wrinkle brow. Taka kneeled slightly to the left side and behind the *Shōgun* with a guard hovering on each of her shoulders.

De Wolfe realized with shock that Suzuki was now wearing the all too recognizable light-blue kimono with the symmetrical embroidery on the chest, and the unknown man wore the robes of the *Shōgun*. They stopped at the doorway and the *Chakunan* announced them, *"The Capitão-sama of Dejima and Commodore Perry of America"*. There were no Japanese words for "Commodore" or "America", so he simply pronounced them as best he could.

The four foreigners bowed and entered the meeting room, the *Chakunan* leading them slowly and formally to stand in front of the dais, and then they all bowed again.

"Where is the *Shōgun*?" de Wolfe asked Suzuki with concern.

"This is the *Shōgun*," Suzuki announced. "*Shōgun* Tokugawa Ieyoshi has joined his ancestors in Heaven. May I present *Shōgun* Tokugawa Iesada, the thirteenth in an unbroken line of great leaders."

De Wolfe and Franz exchanged worried looks. Perry saw their concern, "What's happening?" he asked in English.

"The *Shōgun* has died," de Wolfe whispered. "This is his son, the new *Shōgun*. Our bargain was with his father."

"Oh, that is bad timing. Still, whether it is the old *Shōgun* or the new, I have my mission to complete. We are here, and I say let's get on with it."

De Wolfe nodded in agreement.

The Sergeant Major stood behind them at attention, and Perry murmured over his shoulder, "Parade Rest, Sergeant Major." The Marine shifted his left foot to shoulder width apart and his hands moved behind his back as Perry began, "I come to your Majesty on behalf of the President of the United States, and as a friend."

The translation was cumbersome as de Wolfe put it into Dutch, Suzuki changed that to Japanese, and then the whole process was repeated with the *Shōgun*'s reply.

"He has used the word 'friend', and the *Shōgun* asks if you have properly translated his meaning?" Suzuki asked de Wolfe.

"Yes, I am quite positive that is the correct word."

"The *Shōgun* then asks," Suzuki continued, "if this word has a different meaning in Dutch or in American? Or is it the custom of Americans to bombard their friends with cannon?"

"My sincere apologies, your Majesty," Perry responded following the translations. "But, we were attacked. Is it not the right of any man or nation to defend itself when it is attacked?"

De Wolfe and Suzuki translated, and the *Shōgun* looked Perry up and down, considering carefully. "*Very well*," he finally offered. "*Then tell the Americans to sing.*"

"I am not sure that I understand," Perry questioned when de Wolfe interpreted the request.

Oh, it is quite customary for visitors to sing for the *Shōgun*," de Wolfe assured him.

"And, dance too," Franz offered. "Quite an insult if you do not."

Perry considered, and then bellowed, "Sergeant Major!"

"Sir!" the Marine barked as he snapped to attention.

"Sing!" Perry commanded.

"Aye-aye, sir! Sing what sir?"

"How about that tune from the Mexican War, I've heard your men singing it."

"And dance," Franz reminded them.

"Please respectfully inform the *Shōgun* that it is not our custom to dance to this particular song," Perry explained. "Sergeant Major, if you please."

The Marine began slowly with a loud and clear baritone, and even though only the foreigners of those assembled could understand the words, the emotion behind the melody was clear and filled the room as he stood at attention, tall and ram-rod stiff and stared directly ahead.

> "From the Halls of Montezuma
> To the shores of Tripoli;
> We fight our country's battles
> On the land and on the sea;
> First to fight for right and freedom
> And to keep our honor clean;
> We are proud to claim the title
> Of United States Marine.
>
> Our flag's unfurled to every breeze
> From dawn to setting sun;
> We have fought in every clime and place
> Where we could take a gun;
> In the snow of far-off Northern lands
> And in sunny tropic scenes,
> You will find us always on the job
> The United States Marines."

The large hall fell into silence as he ended, until the quiet was broken by Perry, "Thank you Sergeant Major, Parade Rest," he said softly and the Marine returned to his former position behind him.

Perry withdrew two envelopes from inside his coat and took a step forward, holding the papers out to Suzuki. "These are Letters of Introduction from our President Millard Fillmore."

"What is a 'President'?" Suzuki asked, ignoring the documents.

"He is the man elected by the people of the United States every four years to lead us."

"He is the king?" Suzuki sought to clarify.

"No. Certainly not a king. The people vote and choose who is to lead us. If they do not like him, then after four years they can choose another."

"Absurd!" snorted Suzuki, and the quick dismissal required no translation from Dutch to either English or Japanese.

"It is our way," Perry insisted. "Our President's greetings and our objectives are clearly stated in these letters, the original in English and the second in Dutch. Please accept them with our best hopes and wishes," and Perry extended the documents.

Once again the old man ignored the offered papers. *"My lord,"* Suzuki began, took a deep breath and steeled himself, and then made a clear and strong announcement to all who were there, *"I must protest."*

Perry stood still, the letters in his hand, not sure what was happening and with no way to know what Suzuki was saying.

"I protest your audience with these animals. Look at them, what do they bring that benefits Japan? We can live without sugar. We can live without pins that fold into themselves. We can live without guns and ships that are driven by coal. The only thing that foreigners have ever brought to Japan is death and chaos."

Several of the attending *Daimyō* grunted in agreement as Suzuki continued. *"You have met with them, you have fulfilled any obligations that your father may have had. Now, send them away. Do not accept their letters, and do not meet with them again. I happily offer you my life in protest and to protect Japan from these barbarians. I promise you that I will never live in a Japan further polluted by foreigners. Seppuku is my protest!"*

"Raise your head," the *Shōgun* commanded.

224

"*I cannot my Lord,*" Suzuki turned away.

"*Raise your head and look at me!*" the *Shōgun* repeated, and Suzuki slowly brought his eyes up as tears began forming and then slowly fell down his cheeks. "*You threaten the Shōgunate with seppuku here?*" The new *Shōgun* questioned. "*In this chamber where no dagger or sword may be drawn without instant death?*"

"*My love of the Shōgun is undisputed, and proven through my long and faithful service. Only my love of Japan is greater.*" Tears now streamed freely down his old and wizened face. "*I would never dishonor the Shōgun or his court by baring a blade in your presence or by threatening seppuku here. But, the deed has been done.*"

Suzuki loosened his belt and opened the blue kimono. Across his belly were multiple turns of broad white cloth, discolored by a heavy dark red stain where he had moments before sliced deeply into his bowels, a mortal self-inflicted wound.

"*My service to the Shōgunate is now over, and I will translate no more. Let the foreigners go away unheard, they have nothing to say that we need to hear. Now I will enjoy the absolute freedom that only death can bring. My sole desire today is to show you how easy an honorable passing can be. This is my protest, this is my offering to you my lord. I do not fear death, I welcome it! I only fear the loss of Bushidō, the loss of honor, the loss of everything Japanese that these letters bring.*"

The *Shōgun* spoke sharply with his advisor. "*You refuse to perform your duty? You refuse my commands? There is no honor in defiance.*"

"*I am far past duty, honor or defiance. I will no longer assist in the destruction of Japan, and you no longer have other options to speak with the Dutchmen. Without my translation this negotiation is now over, let them go away unheard.*"

The *Shōgun* appeared frustrated and quickly growing angry as Perry stood still, unsure of what was happening and with the proffered letters offered but not taken, and with no indication of what to do next. The Commodore wondered if perhaps he had done something incorrectly? In the growing ominous silence his diplomatic mission seemed about to come to the same unfruitful conclusion that all others before had.

"*Your Majesty,*" Taka's voice was soft and yet strong from behind the Shogun, "*I speak Dutch. I would be honored to translate on your behalf.*"

The *Shōgun* turned his head slightly towards Taka as Suzuki groaned "*NO!*" through gritted teeth. "*The woman must not speak!*"

The *Shōgun* hesitated for a moment's thought, and then turned back to the front and spoke softly, almost kindly. "*Suzuki-Otona your service is now concluded. We thank you for your loyalty to my father, and to Japan. You may now go.*" The two guards moved quickly from behind the *Shōgun* and assisted Suzuki to his feet and although he was barely able to walk they led him through the paneled doors and away. *"Well translator?"* the *Shōgun* then looked expectantly at Taka as she slowly rose and then kneeled again in the space previously occupied by the old man.

De Wolfe stared at her for a long moment before beginning, "I have been torn in half without you. I have come to Edo to bring you home."

Dr. Franz was grinning and giggling like an imbecile as she answered softly, "I am yours, now and forever."

"What is he saying?" the *Shōgun* demanded as the Americans looked similarly puzzled.

"The Hollander says, your Majesty, that he is now ready to begin negotiations."

"Then let us begin," the *Shōgun* grunted. *"What you ask is most difficult. You have seen that many of my lords would prefer death rather than for me to accept these greetings from your President?"* Taka translated, her voice soothing in contrast to the rough manner Suzuki had used.

"All great endeavors begin in difficulty before they can show rewards," Perry responded. "We all have much to consider." As the discussions progressed Taka continued translating the Japanese into Dutch and de Wolfe expressed them into English, where the responses were once again put back into Dutch and then Japanese. It was slow, but effective.

"And," the Shōgun finally asked, *"What is the recommendation of the Capitão-sama of Dejima?"*

De Wolfe began slowly, "I have come to love Japan and her people. Under the wise rule of the *Shōgunate* they have maintained peace, stability and prosperity for longer than any other nation I have ever heard of. They have remained unchanged as there has been no reason to change. But, that stability has been both your strength and your greatest weakness. As you have held yourselves separate and apart, others have raced ahead."

"Can you even begin to imagine: A road of iron and a steam carriage where you could travel the *Tokaidō* to Kyoto in a single day? A wire that carries the business of government in only an instant to any corner of your islands? Medicines that can heal the sick and ease the injured. Like a tidal wave these things are coming, and they cannot be stopped, they should not be stopped, for they will only benefit the Japanese people."

"But," de Wolfe concluded, "it will not be the decision of the Dutch, nor of the Americans. It can only be the decision of the Japanese. The *Shōgun* may choose to reject these Letters of Introduction and send the Americans away. However, you asked for my recommendation, and I give it to you now: Accept the Letters, listen to the Americans, and then do what will be best for all of Japan."

The *Shōgun* listened to the translation, conferred with her for a long moment, and then Taka spoke again. "Please tell the American Commodore that the *Shōgun* accepts the greeting from his President, and will reflect deeply on what he has heard today." The *Shōgun* motioned and Taka rose, stepped forward and reached out her hand, and then took the letters from Perry.

Taka then continued her translation. "The Americans must understand, of course, how impossible any further requests are at this time. His Majesty will speak with them no more today. However, if they wish to return next year, he and his advisors will be prepared to negotiate - in English." Taka bowed deeply to Perry, and then returned to her position kneeling next to the *Shōgun*.

De Wolfe was unsure what would happen next as the *Shōgun* spoke to Taka again, and then the Japanese woman turned her head to face the Hollander with a slight smile. "The *Shōgun* also asks me to thank the Dutch for their service to his family, and to convey to the Hollander his appreciation for your loyalty, honor, and your understanding of the importance of duty. He has asked me to tell the *Capitão-sama* of Dejima that he will keep all of the promises given to you by his father. "

The *Shōgun* clapped twice and the two guards returned to escort him off of the dais, while the Nagasaki delegation and the Americans bowed deeply and backed out of the meeting hall.

Taka was guided to the Nagasaki House and released to de Wolfe's care that evening.

The White Box

The entire island of Dejima was a ghost town. The shutters were closed and bolted, the storerooms empty, and the Dutch Gate unguarded. Especially evident was the complete lack of activity for the first time in two hundred and eighteen years. The flagship SUSQUEHANNA was anchored in Nagasaki Bay, while the other steamship and sloops of the American fleet cruised just out of sight over the horizon.

De Wolfe, Dr. Franz and Muis waited in patient silence at the wharf in the mid-day shadow of the Dutch flag as two long boats landed and a squad of eight Marines in column were led by Commodore Perry and the Sergeant Major. De Wolfe held a white box tied with a black cord. Together they all marched to the center of the courtyard, stopped, and waited.

A dozen samurai led by the *Obugyō* of Nagasaki and the *Chakunan*, both of them now walking with pronounced limps and with the aid of canes, entered Dejima over the Dutch Gate and spread out across the courtyard.

"Form a line," the Sergeant Major barked, and the Americans fanned in parallel in front of the Japanese with their rifles resting at the right side, the butts on the ground and the left hand touching the tip of the barrel at the Order Arms position, each group spanning the courtyard and facing each other.

"Port Arms! At my command!"

The Marines lifted their rifles to the ready position across their chests and stopped rock-still.

De Wolfe passed the white box to Commodore Perry who held it formally in both hands, and then the American commander advanced alone in front of the *Obugyō*, as the three Dutchmen moved off to the side.

"Ready!"

The Marines lifted their rifles skyward facing forty-five degrees off to the left.

"Fire!"

The discharge of the salute crackled and echoed between the empty buildings, shaking pigeons and sea gulls off of the roofs before clapping away into silence. The Marines returned to the Port Arms position.

Commodore Perry presented the white box containing Abe's ashes to the *Obugyō* and bowed deeply. The *Obugyō* received the box and formally returned the bow. Perry took two steps directly backward, and then saluted the Nagasaki samurai before turning sharply to face the Marines.

"Sergeant Major, when you are ready."

"Aye-aye, sir! About face!" and the Americans spun sharply. "Column of twos! Forward!" They formed up and began marching towards the wharf.

The *Obugyō* bowed and crossed the Dutch Gate into Nagasaki as the Marines arrived at the wharf and began loading into the long boats, leaving the Dutchmen alone as they slowly walked towards the tall flag pole.

"I cannot convince you to leave doctor? The Japans have become a very dangerous place for foreigners," de Wolfe cautioned.

"I have my wife and the clinic, and as you always knew I plan to spend the remainder of my life here. It is my home now. Besides, who would want to hurt an old song and dance man?" He smiled and did a quick few steps, raising a small cloud of dust.

"You have seventeen years of salary due, you would be a very wealthy man in Amsterdam," Muis noted.

"Yes, well I have occasionally taken, shall we say, 'liberties' with the medical supplies here, and you may deduct that from what I am owed. Also, would you see that the remainder is given to my *alma mater* the University of Utrecht? Perhaps they might use the funds to create an educational laboratory of some kind for the practical education of future scientists."

"I shall, doctor," Muis clasped his hand and pumped it energetically. "You are a good man sir."

Franz nodded and gave them a grandiose stage bow before turning away and departing.

"All are aboard for the trip to Shanghai," Muis explained. "The Dutch legation there will assist in making all the necessary arrangements. They may be a bit surprised to see us, but we can be sure of their full cooperation. The Company, however...."

"Of course," de Wolfe responded. "The Company will be most unhappy. The Americans will be back, the Dutch monopoly here is finished."

"You could not prevent it?" Muis asked.

"Prevent it? Why Mr. Muis, I recommended it!"

They arrived at the flag pole and de Wolfe began to slowly lower the Dutch standard that had flown above Dejima for over two centuries. As Holland had risen to become a world power and the center of European art and culture, as vast fortunes had been made, and in some cases lost, throughout war and peace that flag had been the one constant. And, now it was gone, forever.

"I had a plan you know. I came here with such hopes." De Wolfe gently folded the flag and handed it to Muis. "And, in the end, it is all gone."

Muis accepted the flag. "I am an accountant, and the one thing I know to be true is that the books always have to balance." He shook his head. "If you have given anything away, then you must have gotten something in return, even if you do not realize it yet."

"It will all be gone," de Wolfe mused. "Dejima and the men who served here. The work and the sacrifices. The hopes, the dreams, the triumphs and failings of humanity all here on this little island. Gone and forgotten. And, I will be gone with it."

"We live in a world merely decorated with our intentions, but populated by our mistakes," Muis consoled him. "You are the final *Opperhoofd*, and like every man before you, a human being. Each has struggled to find balance, caught between two very different and perhaps irreconcilable worlds. How could any man know what is right? If you have done no better, then I can assure you that you have done no worse."

"It is time to go," de Wolfe said with great sadness.

Muis shook his hand. "What should I tell your wife?"

"Tell her good-bye."

"And, your warning to Dr. Franz? The Dutch are no longer welcome here."

"The Commodore has given me one of their fine American revolvers, and I suppose that I will learn to use those two fine Japanese swords. The *Obugyō-sama* has asked me to begin conducting English lessons. Besides," he laughed, "I believe that it is time the local people are introduced to the pleasures of Dutch beer."

De Wolfe smiled broadly and pointed to the hills behind Nagasaki. "But first, there is a lovely spot up there with a grand view. I am going to build a house."

"God bless you Mr. de Wolfe." Muis turned, boarded the long boat, and was rowed away towards the SUSQUEHANNA as the lone figure walked back into the barren courtyard of Dejima. Waiting at the Dutch Gate were Taka and the baby.

"May I hold him?" Hope rose in the Hollander's voice as he cuddled his infant son. "I want to name him Akio."

"Akio de Wolfe," Taka smiled. "That is a good name."

The new family watched as the Black Ship began to make steam, the paddles spun, and soon started to sail away from the Japans with thick black smoke curling from her stack.

Made in the USA
San Bernardino, CA
31 August 2018